"Welcome home. I heard there was a party." See, she could do friendly, too.

"Oh yeah, it was a wild one." The corners of his eyes crinkled. "Though I think half the people in attendance actually thought it was a party to welcome home my parents from their vacation, not me."

"Can't believe I wasn't invited." As soon as she said the joking words, her lips pressed. She'd meant the comment lightly.

But the sudden swell of tension, the tick in Blake's jaw, her own hard swallow told her they'd both had the same thought.

Of course she wasn't invited.

Because Kingsleys and Hunzikers didn't mix. The one time they'd tried—her sister, his brother—it'd ended in hurt and a shock deep enough to impact the whole town.

Blake's dog jerked on his leash, paving the way for his sudden and stilted, "Well, have a good night."

Her forced nod.

His retreat.

And that's that.

Autumn let out a deep exhale as she watched Blake's walk turn into a run, his dog keeping pace as he crossed the square.

Praise for *Here to Stay*

"Simply adorable . . . you might just fall in love with *Here to Stay*."

—*USA Today's Happy Ever After* blog

"Tagg's signature gentle humor, clean romance, and an integrated and unobtrusive inclusion of faith into the story make for another enjoyable read."

—*Booklist*

"Tagg's writing is sharp and witty, enveloping the reader in the thoughts and feelings of her characters. . . . Melissa Tagg, inspirational romance author, is here to stay."

—*Fresh Fiction*

"With her charming wit and engaging prose, Tagg pens a story of hope in God's dreams for us and ties it all together with sigh-worthy romance. Truly a book and author not to be missed."

—**Rachel Hauck**, award-winning, bestselling author of *The Wedding Dress* and *Princess Ever After*

Praise for Melissa Tagg

"Tagg writes heartfelt and humorous gentle romances with a wisp of faith woven throughout."

—*Library Journal*

"Tagg is one of the freshest new voices in Christian contemporary romance, and brings a level of spunk and originality to a genre in which so many stories can start to sound the same."

—*Christian Manifesto*

Books by Melissa Tagg

Made to Last
Here to Stay

THE WALKER FAMILY BOOKS

Three Little Words: A Walker Family Novella
From the Start
Like Never Before

Here to Stay

MELISSA TAGG

BETHANYHOUSE
a division of Baker Publishing Group
Minneapolis, Minnesota

© 2014 by Melissa Tagg

Published by Bethany House Publishers
11400 Hampshire Avenue South
Bloomington, Minnesota 55438
www.bethanyhouse.com

Bethany House Publishers is a division of
Baker Publishing Group, Grand Rapids, Michigan

Printed in the United States of America

ISBN 978-0-7642-3058-5

Library of Congress Cataloging-in-Publication Data for the original edi-
tion is on file at the Library of Congress, Washington, DC.

Scripture taken from the HOLY BIBLE, NEW INTERNATIONAL VER-
SION®. Copyright © 1973, 1978, 1984 Biblica. Used by permission of
Zondervan. All rights reserved.

Scripture quotations are from *The Message* by Eugene H. Peterson, copyright © 1993, 1994, 1995, 2000, 2001, 2002. Used by permission of NavPress
Publishing Group. All rights reserved.

This is a work of fiction. Names, characters, incidents, and dialogues
are products of the author's imagination and are not to be construed
as real. Any resemblance to actual events or persons, living or dead, is
entirely coincidental.

Cover Design by Eric Walljasper

Author represented by MacGregor Literary, Inc.

17 18 19 20 21 22 23   7 6 5 4 3 2 1

To two of my favorite people in the world,
my grandpa and grandma,
Arnold and Jeane Flessner

1

If the letter—the one that could change everything—didn't arrive today, she'd stop hoping.

Autumn tucked a runaway strand of auburn hair behind her ear and crept across the Kingsley Inn's rooftop on all fours, the dirty black slate tile smudging the knees of her jeans. Sun warmed the tile under her palms despite the late November chill and a lakeside breeze whispering over her face.

Tarping the roof's leaky spot probably would've been a job better saved for someone less queasy about heights. But she'd had to lay off their handyman months ago, which left her playing amateur fix-it girl. She probably looked ridiculous crawling across the roof, but hey, she'd gotten the job done.

Except . . . *Wait*. Autumn scanned the edges of the roof. Where was her ladder?

Gone. And it didn't take a genius to pinpoint the culprit. "I don't have time for this, Harry." Despite her muttered words, a smile tugged at her cheeks as she fished into her pocket for her phone. Twenty-eight wasn't too old to still appreciate a good prank.

Phone pressed to her ear, she took in her rooftop view while waiting for Harry to pick up. Beyond a span of parking lot and lawn, browning grass faded to a pale ribbon of beach, where the turquoise waters of Lake Michigan tussled with the shore.

She *was* getting impatient for word about the potential career move of a lifetime, but pretty Whisper Shore wasn't such a horrible place to linger.

If only she didn't feel as if she'd been lingering her whole life.

"Thank you for calling the Kingsley Inn. My name is Harrison. How may I—"

"Can it, Harry." Her focus snapped back to where her ladder should've been. "You can help me by returning my ladder." Her tone flat-lined, but she had to hand it to the deskman. He'd one-upped her but good.

"Ladder? Whatever are you talking about, Miss Kingsley?"

Ooh, she could just picture him two floors below, leaning against the lobby's mahogany check-in desk, all smug-like. *Weasel.* "Very funny. You should be on that show with the senior citizens who pull pranks."

"Are you calling me old?"

He did have twelve years on her. "Well, if the sweater vest fits . . ."

"And now you're making fun of my wardrobe. I hope you're prepared to sleep on that roof tonight."

Phone balanced between her ear and shoulder, she started crawling again . . . and reached the edge of the sloping roof just as the sound of car tires crackling over gravel carried upward. *Uh-oh*. Had her bride and groom arrived early for their appointment?

She swallowed, chalky dread clenching her throat. She'd been steeling herself for this meeting all week long. *Dylan Porter.* Suddenly the idea of staying up on the roof was all sorts of appealing.

It's been three years. This doesn't have to be awkward.

Yeah, then why the Tilt-A-Whirl case of nerves? "Come on, Harry, let me down. Pretty please?"

"Nineteen years you've known me, and you still can't get it right. Har-ri-son."

On another day she'd have thrown out a few more *Harry*s just to hear the man whine and threaten to quit like always. Of course, he'd never actually go through with it. Harry had been a fixture at the inn since Autumn's preteen years, landing in Whisper Shore when he'd decided to take a year off college. Sometime in the last decade and a half, he'd stopped talking about going back. His love for the inn nearly matched her own.

As, too, she suspected, did his fears about its future.

But the sound of a car door clinking shut kept her from teasing. Her fiancé awaited.

Scratch that. Ex-fiancé.

"All right. Harrison, Harrison, Harrison. Is that better?"

"Yes, Jan Brady, much better. Give me a sec, the other line is ringing."

"But—"

The phone clicked before she could finish. She squinted against cascading sunlight, its brightness along with the front lawn's massive cottonwood blocking her view of the parking lot's newest car. If that was Dylan and his replacement bride arriving early, no way did she want to be caught on the rooftop—windblown and in clothes too dingy for the Goodwill pile.

Autumn sucked in a cold breath and inched over to where the porch roof jutted out from the first floor. The drop wasn't so far. Maybe . . .

But the rattling of the metal ladder against the rain gutter conveniently interrupted that questionable plan.

"It's about time, Harry." Autumn dangled one foot over the edge, found her footing on the ladder rung, then the other. "Can you stall them while I change?" Moments later, her feet thudded to the ground and she turned.

Only it wasn't Harry standing to the side, steadying the ladder while a lawyerly tan trench coat whipped in the wind behind him.

"H-hey, Dylan." The greeting choked up her throat. Really, if ever there would've been a day to call in sick. "The ladder . . . you . . . thank you."

"Autumn Kingsley." Dylan's smile was as devastating as ever, and between the perfectly styled blond hair and his chiseled-as-a-statue's jaw, it certainly wasn't a surprise he'd found a new fiancée—only that it'd taken so long.

Look who's talking. She hadn't been on a date since Zach Dawson coaxed her into sharing his blanket at the Fourth of July picnic last summer, then proceeded to spill the entire contents of his paper plate on her. She'd sat there watching fireworks that were supposed to signal freedom, thinking surely the potato salad in her lap was just one more sign she needed to stop wasting time waiting for her life to start in Whisper Shore.

Dylan coughed.

"Um, sorry I'm dressed like this." She glanced at her tattered jeans. Easier than eye contact. "Figured I'd have enough time to change before you got here, but Harry thought it'd be funny to trap me on the roof."

Dylan's baritone chuckle poked at the tension hovering between them. "I thought you two would've run out of pranks by now."

"Well, apparently my creativity is waning. I went old school this morning—salted his tea."

"What were you doing on the roof anyway?"

Autumn plunged her hands into the pockets of her fleece jacket. It wouldn't do to get into the Kingsley Inn's current financial predicament. Dylan didn't need to know that with tourist season over they now had more empty rooms than full—that Autumn had already dipped into her own measly savings once this fall to pay the mortgage. And next month was looking even more dire. The whole thing was embarrassing.

Owning and managing the family inn may never have been her dream job, but even so . . . who wanted to fail? It's why booking this wedding reception was so important.

And why she held her breath every day when she checked the mailbox, yearning for the letter from the hotel in France. The one that could breathe life into the hope still lurking along under the surface, the hope that eventually life might hold something more. *Travel. Excitement. Adventure.*

"Autumn?"

"Sorry, yes?" She blinked, finally allowing herself to meet Dylan's eyes.

Oh, how she used to gush over those jade irises. But

her fascination with Whisper Shore's most eligible bachelor had worn thin the longer they'd been together. The more he'd talked about settling down for the long haul, the more she'd ached for life outside the confines of her hometown.

Ironic, really. She was the one who longed to escape, but Dylan was the one who had gone off to Detroit, found himself a new life and a new bride, while Autumn was still . . . stuck.

"The roof. What were you doing up there?"

She shook her head, stray hair tickling her cheeks. "Just checking a to-do off the list. So, where's your fiancée? Mariah, is it?" First things first. She couldn't will the Paris hotel to hire her. But she could nail this reception reservation.

Only now Dylan was the one to look away. His focus landed on the inn.

And she couldn't help following his gaze. The inn used to be the glory of the surrounding shore, its sprawling wraparound porch reminiscent of a Southern plantation. Lattice crawled up one side, and the flowerboxes now filled with fall mums under gangly windows added a homey feel.

But did Dylan notice the way the late-afternoon light highlighted a web of cracks in the three-story building's pale yellow siding? Or how about the white shutters in desperate need of a good painting?

He looked back to Autumn. "Mariah . . . isn't coming."

Autumn nudged her chin into the high neck of her fleece. "Do we need to reschedule?"

"No. I already felt bad that we asked you to fit us in the day after Thanksgiving, and now . . ."

Dylan shifted his weight, and a knot of worry tangled through Autumn. *We need this.* Even if that letter finally came and said what she hoped, she still had a responsibility to keep the inn running. "Dylan, it's no problem to reschedule."

"No. I only came out tell you we don't need the appointment anymore." His expression softened, even if his tone didn't. "We won't be holding our reception here."

A testy gust of wind scraped over her cheeks, a dozen arguments jamming in her throat. Dylan had no way of knowing how much she'd counted on booking their reception. On the deposit that could've covered at least a couple repairs.

"Mariah wanted to get married in Whisper Shore since she doesn't have any family in Detroit, and I couldn't help bringing up this place. You have to understand, Autumn, I didn't think you'd still be here. I assumed someone else would be running it by now. After all, you said . . ."

His voice trailed as her own words on the day she'd returned his ring came back to her in snippets.

"I have this dream . . ."

"If I don't feed this restless piece of me now, I'll regret it later. I know I will."

"I'm sorry, Dylan."

Though spoken years ago, the desire, her dreams, hadn't lost their weight. Circumstances had simply delayed them.

"I know what I said." A sigh dangled from her voice now. "But things changed, and—" her forced chuckle came out garbled and fake—"I'm still here."

"And Mariah doesn't like that. As soon as we got to town, well, you know how people talk here."

Oh yeah, she knew. Gossip made its way from the town a mile down the shore to her lakeside inn with lightning speed.

"I tried to talk Mariah into at least coming out to see the place. But then she caught a glimpse of the Hunziker Hotel."

Her jaw pinched as the unwelcome image of their main competitor's pristine building arose. Small-town charm on the outside, sleek and modern amenities galore on the inside.

Autumn's spirits slumped as the front door banged open and footsteps sounded on the whitewashed porch boards. Harry to the rescue, probably. A little late for that.

"Autumn, you'll never guess who just reserved a room in December." Harry's voice tapered off as he came up beside her, his skinny basketball player frame towering over her. "Dylan," he said, greeting stiff and maybe even a little protective. Sweet and brotherly, if unnecessary.

"Hi, Harry. Anyway, I'm really sorry, Autumn. Mariah knows what she wants. And . . . well . . ." He shrugged. "She was gung ho to check out the Hunziker Hotel tonight, but their staff is all busy with the welcome home party for the mayor's son, and—"

This time she couldn't hide her flinch. "Wait, what?"

Dylan buttoned his coat. "Some party at Mayor Hunziker's house."

"The mayor's son?" Harry asked. "Who . . . ?"

Autumn folded her arms, fingers clenched, as a hundred memories of her sister's pained eyes scraped through her mind. "Dylan's talking about Blake, the younger son. You know, the one who's been in all the headlines, with

Miranda Woodruff." Her answer fluttered like a lone leaf clinging to a naked tree.

As if she'd needed one more reason to leave Whisper Shore. Blake Hunziker had finally come home.

After more than half a decade playing adventurous nomad, was it pathetic that coming home felt like the bravest thing Blake Hunziker had ever done?

Blake turned his car onto Cedar Lane. The years away might've reshaped him, but it hadn't changed this street. It was the same as ever. Bony trees casting craggy shadows in the early evening dim. Brick houses rising from expansive lawns, manicured hedges walling each property. The ashy scent of someone burning leaves.

"All right, Kevin. This is it. Last house on the right."

The mutt in the passenger seat only tipped his head, his straggly brown-and-white hair flopping over his eyes.

"Dude, you need a haircut more than I do." It'd be a miracle if his mother allowed the dog in the house. But Blake hadn't been able to leave the mangy animal where he'd found him, stranded along the highway a good fifty miles from Whisper Shore—skinny and limping. He'd stopped by a couple vet's offices along the way, leaving his contact information in case the owners turned up.

Which had been a pretty good procrastination effort if he did say so himself.

Blake parked in his parents' driveway, exited, and rounded the vehicle. He jabbed one arm into the open trunk of his inherited cherry red Firebird—would it never stop feeling like Ryan's car?—and pulled out his duffel bag, the one that had seen more airports than he could count. He slung it over his shoulder, closed the trunk, and moved to the passenger door.

"Okay, Kev, you get to hang out here for a little while. Just until I see how this is going to go down." He unrolled the window a bit to provide Kevin some air and turned, hesitant resolution thudding through him as he covered the distance to his parents' front door, behind which he'd probably find his father's steely eyes and his mother's disappointed frown.

Because surely they'd seen the interviews when they returned from their international vacation. The tabloid covers. Headlines. *TV Host's Husband Exposed As a Fraud*.

Yep, he may only have been back in the States himself for a few months, but it had been . . . an eventful few months.

A restless wind whooshed over his skin as he reached the door. The hair curling out from under his stocking cap tickled the back of his neck. Was it just him, or was the lion's head doorknocker glaring at him? Like it, too, was angry at Blake for skipping town and taking so long to make his "triumphant" return.

Well, I'm here now, Aslan.

No roar in reply, only the sound of Blake's knock puncturing the quiet. And his heart performing a River-dance routine. He shifted as he waited, his duffel bag jostling against his thigh. Another knock. Another impatient shuffle of his sandal-clad feet.

Note to self: November. Cold. Shoes. Finally he shrugged, grasped the doorknob, and pushed his way in.

And then stopped two steps into the house, greeted only by the dark marble-floored entryway. What little sun lingered outside the front door did him no good. Someone had drawn the curtains.

Okay, pause. He *had* called to tell them he was arriving today, right? His mother had answered. Said they were home from their African safari. He hadn't hallucinated that whole conversation, had he? Did they really care so little that he was finally coming home?

"Hello?" He croaked the word, and his bag thudded to the floor. "Helloooo." Singsong this time, sounding like the kid he used to be and not the almost-thirty-year-old playing reluctant prodigal.

A creak. A whisper. And before Blake could make a move, the lights came to life and people, so many people, erupted into cheers, spilling into the entryway from the dining room to the right. His gaze hooked on the *Welcome Home* banner hanging from the base of the second-floor balcony.

And Mom and Dad, standing in the center of the room. Smiling like . . .

Like he hadn't once destroyed their world and then from it, disappeared.

"Whoa." It came out an awed whisper as someone hit the stereo—smooth Miles Davis, his father's favorite. Hands patted his back, chatter sprinkling the room as the party fanned out.

"Son."

Linus Hunziker stepped forward. His linebacker frame had slimmed since Blake saw him last. The silver that once streaked his temples now covered his head. And when had his father traded in his classic leather shoes for something out of an orthopedic catalogue?

Blake met his father's eyes.

The lines etched around Dad's mouth deepened as he grinned and grasped Blake's hand. "Don't ask. Someday you, too, will fall prey to a bossy podiatrist." The handshake turned into a full-blown hug.

Blake stepped back, numb disbelief finally wearing off. "I can't believe . . ."

Mom squeezed in then, nudging Dad out of the way and throwing her arms around Blake's neck. Almost laughably diminutive compared to Linus, Francie Hunziker barely came up to her son's shoulder. Though small, his mother had a fierce side to her. One flash of her brown-almost-black eyes and she'd been able to silence her sons at their wildest. "Hey, Mom," he said over her head.

Dad wound his arm around Mom's shoulders when she moved to his side. Blake pulled the hat from his head, raked his fingers through his shaggy hair—a self-conscious move. He'd expected anger. Maybe tears from his mother. If not because of his disappearance after his brother's funeral, then at least because of his latest stunt. The one that landed him on TV and made his name a household laughingstock.

This . . . happiness? So not in his crystal ball.

Miles faded into a hush, replaced by the brass of Sinatra's "Come Fly With Me." Someone, maybe one of his father's employees, clapped his palm on Blake's shoulder as he scooted past, aiming for the buffet table edged against the base of the open staircase. "Welcome home, Blaze."

His father chuckled at the use of Blake's nickname—the result of one too many accidental fires over the years. The sparklers. The metal travel mug in the microwave.

"I don't get it," he finally sputtered. "I thought—"

"Whatever you thought, let it go. Your mother and I couldn't be happier you're home. Lose the duffel and enjoy your party."

So many questions somersaulted through his brain. Didn't they wonder where he'd been all this time? Why he'd finally come home? What had possessed him to agree to last month's celebrity charade? Emotions—too many to name—pressed in as this place, so familiar and forgotten all at once, blurred Blake's mental vision.

Home. Ryan. And Frank Sinatra telling him to fly.

"Want something to eat?" Mom's voice cut in.

His stomach rumbled at the thought of food. He glanced down at his holey jeans. "I should run upstairs and change first."

Linus reached for the duffel and placed it over Blake's shoulder. "Hurry down."

Blake nodded, then wove through the crowd, returning greetings and smiles. He took the stairs two at a time to the second floor, his sandals flopping against each step.

Music and voices faded as he walked past the doorways to the room he'd called his own for the first eighteen years of his life. Twenty-two if he included the summers he'd spent at home between college semesters.

On a different night he might've trailed to a stop outside Ryan's door, let a rush of memories whisper over him—maybe even wished for a ghost of the older brother he still missed.

But something had changed the moment the lights flickered on downstairs, when he'd heard pride instead of punishment in his father's voice. Reluctance morphed into pulsing determination.

In his old room, posters and basketball trophies had been replaced with generic prints and whatever knick-knacks Mom must've tired of seeing elsewhere. He pulled a pair of wrinkled khakis from his bag. A white collared shirt, too. Closest he had to dressy.

Maybe this whole not-living-out-of-a-duffel thing would stick.

Maybe he could finally be the son his parents had lost. The man Ryan would've been. Work at Dad's hotel, settle down. Meet the right girl—as in, not a celebrity, not a fake relationship.

Not that pretending to be a DIY celebrity's husband hadn't had its fun moments. He'd agreed to the crazy scheme solely to help Randi Woodruff attempt to save her television show, *From the Ground Up*. And honestly, it'd been pretty cool watching her pick up the pieces when the lie of a life she'd built for herself came crashing down.

She'd changed. Found love, the real thing. And faith. Most of that didn't make it into the tabloids, though. And now, almost a month after moving out of Randi's home, the whole thing felt a little like a dream. Well, except for the lingering swirl of media interest—which he'd mostly managed to dodge during the past couple weeks.

But what if he could find the same things Randi had—new life, freedom from the past, the kind of identity he could be proud of rather than a reputation shadowed in shame? It was that hope that'd prodded him home even when worry about his family's—the whole town's—reception crept in.

Blake traded in his sandals for a pair of leather shoes he found in the closet and soon after descended the stair-case. The chandelier overhead cast a whitish yellow glow over the heads of his parents' guests. What were the chances they'd invited anyone under fifty-five?

The clink of silverware against glass stopped him at the bottom of the stairs. Dad lifted his arms to quiet the attendees. "All right, as everyone can see, my son has rejoined the party." His father motioned to him. "Come over here, Blake."

But Kevin was still in the car. He'd hoped to slip out and free the dog. Blake rubbed one hand over his stubble-covered chin, catching the look of anticipation in Dad's eyes. Kevin could wait a few more minutes. He moved to his father's eyes.

"Most of you know Blake has spent a fair amount of time traveling. For a while he led excursions in the Rockies. Then for the past five years he's globe-trotted so much, *Lonely Planet* should hire him. You've probably also heard about his more recent, um, exploits."

Dad paused to allow a sprinkle of polite laughter.

"Blake's an adventurer. And while Francie and I might have appreciated a few more postcards over the years"— Dad gave Blake a pointed look—"we're overjoyed at his return. So I'd like to present him with a gift. Delaney?"

As in Ike Delaney, Blake's old flight instructor?

Dread wormed its way under Blake's skin as Ike moved to the center of the room, something jingling in his hands. The pilot's smile—friendly, exuberant—jarred Blake's confidence. *No, Dad didn't . . .*

"The keys to your Cessna 206. A six-seater with a custom paint job. Took the liberty of naming it: *The Blaze.*"

Chuckles spread through the room as Ike pressed the keys into Blake's hand.

"Now, this isn't a toy. It comes complete with a job

offer—private pilot for the hotel, providing air shuttle for our high-end guests."

His father continued his speech, all gusto, no notice of Blake's heavy breaths. His fingers curled around the keys, metal digging into his palms.

He couldn't make out Dad's words, heard only the roar of wind from an open airplane door. The hum and growl of the engine. Panicked words from his brother's best friend. And his own silent prayers as he scanned the skies from the cockpit, knuckles white on the controls, begging God to let him be wrong. . . .

Nothing.

A slap on his back yanked him back to his parents' home. His father's voice. "Well, Blake, what do you have to say?"

◈

She'd shrug it off. Dylan's cancellation. Blake's return. Just shrug it all off.

From the inn's front porch, Autumn watched Dylan's Lexus motor down the lane toward the road that would lead him south to town and out of sight. So they wouldn't be hosting their wedding reception here. So what.

She turned, jiggling the front door's finicky handle and hefting open the massive door. "So we won't be getting a new storm door anytime soon—that's what." Or new siding. Or fixing the cracks in the dining room ceiling.

From the check-in desk, Harry waved her over as soon as she tripped into the lobby. He'd zipped back inside earlier when they'd heard the phone ringing, leaving Autumn to say her awkward good-bye to Dylan.

A wash of orange sunset spilled through long windows, painting mint-green walls bold and glinting over the waist-high wood wainscoting. The lobby was flanked by a fireside sitting room on one side and the dining room on the other. A wide, open staircase divided the lobby.

Harry gestured again, phone propped against his ear. *Right*. He'd said something about a reservation.

"No, we don't have an indoor pool, but—" Harry offered her a helpless shrug as the person on the other end of the line started talking again.

See, this is why they kept losing guests to the Hunziker Hotel. Because apparently a spectacular view of Lake Michigan couldn't compete with the downtown hotel's spa and indoor pool and oh-so-sturdy roof that probably wouldn't leak if a monsoon hit town.

"Unfortunately, no, it hasn't snowed just yet, but I can certainly try to put in a good word with Mother Nature." Poor Harry was definitely not winning this phone call. Which meant her inn was definitely not snagging this guest. She breathed her dozenth prayer for snow, for guests, then plucked a bottle of Old English and a rag from behind the desk.

"Find me when you're off the phone," she whispered, then headed for the dining room. Might as well check another to-do off the list while waiting for Harry. Guests received a complimentary breakfast in the table-dotted room, and it operated as a restaurant four evenings a week—for guests and the occasional community member who still remembered the inn existed.

Ten minutes later, she'd just about finished polishing the room's baseboards. She paused at the squeak of the swinging door leading into the kitchen, the sight of Betsy's purple old-school Nikes tapping to her side.

"Tell me what you're thinking, kiddo."

"Kiddo?" Autumn looked up from her kneeling position, the lemony scent of Old English wafting around her. "You're only nine years older than me, Bets."

"Yeah, but as your self-appointed big sister or maybe aunt—pick your surrogate family member of choice— I'm entitled to an endearment or two." The inn's chef straightened the apron cinched at her waist. "I saw Harry come in to catch the phone. Before he answered he said Dylan cancelled. How are you?"

"I'm fine."

Betsy tilted her head, black pixie hair held in place by a lace headband. "How fine?"

Autumn capped her bottle of Old English and stood. "So fine someone should write a song about it."

"Autumn—"

"Why stop at a song? Why not a whole musical?"

Betsy's eyebrows peeked under her swooping bangs. "With dancing?"

"And outlandish costumes." She handed Betsy her rag and bottle, then reached around to pull a small notebook from her back pocket. Autumn plucked the pencil from behind her ear, drew a line through the second to last to-do on her list, and added, *Oil kitchen door hinges.*

"I think you're avoiding the topic at hand." Mild reprimand lingered in Betsy's voice. Which is what made Betsy less girlfriend and more nagging babysitter in times like these.

Sometimes Autumn didn't mind it. After all, her own

big sister hadn't stuck around to play the role. But today . . . no thank you. *I don't need advice or a listening ear. I need guests. I need to catch up on mortgage payments. I need Dylan to turn his car around, say he changed his mind. I need that job in France.*

Any or all of it would do. Just some tangible signal God hadn't forgotten her.

"Autumn." Betsy tried once more.

Autumn turned away. Surely Harry was off the phone by now. She tracked toward the lobby, skirting around tables that probably wouldn't see guests tonight. "Don't you have cookies in the oven or something?"

"I think you're more bothered than you're letting on." Betsy trailed behind her.

She sniffed the air as she passed into the lobby. "I think I smell something burning."

Betsy's voice followed her through the doorway. "I think seeing Dylan again, hearing he's booking the hotel instead of the inn, and finding out Blake Hunziker is back all in the same afternoon is enough to fluster even you."

Harry had managed to mention all that before answering the phone?

"You're not even listening to me anymore, are you."

Autumn tugged her hair free of her ponytail, and it fell in a mess of tangles to her shoulders. She sighed. "I'm listening, Bets, I'm just choosing not to let this turn into an impromptu therapy session. Because, seriously, I'm fine."

Betsy's eyes narrowed. "You do realize each time you say it, I'm less inclined to believe it."

Autumn angled around the check-in desk. Truthfully,

seeing Dylan again had been more humiliating than anything. Especially when he'd made that comment about
her "fitting them in" the day after Thanksgiving.

Oh, if he could only see her empty appointment book.
Almost as empty as their reservation spreadsheet—and
that alone would be enough to make her financial advisor swallow his dentures.

But her financial advisor wasn't the one charged with
keeping the Kingsley Inn open. No, that had fallen to her.
And the responsibility seemed just as heavy now—maybe
heavier—as the day Mom had presented her with the
deed. A surprise birthday gift two and a half years ago.

*"I know your Dad would've been proud to hand down
his family's inn to you if he was still alive today."*

It had been all Autumn could do that day to clamp
down her shock and plaster on a smile in a display of
pleasure she didn't feel. Because Mom hadn't known
about Autumn's hopes to leave the Kingsley Inn and all
of Whisper Shore in the dust as she took off on the trip
of a lifetime. Her greatest dream had been to land an
international job. It was the reason she'd called off her
engagement in the first place.

Instead, she'd ended up with a commitment that often
felt just as weighty as marriage. What was that Proverb
about hope deferred?

Betsy leaned across the counter, voice dropping to a
whisper since Harry still spoke on the phone. "Okay,
so Dylan didn't bother you too much, but what about
Blake?"

A clawing irritation finally scraped past her calm.
"Closed subject."

"Autumn—"

"For the sake of what little calm I have left, Bets, drop it." She heard the dark tone of her tight words, saw the flinch Betsy tried to hide with a pause and a shrug.

And then, "Consider it dropped."

Betsy retreated into the dining room, the apology Autumn should've called after her struggling to get out from under the weight of a desperate desire to avoid the topic of Blake Hunziker.

She groaned as she replaced the cleaning supplies in a hidden shelf and then leaned over the surface of the desk, elbows propped, forehead in her hands. She heard the beep of Harry ending his call.

"What'd you say to her?"

Autumn only shook her head.

"You two bicker enough I could almost believe you really are related."

Autumn lifted her head. "Wasn't her. It was all me. I hate it when I'm like this. Snappish and . . . and . . ."

"Irritable?"

"Really, I'm irritable?"

Harry pushed his keyboard out of the way and balanced his elbows beside hers on the counter. "You actually want me to answer that?"

"Not so much."

"Well, this ought to cheer you up. It's what I came outside to tell you." He tilted his computer screen to face her. "Check out who booked the third-floor suite next month."

Autumn leaned in to read the name on the screen. "Dominic Laurent." She straightened, tapping her finger against her chin. "Dominic Laurent, why does that sound . . . ?"

"Think about it. The Laurent family? Ring a bell?"

"Oh my goodness." The screech exploded from her. "Laurent Lodging International. He's one of *those* Laurents?"

"It sounded familiar, so I Googled him as soon as I got off the phone. Definitely one of *those* Laurents."

The ones who owned hotels all over the world—mainly Europe, but lately in the U.S. too. Hadn't they just invested in a resort in Maine, turned it into a five-star destination? "He's staying *here*? Do you think it means . . ." Autumn's words rammed into each other as they tumbled out.

"Yeah, I do."

"But how . . . ?" Autumn broke off at the sight of a pile of mail stashed beside Harry's computer keyboard.

"Maybe they saw our website," Harry said as she reached for the mail. "Or wait, we placed that ad in *Travel International* a few months back. Perhaps they want to invest? Or even buy you out."

Autumn fingered through the envelopes, heart racing and hands suddenly clammy.

"Except you wouldn't really sell, would you?"

Autumn stopped at the oversized envelope with the foreign postage. The words *Par Avion* stamped over the address. The name of the Paris hotel in the corner. This had to be it.

"Oh, this is a weird day." The words came out a whisper. "A weird, weird day."

Everything was happening in twos:

The thorns: Dylan and Blake.

The roses: Dominic Laurent and the envelope from France.

"Autumn?"

Harry's voice pulled her from the fog, and she slipped her fingers over the envelope's return address. She hadn't told him about the job possibility, the phone interview two weeks ago. The nerves eating away at her as she waited to find out if her whole life might change by the time the new year rang in.

"You wouldn't sell, would you?" he asked again.

Focus. Just until they'd finished this conversation. And then she could run home, tear into a bag of Reese's Pieces, and rev herself up to open the envelope.

She looked up. "I-I don't know." She chewed on her bottom lip, hope and excitement and just a tinge of fear tangling into an untidy knot. "But any investment from LLI could keep us from going under. When's he checking in?"

"December 20."

Her breathing hitched. Three and a half weeks to get ready.

Three and a half weeks to save her inn.

Before finally saying good-bye.

2

S o does he still look like a Ken doll?"

Autumn choked on her OJ, giggles pushing through sputters until she finally swallowed. "Ellie Jakes!"

Her best friend leaned over the peninsula counter in Autumn's kitchen, blond curls flowing over her shoulders. "You can't deny Dylan's got the Mattel look down pat."

"Then it's no wonder we didn't last. I'm not Barbie material." Not with her rust-colored hair and freckled cheeks. "Anyway, it may be true, but I'd never say it out loud."

Ellie cupped her hands around her coffee mug. "I think you sorta just did."

Morning sunlight filtered through sheer curtains over the sink and danced in patterns over the peachy-orange wall opposite the window. The room might be small, but between the black-and-white checkered floor and mosaic backsplash, it had personality.

Autumn had made the tiny home her own since moving in shortly after taking over the inn. It had felt like a consolation prize. If she was going to postpone quenching her travel aspirations, at least she could do so in her own space rather than in her childhood bedroom back in town at Mom's. Plus, the two-bedroom cottage was located on inn property, which made for an awfully convenient commute.

What would happen to the place if her still-unopened letter—tucked into the napkin holder on her kitchen table—said what she hoped?

The click of her waffle maker signaled its readiness. "Breakfast time."

Ellie pulled out one of the barstools at the counter, groaning as she hefted herself onto the seat. Her stomach swelled under her polka-dotted maternity shirt. Only two months until Autumn's second honorary niece or nephew was born. "I can't tell you how happy I was when you called this morning. I love my family, but for once it was nice to leave Tim to coax Oliver into eating his breakfast. I don't know what that kid's problem is with oatmeal."

Autumn poured a cupful of batter into the waffle maker. "Um, it's oatmeal. And he's two. That's your problem right there."

"Says the girl who still eats Lucky Charms."

"Hey, am I or am I not making you Belgian waffles *with* blueberries *with* homemade maple syrup?" Fine, so the blueberries were frozen and she'd bought the "homemade" syrup at a local market.

Autumn wiped her hands on her yoga pants, turned, and plucked the letter from the napkin holder. "Here. This is why I invited you over."

"You mean it wasn't for my sparkling company?" Ellie flipped the envelope, hazel eyes scanning the return address, understanding dawning in her gasp and grin. "The Paris Hotel Grand?"

Autumn nodded, folding her sweatshirt-clad arms and leaning back against the fridge. "Sabine said I'd hear within a few weeks. I was beginning to wonder."

Sabine had come to Michigan from France as an exchange student back when Autumn was a sophomore in high school. Though she'd returned to Paris after the school year, they'd stayed in touch through the years. So receiving an e-mail a month back from Sabine hadn't been a surprise.

But what it contained—information about the job opening at the high-end hotel where Sabine worked—had been. So far, Ellie was the only person who knew about the possibility.

Ellie slapped the envelope against the counter top. "And you waited this long to mention it?"

Autumn popped a grape in her mouth from the bowl on the counter. "Thing is, once the letter finally came, I couldn't make myself open it."

She'd tried three times last night, had even gotten so far as to slide her finger under the flap and make the first tear. But it'd stopped there, nerves throwing down the gauntlet and her determination coming up short.

Because a *no* might mean disappointment. But a *yes* . . . ? Who knew a dream potentially coming true could feel so . . . scary. And yet, how long had she prayed for an open door? Somewhat doubtfully, perhaps, but maybe after all this time God was finally throwing one ajar.

"You want me to open it?"

Autumn snatched the letter back. "No, I will, silly. I just want you here to squeal with me if it's good news and cry with me if it's bad."

"It'll be good, and you know it." Ellie slid off her stool and placed one arm around Autumn's waist. At only five foot two, she barely came up to Autumn's shoulders. "I promise I'll do my best to be happy for you—but, Num, if you leave, I'm going to miss you."

"Only Oliver gets to call me Num." She leaned her head on Ellie's. "And thanks."

Ellie straightened. "So you going to open it or wha . . ." She sniffed. "Do you smell—"

"Ahhh, the waffles." With a jerk, Autumn flipped the lid up on the waffle maker, steam—or was that smoke?—billowing in her face. "Ah, man. The first time I make a real breakfast in weeks and—"

Ellie's eyebrows lifted.

"Fine, months, and it's ruined." As in, inedible. The waffle was stuck in charred chunks to the inside of the waffle maker. She'd need an ice pick to clean the appliance before she could make another batch. And it'd need to cool first . . . "So, how do you feel about Pop-Tarts?"

Ellie's snickers faded to an exaggerated sigh. "Beats oatmeal." She nudged past Autumn and opened a cupboard, frosted-glass pane rattling. "Let me toast 'em. You open that letter."

"But Ell—"

"No buts. You've waited too long to open it as is. Besides, I don't trust your recent history with appliances."

Autumn nodded, lips pressed, the taste of resolve mixing with the smell of her burnt breakfast. "Okay.

All right." She slipped her finger under the flap. "Here goes nothing."

She ripped into the envelope and pulled out the letter before she could think twice, heart staccato-ing as she scanned the words.

Dear Miss Kingsley . . . Thank you for your time . . . enjoyed the interview . . . reviewed your experience . . . pleased to offer . . .

At Autumn's shriek, Ellie dropped the box of Pop-Tarts. "You're in?"

A second piece of paper, narrow and telling, floated to her lap. An airline voucher.

"I'm in." She skimmed the rest of the letter. "They want me to start on February 1." *Oh Lord.* Which would mean moving in January. Less than two months. She dropped onto one of the table's mismatched chairs. "I'm going to have to start packing. I need to renew my passport." She hadn't dared renew it earlier for fear of jinxing the job opportunity. "I have to tell Mom. . . ."

Ohhh. Telling Mom. If she contemplated that too long, she'd give herself hives. "And all this on top of Dominic Laurent coming to the inn."

Ellie plugged in the toaster. "Explain that to me again. You think his company might be interested in acquiring the inn? Becoming a majority investor? And you'd get, what? A seal of approval or something?"

Autumn nodded absently, mind spinning as the letter fluttered to the table. "We'd become part of their brand, which would up our standing in the industry. I started Googling investment proposals and packages last night."

If it came to fruition, she wouldn't have to feel guilty leaving for France. The Kingsley Inn would stay intact and her employees would keep their jobs. She'd find a manager to take over her role. This truly could work out perfectly.

She heard the sound of foil crinkling, the toaster lowering, but breakfast had suddenly shifted into a nonissue.

Ellie lowered into the seat opposite her. "I'm proud of you, Autumn. I'll miss you like crazy, but I'll never forget how disappointed you were when things fell through the first time."

She'd had it all planned out after breaking things off with Dylan three years ago. She would quit her job as the inn's night manager—a position she'd held all through community college—take out her savings, and finally see the world the way Dad had always encouraged her to. Maybe she'd find a job at a travel agency or write for an international magazine.

But then Mom had shocked her by handing over the entirety of the inn operation so she could focus on her growing role on the state tourism board. And Autumn hadn't been able to hand it back—not knowing all her mother had already lost, not with the strain already between them. Not when she was the only Kingsley left to take the reins of the family business begun by her father's grandfather.

Well, besides Ava. But her sister hadn't looked back once after leaving town. Autumn blinked away a wince.

"So when would you leave? Would you at least come home for holidays? Have you prayed about this, Autumn?"

The toaster popped.

What was there to pray about? When your dream finally hit the "come true" part, you ran with it, didn't you? "Let's not talk about it now, Ell."

Ellie stood and walked to the counter. "The biggest thing to happen to you since, well, Dylan, and you don't want to talk about it? You don't want to hear my sage wisdom and sound advice?"

"I have Betsy for that. You're the one who's supposed to indulge my reckless avoidance and need for distraction."

Ellie harrumphed. "I think I was just insulted."

Autumn rubbed her palms over her knees. "I just need to let it sink in before talking details." Did her voice sound as shaky as she felt?

Ellie handed her a napkin-wrapped Pop-Tart. She tousled Autumn's still sleep-mussed hair. "All right. Sometimes I forget you like your mental and emotional space."

The toasted pastry warmed her fingers through the napkin. She took a sugary bite, chewing as the crumbs of a dozen to-dos scattered through her mind. Ellie was right. She did need to talk about her plans—with Mom. She needed to whip the inn into better shape than it'd been since she could remember, and she'd have to break the news to Harry and Bets and . . .

Ava. But would her sister even care? After all, she'd been back home all of what, five or six times since leaving town six years ago?

"So what do you want to talk about instead?" Ellie topped off their orange juice. "Ooh, I know. Guess who's back in town."

Her Pop-Tart stuck in her throat. "I heard."

And for one needling moment, twin pangs dueled. Which was worse—the thought of all the geographical and emotional distance between her and her sister? Or the sudden lack of distance between her and the youngest Hunziker?

"Can you believe it? Blaze Hunziker, brave enough to come back to Whisper Shore. And his dad throws him a welcome home party? What do you want to bet he paid the guests to come?"

"Not nice, Ell." But possibly entirely plausible. Who faked a marriage with a home-building show host? Blake-also-known-as-Blaze Hunziker's reputation in Whisper Shore had been rocky enough before he got himself tangled up in a celebrity scandal that read like a reality-TV script.

Autumn only wished she could get as caught up in Blake's most recent shenanigans as the rest of the town. She'd take that any day over the other memories. Ava's tears. Mom's anger. An entire town grieving the loss of its golden boy football star—Blake's brother, Ryan.

And Blake, who could've stopped it all if he'd only listened.

"I changed my mind, Ell. Let's go back to talking about LLI and France and how I'm going to pack and how much you're going to miss me."

And how she'd do everything she could to avoid Blake Hunziker.

◈

Less than twenty-four hours home and he'd already found a way to annoy his father.

At least, Blake assumed that was annoyance written in Dad's creased brow and wordless response. The airplane keys, brick-heavy in Blake's thoughts since Dad presented them last night, now splayed on the glass-top desk between them alongside a silence that expanded like the years since their last real conversation.

Then, finally, "Too much, too fast?"

At least the regret in Dad's voice assured Blake his parents had meant the gift as just that. A gift. Not a purposely torturous reminder.

Blake leaned forward in the leather chair facing his father, palms on the knees of his jeans. "It was a generous gesture, Dad." Which might be the understatement of the decade. "But I don't fly anymore."

The heady aroma of espresso from the machine in the corner of Dad's office niggled Blake's stomach. Shouldn't have skipped breakfast, but he hadn't wanted to put this off.

After six years, he'd lost his taste for avoidance.

Dad pushed aside a folder bearing the Hunziker Hotel logo on the front and fingered the ring of keys. "All you ever used to talk about was having your own plane."

"Used to. Not anymore."

Dad abandoned the keys and pushed his chair back from his desk, sighing with the movement. "You did all that training to get your commercial license. Went to work with that skydiving crew right after college." His pause stretched, strained and uncertain. "If this is about Ryan—"

"Of course it's about Ryan!" Blake's words toppled out before he could control them, hands sliding off his knees and exasperation wheezing through him. Did Dad really have to ask?

Dad stood then and, with the same slump in his shoulders Blake remembered from Ryan's funeral, shuffled to the espresso machine. Linus Hunziker looked nothing like a mayor or successful business owner as he refilled his mug—only a still-grieving father with no idea how to respond to his leftover son.

A flurry of wind rattled against the window behind Dad's desk. The gray and cold that'd had Blake ducking into the high collar of his windbreaker as he walked to the hotel earlier seemed to seep inside now. It matched the office's sharp, angled furniture and chrome accents—a contrast from the building's charming brick exterior that blended in with the rest of the downtown.

Dad turned. "Then what's the plan? If you won't fly for the hotel, then . . . what?"

Over the years Dad had insisted there was always a place for his sons at the hotel. While Blake had never fully committed to the idea, he knew Ryan had planned to eventually move home and help with the family business.

After his football career, of course. The one tragically cut short. All because of Blake's thirst for fun and adventure. Which is why it made sense to leave all that behind, settle down.

"Well, I do have that business degree. Thought maybe I could put it to use here at the hotel." He paused, tracing the stitching along the edge of his chair. "I want a normal life."

He'd never put the desire into words before. Possibly because he'd never had the desire before. Before his brother's death, all he'd ever craved was a good thrill. After, all he'd wanted was to forget.

Now he simply wanted . . . to belong. To have a purpose. Something to convince him there was a reason he was still alive when Ryan wasn't.

"A normal life, huh." Dad's expression hovered somewhere between irked and amused. "Is that why the first thing you did when you came back to the States was play house with a celebrity? Do you have any idea how many media calls we've fielded since returning home?"

Really? He was still that much of a public curiosity? "Dad, I—"

"Never mind. I shouldn't have brought it up." Dad gulped down his espresso and set down the cup with a thud. "Next to our dying tourism trade, your short-lived stint as a celebrity is the most popular conversation piece in Whisper Shore, and frankly, I'm tired of my son being the talk of the town."

Whether Dad intended or not, the verbal punch landed right where it counted—the wound still smarting from the stares and hushed murmurs at Ryan's funeral. *He was the one flying the plane.* Suddenly coming here this morning—coming home at all—felt all kinds of ridiculous.

But he'd been so sure the whisper urging him home had been a divine nudge. God directing his path or something. Then again, maybe he was just as bad at this faith thing as he was the living-a-normal-life thing.

"And," Dad went on, still standing, glancing at his watch, "I'm supposed to meet a council member at the city offices in ten."

In other words, he was dismissed.

Dad straightened his metallic gray tie and reached for his faded leather briefcase, the one he'd carried for as long as Blake could remember.

"Son."

The word was enough to pull Blake to his feet.

"Walk with me."

The invitation seemed a peace offering for an argument they hadn't even had. Which was one more reminder of how long he'd been away. Dad had changed, mellowed. And Blake had missed the transformation.

He followed his father from the office, reminding himself of Kevin just then—a little worse for the wear but eager to please in his own limping way.

Which reminded him, the wayward dog needed a bath. And real dog food instead of table scraps. He still couldn't get over the fact that Mom had let the mutt in the house last night.

"You mentioned an interest in working at the hotel." Dad spoke with a sidelong glance as they trekked toward the lobby. "Truth is, I don't really see you behind a desk."

"Oh." Shouldn't surprise him. He'd suffered through grade school about as well as a grounded bird. But that was then. He'd changed, right?

"I could probably put you at the front desk a few days a week, though, if that's what you want," Dad finished.

Blake's gaze circled the lobby as they passed through. It shined with contemporary fixtures and an upscale aura—slate-colored walls a match for the slew of suits that passed through the hotel on a daily basis. May not have the lakeside view of the Kingsley Inn, but it made up for it in modern appeal.

And when the revolving doors spit them outside, it was like stepping into another century. The cobblestone Main Street echoed old-world, with corner flowerpots and old-fashioned lampposts. The downtown made up of colorful buildings wrapped in perfect right angles around a faded-green town square dotted with trees.

Whisper Shore had quaint in the bag.

Except, in the light of day it all seemed a little . . . tired. And what had Dad said about the dying tourist trade?

"You coming?" Dad was several steps ahead, the short walk to the city offices barely a two-block span. Blake tugged up the zipper of his jacket and picked up his pace to match his father's, sandals he still hadn't traded for shoes slapping against concrete.

"So do you want me to stick you on the front-desk rotation?"

"Not if it means cutting someone else's hours."

Dad shrugged. "Actually, we've been a man short ever since Casey's wife had a baby. He's going to be a stay-at-home dad, and—"

Dad broke off as they neared the teal blue historic building that housed the city offices, its brass sign swinging in the wind from a horizontal post overhead. A voice Blake recognized rose with each beat of the sign's movement.

"Georgie, you can't do it to us. We're barely a month from the festival." Blake would have known his on-again, off-again high-school girlfriend anywhere, even without her telltale Kawasaki parked at the curb. Hilary Gray—arms folded, lips pursed, and hair as black as the leather jacket zipped to her neck. "You can't just leave us in the lurch like this."

She faced off with another familiar face—Georgie Snyder, longtime director of the Chamber of Commerce. Known as much for her penchant for lawn decorations as her militant-like leadership of every community event since, like, the dawn of time.

What was Hils doing arguing with the Flamingo Lady?

"I have given this town my undivided attention for years." Georgie shoved a stack of folders toward Hilary. "I'm not calling off my plans just so I can coordinate a festival nobody's going to show up for anyway."

Dad exhaled an "Uh-oh" before stepping up to the ladies. "What's the trouble?"

Hilary turned to Blake's father. "Oh good, you're here. Maybe you can talk some sense into her."

"You won't change my mind." Georgie pulled on the belt of her coat. "I'm eloping on Sunday and leaving town Monday. That's all there is to it." She spun on her heels and disappeared around a corner before Dad could say a word.

Blake let out a whistle. "The Flamingo Lady's getting hitched?"

Hilary saw him then, eyebrows lifting and arms tightening around the folders Georgie had thrust at her. "So the rumors are true. Blaze Hunziker's back."

Her voice held little welcome. Even less pleasure. *Ooo-kay.*

Dad still stared down the sidewalk. "No wonder you called me to meet with you, Hilary."

Wait, *Hilary* was the city council member Dad had come to meet? The girl who'd worn the label of *rebel* like a badge of honor in high school was now in local government?

"We're out a festival coordinator, which basically means we're out a festival, which absolutely means we can say good-bye to our final tourist boost of the year." Hilary's dark hair swung as she shook her head.

Blake chanced a comment. "Couldn't you just . . . get someone else?"

Hilary drilled him with a glance. "The festival is less than a month away."

Dad's sigh matched the rustling wind. "And this on top of Victoria Kingsley once again . . ." He took a breath and, at Blake's questioning glance, shook his head. "Nope, she's not my biggest problem now. The festival is. Hilary, I'll make some calls. Son, we'll talk later."

Blake nodded, and Dad slipped into the city offices, leaving Blake to face Hilary's stony silence . . . and wonder what the Kingsley family had done now. At least one thing hadn't changed.

The overhead city office sign continued its rhythmic creaking as Hilary glared at him, stack of folders still pressed against her.

"C'mon, Hils. I just got home. At least throw me a *welcome back*."

"Fine. Welcome back, Blaze."

An old truck rumbled by, tires bumping over cobblestone and motor grumbling. "Sorta trying to shake the nickname."

"Not gonna happen. Not here. So, why'd you come back? Couldn't find another celebrity to take up with? What were you thinking, anyway?"

"Long story." One he was starting to believe he'd never hear the end of.

"Not really. You faked a marriage with a TV star. Then she outted you when she fell in love with someone else."

"Thanks for the recap. So you're on the city council?" Gnarled leaves skittered over the sidewalk and between their feet.

She nodded. "Second year of my first term."

"Which means worrying about things like town festivals?"

"Not just me worrying—it's the whole town. Have you seen how many storefronts are empty? The festival was supposed to give us an end-of-the-year income boost. Instead we've lost the coordinator and now we're literally going to have to cancel Christmas. Meanwhile, I've got an AWOL husband and two boys at home who can't figure out why Mom's such a mess."

"You're married?" And a mom? Sheesh, everywhere he looked he was finding evidence of what he'd missed.

"Separated."

"I'm . . . sorry." So Blake wasn't the only one whose life had veered off course. Whatever the shade of loss, the stain was just as permanent. "I wish there was something I could do to help."

Quiet rippled through the square, through its empty gazebo and massive centerpiece of an evergreen. A frosty late-autumn chill still blanketed the morning, the sidewalk under his feet shiny.

Hilary faced him then, looking from Blake to the stack of folders in her hands back to Blake. Her slow grin took on an impish flair—finally a hint of the Hilary he remembered. "Maybe there is."

Cold crawled up the sleeves of Autumn's navy blue coat as she dropped a five-dollar bill on the high window counter of Pete's Snack Shack. Only the twinkle of stringed bulbs around the little building and the glow of streetlamps lit the town square.

"Keep the change."

Grinning down at her from his perch, Pete held out her ice cream cone. "Not a chance, kid."

"Come on, Petey. You deserve it. You'd already turned over the *Closed* sign when I got here, and I *know* I'm the only one who orders ice cream in November. You keep a supply just for me."

Autumn clutched the waffle cone with gloved hands. She fully intended to call Mom tonight. The news of her departure might be better delivered in person, but since Mom spent half her time traveling around the state these days, it was easier to catch her on her cell.

But Autumn needed reinforcement in the form of sugar to fuel her willpower. Something told her it wasn't going to be a fun conversation.

She nudged the five across the counter. "The least I can do is tip you."

"The least you can do is bring a few friends next time." Pete winked, but she didn't miss the hint of sincerity in his suggestion. Wind flickered through his gray-and-white mustache as the man spoke. "I could use the business."

Couldn't they all. A lingering smattering of withered leaves scraped across the sidewalk. "That bad?"

He rubbed his chin, ruddy cheeks evidence of how many years the snack shop proprietor had spent at this window—taking orders and drawing laughs. A town fixture if ever there was one. "Truth is, I'm thinking I might need to close up come winter."

"Aww, Petey."

"Don't look so sad, kid. The supermarket does carry ice cream, you know."

"It's not the ice cream I'd miss most." She'd grown fond of her Saturday night chats with the man. In many ways, he reminded her of her dad—always a story to tell, always the life of a party.

Except not always. Not in the end.

Like her breath fogging in a cloud of white, the image

of Dad's face rose. Not the way she liked to remember him, but the way he'd been in those last couple years, especially the last few weeks before he died. Laugh lines dipping into frequent frowns, sapphire blue eyes—same color he'd passed on to her—more and more often darting and distant.

Time—almost fourteen years—had dulled the sting of Dad's death, but not the effect of what she'd seen and overheard in those last days before the aneurysm that stole his life.

"The last thing I want to do is hurt our family, but I have to do this."

"Nobody has *to abandon his family."*

Silence.

Then, *"Fine, go get the divorce papers drawn up. But don't expect me to step into your shoes here when you leave. I won't run this inn alone."*

Autumn blinked, shucking away the conversation she'd tried so many times to forget. If she could just pretend she'd never overheard, in her memories Dad could still be . . . *Dad.*

Instead of the man who'd once planned to walk away from his family. And Mom, the one who'd barely even fought him on it.

"Take the change, Autumn Kingsley." Pete's voice and the dollar bills he waved in front of her eyes crowded out the unpleasant memory.

"Okay, but only because I intend to come back next week with friends, just like you asked."

"If I'm still open, I'll be appreciative."

Pete waved her off and slid his window closed, leaving her to her cone and a nearly deserted downtown.

Her Jetta rested at the curb, but instead of slipping into the car, she opted for the gazebo. Might do to clear her head a bit. Enjoy the ice cream and the peace of a sleepy Whisper Shore. Maybe read a chapter or two from one of the books weighing down her purse.

After all, fall never held on this long into November. Tonight might be cool, but there was no snowy blizzard or sheets of ice forcing her inside. She should enjoy it while she could.

The crackle of wind through bare branches and the beat of a jogger's footsteps through fallen leaves sounding from somewhere nearby were the only soundtracks to her walk through the square. Intent on reaching the gazebo, she angled around the evergreen that served as the town Christmas tree every year and—

"Whoa, lady!"

The smack came hard and fast. And . . . hard. Her cheek hit into a wall of a chest, and the impact flung her backward, sending her cone plopping to the grass, along with her purse. Her feet tangled beneath her, caught in . . . something. A dog's leash?

The only thing that stopped her from going down was the grip that shot out to catch her. Hands latched onto her arms, fingers warm and tight through the sleeve of her coat.

"Gotcha," the jogger said as he caught his breath. A pair of paws bounded at her side. It *was* a dog. "Down, Kevin. Leave her alone."

Blood, she could taste it. "My nose." She lifted her hands to cover her face.

"Dude, you're bleeding."

"Dude, that's very Sherlock Holmes of you." Finally

she looked up. Swallowed a gasp as her eyes met his. Though the evening's dim light veiled his features, she'd have known him anywhere. The pang traveled from her nose to her heart.

Blake Hunziker . . . looking so much like his brother, it was uncanny—from the dark hair tamed by a rolled-up handkerchief to his height and broad shoulders.

If he weren't a Hunziker, she'd have called him handsome, even in his track pants and running shoes, with a day's stubble shadowing his face. Ridiculously long lashes rimmed his dark eyes.

He dropped his hands from her arms. While she stared, he swiped the handkerchief from his head, shook it, and held it out. "Here. For your nose."

Her gaze passed from his offering to his forehead back to the handkerchief. "But you're, uh . . . sweaty."

"You really think my sweat is grosser than your blood?"

Good point. She accepted the handkerchief and held it to her nose. Hands on his hips, Blake only watched.

"I think you broke it," she said, voice muffled by the cloth, which, amazingly, smelled less like perspiration and more like shampoo. The dog—skinny but looking freshly groomed—sat obediently by his side now.

"Here, let me see. I'm sure it's not broken." He bent his legs and tipped his head down until she could feel the warmth of his breath on her face. He lifted his hand. "We didn't hit that hard."

"Wanna bet?" Autumn inched away, but his hand still connected with her face, fingers tracing from one side of her nose to the other. "I feel like I slammed into a brick wall." But the man had a soft touch. She'd give him that.

"Then I guess my workouts are paying off." He smirked. "Kidding."

She'd have laughed if she weren't so irritated. If he didn't look so "I've just run across town and I'm barely winded." If she didn't have blood on her face and ice cream on her favorite coat.

With two fingers he gently prodded the bridge of her nose once more. "Not broken." He tapped the tip of her nose and stepped back, a telltale crunch signaling the demise of her cone.

"Oh man. My cone, too." And now his dog was licking the thing up. So much for a peaceful walk.

So much for avoiding Blake Hunziker.

"So. Autumn Kingsley."

She lifted his handkerchief back to her nose. "I take back the Sherlock reference. You're too slow on the draw."

"Call me Watson, then." His smile, flanked by annoying dimples, probably should've prompted her own. But how could he be so laid-back after all that had happened between their families? If the longtime business rivalry wasn't enough, then there was the blame, the blowup before his brother's funeral. Their own angry words the day she'd confronted him about Ryan.

"He has a problem, Blake. Ava is convinced—"

"You want to talk about problems? Ava's the problem."

"I recognized you the second we hit, Kingsley," he said now. All casual, no hint of the past heckling him like it did her. "We did go to school together for twelve years, after all."

"Ten. You were two grades ahead of me."

"Fine." His expression turned quizzical. "Why were you eating ice cream when it's forty degrees out?"

She blinked. "Why are you wearing a T-shirt?" One that stretched taut over threaded muscles she wished she didn't notice. No wonder that TV star had picked him for her fake husband.

"Because if I'm cold, I'll run faster," he said wryly, then reached down to pick up her bag. "Man, what do you have in here? Cement?"

"Books, if you must know." Because while he might have the luxury of traveling the world on his family's dime, some people had to live their adventures in the pages of a novel. *Not anymore, though.* It was so, so almost her turn.

"Well, what's the haps? How are things at the inn?"

He really wanted to do this now, play catch-up while her nose bruised and his dog slurped up *her* ice cream? "Things are fine." She reached for her bag and slung it over her shoulder, refusing to wince at the weight of it.

"Nice job on the ambiguity."

"Wow, the man knows big words."

Blake's half-grin floated between amusement and curiosity. "Since I'm sure you're about to ask, I'm fine, too. Just peachy. Running . . . clears my head."

Something, maybe his slight pause or the flicker of uncertainty he probably thought he hid under a teasing exterior, pointed her to the realization then: He remembered just as much as she did.

But he was trying to look past the past, wasn't he? *Six years doesn't erase what happened, Blake.* And yet . . .

She grasped for a softer tone. "*Ice cream* clears my head. And books."

He glanced down to where his dog was finishing off the last of her cone. "Can I buy you another?"

"No, thanks." She lowered the handkerchief once more and tested her nose with a wrinkle. "So . . ."

"So."

"Welcome home. I heard there was a party." See, she could do friendly, too.

"Oh yeah, it was a wild one." The corners of his eyes crinkled. "Though I think half the people in attendance actually thought it was a party to welcome home my parents from their vacation, not me."

"Can't believe I wasn't invited." As soon as she said the joking words, her lips pressed. She'd meant the comment lightly.

But the sudden swell of tension, the tick in Blake's jaw, her own hard swallow told her they'd both had the same thought.

Of course she wasn't invited.

Because Kingsleys and Hunzikers didn't mix. The one time they'd tried—her sister, his brother—it'd ended in hurt and a shock deep enough to impact the whole town.

Blake's dog jerked on his leash, paving the way for his sudden and stilted, "Well, have a good night."

Her forced nod.

His retreat.

And that's that.

Autumn let out a deep exhale as she watched Blake's walk turn into a run, his dog keeping pace as he crossed the square. She looked down to his handkerchief still in her hand, stuffed it in her coat pocket, and sidestepped the remainder of the sticky mess on the grass.

3

The beat of the basketball against the gym floor matched the drumming of Blake's heart.

And here he'd expected to easily school Tim Jakes in their half-court one-on-one match. But the small-town cop, his old best friend, had kept up his game in the years since they played last. Blake had run into Tim last week, the same day Hilary had waltzed him into the city offices and offered him up as Whisper Shore's saving grace.

What a joke.

With one hand, Blake swiped at the sweat across his forehead, while the other dribbled the ball.

"I'm going to call shot clock if you don't move soon, Hunziker."

Tim's razzing drew a smirk. "What, scared?" With the kind of footwork their old coach would've loved, he swept past Tim and landed a jump shot. "46–43." Fifty ended the game. A couple layups and he would claim victory, then guzzle a gallon of water while his calves screamed at him.

Along with his brain. Because sooner or later he'd have to give Hilary, not to mention Dad and the rest of the city council, an answer as to whether he'd take on the Christmas festival in Georgie Snyder's stead.

Right. The guy who'd broken his arm after falling out of a tree and earned a nickname by setting accidental fires. And, oh yeah, who was still the butt of late-night-talk-show jokes. That's who Hilary wanted fronting the town's biggest event of the winter season.

What had he been thinking even staying in the room when she pitched the idea to Dad?

Okay, so he knew what he'd been thinking: Pull this off and the good people of Whisper Shore might finally have something nice to say about him. After all, if things were really that bad in town . . .

Focus on the game. He could figure out his future—and that of his hometown—later.

Tim moved in, Blake guarding him, arms outstretched. But in a flash, Tim backed up behind the three-point line and released the ball. It swished through the net to tie the score.

"Nice."

Gulping in breaths, Tim followed him to the line. "So Hilary and your dad asked the city council to name you the new festival coordinator. Never would've imagined my thrill-seeking friend as an event organizer."

Blake kicked the kinks out of his legs. He might seriously regret this game later. "They all but laughed in Dad's face."

Blake had attended the meeting with his father Monday night, dressed in his best, even though he'd never actually agreed to Hilary's plan. He'd even shaved for the occasion. But he might as well have shown up in jeans and a hoodie for all the serious consideration they gave him.

At first.

But then Hilary had jumped in, cut right to the kicker—a little tidbit she'd failed to spring on him earlier. "He's a media draw, folks. Practically a celebrity."

And just like that, while he sputtered on his water, the tables turned. Suddenly they wanted him—lock, stock and tabloid-weathered barrel.

"So you're doing it?" Tim asked now, knees bent in guard position as he waited for Blake to make his move.

Ball balanced in the crook of his arm, Blake eyed the hoop. "Not sure." Instead of finishing the explanation, he dribbled and drove into the paint.

Two baskets later he closed the deal. Tim shook his head as they lugged themselves to the side-court bleacher. Blake covered his head with a towel, shaking the perspiration from his hair. Dude, he needed a cut. Definitely a shower. "Good game, man."

"Yep." Tim flicked his towel against Blake's leg. "Okay, finish the story. What happened at the meeting?"

Blake cleared his throat. "Well, by the end of it, they offered me a full-time job—Georgie's job at the Chamber—if I can pull off the festival."

"You're kidding."

"I know. Seemed crazy to me, too. And I have a high tolerance for crazy." But that's exactly what they'd done. Hilary had mentioned his business degree, his work ethic, his availability. But the magazines she plopped on the table—all of which had his name in a headline—were what sealed the deal.

He'd wanted to crawl under the table or pull a "Beam me up, Scotty."

"Wow, they must really be desperate," Tim said now.

He smirked. "Thanks for the vote of confidence, Timmy."

"Gonna do it?"

"Dunno." It would've been one thing if they'd asked him to consider the decision based on his experience. After all, he'd led tours through the Amazon, taught ski classes in the Alps. He knew a thing or two about recreation, working with people, even tourism. He'd handled budgets in past jobs, too. And the year he'd spent working for that mega lodge in the Rockies had included obtaining corporate sponsorships for some of their bigger hikes and events. He actually *was* qualified for the job.

But no, the city wanted him for his face. His recent history.

And yet, his misgivings couldn't entirely wipe out the thoughts urging him to at least consider it. Because what if he could finally do something right? Earn back the respect of a town he'd never stopped thinking of as home?

"Truth is, I actually feel like I could do a good job at this festival thing *if* I had a few months to pull it off. But how am I supposed to organize it in three and a half weeks?" Blake lifted his water bottle.

Tim rapped his knuckles on the metal bench. "I've got it. Get Autumn Kingsley to help you."

He sputtered. "Good one." He'd told Tim earlier about running into Autumn over the weekend. How he and Kevin had practically run her down. He'd left out the part about the tension razoring through their brief encounter.

"I'm serious. She's been Georgie's volunteer right-hand person at the past few festivals."

"Our families are like Whisper Shore's own Hatfields and McCoys. My dad was just spouting off about her mom the other day—something about a state tourism grant request she tabled. Name one good reason I should ask Autumn." Well, besides the fact that he'd forgotten how pretty the younger Kingsley girl was. Even in the dark, he hadn't missed that. A sideways grin slipped out at the memory of her feisty blue eyes lit up by the light of the streetlamp.

"She knows how to coordinate events, for one. This town loves her, for two."

But she'd croak before agreeing to work with a Hunziker, wouldn't she?

"Just ask her. You never know." Tim said.

Except that he kinda sorta did. Especially considering the way she'd looked at him Saturday, like it was just yesterday she'd come to him and told him about Ryan's prescription-drug addiction.

"Ava doesn't think you'll listen to her. She asked me to tell you. You're his brother. Do something."

Eventually, finally, he had. The wrong something.

"You know, one of these days, you've got to let it go, Hunziker."

He blinked, Tim's voice yanking him back to the present, to the gym where Ryan had once been crowned homecoming king. Was he so see-through?

"Not that easy." So far from easy, it made planning

the Christmas festival look like a cinch. "Tim, do you, uh . . . you keep in touch with Shawn at all?"

Shawn Baylor had been Ryan's best friend. And the only other person in the plane the day Ryan died.

Tim loosened the laces of his Nikes and straightened. "Not much. He . . . keeps to himself. And I hear he and Hilary are going through a rough patch."

Blake sucked in a breath. *Shawn* was the AWOL husband Hilary had been talking about? His two friends had married—and separated—in his time away . . . and he hadn't even known it. He closed his eyes, feeling the guilt as keenly as if he'd been the one to pull them apart. And maybe he was. Maybe that's why Hilary had bristled when she first saw him.

Maybe Shawn had never gotten over what he'd seen that day.

Just like Blake.

"Do something."

The memory of Autumn's plea all those years ago mixed with the image of Hilary's just the other day.

He stood, chucking off the weight of memories like a practiced shot putter. "You really think Kingsley would help?"

Tim glanced up and shrugged. "Maybe if you ask nice. And call her by her first name."

⸙

Why could she never manage a staff meeting as well as Mom used to?

"People, please!" Autumn waved her clipboard to quell the excitement spreading through the inn's dining room like lava, burning up what was supposed to have been a productive after-dinner meeting. So maybe making the bold pronouncement that they were going to be hosting the most important guest the inn had ever had wasn't her most brilliant idea ever. Should've eased into the news.

"Do something," Harry hissed from the chair next to her. "It's like someone spiked our coffee with catnip."

This must be what preschool teachers felt like.

They were a small but unruly crew—some of the ten staff sitting at the largest dining room table, others perched higher on the stools around a couple tall cocktail tables. The faint tones of Michael Bublé filtered in from the kitchen. Oh, for the calm in his smooth-as-glass voice to infect her staff.

Autumn nudged up the sleeves of her unbuttoned green sweater and forced her voice a notch higher. "Our guest is *not* a movie star. He's *not* on television. And, for goodness sake, he's *not* Pat Sajak." She cast a faux stern glance at Uri, their part-time swing-shift deskman.

"Hey, it was a valid guess." He shrugged from where he leaned against the cherry-hued wall. The man's creased face gave away his distance past retirement age. Autumn had a feeling that since his wife's death last year Uri continued working more out of loneliness than anything else.

One more reason her plan to woo Dominic Laurent had to work. She loved Uri, this whole crew, and each one needed the job. The pressure of the responsibility heated through her, and she tugged off her sweater, wrinkled white shirt underneath, with its wrap belt tied at the side.

"Autumn?" Harry snapped again.

"Okay, I know we're all antsy to call it a day, but we've got more to talk about." She spent the next twenty minutes explaining who Dominic Laurent was, why his visit was so important, what they needed to accomplish in the next two and a half weeks in order to impress the man. Amazingly, something resembling calm and attention settled over the staff as she spoke.

"So the more we can all pitch in, the better. If you've got downtime, find me or Harry and we'll give you a project."

Despite her earlier warmth, a twinge of cold tingled over Autumn's bare feet. She curled her purple-painted toes inside her flats. It might still look like fall outside, but with December moving in by week's end, it was time to tweak the thermostat. And probably reacquaint herself with her sock drawer.

Behind her staff, the dining room's bay windows ushered in the grays and blues of the evening's moody weather. "Does anybody have any questions?"

The sole member of the inn's housekeeping staff raised her hand.

"Yes, Charlotte?"

"If we need Mr. Laurent's investment this badly, I can't help wondering . . ." Charlotte pushed her silver braid over her shoulder. "What happens if he doesn't invest? We've all noticed business hasn't exactly been booming."

Definitely not booming. Autumn could picture the rows of rooms fingering each direction from stairs opening into the second floor. Empty, empty, occupied, empty, empty, empty, occupied, empty . . .

Too many rooms in the inn. Mary and Joseph should have been so lucky.

"Truth is, Char, things are tight. But I have a meeting with our accountant tomorrow. We're going to go over our financials."

She watched the concern ebb and flow over the faces of everyone in the room. It showed itself in twitches and pressed lips, fidgets and clenched fists.

"But I'm sure . . . at least I'm hopeful, things will turn out fine." Her words did little to restore the earlier jovial mood. Or to persuade even her. With every visit to her financial advisor's office, she left less and less convinced she ever should have been handed the reins to the inn. "Well, that's it for the meeting."

Chairs bumped against the hardwood underfoot as the staff rose, quiet in place of the ruckus from before. Autumn dropped into a chair and turned to Harry. "I finally tamed the squirrely masses. Are you proud of me?"

He folded his arms. "Not sure it was you as much as reality dawning on everyone."

She tapped his arm with her clipboard, injecting all semblance of nonchalance she could muster into her voice. "Don't talk like that, Harry. Everything's going to be okay."

"Whatever you say, Pollyanna."

"I'm serious. Think about it: Dominic. Laurent. He fell into our lap right when we most needed a miracle. If that's not divine intervention, I don't know what is."

His eyebrow quirked. "You think God is sending Laurent to us?"

"I sure don't know who else would." Anyway, it's what she wanted to believe. Especially after too many months of wondering if He still remembered her—the girl with the travel itch she couldn't scratch. Autumn stood and tugged Harry up. "Buck up. Good things are on the horizon for the Kingsley Inn." Maybe if she said it enough, she'd believe it.

"And . . . for you."

At that cryptic comment, she met Harry's eyes. He *knew*. "How . . . ?"

"The man from the Paris Hotel Grand accidentally called the inn rather than your cell phone on the day of your interview."

And he hadn't asked her about it in all this time. Was that hurt in his eyes? She lowered her voice. "I'm sorry, Harrison. I was going to tell you. I was just . . . waiting for the right time."

"What's the position?"

"Assistant to the head of guest services." A step down from manager, to be sure. But she'd have volunteered to wash dishes if it meant the opportunity to live in France. To reside in a little flat on a quaint street. To walk to the hotel along the Seine and work every day in a building with a view of the Eiffel Tower.

And on the weekends she'd take the train to surrounding countries. Maybe Sabine would come along and they'd explore historical landmarks and picturesque scenery. And she'd keep her promise to Dad.

"Make sure to see the world, Autumn. You've got the same traveler's blood I do. Promise me you won't make the world wait too long for you."

She couldn't have been more than ten at the time. Dad's stories of his own travels—when he'd worked as a photographer for several years before returning to his hometown, meeting Mom, and taking over the inn after his own father retired—had always seemed so magical.

The magic might have worn off as she got older—as Dad's restlessness started affecting their once-happy family—but not the desire it sparked.

"I received the official job offer last Friday," she said now, waiting for the reprimand or disappointment she was sure to see on Harry's face.

Instead, resignation, and maybe a smidgeon of pride, hovered in his smile. "Of course you got the job."

"Could you not tell anyone? For now?"

He started to nod but was interrupted by a shriek from the other side of the dining room window. They both glanced to where Betsy waved on the opposite side of the glass, urging them outside. "What in the world . . . ?"

Betsy knocked on the window, mouth moving, voice muffled.

Harry chuckled. "Is she saying 'wolf mess'?"

Betsy spoke again.

Autumn's mouth dropped. "No, 'wasp nest.' She found a wasp nest on the porch." She hurried out of the dining room, Harry's footsteps behind her.

The foamy fragrance of Lake Michigan breezed over her as she spilled onto the porch, cold rustling over her bare skin. Should've grabbed her sweater. "Where is it?"

Betsy pointed over her head to where a tangle of netted twigs balled against the overhang. "What do we do?"

"Don't disturb it," Harry said from behind. "Call animal control."

Autumn's laugh was a half snort. "You don't call animal control for a wasp, Harry."

"Well, we can't leave it there. Next thing we know some guest gets stung and has an allergic reaction and we get sued." Betsy fit her hands into a pair of mittens.

"Guys, this is not that big of a deal." Autumn pointed to the nest. "It's cold, which means if there's any wasps in that thing, they're probably dormant. Right?"

Neither Betsy nor Harry wore a look of assurance. "It hasn't been cold for that long," Harry said.

Autumn slipped back into the entryway, pulled an umbrella from the wicker basket just inside, and returned to the porch.

"You are not going to use that." Harry shook his head as he spoke.

"I'm just going to give it a little poke to see what we're dealing with here."

Betsy backed up. "I have a bad feeling about this."

Autumn climbed onto a rattan chair. "Yeah, well, you used to have a bad feeling about kale, too. Remember that?" She gave the nest a tentative tap.

"I don't trust greens I can't easily identify. What's wrong with that?"

"Nothing, except now you eat kale every day in those healthy smoothies you make." Another poke. "So just because you have a bad feeling—"

The nest jiggled.

"Did you do that?" From the corner of her eye, she saw Harry backing up toward Betsy as he asked the question.

"Uh-uh."

And . . . *Uh-oh*.

Suddenly it was alive, moving as a buzzing wasp—or five—kamikazed from the nest. Autumn's scream pierced the air as she jerked, rattan chair wobbling beneath her. The wasps dipped and dived, and she swung the umbrella, losing her balance, Harry and Betsy both yelling behind her.

"Don't let any inside, guys."

She heard the pounding of footsteps on the porch stairs along with the slam of the front door. She crashed into the chair and then felt it—a sting. Fast and harsh in her upper arm. She squealed, standing, gaze darting in search of the offender. The umbrella still dangled from one hand.

"Are you all right, Autumn?"

She whirled at the voice, umbrella pointed like a sword.

Blake Hunziker. Looking for all the world as if he'd just witnessed a comedy routine but was under orders not to laugh.

Perfect, just . . . perfect.

*

"Are you allergic to wasp stings?"

Blake looked from Autumn back to the nest now scattered on the porch floor. A chair lay tipped on its side, and wind chimes dangled from the curved cornice overhead. *And are you off your rocker?* Poking a wasp nest? Why not just take a stapler to her arm? Same effect.

"What?" Autumn glanced around, probably looking for the other two people he'd seen on the porch when he drove up. But they'd abandoned her the second the nest wobbled.

"I said, are you allergic to wasp stings?"

"I-I don't think so. Why do you have an ice cream cone?"

Oh yeah. That. He held the cone in one hand, stickiness dripping down the side. Probably totally un-genius, buying the cone in town and expecting it to last on the mile drive out to the inn. But it'd been the only bribe he could think of.

Because obviously ice cream would be enough to not only wipe out their rocky past but also convince the woman to help him with the festival. *Right.* "Did you get stung anywhere besides your arm?"

"No."

"You can put the umbrella down, you know. I think the wasp's gone."

"Maybe I'm protecting myself from you."

"Ha, funny. What were you thinking, poking that nest? That's like something . . ." *I would do.* But she didn't need to know how many times he'd been stung, bitten, or snapped at in the course of getting too close to an animal's habitat.

All in the past. Risk-taking Blake was gone, and in his place . . . .

Well, so far just a guy with ice cream dribbling over his hand.

"Can I look at your arm?"

She held it up, and with his free hand, he fingered the soft skin around the red spot. Good, the wasp's stinger hadn't stuck in her skin. "You should put some ice on it. Sometimes they swell up. And you need to get inside. It's cold, and you don't have a coat."

A *whoosh* of lakeside air breezed around him as he opened the inn's front door for Autumn. He nudged some stray leaves back outside with his foot and followed her in.

"Sorrysorrysorrysorry," a woman in a white apron flustered as soon as they crossed the threshold. "I know we shouldn't have left you out there, but the wasps . . ." She stopped at the sight of Blake—or maybe the ice cream cone in his hand. Probably both. "Oh. Hi."

"By which Betsy means, can we help you?" the man behind the desk tacked on.

Blake jutted his elbow toward Autumn. "Ice pack?"

"In the kitchen." The man leaned over the counter, a smirk covering his face. "Most guys opt for flowers, by the way." He eyed the ice cream.

"Harry." Pure irritation laced Autumn's tone. Hopefully directed at he-who-must-be-Harry, but by the way she looked at Blake now, he wasn't so certain.

"Come on, let's find that ice pack." He looked around. "Kitchen?"

Both Harry and Betsy pointed the way, and as they stared, he tugged Autumn along by her unstung arm. Dude, kind of an ogling crew she had.

"Y-you brought me ice cream?" she asked as they crossed the empty dining room. Must not be serving dinner tonight? Or were there that few guests staying at the inn?

A row of sconces along the wall offered the only light in the space, the sky's drifting clouds momentarily covering the lingering sunset.

"I felt bad about the other night. Didn't know what flavor you liked, and Kevin wasn't talking, so . . ." He waited for a laugh as he stood in the doorway to the kitchen. Even a chuckle. Okay, a shadow of a smile would do.

But she only stared.

"Anyway, it's kind of melted."

She blinked, finally seemed to focus. "Oh, yes, I . . ." She accepted the cone and brushed past him into the kitchen. "Kevin's your dog?"

"Mine for the moment, I guess." Should he tell Autumn she had dirt from her tumble on the porch all over the back of her white shirt? "I think he's a stray. Funny thing is, I randomly started calling him Kevin and he actually responds to it."

"As in . . . Bacon?"

"No, the kid from *Home Alone*."

She nodded from her spot in the middle of the kitchen. She held the cone awkwardly, ice cream melting over the edges and from the bottom of the cone.

"It's plain old chocolate, by the way."

She bit her lip. "Chocolate's good."

And suddenly he felt all kinds of stupid, which is why he hung back in the doorway as Autumn went to the island counter in the middle of the room, pulled a bowl from a dish rack, and deposited the cone. The kitchen had the feel of a restaurant operation—stainless steel and pots and pans hanging from hooks in the ceiling—and yet, it retained a lakeside quaintness with honey-colored walls, wicker basket decorations, and a chalkboard menu.

The lingering scent of something savory and appetizing set his stomach growling.

Autumn stood over the sink now, running her hands under water, shooting him a questioning glance over her shoulder. He approached her, jutting his sticky hands under the water beside her.

"You really should ice your arm."

"If you say so, Doc." She shook her hands dry, crossed the room, opened a deep freeze, and pulled out an ice pack. She draped it over her arm, then gave him a "now what?" look.

He glanced at the bowl holding the mess of ice cream and soggy cone. "You going to eat that?"

"Well . . ."

"I did drive all this way, Miss Kingsley."

"A whole mile out of town. However did you make it?"

He chuckled at the tease in her tone. Would've been a lie, in that moment, to deny the attraction that crawled up his chest. Between those amazing blue eyes and the flush in her cheeks . . .

Man, remember who she is. Yes. And why he'd come.

"Listen, I didn't stop by only to bring you the cone. I . . ." He watched as she lifted the bowl with her free arm up to her lips.

She paused. "What? You told me to eat it."

"You're going to lap it up like a cat?"

She held the bowl out for him to see inside. "It's practically soup."

"Which most people eat with spoons."

She rolled her eyes. "Then I'd have to wash the spoon." She slurped from the bowl. "Mmm, good stuff."

His laughter bounced through the room. A dimple dented one cheek as she grinned, setting the bowl down. He rounded the counter and came up beside her. He inched closer, she inched away. "What?"

"You've got ice cream on your nose." He swiped it away with his finger. And when he looked down at her, caught a whiff of her hair—something appley and sweet—suddenly he really, really wanted her to say yes to helping him. Last name or no.

"You, um, were saying?" she prodded, left hand now covering the ice pack on her right arm.

Was it wrong to give in to the instant urge to drag out this conversation? Linger in the company of the first woman to pique his interest since . . . who knew when.

He cleared his throat, shifted his weight from one foot to the other. "You know the Christmas festival?"

She nodded. "Of course. It's my favorite time of year around here."

Good. He had that in his favor. "Well, turns out it's on the brink of not happening this year. The coordinator went off to get married, and—"

"Georgie really did it? She'd been talking about this guy she met on the Internet. Wow."

"And anyway, they—the city council—want me to take over."

"You?"

"Me."

"You."

"I know I'm not Georgie Snyder, but I'm available and apparently the only willing stand-in." He'd decided to leave out the part about being a media draw. Because hadn't his fifteen minutes of undeserved fame stretched long enough already?

Autumn's eyebrows raised. She was waiting.

"I was hoping maybe you'd be willing to co-coordinate it with me." He rushed through the request, words tripping over each other.

"Me?"

"You."

"Me."

"I think we just had this conversation." He chuckled. "Look, I know it's out of the blue, but it was actually Tim Jakes's idea. He said you helped Georgie sometimes and obviously you run this place, so you're organized and stuff." *Just say yes.*

Because, media and the city council's motivation aside, sometime between that basketball game with Tim and now, he'd pushed a few steps past his reluctance. Far enough to realize he'd just been handed the chance to grasp the very thing he'd come home for: a place to fit and a purpose to fulfill. Maybe even the possibility of a full-time job. What if this was God answering his prayer for direction? Plus, what was it Hilary had said after the meeting?

"You've got the chance to play town hero, Blaze. Seriously, if you had any idea how much our small businesses are struggling . . ."

Town hero. The words tasted sweet.

Only he needed help to make it happen.

Autumn laid down the ice pack and folded her arms. Not a good sign. "Blake, it was . . . nice of you to think of me. And to bring out the ice cream. But between running the inn and trying to keep up with repairs since we don't have a handyman, I don't have a spare second. And I've got this VIP coming . . ." Her gaze shifted to the window. "All that and I've got some other pretty big things on my mind lately."

He wanted to ask what, but why should she tell him? So they'd shared a few laughs over melted ice cream. It's not like they were friends. "I could make it up to you. You mentioned repairs. I can help." Hadn't he spent a month watching a celebrity DIY guru at work?

"Blake—"

"And I'll buy you another cone. And books—you said you like books."

She nibbled on her bottom lip.

She's thinking. That's good.

"Why ask me, of all people?"

"Like I said, Tim Jakes suggested it." A sliver of moonlight now streaming through the window painted streaks of reddish-gold in her hair. "And maybe it would be good. For our families, I mean. Maybe even the whole town . . . to see some closure."

From the sudden stillness in Autumn's stance, the way she hugged her arms to herself, he knew he'd hit a nerve. But whether or not it was a good one, who could know? Because she didn't say anything. Finally, when the silence stretched, he gave into the question that had poked him ever since running into her on Saturday. "Autumn, is Ava still in town?"

"Why?" Her one-word question was barely a peep.

"I always wondered why she didn't come to Ryan's funeral."

She snapped into focus. "Are you kidding?" Anger—or was that hurt?—fueled her gaze. "After your father, the mayor of this town, practically called her out right in the town square, in front of everyone. Blamed her for breaking Ryan's heart when all she ever tried to do was help him get—" She cut off her own words.

"I remember that." And he remembered feeling embarrassed for his father. Even worse, devastated by his own guilt. Because while Dad blamed Ava for Ryan's reckless actions, Blake blamed only himself. "I'm not saying Dad was right. But he'd just lost his son."

"Yeah, well, none of it was Ava's fault."

Her words burrowed under his skin, gnawing and sharp. "I know that." He could hear the darkness in his own voice. "I know." And Autumn had no way of knowing how his heart choked on the truth. Why were they even having this conversation?

He searched for the words to close the topic he never should have opened.

But Autumn spoke first. "I think closure might be a pipe dream, Blake."

"Maybe." But inside, his heart and his brain protested. Because if that was true, then his whole reason for coming home in the first place was a hopeless quest.

4

The blaring of her phone yanked Autumn from an already restless sleep. She rolled over with a groan, legs tangled in her flannel sheets.

Before she could bring herself to reach for the phone, the ringing cut off. She waited for the trill to signal a voice mail, but instead, seconds later, the ringtone began again.

"Fine. I hear you." She pulled herself up and grabbed for the phone on her nightstand. "The inn better be on fire, Jamie, or some other disaster for you to be calling at . . ." She glanced at her alarm clock declaring the time in bright red numbers. "Five thirty a.m."

"I'm sorry, Miss Kingsley. So sorry."

How many times had she told the college kid who manned the desk at night to call her Autumn? She stood, bare feet padding over the chilled floor, a picture of Jamie's freckled face prompting reproach at her tone. "Nah, I'm sorry, Jamie."

She reached for her robe. Ooh, why the ache in her

arm when she thrust it through her sleeve? Oh yes, the wasp sting. *And Blake.* A replay of last night came swooping in.

Including the memory of how awkwardly their conversation finally ended. Her stammered decline. His disappointed nod. Her surprise at her own regret. She had always enjoyed Whisper Shore's regular lineup of festivals—the Christmas one best of all. Might have been fun to help again.

If not for the timing. And the person doing the asking.

Though, Blake wasn't so bad. In fact, she'd even had the crazy thought—in a completely platonic, distant observer sort of way—that he'd looked kind of cute standing in the middle of the lobby holding that ice cream cone.

But as she'd second-guessed her decision on the short walk from the inn back to her cottage last night, she'd remembered all the reasons any association at all with Blake Hunziker went on the bad-idea list. The business competition. Ryan and Ava. The fact that just last week she'd heard rumblings about Mayor Hunziker blaming Autumn's mother and her role on the state tourism board for Whisper Shore's lack of grant funding.

Hunzikers and Kingsleys didn't go together. That's all there was to it.

"So no fire?" she asked Jamie now.

"No, but you gotta get over here."

She caught her reflection in the full-size mirror attached to her closet door. "Jamie, I've already grouched at you this morning. I have no desire to add to that by scaring you with my morning hair." Which totally had the bird's-nest thing going on. "What's wrong?"

"It's an emergency." The line shuffled for a moment,

and she heard Jamie's muffled voice, as if he cupped his hand around the speaker. "I'm so sorry. I'm getting our manager now."

"What kind of emergency, Jamie?" she asked.

"Just get over here." He hung up.

Another glance in the mirror. Her white-and-pink-striped pajama pants peeked out from under her lime-green robe. Fuzzy slippers, makeup-less face. Surely she had time to change. *But if it really is an emergency . . .*

With an exaggerated whimper, she pocketed her phone and hurried through her chilly house. She grabbed a knit scarf from where she'd left it on the kitchen table last night, pulled on matching mittens, and stepped outside.

A lazy morning fog drifted from the lake, and frost-covered grass slicked under the soles of her slippers. Times like these she wished she'd rented a place in town. Living so close to the inn meant she was at the business's beck and call.

She entered the inn from the back door and trailed down the hallway. She found Jamie in the lobby, hands sunk in his back pockets as he faced a disgruntled guest. And what was that noise? A thumping, loud, from out-side.

"I really do apologize, Mr. Glass."

The guest thumbed his salt-and-pepper mustache, rumpled long-john shirt evidence of his disturbed sleep. Jamie glanced over his shoulder, following the man's focus. "Oh, good."

"What's going on?"

Jamie jabbed a finger toward the ceiling. "That. It's waking everyone up. I tried to get him to stop, but he just laughed at me."

"Who?"

Another thud.

"Some guy who said you knew he was going to be helping out around the place. I asked for a work order, but like I said, he just laughed."

Who in the world . . .

Thump.

Her eyes narrowed. Of course. "Mr. Glass, I echo Jamie's apologies, and assure you, I'm going to take care of this."

The man gave a gruff thanks and shuffled toward the open staircase.

"I'm sorry, Miss Kingsley. I tried to take care of it. As soon as I woke up and heard the hammering . . ." He broke off, sheepish expression taking over.

She held back a chuckle. If Jamie didn't realize she knew how often he slept through his shift, well, she'd go ahead and let him keep thinking what he wanted. Anyone else might deserve a scolding, but the guy worked five nights a week while keeping up a full course load at a college forty-five minutes away.

One more reason not to give up on her inn. One more reason to secure its future before leaving for France.

"Don't worry about it, Jamie. I'll take care of this."

She marched to the front door, jerked it open, and stomped down the stairs, neck craning for a view of the man she knew she'd find plodding around the porch roof.

"Blake Hunziker, *what* do you think you're doing?"

His head appeared over the edge, dark hair flopping over his forehead and brown eyes dancing in the light of the sunrise. "Patching your porch roof. What's it look like I'm doing?"

"More like what it *sounds* like you're doing. Which is performing a jig at the crack of dawn when my guests are trying to sleep." She crossed her arms, cutting off the morning chill from breezing up the wide arms of her robe.

"Wanted to get an early start. Busy day today."

"What, you've got other inns to terrorize?"

His grin faded just the slightest. "Red, the first big snow of the season is going to cause a flood on your porch. I don't know how you managed through the summer rains."

They'd learned to duck the drips falling from leaky spots, that's how. She'd done as much patching as she could. And . . . Wait, what had he called her? "Red?"

"It fits. How's your arm by the way?"

"Blake, I—"

The front door opened, and Jamie hurried out. He brushed his fingers through his hair in a worried move as he hustled down the porch steps. "Now somebody called the front desk about all the yelling."

Blake's head and shoulders disappeared.

Jamie's head tipped. "What are you going to do about him?"

"Guess I'm going to go up there and make him come down." Because that's what managers did, right? Solved problems.

And Blake Hunziker? *Problem* with the capital-est of Ps.

Slippers brushing through frosty grass, she headed for the ladder. For the second time in less than a week she'd brave her fear of heights and conquer the climb. This time, at least, irritation powered her determination.

Seconds later, she peered over the edge of the roof to where Blake sat cross-legged, eyes on the horizon.

"Hand over the hammer, Hunziker."

He blinked, almost as if stunned out of a moment of reflection. But he covered it with a lazy smile. "Come and get it."

With an annoyed huff, she hefted herself onto the roof. *Don't look down, don't look down.*

"Nice PJs, Red."

She looked down.

Her robe gaped open to reveal the flannel pajama top underneath. Lovely. "Has anyone ever told you you're exasperating?" She scooted to his side, feeling stares from the second-floor windows and the tingle of winter's approach in the air.

"Has anyone ever told you it's dangerous to crawl around on rooftops in slippers?"

She stopped in front of him, knees digging into the porch roof. This thing would hold both of them, right? Autumn reached for the hammer at his side, but Blake's fingers closed around it first. "Not so fast."

Eyes narrowed, she made another attempt, but he slid it behind his back. In her failed lunge she ended up inches from his face, balanced on one arm and disarmingly aware of the still-wet tips of his hair and the soapy, mint smell clinging to him.

He only grinned at her, flecks of gold twinkling in his eyes.

She gulped, straightening, backing up . . . finally turning to plop down at his side.

"Giving up that easy?"

"I'm on a roof in my pajamas. Give me some credit."

His laughter floated away with the breeze, and she followed it with her gaze. From the porch roof, the view of the lake was stunning—threads of blue and foamy white weaving up to a fiery sunrise. She'd completely missed the beauty of it in her rush from her house. But now it pulled her focus in a gentle tug.

"Why are you up here, Blake?"

"I told you last night I'd help out around the place. It's obvious you need it." He fixed his eyes on her. "And I need you. Please help me with the festival."

So he wasn't giving up. The sincerity in his voice, the hint of a plea, was almost enough to push past her resistance.

But how in the world was she supposed to help co-ordinate an event when she had an inn to run? Dominic Laurent to wow. A move to prepare for.

"Do you have any idea what goes into planning the festival? We're less than four weeks out. It's a massive undertaking." And how were they supposed to work together with the past glaring like a theater marquee between them?

"Georgie already had a lot of it in the works. We'll pick up where she left off. Besides, I like a challenge."

Yeah, well, she already had enough challenges star-ing her in the face. Even so, something about the mix of enthusiasm and desperation in Blake's countenance halted an outright refusal.

There was more at stake for him in this whole thing, wasn't there. She wasn't exactly sure what, but for a moment there, his goofball exterior faded to reveal a man with deeper layers.

"You know, before you came up that ladder, I was sitting here thinking about how Ryan and I used to go up into our parents' attic and climb out the little window onto the roof. We did it all the time in the summer, never once got caught."

She blinked at his sudden shift in topic. "And you'd do what?"

He shrugged. "Nothing really. Just sit there, talk. He'd talk about football, I'd talk about flying. We'd both talk about girls. Did you know he had a crush on your sister as early as seventh grade?"

"I had no idea." Except it wasn't that surprising, really. Ava—tomboy tendencies and all—was the family beauty, the one all the boys fell for. And once she and Ryan had braved their way past the barrier of family rivalry, there'd been no tiptoeing. Oh no, they'd practically barreled their way into a relationship, regardless of parental consternation. They'd been so blissfully happy, Autumn had figured an engagement wasn't far off.

But that was before Ryan's football injury his senior year of college. The surgery. The end of his NFL prospects. The painkillers.

"Of course, he didn't get up the nerve to ask her out 'til college, and then——" Blake broke off, fists balling where they dangled over his bent knees. "Anyway, sorry I came too early." He slid the hammer to her. "Truce?"

She wrapped one hand around the wood handle, the sleeve of her robe flopping at her wrist. Then, still holding on, she scanned the surface of the porch roof, Blake's quick handiwork obvious. "Truce, and thanks."

"For the record, I'm happy to help with anything around here even if you say no to the festival."

"But . . . why?"

His gaze returned to Lake Michigan. "Because I had the chance to help once . . . and didn't."

She knew then, he was talking about the day she'd sought him out over spring break. She hadn't wanted to, but Ava had begged. *"Please, Autumn. I promised Ryan I wouldn't tell his family. He's already mad at me for confronting him. But I didn't promise I wouldn't tell mine. Maybe if you talk to Blake . . . tell him what I saw."*

So she'd given in. Told Blake about the orange bottles Ava kept finding in Ryan's apartment—the ones with someone else's name in the prescription. He'd brushed her off, disbelieving. It was the last time she'd seen him until his brother's funeral, three months later.

Looking at Blake now, maybe really seeing him for the first time, she didn't see the adventurer, the goof-off unable to take anything seriously. She saw a regret-filled man still tortured by the loss of his brother. Compassion, unbidden and surprising, unfolded in her.

He released the hammer. "Come on, it's too cold for you to be up here without a coat."

"*You're* not wearing a coat."

"Do you argue about everything, Red?"

"I do about nicknames that come from nowhere."

He reached over to muss her hair. "Not from nowhere. In the sun, it's totally red."

"It's auburn."

He stopped at the ladder. "Ladies first."

After he'd helped her over the edge, she stopped, glanced up at him. "All right, I'll co-coordinate the festival with you."

The dimples in his cheeks deepened as genuine gratitude overtook his expression. No teasing or playfulness now. "Seriously?"

"And if the offer still stands for help—"

"It does. Mornings I'll help out here. Afternoons we'll work on the festival. Deal?"

She stepped down a rung. "Let's flip-flop it. Festival in the mornings."

"And she doesn't think she has a problem with arguing."

Not with arguing. But very possibly with agreeing to things that were probably a really bad idea.

He had a feeling Autumn Kingsley didn't even know why she'd said yes.

But all that mattered was, she'd said yes. Right?

Blake hopped the curb, the sticky sweet smell of glaze and fruit pastries greeting him he passed under the awning of Gable's Bakery. When he entered, a bell above the door chimed in tune with the growling of his stomach.

Just like he recalled, an eclectic mix of tables and colored chairs dotted the downtown bakery. Bright yellow walls contrasted with the overcast shadows of the morning. But there were fewer patrons than Blake remembered from his youth.

And the few people who did fill seats offered furtive glances rather than smiles. *Riiight*. So he probably shouldn't expect a visit from the welcome wagon anytime soon.

"Blake Hunziker, it's about time you stopped by." Kip Gable, the bakery owner, raised a sloshing coffeepot in greeting. He stood next to a booth, his apron covered in flour and the same Whisper Shore Ravens cap he'd always worn atop his head.

"Blake? Well, I'll be." The patron in the booth next to Kip rose, bobbing her silver-almost-blue hair as she turned.

"Mrs. Satterly." Blake skirted through the maze of tables to reach the elderly woman. His first-grade teacher still had the stature of a woman in charge of her classroom. "You still eat breakfast here every day?"

"Like clockwork," Kip said, filling her cup.

"You're old enough to call me Pam now." She clasped Blake's right hand in both of her own. Thick veins ribboned over her frail hands, and yet their warmth matched her welcome. "You'll sit with me, won't you? I'm so happy you're home."

One more roving glance around the place and he lowered into the vinyl seat. "You might be the only one."

She harrumphed. "Don't let them bother you. Half of them haven't had their caffeine yet and the other half are too stubborn to know they need it."

Blake's chuckle was accompanied by the clink of a mug atop the table as Kip placed it in front of Blake. He filled it to the rim with the muddy coffee the bakery was known for. "Besides, you're the closest thing we've got to a celebrity. They're all just curious. What can I get you to eat?"

"I'm not too late for breakfast, am I?" His mouth watered.

"For one of the Hunziker boys, I'd serve breakfast at sunset."

Both Blake and Ryan had worked at the bakery part-time all through high school—part of their father's desire to instill a solid work ethic in his sons. Of course, Ryan had cut back his hours every football season. And never one to hole up when the outdoors beckoned, Blake snuck out early more often than not during the summer.

"In that case, I'll have some of your chocolate chip banana pancakes."

Kip saluted. "You got it."

When the baker retreated, Blake nudged his coffee cup away. "Don't tell him, but I'm one of the world's few non-coffee drinkers."

Mrs. Satterly grinned. "I'm a three-cup-a-day woman myself. It's why I've lived so long. Did you know I turned eighty-six last month?" She reached for Blake's cup and poured into her already half-empty mug.

They chatted for a few minutes until Kip returned with a plate of pancakes.

Blake glanced from Kip to Mrs. Satterly as the bakery owner set the plate in front of him. "Dude, I've missed small-town life."

Mrs. Satterly offered a teacherly raise of her eyebrows. "That's what you get for leaving us, Blake Lucas Hunziker."

"Been forever since someone used my middle name."

Kip slid into the open space beside Mrs. Satterly. "Better than that old nickname. Blaze. Just not right. A kid sets an accidental fire or two—"

"Or five," Blake inserted before biting into a syrupy pancake.

"And he's branded for life. No wonder you set off for greener pastures." Kip spoke in lighthearted tones, but Blake had no doubt both the baker and Mrs. Satterly knew full well his real reason for staying away so long.

"So tell us, what're you aiming to do now that you're back?"

"Well, believe it or not—"

"I thought that was you."

A shadow fell over the Formica table in sync with a voice that carried Blake back decades—to hot summer nights sleeping outside, only the thin plastic of a pup tent between him and the dewy ground. Blake, Ryan, Tim, and Shawn—pals since their first Boy Scouts camping trip—swapping ghost stories.

He looked up to see Shawn's dad, his long-ago scout troop leader with arms crossed over a paunchy stomach that hadn't been there last time Blake saw him. Blake stood, held out his hand.

"Mr. Baylor, wow. Been a long time."

Gone was the paternal gentleness that used to make the man a hero and friend among Blake and his friends. Instead, an unmistakable surliness darkened his eyes.

Blake glanced down at Mrs. Satterly. She gave him a tight, *hang in there* half smile. He dropped his hand.

"How's um . . . how's Shawn?"

The second the question came out, Blake wished it back. Because if William Baylor had been gruff a second ago, now he sizzled. "You want to know how my son is? He's been on depression meds off and on for almost six years now. Refuses to do anything with his life. Won't step on a plane for the life of him. Walked out on his wife." Mr. Baylor stepped closer. "That's how Shawn's doing."

Blake could feel the eyes of every customer in the bakery on him. And suddenly the smell of breakfast food turned sickly sweet, enough to set his stomach churning, as the memory of Shawn's panic the day of Ryan's accident bulleted through him.

"Something's wrong, Blake. Something's wrong. I don't see his chute. He's not pulling."

Blake closed his eyes now.

Oh, Shawn. The thought of his friend, his brother's *best* friend—the only one whose taste for adventure ever rivaled Blake's—morose and inactive bruised whatever conviction he'd had just minutes ago that something good might come of his return.

"Mr. Baylor, I'm truly—"

"If you try to apologize to me, kid, I swear my fist will be in your face before you finish."

"William Baylor!" Mrs. Satterly jerked, only Kip's hand on her arm stopping her from rising from the booth.

Blake's focus faltered under Baylor's stare, floundering over the heads of bakery patrons and booth backs, toward the back wall where town mementos ornamented the space. And there, near the center, Ryan's football jersey from the year they'd taken State.

Baylor's growl drew him back. "I didn't come over here for an apology. Only to tell you to stay away from Shawn. It's bad enough you're back in town, driving around in that showy Firebird. Last thing he needs is to see it, see *you*, and be reminded."

With that, the man lurched on his heel and stalked from the bakery, awkward silence dragging as Blake stood frozen beside the table.

Grady Lewis couldn't be saying what Autumn thought he was saying.

The oversized leather chair squeaked as she crossed one leg over the other, its high arms walling her in. Across his mahogany desk, her family's longtime financial advisor peered at her through thin-rimmed spectacles. Waiting, probably, for some sign she'd processed his words of doom.

"You're saying we should close one of this town's most historic sites?"

Grady folded his hands, arms outstretched on his clutter-free desktop, narrow shoulders hunched. "Hopefully only for the winter season."

Each tick of the grandfather clock in the corner lanced her confidence. Why hadn't she suggested they meet at her office instead, where generous windows ushered in sunlight and an ever-calming coastal view? Where it might be a little harder for Grady to look her in the eye and suggest cutting off her great-grandfather's dream.

Even if only until spring. "But how will no income for three or four months help us?"

"The inn has always operated in the red the first three, four months of the year. Profits during high-tourist season made up for the loss in the past. But that wasn't the case this year." Grady nudged his glasses with one finger, then spread a series of papers across his desk. "I've noted estimates here. Why, in staff costs alone you're looking at a sizable savings. Add in electricity, water—"

"Wait, you're suggesting I lay off our staff?"

"You didn't think you'd pay them to do nothing, did you?"

What she'd thought was that Grady would tell her the bank had agreed to one final mortgage extension or short-term loan. Just enough to keep them going until Dominic Laurent saved the day.

And yet . . .

Grady's numbers told a story she couldn't ignore. The Kingsley Inn was inching toward a financial sinkhole it might not be able to climb back out of—especially if next tourist season fell as flat as this past summer. Didn't help that along with the inn, she'd inherited a mortgage and bank payments. Dad had taken out a large loan in the late '90s to renovate the inn. Then after he'd died, Mom had been forced to take out a second mortgage when business slowed.

The fiscal responsibility of it all too often felt like a dragon breathing down her neck. It had only fueled her antipathy, the irked piece of her that had wondered how Mom ever thought handing the Kingsley Inn and all its debt to her could ever feel like a gift.

Autumn's cell phone interrupted her morose thoughts, jarring her and prompting a sigh from Grady. Oh yes, she'd forgotten how much the man disliked cell phones. "Sorry." She reached into her purse to silence the thing.

Grady removed his glasses and rubbed his eyes, the age spots on his cheeks stretching with the movement. The man had a gruff manner and a no-nonsense way about him, but he wasn't cold. He wouldn't suggest something this drastic without good cause. In fact, if she knew Grady at all, he'd probably lost sleep before deciding on his recommendation.

"If we close, what if we don't open again? If my employees go off and get other jobs . . ." *And I'm not around to make sure everything's ready come spring.*

Because she wouldn't be. It'd be someone else at the

helm by then. Maybe even Ava. The hazy hope that her sister might finally be ready to contribute to the family business had solidified sometime in the past couple days.

Yes, Ava lived in Minnesota now—worked half time as an adjunct college instructor and half time in the college's athletic department. But maybe she would consider taking a turn running the inn. Autumn had even tried to call her sister yesterday under the guise of finding out when Ava planned to come home for the holidays. Surely she'd hear back soon.

But a thread of worry knit through her, same concern that always hit her this time of year—that one of these years Ava wouldn't come home at all. They'd grown so distant.

Grady leaned forward. "Do you have a better idea, Autumn?"

Actually, she did—namely, Dominic Laurent. But now Grady's concerns blasted a hole in her optimism. Because why would the Laurent company invest in a failing business? Surely they would take one look at the books, the late payment notices from the bank, and run the other way.

"There has to be something we can do." The conviction came out breathy and closer to pleading than she liked. "The festival is coming up. That usually fills us up during Christmas week. That's something, right?"

"Heard it might be cancelled."

Autumn shook her head, latching on to the tiniest thread of opportunity at the interest in his voice. "Blake Hunziker's heading it up. Well, and me too. We're co-coordinators."

First time she'd said it aloud, and it sounded hilarious. Two inexperienced adults who just happened to be from feuding families organizing the most important event of the winter season. What had the city council been thinking?

What had *she* been thinking?

That Blake has an endearing smile and a deeper layer underneath all that crazy—that's what. She'd seen it last night when he'd mentioned closure. She'd seen it this morning when he reminisced about his brother.

As for the smile . . . Well, the right smile could get under a girl's skin, and he'd gotten under hers long enough to extract an agreement from her. Hopefully it'd be worth it.

From her purse, her cell phone vibrated a second time.

"Young Hunziker's taking the helm? That is a surprise." Grady perched his glasses on his nose. "Though not quite as surprising as you working with him. Your mother know yet?"

There were several things her mother didn't know yet. "Waiting for the right time."

"Wait long enough and there might not be a right time, young lady."

There he went, slipping into fatherly mode. She didn't mind it, not really. But sometime it might be nice to feel independent. Maybe that's why travel was so appealing. Here in Whisper Shore, there'd always be her mother, Grady, even the memory of her father, watching over her shoulder.

Abroad, she'd make her own moves. No regrets, no wondering what she might be missing while holed away in a role she'd never asked for, in a town she'd never had a chance to leave.

"Autumn, perhaps if we let Victoria know—"

"No."

"The Kingsley Inn may have been your father's family business, but your mother cared—cares—about it, too."

"Then why did she hand the whole thing over to me?" *Without even asking if I wanted it.*

The grandfather clock continued its slow click. "She meant it as a gift. Surely you know that. And I believe if she knew how it was struggling financially, she'd want to help. Don't you remember how hard she worked to keep it going after your father's death?"

It'd happened so fast. The aneurysm one day. A funeral three days later.

Her voice quieted. "I know. I remember." Remembered how Mom poured herself into the business as if holding on to the inn somehow meant holding on to Dad. But none of it had made any sense . . .

Because Autumn had overheard that conversation only weeks before Dad died. They may never have gotten around to telling their daughters, but it didn't change what Autumn knew: They'd planned to divorce. Dad planned to leave. Mom planned . . . who knew what?

"I won't run this place without you."

But she had. And Autumn hadn't known what to feel about that. About any of it. All she knew now was she wasn't ready to tell Mom how dire things really were. Not when she knew Mom probably couldn't help anyway, having already sunk most of her own savings into the place throughout the years.

"Autumn, you still with me?"

"Still here. Still trying to figure out some way to make this work."

Behind Grady's head, a small window peeked out onto the quiet of Main Avenue. Cars turtling by in slow movements of color. The occasional passerby with chin tucked against the cold and hands hidden in pockets. Trees mostly absent of their leaves, as if waiting for winter's covering.

Across the street, the gold letters of the Hunziker Hotel sign mocked her.

"I can't close, Grady. Not yet." Not when there was still the hope of Dominic Laurent. Even if she couldn't make all the repairs she'd started dreaming about ever since Blake offered his help. She'd been hopeful Grady might help her find enough wiggle room in their operating budget to pay for a quick sprucing up.

So much for that plan.

But she wasn't giving up. She'd keep their doors open—at least until Laurent's visit.

Minutes later, they shook hands and she returned to her car. Forehead against the steering wheel, she let out the groan she'd held at bay in Grady's office. *Lord, we just need a Band-Aid, something to tide us over.*

Did he hear?

Straightening in her Jetta's cloth seat, she remembered her silenced phone. Maybe Ava had called back. She pulled it out. Four missed calls. None from Ava. But three from Betsy.

Uh-oh.

She tapped Betsy's name and waited as the phone rang. *Please, not a stove fire or a broken appliance we can't afford to replace or—*

"Autumn, you saw my calls." Betsy's tone was low, raspy.

"Bets, what is it?"

"It's Lucy."

At the name, she pictured Betsy's younger sister—her beacon of a smile, straight, strawberry-blond hair framing her face, almond-shaped eyes that most often shined with innocence . . . but now and then flickered with mischief. "She's not sick, is she?"

"No, just . . . homeless."

5

His instinct was to cut and run.

Less than a week home, and Blake was already thinking about packing his bags—the result of William Baylor's assaulting words. He rubbed tired eyes with his fist and rounded the corner of the Kingsley Inn.

He'd told Autumn yesterday that he'd stop by so they could talk over their festival to-dos. It wouldn't be right to leave her hanging, even if he was considering dropping the whole thing. When he'd stopped at the inn's front desk a minute ago, Harry had directed him to her cottage. "Yellow paint, white trim, just like the inn."

The glass had rattled in the inn's front door when he pulled it closed behind him. The creaks and groans of the porch floorboards, paint chippings wrinkling the wood railing . . . this old building was showing its age. No wonder stress laced Autumn's tone when she talked about her business.

A burly wind raced past him as he made his way toward the cottage nestled in a grove of bare trees at the boundary of the inn's expansive back yard. Overhead, pillowy clouds hinted at snow, even if the forecast nixed it for today.

He neared the entrance just as a crash sounded from inside the cottage.

He rapped on the front door. "Kingsley, it's me. You okay in there?" No answer.

What if she was hurt and that was why she wasn't answering? He tried the doorknob. Unlocked. "I'm coming in. Not a burglar, so don't take a baseball bat to me or anything."

The door opened into a small entryway that widened into a living room. A hodgepodge of mismatched furniture, throw pillows, and black-and-white pictures on the walls—all street scenes and foreign landmarks—gave the room a vintage feel. He turned down a narrow hallway, following the sound of scuffling coming from what was probably Autumn's bedroom.

He stopped in the doorway . . . and covered his mouth with his fist to stop a howl of laughter.

Tipped over and broken, a tall wicker hamper extended from an open closet. And Autumn lay caught inside up to her waist with open shoeboxes and clothes littered around her.

"Don't you dare laugh."

"I'm not laughing." Though his voice sounded like a mouse from trying to hold it in. "Let me help you, Red."

He thought she might argue, but instead, she only released an irritated puff that fanned her mussed bangs. He bit back another laugh and pulled the hamper away, freeing her legs, then held out his hand. He could practically taste her reluctance when she placed her palm in his.

The woman was cute, no denying that—freckles, unruly hair. And when she was annoyed, she was downright adorable. The thought was all sorts of forbidden—considering their history and all, considering the great failed experiment in love that had been Ryan and Ava.

Still, when he pulled her to her feet and she came up just inches from his face, the closeness set his senses on alert. He'd spent so many years pushing people away, running. So why the sudden desire to, for once, pull someone in? Especially this someone?

He coughed, stepped backward.

"You know, normally people ring the doorbell before walking into someone's house."

"I knocked."

"And then barged in."

"'Barged in' would be breaking down your door. I was playing hero to your damsel in distress. Which is apparently becoming a theme with us. Bloody nose, wasp sting, closet mishap."

She only rolled her eyes, but if he wasn't mistaken she hid a grin as she turned to pick up her hamper.

"What happened anyway?"

"I was trying to get those plastic tubs." She pointed overhead.

"A step stool might have been the better choice." He brushed past her and pulled the tubs down. "There you go."

"Thanks." She placed them on her bed, its bright green duvet the main splash of color in the room otherwise decorated in black and white.

His forehead scrunched. "So you packing or some-thing?"

"Just need to store some books."

"Books."

"You know, covers, pages, spines."

He looked around the room. "And where are these books?"

"In my spare bedroom." She reached for the tubs once more, but he snatched them up first.

"I'll help."

"That's okay, Blake. I'm sure you have things to do."

"My things to do involve talking to you about the festival. We can do that while I help you box your books."

She bit her lip, indecision clear, but finally shrugged and sashayed through the bedroom doorway. "You haven't seen how many books I've got."

He followed her down the hallway, into a second bed-room. And whoa, she wasn't joking about the books. Shelves lined two of the room's walls, filled with paper-backs and hardcovers. A daybed edged up to a third wall underneath a square-paneled window.

She stopped in the center of the room. "See what I mean?"

"You put new meaning to the word *bookworm*. More like a book . . . boa constrictor."

She chuckled. "I'd take offense at that if it wasn't absolutely true."

"So how much are we packing up?"

"As many as we can fit into these tubs until I find more boxes."

He swept an armful of books from the nearest shelf. *Anne of Green Gables* faced up on the top. Typical girl

fare. But the one underneath, a Winston Churchill biography, was interesting. "Any particular reason you're
packing them?"

"I need the space."

"For . . . ?" He lined the bottom of the tub with books.

"A houseguest. You know Betsy, my chef? Well, her
sister Lucy—" A knock sounding from the front door
cut her off. "That's probably her now." Her focus shifted
from her half-filled tub to the still-almost-full shelves.

Another knock. "Go on. I'll keep working."

She turned before exiting the room. "By the way,
Blake, hear that knocking?" Teasing tugged at the corners of her mouth. "Notice how they're waiting for me
to answer the door before barging in?"

He tossed a paperback at her retreating form, then
stood, a grin of his own leading the way back to the
bookshelf. But instead of hooking his arm around
another bundle of books, he paused, gaze drawn to a
framed photo serving as a bookend. The faces of Autumn and her family stared back at him from the porch
of the inn—all smiles and carefree poses, arms locked
around each other.

He picked up the frame, his scrutiny moving from
Autumn's little-girl grin to her father's face, awareness
creeping through him. He'd forgotten about her family's loss.

"And this will be your bedroom, Luce—if you decide
you'd like to stay here, that is."

He turned at the sound of Autumn's voice and shuffled steps entering the room. A man followed Autumn
in, along with the young woman who must be Lucy.
Straight blond hair hung in pigtails on both sides of her

heart-shaped face. She peered around the room with interest, movement slow but smile steady—features both endearing and telling.

"What do you think?" Autumn asked Lucy. "We'll clear out the bookshelves, and I'm going to clean out the closet, too. It'll be all your own."

"I can't stay at Hope House?"

Blake recognized the name of the nonprofit in a neighboring town—a home for adults with Down syndrome or other developmental challenges.

The man beside Lucy placed his arm around her shoulder. "I'm afraid not, Luce. But I think you'd really like it here. It's right by where Betsy works, and you can come to the house and see your nieces and nephew whenever you want. We're all excited about having you so close."

Must be Betsy's husband.

"Is he staying here, too?" Lucy pointed at Blake.

At that, both Autumn and the man chuckled. "No, this is my friend Blake. He's just helping me get the room ready for you. If you decide you like it, I'll have it all ready when we help you move tomorrow."

Lucy stepped forward and jutted out her hand. "Hiya, Blake."

"Hiya, Lucy." He mimicked her greeting and didn't have to work for the warmth in his voice. Partially because Lucy's sweet demeanor naturally drew it out of him.

But, too, because he couldn't stop the rush of respect toward Autumn. Opening up her tiny home. Reaching out to a friend's sister. Watching Lucy with as much care and concern as if she were family.

Lucy glanced around the room once more. Nodded. And then, "Okay."

Autumn's lips spread. "Good."

"Can we go say hi to Betsy now?"

Autumn and Betsy's husband laughed at the quick change, and seconds later, as she walked them back through the house, he heard Autumn promising to help pick up Lucy's things tomorrow.

Blake was loading up another box of books when Autumn returned. And she must have read the question in his eyes. "Hope House is closing. Betsy and Philip live in a three-bedroom house with four kids. I have this spare room. So . . ."

From his kneeling position he looked up at her, pretty sure the wave of admiration surging through him was visible on his face.

"Anyway, I thought it might feel a little more like home if my stuff wasn't crowding the space."

He held her gaze. "You're something else, Red."

Embarrassment flitted through her eyes, and she turned to the shelf. "It helps that she already knows me. She spent a lot of time at the inn before moving to Hope House. And I hang out at Hope House a couple times a month and lead a book club for the residents."

He dropped another load of books in the tub. "They got the right woman for the job."

"Lucy's the biggest reader in the group. It takes her a while to get through a book, but she has this uncanny ability to pick up something surprising in a story, to sum up a theme or insight in such a clear way you wonder why you didn't see it yourself."

"You like her."

"A lot. So you wanted to talk about the festival?"

He'd come to tell her he wasn't sure he was up for it anymore, that it was too hard knowing William Baylor wasn't the only one in this town just waiting for him to fail.

But Autumn's commitment to others, and her expectant expression as she watched him, suddenly made him very much want to succeed.

"I thought maybe we should start by going over Georgie's notes, then making a to-do list."

She grinned. "A to-do list. You might just be a man after my own heart, Blake Hunziker."

Okay, so he wouldn't quit.

Why would Dylan Porter come back?

Autumn covered the distance to the inn, cold poking through the thin fabric of her gray sweater boots and frosting her toes. Black leggings and a jean skirt hadn't been the most practical outfit for cleaning out the spare bedroom, but she'd planned to head in to work at lunch.

Hadn't planned on the call from Harry, though, letting her know Dylan and his fiancée were waiting for her at the front desk.

The belled wreath on the inn's back door—the only Christmas decoration they'd put up so far—jingled when she entered. At the sound, Betsy turned from the stove, the smell of her signature mushroom soup wafting. "Why's *he* here?"

Autumn's appetite niggled. "No idea. Harry didn't say. Maybe he changed his mind about the reception." Or rather, changed Mariah's mind.

"I mean Blake. I saw him walk past the back window to your place."

Autumn stopped short. "Came to talk festival business." Except that they hadn't. They'd packed books to the tune of their own banter after Lucy and Philip left. He'd called her a book nerd. She'd called him a show-off for seeing how many books he could carry at once.

And all the while, she hadn't been able to clear her mind of the way he'd looked at her when Lucy stopped in—warm and admiring. It'd been enough to turn her common sense to mush for a minute. Or sixty. Wow, had an hour really gone by while they worked?

"You left him at your house?" Betsy swirled a spoon through the oversized pot on the stove.

"He's boxing up my books to make room for Lucy."

At that, Betsy's fingers uncurled from around the ladle and she turned. "What you're doing for Lucy . . . we're beyond grateful."

Autumn moved to Betsy's side. "You know I'd do anything to help you guys—and I adore Lucy." She looked down, nudged a crumb on the laminate floor under the stove. "Well, duty calls." *Lord, help me.*

She left the kitchen but halfway through the dining room slowed her steps. She reached down to pull up the fabric of her boots, then gulped in as much resolve as she could muster and passed into the lobby.

"Dylan, hello. What brings you by?" *Yikes, too much perk. Tone it down.*

"Morning, Autumn." He stepped aside to reveal the woman who was clearly his fiancée. Pixie-cut hair, striped scarf, rosy cheeks. At 5'8" Autumn had at least four inches on her and probably five times that in pounds.

Suddenly she felt like a Raggedy Ann doll next to . . . Barbie. Which was way too ironic considering Dylan . . .

"Autumn, this is my fiancée, Mariah Bates."

They shook hands, Mariah's once-over swift, her "nice to meet you" stilted and uncertain. Clearly, the woman wasn't excited to be there. And yet, as her gaze moved around the lobby and over the ornate open staircase winding toward the second floor, veiled appreciation played over her face.

Even in its weathered state, the inn still breathed with stately charm. A surprising shoot of pride flickered through Autumn. "What can I do for you?"

Dylan cleared his throat. "We've been talking about our reception location. I felt badly about cancelling last week."

"Oh, please, don't worry about it. It was—" she met Mariah's eyes—"understandable."

"Turns out the Hunziker Hotel is already booked on the date of our wedding. I know showing up out of the blue like this probably doesn't work into your schedule, but I wondered if you'd mind if I showed Mariah around."

Hope slid in, gooey and warm. She could handle being Plan B. Especially if it meant a deposit. Her own words to Harry came floating back in: "*Right when we needed it most, Dominic Laurent fell in our lap.*"

And now this.

"I wouldn't mind that at all."

Dylan's eyes brightened. "We're thinking of an outdoor reception, but it'd be good to look at the guest rooms. Dining room, too. Might make a good rehearsal dinner space."

Mariah snaked an arm through the crook of Dylan's elbow. "My man is quite the event planner."

Was it Autumn's imagination, or did Mariah place special emphasis on the *my*?

Dylan patted her hand on his arm. "I just want to make our special day perfect."

Mariah eyed Autumn. "He's always so thoughtful. I admit, I was concerned when I found out Dylan's ex-fiancée ran this place. But he assured me things ended a long time ago."

Autumn's eyebrows lifted. "Uh, yes."

"I realized I was being silly. After all, Dylan couldn't possibly be more committed, loving. We're like . . . Romeo and Juliet."

Okay, honey, you made your point. "Right. Well, I—"

"There you are, Red."

Autumn gasped, turned. *Oh no, please no. Blake?* How long had he been here? And why was he hurrying to her side, flashing that smug, dimpled grin, then . . .

Kissing my cheek? Warmth rushed up her neck and flooded her face.

Dylan glanced at Autumn. "Red?"

Blake pulled her close, crushing her to his side. "My pet name for her," he practically cooed. "Between her hair and her fiery spirit, it fits, don't you think?"

"I, uh . . ." Dylan stammered.

She felt the ribbon of muscle in Blake's arm around her back. *Too close.* And he smelled like a forest, if a forest could smell so clean and . . . masculine. *Oh, please . . .*

"And you are . . ." Dylan prodded. Right, Dylan hadn't moved to town until after Blake left.

"Blake Hunziker. Nice to meet you." Blake ran his

hand up and down her arm. And she was torn between pulling away and . . . What? Snuggling up? *You are not enjoying this. You are not enjoying this. You are not—*

She met Blake's eyes, read the "play along" in his wink. "Yes, uh, yes. This is Blake. Blake, meet Dylan Porter." Such a bad idea.

"Oh, the ex-fiancé."

He knew? Betsy must have said something.

"Well, thanks for leaving Red here for me."

"I wasn't the one to—" Dylan froze midblurt as Mariah shot him an accusing glare.

Blake's hand stilled on her arm. Ha, so he didn't know everything.

"Well, Dylan and Mariah, please feel free to look around at your leisure. I'll have Harry open up a couple rooms upstairs. Look around the yard, too."

Dylan glanced once more at Blake, then her. "Thanks."

Mariah only nodded. Harry stepped in then, gesturing toward the staircase. Only when they'd started up did Autumn yank away from Blake. "*What* was *that*?"

"Good acting. Just making sure I haven't lost my touch since Randi Woodruff."

She'd have pinched that grin right off his face if she could have. If a pathetic piece of her hadn't halfway enjoyed the past three minutes. She folded her arms. "Who knows what Dylan thinks now?"

"I wasn't acting for Dylan. It was for the snarky blonde. Romeo and Juliet? Do you think she even knows how that ended?" He took a step closer, peering down at her. "Besides, tell me you didn't get a kick out of the surprise on both their faces."

"Don't know what you're talking about."

"Say it, Red." He reached around to his back pocket, pulling out a curled copy of a magazine. "Or I'll have to tease you mercilessly about what I found on your bookshelves. It's why I came over."

She groaned as he held it up it by its corners in front of her, his own face grinning from the cover. The only tabloid magazine she'd ever purchased in her life and, of course, he'd found it. The headline mocked her: *Randi Reveals Handsome Mystery Husband*. She reached for it, but he snatched it away.

"*You* bought a magazine with *me* on the cover." If she'd thought he was smug before, he was Cheshire cat pleased now.

"I happen to like Randi Woodruff's TV show."

"Right."

She swiped for it again, but he held it over his head, eyes dancing with amusement. "Why'd you save it?"

"Because I figured it'd make a nice target for a game of darts."

"Ooh, good one."

"Why you—"

"It's just not going to work, Dylan."

At the sound of Mariah's voice trailing from the staircase, Autumn lost her footing, only Blake's chest keeping her from going down. "Make that five."

At his whisper in her ear, she elbowed his stomach and straightened. "Five what?"

"Five saves: bloody nose, wasp sting, closet mishap, playing boyfriend, catching you."

By the time he finished with the list, Mariah was out the front door and Dylan had halted in front of them, apology brimming in his expression. "Sorry, Autumn."

"You didn't look around for more than two minutes."

"She's used to five-star resorts." He shrugged. "She'd rather change our date and book the hotel."

The indignation she should've felt at Dylan's words was no match for the humiliation punching through her. Dylan might as well have labeled her inn a clay pot compared to the Hunziker Hotel's crystal vase. And with Blake right there. . . .

"I thought bringing her here might do some good. I got the feeling when I was here the other day . . . Well, anyway, I thought it might help you out."

She felt herself stiffen. "I don't need your help." Oh, but she needed his deposit.

Dylan shook his head and followed Mariah out the door.

"Man. Rude."

She pressed her eyes closed at Blake's exhaled words, turned to face him. "I know, I shouldn't have said—"

"I meant the chick. And Dylan, all condescending. You *don't* need his help. Tell ya what, festival plans can wait until tomorrow. We'll spend all today on inn projects."

Irritation clashed with appreciation. But emotions aside, she couldn't ask Blake to dust or polish woodwork or rearrange the furniture in the den. Any project worth his time would take money. Money she didn't have. She should've told him as soon as he'd stopped by this morning. "Blake—"

"Although, I will add it to the ever-growing list of heroics: Six, spends whole day helping at the inn. So what's up first? I'm not good with anything plumbing or electricity related, but give me a paintbrush, a hammer, whatever. We made a deal, and I'm ready to work."

She stepped back. "I need to call our deal off."

"If it's about me pretending in front of Dylan—"

"It's not. Believe me. That's my past. I've let go."

"Then give me a project."

"You don't understand. I don't have a project for you because I don't have money for a project." She waved her hands. "Yeah, we need new carpet in half the guest rooms, and the third-floor suite could use a makeover, and if I could, I'd replace every window in the inn. But I don't know what I was thinking making a deal for your help fixing up this place when I can't even afford to keep it open. The bank said no to a loan, which is understandable, since I am behind on the mortgage payments, and . . ."

She shook her head, stuffed her hands in her back pockets. Should've stopped herself. She didn't want pity.

She just wanted to save her inn, secure everyone's jobs, keep believing that everything would work out so she could leave for France without disappointing anyone.

Because she wouldn't do what Dad had planned to—leave a broken mess in the wake of desertion. She wouldn't.

"Don't worry, I'll still help with the festival. Leave me Georgie's notes, and I'll take a look."

Blake grimaced. "That's not what I'm—"

Harry entered the room then, muttering something about another crack in the dining room ceiling. "I don't think we can just keep plastering the cracks. Come look, Autumn."

She gave Blake a parting shrug and, as she followed

Harry from the room, tried to convince herself it wasn't disappointment she'd seen on Blake's face.

◌

Clearly making the phone call had been the right choice. Blake reached down to ruffle Kevin's shaggy hair as Jessie Banks circled the Firebird in his parents' driveway. "Ooh, I've been waiting years to get my hands on this baby." Jessie ran her hand along the hood of the car as she rounded it. She wore a bandana over her gray hair and baggy overalls under her plaid coat.

He hadn't expected when he asked Mom for her antique car hobbyist friend's phone number that the woman would insist on stopping by that very night. But apparently Jessie Banks had been eyeing Ryan's classic Firebird for a long time. She looked at it as if it were a diamond necklace.

The sound of the wood swing's creaking drifted from where Mom watched on the porch.

"I know you once offered to buy it from Ryan," he said.

"That I did. He looked at me as if I'd just offered to hack off his right arm. He loved this car."

So true. When Ryan died, Blake had assumed his parents would store the Firebird, or maybe sell it. Instead, they'd given it to him. When he'd tried to refuse, Dad had taken him aside, given him a talk about the importance of not slumping into denial.

He could still hear the buzz of his own unspoken replies. *Denial? I watched the accident. I flew the plane. I couldn't be in denial if I wanted to.*

Instead, he'd accepted the keys and when he'd left

town just days after the funeral, it'd been behind the wheel of the Firebird. Of course, in the years since, the car spent more time in storage garages than on the road.

"Before we talk offers, I need to know, Blaze—are you sure about selling?" Jessie pulled off her bandana and swiped it over a dust mark on the car.

The fiery hues of sunset filtered through clouds and bare branches to streak the car's shiny surface. "Yes, I'm sure."

Because there was something oddly attractive about the idea of picking out his own ride. Maybe a soft-top Jeep or old Ford truck. Something sensible, of course, to fit his new life. But with a little fun to it, as well.

Something that wouldn't draw William Baylor's, or anyone else's, ire when he drove it down Main.

Kevin left his side and bounded up the porch steps toward Mom. Funny how the mutt had bonded with his parents. Mom reached down to pet Kevin, then met Blake's eyes.

Was *she* okay with this? Or did she feel like he was giving away a piece of Ryan's memory? And what about Dad? He hadn't even thought to call him.

Jessie beamed. "Then let's talk numbers." She rounded the car once more then angled to face him. "Have to be honest. What I can afford to pay you isn't anywhere close to what you could probably get if you advertised. You wouldn't believe what some enthusiasts would plunk down." She tapped the roof of the car. "Especially for a 'bird with this kind of detailing."

"I'm not looking to make a bundle."

Jessie gave him a figure—one that sounded good to him. And within minutes, they sealed the deal. Just a little paperwork and they could call it done. Jessie waved to his mom before shaking Blake's hand once more. She'd have a check to him within a few days. Which meant tonight he needed to find the vehicle title and registration and work out all the details—not to mention carve out time to shop for a new ride.

After Jessie drove off, he turned back to the house, but Mom had already gone inside—Kevin with her.

Inside the house, the smell of chocolate chip cookies led him to the kitchen. Mom turned from the stainless-steel stove when he walked in, hot pad over her fingers and pan in hand. "I suddenly remembered I'd popped these into the oven before Jessie arrived," she said as he trailed to the middle of the room. She set the pan on the counter and turned.

"You baked?"

The recessed lights overhead spotlighted Mom's eye roll. She tossed her hot pad at him and laughed. "Don't sound so surprised. I am the only one allowed to make fun of my kitcheny skills."

"Why would I bother making fun of your cooking ability when I could tease you for using words like *kitcheny*." He reached for a cookie but stopped at her playful swat.

"So nice to have you home, son." Mom's voice dripped with sarcasm, but he didn't miss the smile she shot his direction. Everybody'd always said he got his sense of humor from his mother, while Ryan got Dad's serious streak.

Mom pulled a plate from the cupboard and motioned Blake to sit. Felt like old times, sitting at the table in the kitchen Mom rarely actually cooked in. Modern appliances couldn't steal the homey feel of the room—basket of fruit in the middle of the table, the refrigerator plastered with photos, wood sign with the words *Bon Appetit* hung over the doorway—where Mom used to sit with Ryan and Blake after school. The rule had been one Oreo for every tidbit they told her about their day.

Now Mom placed a plate in front of him with two gooey cookies. He took a bite, gasping when it hit his tongue, sputtering. "Whoa. Warm."

Mom poured him a glass of water. "That's what you get for mocking your mother."

He gulped the cool liquid. "Tasted good. Even if I do have third-degree burns in my mouth."

"Well, it better taste good." Mom reached for something at the back of the counter, held it out in front of him.

And he burst into laughter. A plastic tub full of Pillsbury cookie dough.

He was halfway through the cookie when Mom sat down across from him. He could feel her stare as he ate, heard the unasked questions she let linger between them. Mom had always been amazing like that—without a word able to draw him out.

"You want to know why I decided to sell the car so quickly."

"Or not quickly, as it were. You've had it for six years now."

True. "Always figured I would eventually. I don't have enough car appreciation to own something so fancy." He finished off the first cookie and looked up. "Think Dad will be mad?"

Mom nibbled on her own snack. "You're almost thirty

years old, Blake. The time for determining your actions based on your father's and my approval is long since passed."

"Just don't want him thinking it was some act of denial. Truth is, a friend said something to me about not holding on to the past."

"That's my past. I've let go." Autumn had said it as if it were easy.

He fingered the rim of his plate. "Anyway, I guess she got me thinking."

Mom's eyebrows raised. "Ah, she's a she. I like this."

A rush of warmth passed over him. "It's not like that."

"What's her name?"

"Mom . . ."

"I just want to know if her first name would go well with your last name."

Frankly, it was probably *her* last name that'd cause the most shock if he were to say it. Dad had literally burst a blood vessel in his eye the day he found out Ryan was dating "that Kingsley girl."

Oh no. Kingsleys and Hunzikers weren't meant to mix. *And is it stuffy in here?* "Did you remember to turn the stove off?"

Mom jumped from her chair. "Goodness gracious, you'd think I left my brain in bed this morning." She marched to the stove, poked a button, and turned to face him. "Anyhow, because I'm a good mother who now and then chooses to respect her son's privacy, I will refrain from mentioning the fact that you're blushing right now and stop fishing for information."

"Well, that's a relief."

"And for the record, no, I don't think your father will

mind. Besides, he has more on his mind to worry about than what vehicle you're driving."

Of course. The hotel. The town. Was he up for re-election anytime soon? One or all of them must be the cause for the dark circles under his father's eyes and the tiredness that seemed to pull on his features.

"You know what, Mom? I think I'll start checking into townhouses. I should get out of your hair."

Mom used a spatula to drop another cookie onto his plate. "You're not in our hair. We even like Kevin." She sat once more, then leveled him with a serious look. "But if you want to do something to make your father happy, here's a thought: go see that plane."

A bite lodged in his throat. "Already gave the keys back to Dad."

"They're in his top dresser drawer."

"Mom, I—"

"You don't have to fly it. Just take a look. Your father spent hours poring over custom paint options."

"It's too much of a reminder." He'd only see Ryan jumping and hear Shawn yelling and . . . He closed his eyes, willing away the sudden smell of the airplane's interior fusing with crisp sky air, the taste of fear and the numb of shock.

"What if it helps you remember the good times?" At only his sigh for an answer, Mom's shoulders dropped. "Please, Blake, just go see it." She turned then, walked from the room.

A shameful weight settled over him. How could he ignore such a simple request? Maybe she had a point. Maybe seeing the plane would help him remember the good times.

But he could remember those anywhere. Like sitting out on the porch roof of the Kingsley Inn, Autumn at his side. No, he didn't need to sit in a cockpit to remember the good stuff.

But speaking of the inn, that reminded him. After another heaved sigh, he reached into his pocket and pulled out his phone. Only took a couple rings for Hilary's voice to sound on the other end.

"Hey, Hils, question for you. Does your oldest brother still work at the bank?"

6

The rumble and hum of a puddle-jumper's ascent whooshed overhead as Blake trekked from the Whisper Shore Municipal Airport office building toward Hangar 7. Wispy clouds hazed the sun and fiddled with the pattern of the airplane's vapor trail.

Blake used to dream about this—claiming a hangar spot and Cessna all his own—back in the days when he was taking flying lessons from Ike Delaney. Used to imagine himself flying the skies on secret missions for one government entity or another.

Now only apprehension and a touch of nausea accompanied his walk to the hangar.

Blake thudded to a halt in front of the metal building that stored his parents' well-meaning gift—the plane he knew he'd never fly. He hadn't been able to get Mom's pleading expression from his head. So after a morning spent walking the entire downtown—talking to business owners, figuring out who planned to host a booth at the festival, convincing those who were reluctant to give the event a chance—he'd forced himself to make the drive out to the small airport.

A gust of wind chugged past him now, rattling the hangar frame.

"You going in or what?"

Delaney. Blake turned to see the pilot covering the distance to the hangar. "I didn't see your truck at the office."

"Took an early lunch. Just pulled into the lot when I saw you lugging out here." Delaney stopped in front of Blake, the camo jacket he'd worn as long as Blake had known him buttoned halfway up. The burly man had the girth of a wrestler, but the gentleness of a teddy bear. "Didn't get to hug you at the party last week, Blaze. Or was that two weeks ago now? Took you long enough to get out here."

Blake stepped into the older man's offered embrace. "I've missed you, Ike." Missed their talks. The pilot had somehow become Blake's go-to mentor during his angst-filled teen years, when he'd sullenly considered himself a second-class Hunziker compared to his perfect football-star brother.

How idiotic he'd been. So much he'd taken for granted.

"Correct me if I'm wrong, but you weren't too over-joyed about the Cessna when your father made the pre-sentation." Delaney stepped around him and gave the hangar door a hefty pull, sliding it open.

"I haven't flown since . . ." Should it really still be so hard to produce the words this many years after the accident? He stepped into the hangar, blinking as he adjusted to the dark. The oily smell of gasoline mixed with metal and dust, at once familiar and jarring. He used to think of it as the scent of adventure.

"Doesn't mean you can't pick it back up." Delaney slapped on the lights as his words bounced against the metal walls. "If you want to."

And there it sat. The sport-utility Cessna 206 with the 310-horse turbocharged power plant. Blake could rattle off the specs like his own birth date. With a high-wing design, black nose, and white body, it was a thing of beauty.

"It's perfect," Blake murmured. It had the body of a bird and the words *The Blaze* printed in red script near the tail.

"Got the keys?"

Blake shook his head. "Gave 'em back to Dad." There wasn't a chance he was going to sit in that cockpit. Not a chance he'd curl his fingers around the controls or prop his feet on the steering pedals. No, he'd only come to appease Mom.

"What'd you do that for?"

"Told you. I don't fly anymore." Except . . . except maybe for the first time since Ryan's accident, a prick of desire needled him now. Barely enough to sting, but it was there.

Delaney clapped a palm on Blake's shoulder. "Nope, you said you haven't flown since your brother's death. Not the same thing as saying you don't fly anymore."

"You can't understand, Ike."

"You'd be surprised."

Blake's voice hit a low note. "I watched my brother fall to his death in a skydiving accident." Had he ever said it out loud? "You know what *that* feels like?"

"I know what it's like to hurt, son." Delaney's gaze seared through him.

It was a pointless conversation. Delaney hadn't been there, didn't know the whole story. Blake's conscience still got a kick out of stabbing his dreams. By day he could usually ward off the flashbacks with enough effort. At night, he was powerless.

And in the mornings when the dreams faded away, they always left the same thing in their wake—accusation, his familiar bedfellow.

He'd convinced Ryan the jump was just what he needed to clear his head after the loss of his football career—an injury his senior year in college—and his girlfriend, too. Ryan had listened, jumped, died. Simple—and devastating—as that.

Except it wasn't quite that cut and dried. There'd been questions after the accident. Drugs—not the prescription kind—identified in his brother's system. Hard to know whether it had been the drugs or a possible defect in the chute that caused the accident. And then there was the question no one voiced, but certainly everyone entertained: *Was* it an accident . . . or a choice?

After all, Ryan had lost so much. What if he'd finally just given up . . . and opted not to deploy his own parachute?

They'd never know. Blake forced his fists to loosen and his fingers to stretch. But what did the *why*s and *how*s matter now anyway? Ryan had died a death orchestrated by Blake's recklessness. Nothing could change that.

Blake swallowed the familiar lump clogging his throat.

After a moment of strained silence, Delaney folded his arms and leaned against the hangar wall. "Why'd you come home?"

Blake ran one hand along the underbelly of the plane.

"Tired of playing nomad. Got this feeling in my gut it was time." This was safer—light conversation, catching up.

"And now that you're here?"

Blake shrugged. "I'm coordinating the festival. You heard that, right?" In the past two days he'd lined up musicians and entertainment. Ordered strings of lights and decorations. Started piecing together a schedule. He was beginning to think he might actually have a knack for organizing events.

Or maybe it just felt good to be entrusted with something important.

And so far, he'd managed without Autumn's help. He'd called the inn a couple times since Wednesday morning's incident with the Dylan dude. But Harry answered every time and insisted she was busy. Couldn't help feeling badly that their little deal hadn't worked out. He might be managing the festival just fine, but Autumn seemed to really need the help around her inn.

"Somehow never took you as the party planner type." Delaney pulled off his baseball cap, scratched his scalp, and then replaced the hat.

"Maybe not, but it's something to do. Dad's hoping it will impress the state tourism board if he can get some board members up here. Said there might be grant dollars in it if we do." Apparently he had invited the board members behind Victoria Kingsley's back. The family feud lived on.

Blake faced the front of the plane now. Like a live being, it stared him down through Lexar-glass eyes over a pointed nose.

Could he take to the skies once more?

"I've got another set of keys in the office," Delaney offered. "I can be back in five."

Maybe he could do it. Bleach the past from his mind, and in its place, the white of the clouds and the thrill of the flight.

He considered the thought for all of a minute before shaking his head. It wasn't fear that racked his nerves . . . but certainty. He didn't belong in the skies anymore.

Which begged the question—where *did* he belong? Once the festival ended, would there be a place for Blake in Whisper Shore anymore? Sure, there was the promise of the city job. But did a job equal purpose? Belonging?

Delaney leaned against the side of the plane, studying Blake. "You seem more pensive than I remember. I mean, you were always the dreamer-type, even as a kid. Always thought there was a sort of visionary in you. But feels like . . . like your spark might've gone out some."

Some? "I don't want to be a dreamer, Ike. I want goals—like what Ryan had. While I was off planning my next big adventure, he was always solid, focused—football, then someday, the family biz."

Ike propped one hand against the body of the plane. "What you don't realize, son, is that being a dreamer is a gift. Being able to see something as it could be before it is . . . Not everybody can do that."

"If it's so great, why can't I do that with my life? See what it could be. Or should be."

Ike grinned. "You don't have to figure out everything you're meant to do today. You're all of, what, thirty years old?"

"Twenty-nine."

"Plenty of time. Pray about things. If God likes an

idea, He'll see it through. If He doesn't, He'll let you know. That's for sure."

Ike made it sound so easy. "And in the meantime?"

"You do whatever God puts in front of you. Best way to live life. You don't have to see every open door on the way to your end goal—just the one staring you in the face."

"If you mean the Cessna, I—"

"I mean whatever it is."

Hope House usually rang with laughter and cheer, but today only silence echoed against the beige interior walls of the home. Autumn forced herself to swallow the disappointment threatening to show itself on her face. Lucy would need her smiles.

Blake walked beside her, cocoa eyes scanning their surroundings as they walked into the living room. After the forty-five-minute drive from the inn down to Traverse City, she was still trying to figure out how he'd ended up with her.

One minute she'd been racing around the inn, completing chore after chore—every day brought them closer to Dominic Laurent's arrival, and every day she felt further behind—the next she was sitting in Philip's truck with Blake at the wheel. Apparently two of Betsy's kids were sick and Philip was working.

"So why's this place closing again?" Blake took a second look around. Couches and comfy chairs filled the space, accompanied by calming watercolor paintings on the walls.

"Government funding. Or lack thereof." They checked

in at a small staff office and then settled onto the red couch where Autumn usually led her reading group. "It was nice of you to come help move Lucy. Though I still don't get why Betsy didn't call me. I was planning to come with her anyway. Probably could've done this myself."

Blake's doubtful look told her he hadn't missed her frantic state when he'd found her at the inn. She swallowed another shot of humiliation, same flavor as the other day when she'd admitted her financial predicament.

"She knew you'd need a truck to transport Lucy's stuff. Philip's truck is manual."

"I can drive stick."

"Not from what I hear."

She crossed her arms. "One teensy-tiny intersection incident."

"Betsy said you held up traffic for ten minutes, Red. And that Philip told her never to let you drive their truck again."

"Betsy's got a big mouth."

It looked like it was taking every ounce of self-control in Blake not to laugh. Cheeky man. And how was it that he could make a pair of worn jeans, black Henley, and navy puff vest look so . . . good? And seriously, sandals? On a day that wasn't supposed to get warmer than forty degrees?

Or maybe the better question was why she couldn't stop noticing every little detail about the man. Like how his dark hair brushed the tips of his ears. Or how his presence had dominated the small cab of Philip's truck on the drive, practically stealing the oxygen from the space.

"So aren't there grants they could apply for?" he asked now. At least he was kindly changing the subject.

"I guess the funding stream must've run dry." Leaving Lucy and the other Hope House residents out in the cold.

Through her volunteering, she'd come to know all the inhabitants of the house. Five of the eight occupants had Down syndrome. The three others had varying developmental challenges. All of them had wriggled their way into her heart.

Fletcher with his impeccable manners, who never let her open a door herself.

Jillian, who always crocheted while Autumn read. She'd given Autumn a rainbow-colored scarf on her last birthday.

Brandon, the youngest of the group at eighteen. Autumn happened to be there the day his parents brought him to Hope House. She'd seen the fear on their faces—a fear Brandon hadn't shared. He'd spotted the reading group right away and bounded over. When he saw the book they were reading—*The Magician's Nephew*—he'd clapped his hands and exclaimed that he'd already read it. Twice. But could he still read it with them?

And as he'd settled, as Lucy offered to share her copy with him, Autumn had seen his parents' anxiety shift to comfort.

"They're like a family here." The sound of pop music filtered through the ceiling from the second floor. Probably Jessie's. At thirty-five, she'd never outgrown her love of '90s boy bands. "It kills me to think of how hard it's going to be on all of them as they separate."

"Maybe they can all get together once in a while."

"Ooh, I could have them all out to the inn. And maybe somehow keep up our reading group online."

But as soon as the words left her lips, a reminder of

her own massive life change came zooming in. Even if all the Hope House residents were staying in the area . . . she wasn't.

For once, the thought of leaving Whisper Shore pinched instead of hugged.

Lucy rounded the corner from the stairway then, ponytail bouncing behind her, CD in her hand. "Hiya. Jessie gave me a CD of Backstreet Boys. I told her I only listen to music on my iPod, but then I said—" Lucy broke off for a moment at the sight of Blake standing with Autumn, but only for a moment. "I said maybe Autumn has a CD player because she's older than me."

The case manager, Angela, chuckled as she passed by. "Feel free to head up to her room. Everything's mostly packed."

Autumn pulled Lucy into a tight hug. "Have you said all your good-byes?"

Lucy's lips turned down. "Yes. Fletcher cried."

Probably because the man had had a crush on Lucy from the day he moved in. It just wasn't right—such a wonderful nonprofit closing its doors. What she wouldn't give to throw a couple million dollars Hope House's way, play benefactress instead of simple volunteer.

Why was money always such a hassle?

"Anyway, do you?"

She blinked, attention returning to Lucy, who waited for an answer to a question Autumn must have forgotten. "Do I what?"

Lucy's giggles sprinkled over Autumn's morose thoughts of moments ago. "Have a CD player, silly."

"I do indeed. Come on, let's go get your stuff. Do you remember Blake?"

Lucy nodded uncertainly. "Your boyfriend?"

Autumn choked, her gum lodging in her throat.

At her sputtering, Blake raised his eyebrows in a tease. "All right there, Red?"

She swallowed, gum knocking its way to her stomach. Coughed and then, "Blake is my friend, Lucy."

Lucy nodded a second time, reluctance gone. "Okay. Let's go."

As they followed her up a staircase, Blake's voice drifted over her shoulder. "Thought I might have to do the Heimlich there for a sec, Red."

The skirt she wore over her leggings and boots swished over her knees. "You'd like that, wouldn't you? One more heroic act to hold over my head."

"I don't know why her question flustered you so much. That's all."

The guy was exasperating.

The guy was funny.

She'd have reached back to give him a punch, but that would mean touching him, and the walled stairway felt like close enough quarters as it was. *Dylan's teasing never did this to me.*

Probably best not to camp out on that thought too long.

At the top of the stairs, a wallpapered corridor was lined with doorways, and the sound of movement came from the openings. Something of a hush clung to the air. Moving day—not something to be celebrated in this instance.

They were halfway to Lucy's room when Lucy stopped, concern sketching across her face at the muffled noise coming from the room in front of her. The door was halfway closed, revealing a handwritten name badge on the door that read *Fletcher*.

Lucy turned to Autumn. "He sounds sad."

Frustration edged the groans and quick spurts of words coming from the room. "Can't do it . . . not right . . . hate this."

After glancing around and not seeing any staff or case managers, Autumn stepped forward to nudge open the door. "Hey, Fletch. Everything okay in here?"

He stood in the center of the room, a long striped bed sheet knotted in his arms. "Miss Kingsley!"

No mistaking the red circles around his eyes or the way his lower lip quivered even as he smiled.

"Hard day, huh." Her words felt so inadequate for the pain Fletcher must feel. As for the sheet, had he been trying to fold it?

"Hey, buddy, can I help you with that?"

Autumn turned, surprised at Blake's voice cutting in as he edged around her.

At first, Fletcher drew back, hesitation spelled out in rounded eyes and clamped lips. Blake *was* a stranger and his size seemed to dwarf Fletcher.

But then Blake glanced around the room, a slow smile spreading over his cheeks as his gaze targeted a poster on the wall. "Oh man, you're a Ninja Turtles fan, too? I used to watch that every single Saturday."

And just like that, Fletcher uncurled. "I watch it on DVD."

"No way, really? I'm Blake, by the way." He held out his hand, and Fletcher quickly dropped the sheet to stick his palm in Blake's.

And something in her heart hiccupped at the sight of

their handshake. At the way Blake reached for Fletcher's sheet and offered to help him fold it. At his, "I'm no good at folding, either," and the spark in Fletcher's eyes that signaled his gratitude and trust.

"There's nothing sexier than men doing laundry."

Autumn whirled. "Lucy!"

Lucy shrugged innocently. "I heard Angela say it once."

With a giggle Autumn moved to the doorway, glancing behind her once more to see Blake moving on to the comforter piled at the foot of Fletcher's bed.

Fine, so maybe Lucy—Angela, whoever—had a point.

Before she could reprimand herself for even thinking that, her phone blared from her pocket. She pulled it out. *The bank?* "Uh, gotta take this guys. Just a sec."

She stepped out of the room, tapped her phone to answer the call.

And was still speechless when it ended a few minutes later.

"Everything okay?"

Blake stood in the doorway now, the sound of Lucy and Fletcher's laughter drifting from behind him.

A choir of surprise and delight sang inside her. "That was the bank. They're approving a short-term loan. It doesn't . . . it doesn't make sense." She dropped her phone in her purse. "They said no the other day. A firm no, according to Grady."

As if contagious, she saw her own happiness reflected on Blake's face. "That's awesome, Red. Don't try to figure why it happened, just be happy it did. Now you can put me to work. After we get Lucy moved, that is. And after we celebrate, that is."

"What? Oh no, I have way too much work to do.

Especially now that there's money to do it with." Dominic Laurent would arrive before she knew it. But finally, hope that everything might work out didn't feel so far out of reach. "Anyway, you've seen the state the inn is in."

Blake folded his arms, the fabric of his cotton shirt pulling taut under his vest. "And I've seen the state you're in. You need a break. Time to enjoy the thrill of winter in Whisper Shore."

"Winter? We haven't even seen a speck of snow yet." She mimicked his crossed arms, leaning against the hallway wall. "Besides . . . thrill? In Whisper Shore?"

"They're not mutually exclusive, believe it or not. You need to have a little fun."

"I have plenty of fun in my life, thank you very much."

He gave his doubt full exposure. "Really? What'd you do last Friday night?"

"None of your business."

"None of my business because it was so scandalously fun you can't tell me, or none of my business because it involved a book and a cup of tea?" He motioned raising a teacup, pinky up, on that last part.

Scary, really, how close he was. But no way was she letting him know that.

"Celebrate with me tonight, Red. And then it's inn and festival business from here on out." He ducked his head back into Fletcher's room then. "Ready to start hauling your stuff, Luce?"

When he turned back to her, his dimpled grin was still in place. And she couldn't help asking. "Why?"

"Because I think you, my dear, might be my open door."

"Because I think you might be my open door?"

Blake said the words out loud for the dozenth time that day. And for the dozenth time, he pictured Autumn's puzzled expression and felt his cheeks reheat. What kind of idiot said something like that to a girl? Especially one he had to, like, see again?

Blake rounded the Firebird—probably one of his last drives in the thing—and moved to the back of the car. In the distance, Lake Michigan lapped at the shore in the lazy shallows.

Thing is, even if he shouldn't have said the thought out loud, he'd meant it.

"You don't have to see every open door on the way to your end goal—just the one staring you in the face."

Ike's words from that morning had played over and over in his head as he'd driven from the airport. Then Betsy had called and he'd found himself driving Autumn to Hope House. He'd filled her in on his progress with the festival on the way, and then they'd met up with Lucy and Autumn had gotten her news from the bank. . . . *Thank you very much, Hilary's brother.*

And just like that, standing in the hallway of Hope House, the thought hit him. Maybe Autumn was his open door. This woman who had listened to him go on about the festival, had taken time out of her day to pick up Lucy, who was working herself to the bone trying to fix up her inn in time for some investor so she could save her family's business and her employees' jobs. Suddenly he wanted to just . . . be there for her. The way she was there for so many others, him included.

Finally, after driving back to the inn and unloading all Lucy's things, he'd worn Autumn down and convinced her to take a couple hours off to celebrate her good news. Now he just hoped she actually showed up.

Blake's feet sunk into the glinting sand of the dunes when he reached the trunk. He pulled it open and reached inside for his sand-board, along with two oversized *For Sale* signs he'd picked up at the hardware store. Perfect for what he had in mind.

Autumn was just pulling up in her Jetta when he closed the trunk. She emerged, wearing a pair of impractical boots and a lightweight coat, indicative of the unseasonably warm weather. She looked wary. And cute.

What were the chances she'd forgotten his awkward words earlier?

"Hey, Blake."

"You came."

She eyed the board under his arm. "I said I would. Besides, I kind of owe you, after all your help today."

"You don't owe me. You do, however, owe yourself. I can't believe you've lived this close to the dunes all your life and have never done this." He started plodding up the nearest hill. A gentle breeze raked through his hair, and the sunlight glimmered off the quartz in almost snow-white sand.

"I usually wait for snow to go sledding." She fell into step beside him. "You should know, I'm not athletic. At all. I tried to go out for basketball in middle school, and Coach Harris told me I should try the debate club instead."

Totally understandable.

"Couldn't we go see a movie instead? That's fun. You said you wanted me to have fun."

"Nope. Clearly you've not experienced all our little

coastline has to offer. And don't worry, you're not going to break any bones."

Her footsteps behind him stopped and he turned. Wow, her face was almost white. "I hadn't thought of that."

He'd have laughed if she didn't look so stricken. If his legs weren't burning from the climb. Dude, it'd been too long since he'd had a good hike.

"There's nothing to it. You'll see."

She gave a hesitant nod and finally started walking again. "Tell me something. How many times have you broken a bone in your life?"

"I'd rather not say."

"Tell me."

"Privileged information."

"All right, then, how many fires have you set?"

"What's with the Spanish Inquisition?" He reached the top of the slope.

She shrugged as she caught up to him. "I need to know these things before I trust you to give me a snow-boarding lesson."

"Sand-boarding. And you mean, if I tell you how many bones I've broken or how many fires I've set, you're suddenly going to trust me?"

She jutted her chin out. "Maybe."

"All right then. Six and four."

"Six bones and four fires or four bones and six fires?"

"That's for me to know and you to go crazy trying to figure out. But for now, we board."

"Blake—"

"Pipe down." He dropped his board in the sand. "Now, this isn't going to be quite as exciting as if we were at, say, the Kobuk Sand Dunes in Colorado or Alaska's Great Sand Dunes National Park. Or even better, Egypt. Actually, sand-boarding is believed to have originated in Egypt back in the time of the pharaohs. Supposedly they slid down dunes on pieces of wood."

Autumn only eyed the slope in front of them.

"Boarding down Michigan dunes is like the bunny hill at a ski resort. Still fun, though."

"Right. Fun." Autumn pursed her lips.

"And for the record, this is a waxed Maven 105 centimeter board. I know you were intensely curious about that." He laughed, stepped into the footpads, tightened the neoprene straps, and straightened. "I'll go down first, just to show you there's nothing to be scared of."

He twisted his ankles to "skate" toward the precipice of the dune. "First time down, it's better to go on your heels. Pull up your toes to keep it slow."

It'd been a few years since he'd done this, but the hill was child's play. Still, probably smart to take the first run slowly, just to test the sand.

"Shouldn't you wear a helmet or something?" Autumn tucked her hands into the wide pockets of her coat.

"You worried about me, Red?"

"Well, if you break your neck, who's going to install my new storm windows?"

"Touching." He chuckled. "Don't worry your pretty little head. If I biff it, worse thing that'll happen is I'll swallow a little sand."

With a flick of his ankles, he started down the hill, easing the pressure on his heels to gain speed. Sand hummed against his board, spewing up on both sides, and the landscape blurred as he angled down. It was nothing like snowboarding down the Alps, but the wind pushing against him, the slick hill moving underneath him as he used one foot and then the other to weave and descend, it was thrill enough for an impromptu afternoon outing.

"Whoo!" Close to the end of the hill he leaned back on his heels and eventually slowed.

He caught his breath at the bottom of the hill, the sound of water slurping at the beach not far away replacing the whir of his board on the sand. He glanced up the hill—it was too far away to see the features of Autumn's face, but he'd have bet money she didn't look away once as he slid down the dune. He knelt down to unstrap his feet and made his way back up the hill.

He gave a sweep of his arms when he reached the top. "See? Nothing to it."

"It did look fun."

His grin widened. "She can admit it. I'm impressed. Now it's your turn."

"Didn't say I was ready to go down." She folded her arms. He was about ready to name it her signature move. Honestly, stubborn looked good on her.

"I'm not going to have you go down on the board." He reached for the *For Sale* signs he'd modified before driving out to the dunes. He'd attached hefty string to both the fronts and backs of the signs, the ones in front longer. "Saw this on the Web. Never tried it, but apparently it works good."

"You've never tried this?"

Did the woman know she squeaked when she got worried? "Never fear, Red. You're going to love this." He looked for the steepest section of hill and tugged Autumn along with him, the signs swinging at his side.

"It's going to be more like tobogganing down a hill than boarding."

He positioned one board underneath himself, legs out to keep from sliding, and pointed to her sign. "Sit."

She obeyed, despite the hesitance still hovering in her face.

"That's a good girl. Now, here's what we do. Feet go toward the front of the sign. Hold on to the front string with one hand. The back with the other."

He could almost hear her uncertainty. And yet, she didn't scoot off the sign. Instead, she peered down the slope as if outlining her path. Same look she got when poring over one of her to-do lists. Finally, she nodded. "All right. I'm ready." She tucked her feet onto the sign.

"I'll give you a boost."

"No really, that's—"

But he reached out before she finished, pushing the back of her sign until it wriggled in the sand, teetered, and zipped down the slope. The imprint of Autumn's makeshift sled ribboned down the hill. Her shrieks floated behind her along with her bouncing ponytail.

But he had to give the woman credit. She held on as she slid down, squeals turning to giggles until she thudded over a lump in the sand halfway down. Suddenly the sign slipped out from beneath her, and she flew into the sand, rolling.

He was on his own sign in a second, steering down the hill until he reached her. She still lay in the sand, hair splayed around her and sign out of sight. Was she moaning or laughing?

"Autumn!" He flung off his sign and crawled to her side. "You okay? You hurt?"

She was moaning *and* laughing. "I am going to have a bruise the size of a mountain tomorrow."

There was sand in her hair and on her face, and one hand held her opposite wrist over her stomach. "You *are* hurt."

She sat up then, still cradling her wrist. "I'm fine. Just twisted it a bit."

His heart was still hammering. Not from the slide down, but from the panic. He'd brought her here. He'd coaxed her onto that stupid makeshift sled. He'd pushed her down.

Just like . . .

"Whoa, Blake, you're going white."

"I'm fine." He sounded like her now. Only his voice felt muffled to his own ears, the setting suddenly distant and hazy.

"I don't think you are."

He squeezed his eyes closed, wishing away the image of his brother, willing his heart to steady. He shouldn't have done this. Should've realized she could get hurt.

"Blake, talk to me."

When he opened his eyes, her face was only inches from his, concern written in every feature. "Sorry," he whispered.

"You scared me. You got pale and your eyes unfocused and . . ." She sat back, legs folded underneath her. "Y-you were remembering, weren't you?"

She said the words so softly, it was as if the wind carried them away. And all he could do was nod.

Autumn looked over his shoulder, blue-eyed gaze scanning the landscape before returning to meet and hold his. "I can't . . . I can't imagine."

Why couldn't he find words? Why wasn't he pushing past this moment like usual, defying the memory-invoked emotions before they could freeze him?

"It wasn't your fault, Blake."

And why couldn't he argue like he normally would? *I didn't listen when you tried to tell me about the drugs. I took him skydiving. I watched him jump.* The arguments formed in his throat but refused to come out.

Autumn reached out and rubbed his arm, then held out the wrist she'd cradled before, twisting it in front of him. "See? It's fine."

He blinked and finally forced words. "Well, maybe a movie wasn't such a bad idea."

She squeezed his arm and scooted back. "Let's go down the hill a couple more times. And then after, let's see if the hardware store's still open. I've got some hardwood floors to varnish, and you promised to help."

She stood. He blinked again and rose, realizing as he did, for once, he'd made it through a memory without despair claiming the rest of his day. And Autumn . . . She might be the reason why.

"So come on, tell me." She tossed the words over her shoulder. "Six fires and four bones or four fires and six bones?"

He double stepped to catch up to her. "Yeah, actually, probably neither. I'm six foot four, so those were the first numbers to come into my head."

Her glare was as great as her smile.

7

Autumn smelled her mother before she saw her. Chanel No. 5. And tart disapproval.

"Why is there an orange rug in the entryway?" Victoria Kingsley's voice pealed through the first floor of the inn. The click of her heels almost drowned out the groan of wood floors desperately in need of replacement, the faint buzz of the lobby's soft lighting.

"Autumn!"

Don't do it, Autumn. Don't do it.

She did it. Ducked behind the desk before Mom spotted her. She'd known Mom was due to arrive home Sunday night from her latest round of meetings in Detroit. Had guessed she'd probably stop by the inn for breakfast that morning. Promised herself she'd finally spill her news.

Didn't make the idea an appealing one.

"What are you doing?" Harrison's hiss sounded from above.

"Your shoes are shiny. Do you get them professionally polished?"

His narrow eyes shot bullets of amusement as he crouched down beside her. "You are insane."

"No, I'm hiding." Wasn't proud of it, but she could admit it.

"Autumn!" The dinging of the front desk bell joined her mother's shrill tone.

Harrison raised his eyebrows.

Well? Autumn rose.

"Autumn, what were you doing down there? Didn't you hear me calling?"

"Morning, Mom."

Victoria's white-blond hair—the same shade as Ava's—was flat-ironed ramrod straight, her makeup airbrushed perfectly. Mom smoothed one hand over her crisp blue blazer. "How's capacity?"

Mom may have deeded the inn over to Autumn, but she'd never entirely let go.

"We were at sixty percent over the weekend. Christmas week we're almost fully booked, but we're looking at a couple potential under-forties until then. How was your trip?"

"Meetings. More meetings. Anything interesting happen here?"

Harry snorted from where he still crouched, and she gave him a kick. "Let's have breakfast and I'll fill you in."

"All right." Mom nodded. "Might as well let Harrison come out of hiding."

They both grinned at the gasp coming from down below. Autumn stepped from behind the desk and walked with Mom into the dining room. Though in need of an upgrade, the space was a mix of elegant and earthy—decorated in greens and blues that played nicely with the ornate crown molding. Cream-colored curtains pulled aside allowed morning sunlight to pour into the room.

If only there were more than a sprinkling of guests filling the tables. But if they could just keep holding out, surely the festival would pull the tourists in. *Festival. Dominic Laurent. Festival. Dominic Laurent.* Her dual-sided hope in mantra form.

Mom stopped at a table in the corner, peeling off leather gloves. "You might consider getting rid of that orange rug in the entryway. Thanksgiving is long since over."

Autumn swallowed the sigh that climbed up her throat. "We plan to put up Christmas decorations later this week. I believe Betsy's serving cinnamon rolls and fresh fruit today. I'll grab us some."

"You really should let your waitstaff do their job."

Waitstaff? Didn't Mom remember how much they'd had to whittle down their employee numbers in the past couple years?

"It's no problem. Just give me a sec."

The sweet scent of Betsy's iced cinnamon rolls enveloped Autumn as soon as she stepped into the kitchen. *Heaven.* "Hey, Bets, can I steal a couple plates?"

Betsy stepped back from the glass-fronted refrigerator, fruit tray in hand. "Of course. Breakfast with Vicki, yeah? You going to tell her about Laurent?"

"You betcha." The only question was whether to share the good news about LLI first and hope it cushioned the part about her move to France, or vice versa.

Autumn grabbed a pair of tongs from a drawer and placed cantaloupe slices on each plate. "Wish me luck."

She pushed through the swinging door and returned to the table. "Here we are, Mom."

Mom sighed as Autumn lowered the plates. "My mouth is watering. My waistline is protesting."

"Listen to the former, ignore the latter." Autumn sat. "I'll pray." They bowed their heads. "Dear God, thank you for this day, the sunshine, the food, and the chance to spend time with Mom." *And please, please help her not get mad about France. . . .*

The ornate clock hanging on the wall stared Autumn down. She picked up her fork. Set it back down again. *Just get it out.*

Fine. France first. "Mom, remember in high school when I had that exchange student friend—Sabine from France."

Mom closed her lips around a bite of Betsy's roll, an "mmm" following her swallow. "Yes, of course I remember. You insisted we buy a bread maker. You wanted fresh bread every day."

"Yes! Because Sabine always made it for her host family." Autumn could still smell the yeasty smell in the air when she'd hung out with Sabine at her host house.

And she could still taste her own imagined carefree abandon, the dream something as simple as fresh bread had embedded in her. Sabine's talk of France had enchanted her. She'd begun daydreaming about studying in France her junior year. Started picturing herself strolling down a French village street, sundress swishing around her legs, the cadence of a foreign language humming around her.

But then . . . then she'd overheard the word *divorce* falling from Dad's lips. And worse, his sudden death.

So, no, she'd never gone. But the hunger had continued tunneling in her soul in the decade since—to see and feel and experience another life, in another place.

"What about Sabine?" Mom sipped her coffee.

"Well, she works at an upscale hotel in Paris now. There's a job opening there."

Mom's coffee mug thumped against the table as she set it down, attention suddenly sharp. "And?"

"And I've been offered the position."

Her words seemed to dangle in the air before thudding down. She waited one second, two, three for Mom to jump in. To congratulate her. Or chastise her. Something.

Nothing.

Why? Why was it always like this between them? Stilted and awkward.

"I have a plan for the inn. Took out a little loan to spruce it up. And I've left a couple messages for Ava. Remember how when we were younger, she was the one who always talked about running the inn someday?"

Finally, Mom spoke, her interruption severe. "Autumn, listen to me. Ava's happy in Minnesota."

"Yes, but I—"

"Much happier than she'd be here, surrounded by memories of the boy who broke her heart and his family who treated her like mud. I'll never forgive them for that."

Autumn pushed her plate away, Friday's sand-boarding episode with Blake sailing through her memory. Those minutes, sitting in the sand, watching him remember. "Ryan *died*. They deserve our sympathy, Mom."

"I can't believe you're defending them."

"And I can't believe . . ." What—that her mother was still angry at the entire Hunziker clan? It shouldn't surprise her. The angst between their families was like a proud, unbreakable statue standing in the middle of town. She'd only been helping Blake with the festival for three or four days, and already she'd heard at least a dozen times—*"A Hunziker and a Kingsley working together?"*

Ryan and Ava's fling had only exacerbated the rivalry that had existed before they were born. Going back to when the Hunzikers built their hotel and started stealing the Kingsleys' guests.

But shouldn't there come a time when they all bucked up enough to put the past behind them? Move forward. "I heard something about a state grant, Mom. And that you are blocking it just because of Mayor Hunziker."

"You heard wrong."

"Shouldn't you care more about the town than an old grudge? And what about the inn? Helping the town is helping us."

"I can't show favoritism, Autumn." Mom's fork clinked against her plate. "Besides, you accuse me only minutes after telling me you're abandoning the inn."

"Well, I'm not the first one to do so, am I?"

The brash statement escaped before she could stop it, its impact stilling them both.

"I didn't abandon it," Mom finally said, voice steady despite the tension rippling between them.

But maybe Autumn hadn't meant Mom. Maybe she'd meant Dad. Or Ava. All three of them. And she had to wonder why she even worried so much about the inn when all the rest of them didn't. *Why am I am the last one holding on to something everyone else already let go of?*

But no answer came in the seconds as she watched Mom spread her napkin over her plate, shake her head as if brushing away the crumbs of this conversation, and stand. "Do what you will, Autumn. But don't count on your sister to step in and take up where you leave off. She's got a new life now."

And I'm still waiting to start mine.

The same old cry of desperation pushed through her. But there wasn't any point in putting voice to it. It seemed there was no getting over the strain of Dad's death, Ava's flight. Worse, the secret they both knew but never talked about. Sometimes Autumn wondered if telling Mom she knew about the planned divorce would open up the lines of communication.

But for all she knew, it'd do the opposite. Wedge them even further apart.

"Mom, there was something else. Better news, actually. Does the name Dominic—"

She broke off at the sound of yells coming from the kitchen. And then, "Fire!" Betsy, frantic, hurried into the dining room. "It's the cottage, Autumn."

Where was Autumn?

The conference hall of the Whisper Shore town hall buzzed with impatient energy. Eleven people had shown up for tonight's meeting—all local business owners and community members Blake and Autumn had recruited to help with the festival.

"We need everyone to feel invested in this," Autumn had said Saturday as they worked together. "In the past, this was Georgie's event. Now the rest of us need to own

it. Plus, it's only two and a half weeks away. We need all
the help we can get."

He'd teased her about the light in her eyes, the energy
in her voice, when she'd pitched the idea. And yet, he'd
loved the fact that she was finally as excited about the
festival as he was.

So why was he worrying she wasn't going to show up?

The scrapes of folding chairs mixed in with chatter
and the gurgling of a large coffeepot in back. A woman
dropped into the chair to Blake's right, her elbow pressing into his side. Mrs. Hathaway, the longtime town
librarian. She flung her scarf away from her face, its
staticy fuzz scratching over Blake's cheek.

"Sorry, Blaze." Mrs. Hathaway plopped her purse
atop the table.

He might be able to throw a festival together, but
escaping his nickname was apparently not in the cards.
"No problem, Mrs. Hathaway."

Blake pulled a box of Tic Tacs from his pocket and
clicked it open. He tossed back a mouthful. Nerves jos-
tled his empty stomach. *Where are you, Red?*

And when had he slipped into this unlikely depen-
dency on her? He could handle this meeting alone. Even
if he did have that new-kid-in-school feeling poking at
his insides.

He'd placed packets at each seat around the table—
budget numbers, town-square layout, schedule of events,
all clearly outlined.

Blake rubbed his hands together, the chill of the outdoors not entirely barred from the room. Brown-paneled
walls gave the meeting room a closed-in feeling. Framed
aerial photos of Whisper Shore lined three of the four

walls. On the fourth, headshots of the town founders stared down the crowd.

"All right, everyone, thanks for taking time out of your evening to meet. Let's get started." Surely Autumn would show up any minute now.

Voices hushed, replaced by the squeaks of metal chairs as the committee members settled.

"First of all—"

The meeting room door pushed open, and William Baylor entered. "Sorry, I'm late." He offered the gruff apology, then dropped into the last open chair.

Oh, man. Why had Autumn invited him?

"Uh, thanks for joining us, Mr. Baylor." He supposed it made sense, the man being the town's parks and rec manager. They'd need his help with wiring the park for sound and decorations. Didn't mean it was going to be easy working with him.

Baylor only grunted in acknowledgment, eyes on the packet in front of him.

"Okay, well, I can't tell you all how much I appreciate your willingness to help with the festival. This is very last minute, but we're working hard to make sure it's the best event this town has ever hosted."

This is where he would've waited for Autumn to jump in, impress them all with the finesse of someone used to running her own business.

"My co-coordinator and I made several lists. I'm not sure where Autumn is, actually, but . . ." Did he sound as unpolished as he felt? Why couldn't he have the confidence he'd had on top of that dune, convincing Autumn to brave the ride down? "Anyway, if we keep on schedule with everything on these lists, we'll have no problem pulling this festival together in time. Thankfully Georgie got the ball rolling weeks ago. We can talk about assignments and all that later, but first . . ."

He paused at the site of Mindy Turner's raised hand. As the president of the ladies league, she was the perfect person to head up decorations for the festival. "I'm sorry, Blaze, but before we dig in, I just have to ask, what's Randi Woodruff like?"

"Um, what?"

She flipped her dark curls over her shoulder. "I know I'm not the only one wondering. Probably half of us agreed to join this committee solely out of curiosity."

"That's not really—"

"Can she really build houses?" Bert from the hardware store tapped his coffee mug against the tabletop.

Blake had to work not to roll his eyes. "She can really build houses, Bert. And Mindy, she's a very nice person. Let's move on."

"How'd it feel losing her to the reporter?" Mindy again.

Maybe the ladies league wasn't so vital to the festival. "I didn't lose her to the reporter. I never had her. It was strictly professional, beginning to end."

"Because it's so professional to fake a marriage."

William Baylor. Of course.

"Look, folks, we're here to talk about the festival. Autumn and I had a brainstorm the other night, and we're pumped to let you in on it." He rushed into the new topic before additional questions could pop up. "I know every year, businesses that commit to booths at the festival put down a deposit. That money, in the past, has been used to hire someone to serve as the festival emcee, right?"

"Ahh, Channel 16 meteorologist Lillith Dunwoody," Bert piped in. "What a beauty."

"He's twice her age, silly man," Mrs. Hathaway quipped beside Blake.

"She gets her forecast right at least fifty percent of the time, to boot," Bert added.

"Well, anyway," Blake continued, "we have a proposal. Instead of spending the money on an emcee, what if we take that money and use it to spruce up the square. Repaint the gazebo if the weather holds, replace our out-of-date Christmas decorations. We'd have to work fast, but if everybody pitches in, we could do it. What do you think?"

He waited for a smattering of approval. Instead, only the sound of the wind flapping against the building. The groan of the coffeepot. An uncomfortable cough from across the table. Why didn't anyone say anything?

Finally Mrs. Hathaway gave his hand a motherly pat. "Blaze, giving the square a facelift is a nice idea. But the fact of the matter is, we're not the town beautification committee. You asked us to help with the festival. And in the past, Lillith Dunwoody has been a real draw."

His knuckles rapped against the table as he turned his hands palms up. "Well, did anyone consider asking her to donate her time? This is her hometown after all."

"Now, how would that look after seven years of paying her?" She may not have meant to sound condescending, but Mrs. Hathaway's tone was enough to dry up Blake's confidence.

He closed his eyes, pressed his lips together. And when he spoke again, his words were measured. "I am sure that Lillith Dunwoody has done a wonderful job. And I am sure, like you said, she is a real draw for folks in this community. But she's a far cry from a celebrity who's going to lure tourists from farther away than a thirty-mile radius."

"And I suppose you know all about celebrities." Baylor's blurted words stilled the room. He stood, rounding his chair and propping both hands on its back. "I can't be the only one here who's wondering why I'm listening to the plan of a boy who spends one week in town and decides he knows what all we're doing wrong. As if he's never made one misstep—or a hundred."

Gasps popped like hot corn kernels across the room, then fell at once as a weighty tension shrouded the space. So many faces staring at him, a mix of disapproval and embarrassment hovering like a sticky mist.

The silence pulled rubber-band taut, and suddenly he was sitting in the front of First Church again, Ryan's coffin just feet away, feeling the disapproval of those in attendance who'd heard the details of Ryan's death, hearing the whispers. *"Blake was flying the plane."*

He grasped for control, an intelligent response, anything. "I don't think you all understand. My dad is working on getting some state tourism board members to the festival. There's grant money on the table. If we impress them—"

"Everybody knows we don't have a chance at a grant," William Baylor interrupted. "We haven't been taken seriously in years, not compared to Ann Arbor or Mackinac."

It was all Blake could do not to bang his forehead against the table.

"Besides, Victoria Kingsley would rather fund a

popcorn stand in Poughkeepsie than do anything that might make your father look good."

They all stared at him when William finally finished. Waiting for a reply. One he didn't have.

∞

"Autumn, are you still awake?"

Mom's voice muffled past Autumn's closed bedroom door. Autumn tapped her toothbrush against the side of the sink in her bathroom. "Yes, Mom."

She sidestepped the pile of soot-stained clothes at her feet, where she'd traded them in for flannel PJs. The white lights over the mirror highlighted the mascara smudged under her eyes, the result of a too-long day coming to a too-distant end.

Faulty wiring had caused the fire in her cottage's kitchen. Thankfully, Lucy had called 9-1-1 as soon as she saw the smoke wafting from the vent. The damage was minimal, contained mostly to the kitchen. But with the smell of smoke heavy and the electrician unable to immediately fix the wiring, she and Lucy had relocated to Mom's.

Autumn crossed her childhood bedroom now and opened her door.

Mom leaned against the doorframe, hair pulled away from her face and sharp cheekbones cleared of makeup. Autumn steeled herself for the lecture sure to come as she bunched her hair into a ponytail behind her head and stretched a band.

"Autumn, I . . . wanted to apologize."

The hair band snapped, and her hair spilled over her shoulders. *Say again?*

"For this morning. At the inn. The things I said."
Discomfort sifted over Mom's face.

"Well . . . thanks. I mean . . . apology accepted."

Mom nodded and turned.

"Mom?"

"Yes?"

"Even if Ava won't come back, I'm still going to try
to figure everything out. There's this man coming—
Dominic Laurent, from Laurent Lodging International.
He must've seen that ad I took out in a few magazines
last summer. I think this could be a great thing."

She couldn't translate the shift in expression in Mom's
eyes. She'd expected at least a glimmer of relief. After
all, she was still looking out for the best interest of the
inn. That's what Mom had been concerned about, right?

Mom tightened the robe of her belt. "It's been a long
day. I'm going to go check on Lucy and then turn in."

She turned, and Autumn released the sigh building
in her. Why is it they had so much trouble talking? Just
being a mother and daughter. It had started long before
Ava ever left, before anything happened with Ryan or
the Hunzikers . . .

It's because we've both been pretending for years.

The thought chugged through her, heavy and poignant and . . . true.

Ever since Dad died, Mom had pretended things had
been perfect between them, that divorce had never been
on the table. But mother and daughter still bore the hurt
of it. Separately. Because neither chose to talk.

"Are you all settled in, Lucy?" The sound of Mom's
voice drifted down the hallway followed by the muted
tones of Lucy's answer.

The click of Mom's bedroom door cut into the quiet. Autumn closed her own door and returned to the little bathroom connected to her room. She grabbed a washcloth from the cupboard over the toilet and ran it under warm water.

She was grateful Mom had been quick to offer to put them up, hadn't even blinked when Autumn mentioned Lucy was now living with her. Autumn paused, washcloth lifted halfway to her face.

What if Mom's sadness didn't only have to do with her worries about the inn, but about Autumn's leaving? Considering all she'd gone through with Dad, considering Ava's distance . . . did Autumn's plan feel like the final break in their family tree?

I don't want to hurt her, God. But if I don't get out and start living my own life now, I never will.

And she could end up just like Dad, trapped in a headlock of regrets. *I have to go.*

She scrubbed at her face, hard, smearing away her makeup and leaving in its place, splotches of red.

"Have you prayed about this, Autumn?"

Autumn had waved off Ellie's question the other day, because, well, yes, she'd prayed . . . but only halfheartedly. Never listening long enough for an answer.

Because she couldn't risk the answer being "Stay."

But God wouldn't actually ask her to give up France, would He? Not after she'd waited this long. Of course, maybe the real problem wasn't so much what God might ask of her . . . but whether she'd even hear it, if He did answer. Somehow in the past months of financial worries—or maybe the past years of listless longing—she'd lost her ear for His voice.

Or maybe He'd just stopped talking.

She wrung out the washcloth and slung it over a towel bar. The bathroom, decorated in warm earthy tones, had always been her favorite place to think before moving to her cottage at the inn—especially in the deep, oversized tub.

But tonight she'd been too tired to even fill the tub. Autumn picked up her pile of clothes, then paused. *What was that?* She waited, heard another sharp rap.

She padded out of the bathroom, shuffling in her slippers. One more rap . . .

She dropped her clothes, clamping a fist over her mouth. A face at her window. Heart hammering, she stalked to the window and thrust it open. "*What* do you think you're doing?"

Blake perched on the overhang that sheltered the side porch. His cheeks were red—either from the exertion of his climb or the cold. Probably both. Crazy man.

"I wanted to talk."

Thank the Lord she'd skipped that bubble bath. "You haven't heard of a phone? Or, you know, like a front door? How did you even know I was here?"

He climbed in the window. "Called the inn. Jamie said you were staying here tonight. You never gave me your cell phone number, so . . ."

Autumn flounced over the clothes she'd dropped and walked to her desk. She scribbled down her number and pulled the Post-it from its cube. When she turned, she was face-to-face with Blake. Did he have to stand so close? She stuck the Post-it to his light blue button-down shirt. "There. My number."

He peeled it from his shirt. "So you want me to climb

back out the window, go stand at the curb, and call you from there?"

She folded her arms instead of answering. Swell, she'd chosen her white pajamas with pink and red hearts. Second time he'd seen her in her PJs, and it wasn't any more pleasant than the first.

Suddenly the humor seeped from his expression and he turned serious. "Where were you tonight? I needed you at that meeting."

She inhaled. The meeting, she'd completely forgotten. "Blake, I'm—"

"And why didn't you tell me you invited William Baylor? The man can't stand me. In fact, newsflash: Most of the people on that committee can't stand me. They don't like me. They sure don't like my ideas. And the one person I thought might back me up didn't even bother to show."

"I'm so—"

"I needed you there."

If he'd let her get a word in edgewise, she might explain. The fire, Lucy, Mom. But behind the anger in his voice was something surprising and . . . raw. For some reason, his shoulders didn't seem as broad tonight, not with his arms hanging limp at his side and his stance sagging like a man fatigued. He ran a hand through his disheveled dark hair, then pinned her with his gaze.

"Blake, what happened at the meeting?"

"Nothing worth reliving. It was a mess."

"I'm really sorry." The apology tumbled from her, so sincere it surprised her. "You're right, I should've been there. I shouldn't have made you face them all yourself."

Listen to yourself, Autumn. He's a man. He doesn't need coddling.

That was probably part of the problem. His . . . manliness. His dark eyes, his height, that unshaven jaw that could've starred in a shaving cream commercial. His presence in her bedroom set all her senses on edge.

"We can have another meeting."

Blake's eyebrows lowered. "Not sure they'd show up."

There was that maternal feeling again. Except the way he captured her gaze, the way she couldn't look away . . . *Oh, boy,* not *maternal.*

She broke eye contact and took a step back. "There was a fire at my house today. That's why I'm here."

He blinked, jaw dropping. "Are you serious?"

"Nothing major. Kitchen wall's a little black. Something wonky with the wiring."

He palmed his forehead. "And that's why you missed the meeting. I'm an idiot."

"You're not. You didn't know. And I should have remembered to let you know."

"I practically bit your head off."

She bobbed her head from side to side. "Eh, still attached. Still working."

His grin turned on then, and he took a breath, gaze wandering around the room. She followed his vision, trying to see the room through his eyes.

Built-in faux bamboo bookshelves lined two of the four walls. The other two walls were painted a vibrant grass green. Her white bedspread matched the area rug underfoot. An antique trunk took up the space under the window—or in Blake's case, the entrance.

"More books," he observed. He pulled a book from

one of the eye-level shelves. "*Swiss Family Robinson.* Like the movie?"

"That's backward, but yeah."

"Ryan and I used to pretend we were Fritz and Ernst. I always wanted to be Fritz, but Ryan forced me to be Ernst because I'm younger." He scanned the rest of the shelf. "Lot of biographies. Lots of travel books. Mostly fiction."

She stepped up to the shelf. "My dad encouraged my bookworm tendencies. He loved reading to me— *Robinson Crusoe, Gulliver's Travels, Peter Pan*, anything to do with adventures." She shrugged, remembering the smooth tone of Dad's reading voice. The way he'd close the book when a chapter ended, then ask Autumn where she'd travel if she could. Which character she liked best. Which one she'd most like to meet.

Blake tapped a book back into place, eyes on her as he did.

His study sent her into self-conscious mode, and she reached up to slip her hair behind her ear. "Hey, let me show you something cool." She nudged him out of the way, then found the hidden clamp inside one bookshelf. Just a minor push and the whole section of the shelving, from floor to ceiling, moved. "Hidden passageway."

Blake perked up. "No way."

"Yes way. My Dad made it when I was little." She ducked in. "Come on."

Her hand found the switch inside the adjacent room and light filled the space. Ava's bedroom, just like she'd left it last time she was home—last Christmas. "Dad thought it'd be fun for us to have a secret entrance to each other's room. Ava and I were by far the most popular on the sleepover circuit in grade school."

"I bet." He turned a full circle, probably laughing inside at the pink and lace décor—which was especially funny considering Ava's tomboy demeanor and love for football. "I don't remember your dad all that well."

"Well, it's not like our families mingled."

He grinned, but only for a moment. His eyes seemed to latch on to something on Ava's closet door. He walked over, fumbled through the items hanging from the hook on the back and pulled off a jacket.

Autumn inhaled sharply. She'd forgotten.

He turned to face her, slowly. "My mom . . . she looked for this before the . . ."

Funeral. Ryan's college letter jacket. Why hadn't she or Mom or especially Ava had the decency to return it to the Hunzikers?

"I'm sorry. We should've . . . I never thought to . . ."

He just stood there, holding the coat in one hand, like a man frozen. And before she knew what she was doing, Autumn closed the space between them. In a tentative move, she threaded first one arm, then another around him. Her cheek found the crook between his neck and shoulder and she just . . . stayed there.

He smelled of soap and his chin scratched her forehead. Warmth slid from her head all the way through her, down to her toes, leaving winged flutters in her stomach. *Lord, what am I doing?*

But right when embarrassment threatened to push her away, Blake circled his own arms around her. Tight, as if holding on for life. She could feel the staccato of her heartbeat. Or was that his?

"Blake, I'm . . ." Her voice was muffled, her thought directionless.

I'm what? Sorry, for the hug? No, not really. Suddenly way too aware of how perfectly she fit into his hold? *Yes. Definitely, yes.*

"You don't have to say anything, Red."

So she didn't.

8

"Honestly, Red, when we made this deal, I was thinking more along the lines of hefty, manly projects. Bob Vila–type stuff."

Blake's flustered voice came from the other side of the fake Christmas tree only half assembled in the Kingsley Inn's long den.

"Instead, I'm playing interior decorator while your tree attacks me." A branch rustled, and Blake's exaggerated groan drew giggles from Lucy, who dug through a box of ornaments on the couch.

Autumn leaned against the fireplace mantel, hiding her smirk behind the manual they'd found in the bottom of the tree box. "You call it attacking. I call it protesting. You're putting it together wrong."

A fire crackled in the fireplace, and the buttery aroma of popcorn still lingered in the air, even though they'd already eaten every last kernel.

Blake appeared from the behind the tree, fake pine needles decorating his shirt. "I don't need a manual to tell me how to put together a fake tree."

She looked from Blake to the lopsided tree and back to Blake. "I'd argue that point, but then you'd launch into another diatribe on how I always argue."

"You do."

"I don't."

"Score one for the Hunziker team." He drew a tally mark in the air. "And anyway, like I was saying, I . . . am a man."

"Uh, yeah, nobody was questioning that." Hadn't she lain awake until after midnight last night thinking about that hug in Ava's bedroom, trying to shake off the feel of his arms around her? Or, well, fine—replaying those minutes pressed against him over and over while simultaneously trying to convince herself she *hadn't* relished every second. Wishing she could get his dimpled smile and perfect torso and dark eyes out of her head?

And that was another thing. Where did he get off having such luscious eyelashes? A mascara ad would kill for those lashes.

Manual in front of face. Hide blush. Get a grip.

Maybe it would've been better to relegate him to some other job today. It'd been distracting enough trying to get through their festival to-dos this morning while holed up in her office. But at least they'd made progress. Despite the messy meeting he'd described to her the night before, things were moving along.

"I am a man," Blake was still talking. "And I should be doing something masculine. Like ripping up old floorboards or knocking down drywall or installing crown molding."

She lowered the manual. "Installing crown molding is

masculine? Didn't you just spend four weeks living with a *woman* who does all that for a living?"

He picked up a loose branch from the floor. "Fine. But if you ask me to pick out new potpourri for the guest rooms next, it's not happening."

Autumn stifled a laugh and plopped next to Lucy on the couch. "Lucy, never let a man tell you what is and what isn't *women's work*."

"Oh, I won't, Miss Autumn." Lucy's face was pure seriousness.

"And Lucy, never agree to deals with feisty women before reading the fine print." Blake batted at a branch jutting from the tree.

Lucy only giggled at that. She'd giggled at everything Blake said. The man had charmed her within seconds of stopping by—just like he had his adoring public during the month when Randi Woodruff had paraded him around as her husband. Autumn would never admit it to him, but she'd caught a couple of the TV interviews he'd done back in October. He had the kind of face cameras loved.

But it wasn't a phony role he played as he interacted with Lucy today. He seemed to take special care to make her smile—complimenting her bell-shaped earrings and promising she'd get the privilege of placing the angel atop the tree. At the same time, he didn't treat Lucy as somehow different or in any way beneath him.

"Ooh, I like this one," Lucy said as she pulled an ornament from the box beside her.

Autumn recognized it immediately. The ball was swirled in glittery blue and green, made to look like a globe. "There's a little on-off switch on the bottom."

Lucy found the switch and turned it on, holding the ornament by the gold hook at the top. The globe twirled beneath, the hum of its tiny motor joined by the lilting melody of "What a Wonderful World."

"My sister and I bought that one for our dad when we were kids."

Blake stepped away from the tree. "Because of all his traveling stories."

Eyes still on the ornament, she nodded. "He usually left the holiday decorating to us and Mom, but he always insisted on hanging that ornament himself."

Lucy held the ornament toward her. "Then you should hang it."

Funny how such a little piece of glass and metal could erase the years and draw so clearly a picture of their happy little family as they used to be. But as quickly as the image appeared, it scratched away.

And just like they always did, the questions scribbled through her mind: Had Dad always been unhappy? How long had he been planning to leave? Would he really have gone through with it?

Autumn stood. "I'll let you do it, Luce."

Lucy shrugged and bent over to place the globe next to the other ornaments she'd arranged in neat rows at her feet. No shrug from Blake, though. No, instead his gaze pierced her with uncanny understanding. The heat of it flustered her, and she reverted her focus to the window.

A late-afternoon sun slipped through the sheer fabric dangling down from the gold-knobbed curtain rods over the windows.

Autumn blinked. "Well, we should get this finished. This room is going to look spectacular when we're done.

We'll string lights around the tree and over the mantel. We'll hang stockings and put up the Nativity. It'll be the perfect mingling spot for the Christmas party."

Every year the Kingsley Inn hosted a Christmas party— a mix of guests and community members. It hadn't been as big these past years as it used to be, not with hotel numbers dwindling and Whisper Shore losing some of the holiday magic that used to light up the town.

But this year . . . This year she was going to do the party up right. It would be Dominic Laurent's first night in town. And she aimed to show him the Kingsley Inn could still be the life of the shore.

"So am I invited to the party?" Blake was back to poking branches into their spots on the tree.

"Sure, if you want to come. But if you do, you have to be on your best behavior. I've got that potential investor coming, you know."

Blake rearranged a couple branches to fill in a see-through spot on the tree. "Right, right. Dominic Somebody-or-other."

"He is, by far, the best Christmas present I could receive this year. Well, that and the return of Whisper Shore's annual snowball fight. Remember that?"

"Of course I do. Who do you think still holds the records for snowball-toss yardage?" He flashed a smirk. "If Mother Nature would ever give us some snow, we could resurrect the tradition. But I promise to behave at your important Christmas party. I won't even call you Red, if it helps."

"Very good." Although, she'd kind of gotten used to the nickname.

"*Honey* or *sweetheart* or *muffin*, maybe. But not Red."

"Blake."

"What?"

He did the completely innocent look so well.

"Hey, Miss Autumn, I think your mom's here." Lucy pointed out the window.

Autumn's gaze zipped to the window.

Ohhh, not good. Not good at all. Mom emerged from her SUV, long black coat cinched at the waist, high-heeled boots peeking out from underneath. Autumn spun, pointing at Blake. "You need to leave."

"Uh, and go . . . ?"

"Anywhere. Away. My mom would rather run into Fidel than you."

"Castro?"

"You know any other Fidels?"

His smirk resurfaced. "Ooh, I could hide in the tree."

Think, Autumn, think.

"Come on." She snatched his arm and dragged him to the lobby. Staircase. If she could get him up the stairs before Mom climbed the porch steps . . . "Go up."

She pushed him. Did the man have to be so . . . big and strong and stuff? But at least he took the steps two at a time, throwing a couple glances over his shoulder as she chased him up. "Then what? I climb out a second-story window?"

The front door creaked open.

Autumn yanked on the door of the first guest room. "In there."

The cinnamon scent whiffed from the room, where a canopied bed stood front and center. Blake ducked his head into the room, then turned back to Autumn, held up both hands in a halting gesture. "I'm flattered, but really, Autumn, I'm not this kind of guy. We haven't even been on a real date." Laughter danced in his words.

"You crazy . . ." But for just one moment, facing Blake in the doorframe's embrace, his breath on her face, the barely-there hint of spicy cologne, the man's broad shoulders filling up the space . . . Well, for just a second, he wasn't crazy Blake Hunziker.

He was the guy who made a fake-pine-needle-dotted black sweater seem like the most masculine article of clothing ever.

Whose teasing she'd honest-to-goodness begun to crave.

Who'd stood in Ava's bedroom last night wearing vulnerability like a second skin.

And who she was starting to like way, way, *way* too much for her own good.

"Just s-stay here 'til I come back." And who turned her into a stuttering idiot.

⁊

Of all people, Victoria Kingsley had given him the idea.

"I don't know about this, Blaze." The assistant city manager led the way through the beige-colored walls of the Whisper Shore city offices. The aroma of donuts trailed them through the maze of hallways. At least one town tradition hadn't fallen by the wayside—Friday morning refreshments at the town hall, open to the public. "You realize I could get an earful from the council if I do this without approval?"

Blaze unzipped his hooded jacket and followed Joe Lemon into a room stacked with computer monitors and equipment. "I'll take the blame if anyone gives you any grief. I promise."

Last night, from his hiding place in the guest room at the top of the stairs, he'd caught snatches of Autumn and her mother's conversation. Which reminded him, he should talk to Autumn about adding soundproof insulation in the guest rooms. It's the first improvement *he'd* make at the inn if it were his place.

Not that it was. Even so, after a week and a half of spending nearly every day at the inn, he'd started to feel a part of the place.

"We'll have this place looking like a Thomas Kinkade Christmas painting in no time, Mom."

"All you need now is Christmas music."

Their voices had drifted up the open stairway, and the idea hit him.

Joe paused in the middle of the computer room now, one hand on his hip. He adjusted his cap with the other. The longtime city leader had a Barney Fife appearance, complete with creases bordering his half smile. "I will admit, I have missed the music. The Andrews Sisters come holidays. The Beach Boys during the Summer Splash Festival each July." Joe removed his hat, ran a hand through thinning gray hair, then plopped the cap on again. "Never thought you young'uns put much stock in it, though."

"You kidding? We used to take bets as to how many times in a day we'd hear certain songs." The speakers placed throughout town had dished out one Christmas classic after another, every weekday in December, nine a.m. to five p.m., as far back as Blake could remember—and then it stopped. "I made a good hundred and twenty dollars one year off Bing Crosby's 'White Christmas.'"

Joe dropped into a chair and turned on the one computer monitor in the room. "Let's see if I remember how to run this here thingy."

Blake peered over the man's shoulder. Far as he could tell, the ancient system was simple—open up the set list, pull up the central controls for the off-site computerized speakers, hit Play. "Who made the decision to stop playing the music?"

"Don't rightly know. Don't know that anyone made the actual decision. Some things just fade away, you know?" Joe slanted closer to the monitor, eyes squinting. "Ahh, there it is. The old Christmas playlist."

A few more clicks of the computer's mouse and Joe leaned back in his chair, raising his arms and lacing his fingers behind his head. "Here we go. Starting with a goody—'Baby, It's Cold Outside.'"

One of Mom's favorites. Would she hear it from home? "How do we know if it's working?"

Joe spun in his chair and chuckled. "Open the window, of course."

"Right." He crossed the room and unlatched the locks of the lone window, then pushed the glass to the side. He leaned his ear to the screen, cold threading through to settle over his face. "I don't hear anything."

Joe's chair creaked as he turned back to the screen. "Drat." A few clicks, and then, "Now?"

Only the distant honking of a horn and the murmur of cold seeping through the screen. "Nothing."

"Well, something's not right. Let me fiddle around, see what I can do."

"If you can't, that's all right. I just thought it might be

a nice throwback to the good old days in Whisper Shore. Better yet, a happy note of things to come."

"I'll keep working on this thing, and if we're lucky, you can start taking bets on songs again."

Blake clapped Joe on the shoulder and offered his thanks, and minutes later he was on his way, trekking down the sidewalk toward his parents' house. Winter had finally settled in temperature-wise—it burrowed through his coat to send a shiver down his spine—but still no snow. Only a beige carpet of dying grass underfoot and evergreen trees waiting for a frosty cover.

He was starting to worry Michigan wouldn't get its winter wonderland in time for the festival. A burly wind hurled through, scraping over his cheeks, and he picked up his pace as he turned onto a residential street.

"Afternoon, Blake."

He paused mid-sidewalk, glance shifting to the lawn where Mrs. Satterly stood. She held an armful of sticks. "Mrs. Satterly, you shouldn't be doing yard work in this cold."

"Don't be silly, Blake. I'm as spry as they come, and the exercise does me good." Her neon-pink coat glowed against the paleness of the day.

He crossed the lawn. "Why don't you let me take over?"

"That's very gallant of you, but frankly, I was just asking myself why I'm even doing this when we're supposed to get even crazier winds overnight. Let's go inside. I'll make you a cup of something warm."

She patted his cheek and led him up to the side door of her two-story brick house. The heat blasted him the second he entered. Felt like summer around the equator.

But it didn't seem to bother Mrs. Satterly, because she left her coat on as she ambled to the kitchen.

"It's too late in the day for me to drink caffeine, so I hope you're okay with decaf," she said as she filled her coffeepot with water.

"But I don't . . ." Oh, well, if Mrs. Satterly wanted him to drink coffee, then, he'd drink coffee.

But she paused. "Oh, that's right. It's beyond me how a boy gets to be your age and doesn't drink coffee. What can I get you instead? I can heat some milk for cocoa. There's a jug of apple cider at the back of the fridge, but I'm guessing it's fermented by now. 'Fraid I don't keep any soda around."

"Please, I'm fine. Don't go to any trouble." Was it just the brightness of the kitchen lights that gave her cheeks a sallow tone?

"How many times do I have to tell you to call me Pam. You'd think you were the senile one."

"I'd hardly call you senile . . . *Pam*." He punctuated the last word with a chuckle.

"True. My mind's sharp, even if the ticker's not."

He swiped a bead of sweat from his forehead and shrugged out of his coat. "Your . . . ticker?"

She plopped a pan of brownies in front of him, ignoring his question. "Tell me about the festival." She reached for a glass from the sink, walked to the fridge, and pull out a milk jug.

"Well, we're doing a few new things this year. Ceremonial tree lighting, for one. And, if we can manage to get some snow, sleigh rides. I—"

"That's a wonderful idea." She set the milk on the table and clapped her hands together. "I will never forget when my Paul and I took a sleigh ride. It was back when we lived in Illinois, and . . ." She trailed off with a wave of her hand. "Oh, there I go. Paul's been gone fifteen years, and I still can't stop telling stories about him. Go on." She filled the glass to the brim and pushed it his way.

"No, I want to hear your story. I didn't realize you lived in Illinois." He pulled at the high collar of his sweater, warmth reddening his cheeks.

"Oh yes, for the first two decades of our marriage. Lived out on a rural property with a barn and everything. Someone else rented the surrounding acres and worked the land, but all the same, we liked to consider ourselves farmers. Kept a few chickens, had a garden, that sort of thing."

She sat in the seat next to him. "On our tenth anniversary, Paul surprised me with a sleigh ride. He rented it, and we rode in the back while the owner drove it." The memory danced in her eyes as her voice softened. "Full moon that night. We rode all over the property. Incredibly romantic."

"Sounds like it."

"What I wouldn't give for a chance to see that farm again." She looked up. "I've always wondered about the couple we sold it to. We joked as we drove that U-Haul up to Michigan that the couple reminded us of us at that same age."

She laced her fingers in her lap. "We were never able to have kids, you know. Which was hard at times. And we didn't travel the world or live exotic or eclectic lives." Her gaze moved to the window, flurries of white racing past. "But I never felt . . . incomplete."

Blake stopped chewing and set his brownie on the table. This moment felt sacred. Mrs. Satterly's words, heavy with importance.

"I think it's because Paul and I, we shared an awareness that life's greatest adventure is love. Loving each other, loving others. And being loved—first by God, then by each other. There's no better purpose."

Her words hung in the air, rich and touching, a soothing cool for the heat of her house.

And the weariness in his heart.

Because after years of running, wishing he knew where he belonged and what to do next, searching for a purpose to make up for the pain of his past, *incomplete* had become a place he knew intimately.

And love too often felt like something lost.

He lifted the brownie once more, took a bite, unsure what to do with the swirl of emotions pooling through him.

"I'm sick, Blake."

Her words pierced the moment. Crumbs turned to dust in his mouth, and he couldn't swallow. "What?"

"Don't talk with your mouth full." Her gray eyes brimmed with clarity and calm.

He took a drink of milk, forcing the bite down with the gulp. "But you . . . you said you're spry. You were doing yard work."

"I fatigue quickly. I would've quit in another five minutes if you hadn't come along. But I'm not going to just sit around waiting for the inevitable."

Inevitable? The word soured the second he tasted it. "What kind of sick?" But even as he asked, her cryptic comment from only minutes earlier returned. "*My mind's sharp, even if the ticker's not.*"

"Sick enough to make the most of every day I've got left. To not hold back."

"Why . . . did you tell me?"

"Because the Christmas festival was Paul's and my favorite event of the year. And this . . ." For the first time in their conversation, she faltered. But her recovery was quick. "This will likely be my last one."

*

"So then, he starts telling me all these ideas he has for making our third-floor suite, in his words, 'beyond awesome.'" Autumn sliced into the tomato on her cutting board with more force than necessary.

"Girl, you're worrying me. How about I take over dicing vegetables?" Ellie tucked a stray ringlet behind her ear from her perch atop the barstool on the other side of Autumn's mom's kitchen counter.

Mom and Lucy had gone to the diner for dinner. But tonight was one of Autumn's twice monthly best-friend dates. With Autumn's busyness at the inn and Ellie's full mom schedule, they'd decided long ago to intentionally set aside a couple nights each month to hang out.

"So then Blake tells me we need to install a Jacuzzi in the bathroom, swap out the queen bed for a king and, get this, build a balcony, knock out half a wall, and stick in French doors leading to said hypothetical balcony."

Which is when she'd called him crazy. He'd thanked her for the compliment. And she'd realized, even in her annoyance, that maybe she kind of liked crazy. Which only annoyed her all the more.

"What's so bad about that? I'd book that room."

"It'd cost a fortune—that's what. I'm trying to keep

the inn's doors open." Another spear into the tomato. Blake Hunziker wore *exasperating* like a floppy overcoat. He and his ideas.

Ellie nabbed a cucumber from the salad bowl before speaking up. "Hon, you need to take a breath. And I'm not kidding, hand over the knife."

Autumn rolled her eyes and surrendered the knife.

Honestly, she had to get Blake out of her head. Sure, he'd helped her turn the first floor of the inn into a Christmas paradise today—despite his complaints. And then he'd spent another hour helping her rearrange the furniture in the master suite where Dominic Laurent would stay.

But the whole hour he'd needled her with ideas about how to make the space better, as if he had some personal stake in her inn. Why it rankled her so, she didn't know.

Or maybe she did. Maybe it frustrated her that she *liked* his ideas. Wished she had the kind of vision he had. Wished she could wave a magic wand and turn his ideas into reality. Knew she couldn't.

Ellie's knife scraping against the wooden cutting board drew Autumn back. Ellie used the utensil to nudge the cut-up tomatoes into the salad bowl. "You have to admit, his ideas are good, even if you can't afford them."

And then there'd been the way he teased her when she'd hidden him away in that guest room. It'd been a teenage move, but the thought of Mom encountering him had been too much. "He just . . . drives me crazy."

"So I've noticed."

She didn't like the layer of suggestion in Ellie's voice.

"And it's not the only thing I've noticed."

"By which you mean . . ."

"The man has done a little filling out over the years, is all I'm saying. I'm a married woman, of course, so I'll leave it at that. Other than to say, if you weren't so irked by the guy, I might be pointing out his TDH qualities and telling you to go after him."

Tall, dark, and handsome? Blake? Fine, so the description fit. The insinuation, not so much. "Right. Because Hunzikers and Kingsleys go together so well. Like ketchup on strawberries."

"Are you the ketchup or the strawberry?"

"Ha. Funny."

Autumn grabbed three kinds of salad dressing from the fridge and dropped them on the counter. Ellie pushed a plate heaping with salad at her. "Why did we decide to have salads? I feel like Tater Tots. Let's have Tater Tots."

Ellie held up her fork like a teacher pointing a ruler. "No. You told me last week you were giving up foods that come out of a bag."

Autumn wrinkled her nose. "This lettuce came from a bag."

"But it's not frozen."

"Fine. Salads. Yum."

They climbed onto the stools around the island, and Ellie bowed her head. "I'll pray."

Autumn nodded and lowered her gaze as Ellie began. "God, thank you for this meal—even if it's not Tater Tots—and the chance to spend time with Autumn."

When Autumn opened her eyes, she gulped in the warmth in her friend's eyes. Shirley Temple curls framed Ellie's face and a circle of orange stained her T-shirt—probably something Oliver had spilled. "You do realize you're the best friend ever, right, Ell?" She forked a piece of lettuce. Lifted it to her mouth. Wrinkled her nose. "And I changed my mind. We're having Tater Tots." She stood.

Ellie's fork clinked against her plate as Autumn fished in the freezer for the bag she'd stuffed toward the back. She'd insisted on purchasing groceries as a way of thanking Mom for letting her and Lucy crash there.

"So much for determination," Ellie quipped. "Hey, I almost forgot, we got Oliver's two-year photos back today. I brought you a five by seven." She reached for the purse hooked around the back of her seat and pulled out a photo. But when she twisted back around, her face scrunched.

"You all right?"

Ellie held her arm to her stomach, wincing once more. "Must've turned too fast."

Autumn dropped the bag of Tots on the counter. "You sure?"

Ellie blinked, nodded. "Yeah, just a weird moment." She slid the picture to Autumn.

Oliver's smile bubbled from the photo, his reddish-blond cowlick adding extra cuteness. "Oh, he's so adorable."

Autumn had gotten used to the stir of longing being around a pregnant Ellie or her son produced. *Someday.*

"Ooh, I've got the perfect frame. Just a sec. Stick the Tots in the oven while I'm gone, will ya?"

She left the kitchen, trailed past the massive antique table swallowing up the dining room and toward the staircase to the second floor. In her old bedroom, she stepped over a pile of laundry she'd meant to throw in the washer for three days now, and plucked a frame from the overcrowded vanity surface.

Ava smiled at her from the photo. A senior photo, taken on the veranda of the inn. This is how she liked to remember her sister—smiling and wind whipping through her blond hair. Eyes clear, not downcast and sullen like they were in the days after Ryan's death.

She set to work prying the back off the frame. She slipped out Ava's photo, then paused when a second photo fluttered to the floor.

Huh, there'd been a picture behind Ava's? She reached for the photograph. From the glossy surface shone the Kingsley Inn in all its once-glory. Yellow exterior clean and bright, white-washed wraparound porch inviting and in perfect repair. And on the front steps—Mom, Ava, Autumn . . . even Dad. This photo was *old*.

You loved this place, Dad. I know you did. And yet you were just going to leave it.

But wasn't she doing the same?

No. No, this is different. I'm not abandoning it. The opposite, really. Everything she was doing now—fixing it up, throwing the Christmas party, helping with the festival, prepping for Dominic Laurent—was in an effort to secure the Kingsley Inn's future.

And what if Dominic Laurent wants to buy you out completely? What if he wants to change the name and the entire feel of the place?

Did it really matter? As long as everyone's job would be safe?

"Autumn?" Ellie's call sounded from the first floor.

"Just a sec. I'm coming." She set the old photo on the dresser, an uncertain tingle traveling to her heart.

The tingle turned to alarm halfway down the stairs when she heard Ellie's gasp, a pan crashing to the floor.

9

The morning was barely over, and fatigue already clawed at her. Apparently, a toddler did that to a person.

Autumn lifted her head from the steering wheel. She pushed open her door and stepped into muted sunlight, gray clouds shadowing the lot. At least Ellie was okay. The early contractions weren't unusual, but the doctor ordered bed rest for a few days—to which Ellie had practically filed a court appeal. Poor thing.

Autumn opened the back door of her car and ducked in. "All right, little Oliver. Auntie Autumn has one more hour with you before your daddy gets off work."

It'd been the least she could do—offer to watch Oliver so Ellie could get some rest after spending five hours last night at the hospital. She'd bugged out of helping Blake map out the festival booth arrangements.

"I wanna see the water."

Oliver pointed over her shoulder to where Lake Michigan dabbled with the shore, edging in and out against the sand. One look at the sky and she could tell a mix of rain wasn't far off, maybe even the snow they'd all been waiting for, if the morning's unseasonably warm temperatures dropped as predicted.

"I don't know, Oliver. You're not dressed for playing outside." She should've grabbed playclothes at Tim and Ellie's. But she hadn't been able to resist the adorable corduroy pants and little Converse All-Stars she found in Oliver's bedroom.

"Pleeease."

Her gaze hooked on the figures walking down by the beach. Lucy and Betsy. And they weren't alone. Apparently the warmth had coaxed several of the hotel's guests outside. She recognized the Hammersmiths, a retired couple who visited the shore every December. And farther down the beach, a younger married couple. Autumn had checked them in yesterday, and if they hadn't told her then, she'd have known now that they were professional photographers by the cameras and elongated lenses they both held, pointed toward the landscape.

"Please, Num," Oliver repeated.

It was a gorgeous day for December, but she expected it wouldn't last long. "Okay, but just for a few minutes."

As they approached, she saw that Lucy had abandoned her shoes in the grassy knoll that faded into sand and rock. The frothy scent of the water engulfed Autumn as she reached Lucy and Bets, sandy wind pricking her skin.

"Hey, girls. Barefoot in winter, huh, Luce."

"I love the feel of sand."

The weight of Oliver pulled on her arms, and he jiggled in an effort to get down. She let him slide down her side but held on to his hand. "What happened to making Christmas cookies?"

Betsy held up a bandaged hand. "Word to the wise: hot pads were invented for a reason."

Lucy was kneeling down now to smile at Oliver. "Can I have a high-five, buddy?"

Autumn released Oliver's hand so he could play patty-cake with Lucy as another windy howl chugged through the water, sending it closer to where they stood. The swirls of gray and white in the sky tinged her with unease.

Or maybe those were simply leftover feelings from last night. The doubt, circling around in the back of her mind like a seagull that couldn't decide where to land. Causing her to question, for the first time since receiving her Paris job offer, whether she really wanted to leave Whisper Shore.

Of course, I do. I've been dreaming of this forever. Sure, I love the inn and my friends and this town. And she'd miss them, yes.

"Again." Oliver giggled from where he plunked in the sand.

"Patty cake, patty cake, baker's man . . ." Lucy's voice lilted.

"Can you believe this day?" Betsy's voice poked into her thoughts. "Thermometer hit fifty degrees at noon. Yet they're saying by midafternoon, it'll be snowing and . . . Hey, look who it is."

Autumn followed Betsy's bandage-wrapped point. Past the Hammersmiths and the photographers, another couple roamed the beach, hands held. Dylan and Mariah.

"And on that note . . ."

Betsy patted her arm. "Let's go inside, guys. I'll make

you some of my homemade hot chocolate. It's like a Hershey bar sliding down your throat."

"Not yet. I want to go wading." This from Lucy.

"Brr, seriously?" Autumn shivered just thinking about it. "Your feet will turn blue. Lake Michigan is nippy enough in the summer, but in the winter it's downright biting."

"I want to."

Betsy shrugged, an impish grin breaking out on her face. "Well, in that case . . ." She kicked off her shoes and bent over to peel her socks off.

Autumn lifted Oliver once more. "You two are crazy."

"Me too! Me too!" Oliver called as they watched Lucy and Betsy toe the water.

"I don't think so, kiddo. I have a feeling your mom would not be happy about it."

"You wade in while holding him, Autumn," Betsy called.

"Uh-uh. No way. I have no desire to freeze my feet off." But even as the argument climbed up her throat, a distant memory floated in. Cloudy at first, but clearing until she could almost hear his voice. Dad's.

"Come on, girls. I dare you."

She couldn't have been older than eight or nine. Ava, ten or eleven. They stood on the shore, cold breeze flickering through their pigtails as Dad coaxed and laughed. *"I double-dog dare you."*

Dad used to try to get them to swim in Lake Michigan in the winter. Drove Mom crazy. She'd tell him it was asking for pneumonia, and he'd wave her off and promise her they'd take hot baths after.

The memory tasted crisp and new. Dad stripping off

his coat, running in. She could still feel her own reluctance, the pull of fear as Ava rose to the challenge . . .
and she shrank back, standing on the shore with Mom.
Watching as Dad and Ava floated in the water on their
own private adventure.

She locked gazes with Oliver. "All right, buddy. But
I'm only going in as deep as my ankles."

His eyes lit with delight, as if he understood.

She ditched her shoes and socks, rolled her jeans, and
picked up Oliver. Her feet sank into squeaky white sand,
its quartz content causing it to gleam in the sun. In the
distance, dunes rose like tiny mountains sprinkled with
beach grass and sand cherries.

"Hurry, hurry." He clapped.

Lucy and Betsy were already shrieking as they skipped
through the water. "Okay, here we go."

Cold, wet sand squished between her toes as the
first lick of foamy water over her feet prompted shivers. "Brr." Oliver giggled at that. Two more steps and
the chill reached to her ankles. Her squeal pierced the
air. "More, Num!" To the tune of Oliver's laughter, she
splashed around for a few minutes before tiptoeing out
of the water.

She hadn't lasted long . . . but she'd done it. *Wonder
if Dad could see. . . .*

Betsy flustered over. "I think my internal organs are
turning to ice."

Still giggling, and now on dry sand, Autumn set Oliver
down and rubbed her hands over her arms, settling the
goose bumps trailing her skin underneath her jacket.
Chills beat through her body, but watching Lucy kick
through the water was worth it.

And knowing she'd gone in satisfied a curiosity about herself she hadn't even known she had.

Betsy picked up her shoes. "I'll take Oliver inside and start heating up that cocoa. Stay with Lucy 'til she's ready to come in?"

"Sure thing."

After Betsy left with Oliver, she knelt down to brush the sand from her toes and unroll her jeans.

"Wading in the winter. A surprising Kingsley hobby?"

Autumn jumped at the voice behind her. A shadow joined hers in the white sand, and she spun.

Blake stood with arms folded. His fitted military-style jacket didn't hide the knot of his muscles. Curiosity danced with amusement in his dark eyes. And for a moment, she was back in the doorway of the guest room she had hid him in, every nerve standing at attention.

"Uh . . . hey."

Blake looked behind her. She turned, saw that his gaze had landed on Lucy, now back at the end of the shore, peering into its aqua translucence. "Are you two still staying at your mom's house?"

She stood up, bare feet turning numb. "Yeah. Until I can get an electrician out to check out the wiring, I'm not comfortable moving back in."

He nodded, not quite looking her in the eye.

"So . . . did you stop out here for any particular reason?"

He looked tired. Why did he look so tired? Sure, he'd been running around on festival errands for days, in between helping her at the inn. But today he seemed . . . worn down.

"I got some news yesterday." He ran his fingers through

dark hair tousled by the wind. The scent of his aftershave mixed with the cold.

"What kind of news?"

"The kind that . . ." His lips closed around the finish of his sentence. "Listen, you free tomorrow night?"

"Well, I've got the Christmas party in just a few days and . . ." Now she was the one to cut off, the puddle of hope and sadness in his expression stilling her.

His stare was intent. "I was thinking that—"

But Lucy's piercing voice interrupted. "Miss Autumn!"

Both Autumn and Blake spun at the panic in her tone. And then a scream from down the beach.

❦

Blake could sense the swelling of Autumn's panic.

It nearly matched his own. Lucy was frantically pointing to the water. Not far away, Mariah yelled Dylan's name.

Autumn's fingers hooked around Blake's arm. "He can't swim. Dylan can't . . ." The wind whipped through her hair. She stood so close loose strands tickled his cheek.

The low grumble of dense clouds tracking overhead fed his own worry. He'd heard snow and wind were on the way today. Was the storm setting in already?

"Dylan!" Autumn matched Mariah's call, plowing her way to the lakeside, alarm anchored in her voice.

Mariah was running toward them now.

Autumn fought with the zipper of her fleece coat. "Drat this thing."

"What are you—" He dropped the question, and instead took over for her. He pried her fingers away, then loosened the zipper from where it had stuck on the fabric. "There."

Autumn's breath came in warm, rapid puffs. "Thanks." The second he removed his hand, she jerked the zipper the rest of the way down and floundered out of her jacket.

And then it dawned on him, what she intended to do. "No, Red."

Mariah reached them then. "My hat . . . the wind . . . He went in after it, and then . . ."

Blake scanned the lake, hurried gaze finally landing on the bobbing figure a ways out from shore.

"I'm going in." Autumn looked frightened but determined.

"No, you're not." He was already peeling off his own coat, kicking off his shoes. "I am."

"I've had lifeguard training. I'm a great swimmer." She stepped into the water.

Blake sprang toward her. "Stay with Luce and Mariah." Fear puddled in her eyes and she attempted to push past him, but he caught her in his arms. "Trust me. I've got this."

And before any more precious seconds could tick by, he pushed her away and plunged into the water. Water stung through his clothes, icy and sharp. He plummeted under, heading the direction of the flash of color he'd seen before pitching into the lake's sudsy blue.

Cold sliced over and into his body, and the force of the water battled with his determination. With strained strokes he pushed his arms forward and back, kicked his legs with every ounce of strength in him.

What would it have been like to rush after his brother

like this? To dive through clouds instead of waves? To reach into cavernous skies and pull Ryan to safety?

Blake jutted his head above the surface, gulping for air, scanning the lake. There, just a little farther. Dylan bobbed, water up to his neck, the skin of his cheeks white. "I'm coming. Keep treading."

Once more, he barreled under and kicked his way toward him. His lungs pulled taut. How had Dylan ended up so far from the shore in so short a time?

It was the same question he'd asked himself over and over about Ryan. How had his brother drifted so far from hope and happiness so quickly, so fully? Oh, Blake had known he was hurting, but not that the ache went so devastatingly deep. When he'd convinced Ryan to go skydiving, he'd honestly thought the diversion might be enough to snap his brother out of it. How could he have known Ryan would come home in a coffin?

But I should've. I should've seen the signs.

As he heaved through the water, the memories hit him just as they had so many times before: Ryan watching hours and hours of game tape. Staring at the photos on his cell phone when he thought no one was looking. Looking straight into Blake's eyes, mouthing his good-bye before stepping from the plane.

The sky groaned, the sound muffled by water rushing past Blake's ears. Thunder. Odd for December. Dangerous for him and Dylan.

He burst through the surface, gasping for breath, opening his eyes. Through the rivulets catching in his eyelashes and running down his face, he saw Dylan.

He approached carefully. At least the guy wasn't panicking. "I've got you, Dylan. Hold on to my arm and kick. We'll go back together." The first pricks of sleet hit his forehead, then disappeared into the water around them. "We need to hurry." If the snow picked up in this wind . . .

Blake pushed against the water, the added weight of Dylan slowing his movement. But he was kicking as well. "I-I lost my balance and swallowed water, and when I came up . . ."

Dylan should stop talking. He could explain once they'd reached dry land. But Blake was too tired to issue the order. *Just keep swimming. Keep pressing forward.* The hope of rest and their safety pulled him on.

That and the thought of Autumn waiting.

Please, God, don't let her have come in, too.

Not with the sleet now falling in steady rhythm.

He shook the hair out of his eyes and looked to the shore. Though his heart hammered, relief pulsed through him at the sight of her, arms hugging her middle. She'd listened to him. Trusted him.

One, two, three more hefty kicks and they reached the point at which both Blake and Dylan could touch the sand with heads above water. The man's heavy breathing sounded at his side. *Thank you, God. Thank you.*

Mariah rushed into the water. "Honey, are you okay?"

Behind her, Autumn still waited with Lucy. Wind and sleet pasted her hair to her face and landed in splotches on her lavender fleece. But she'd never looked more beautiful.

The thought smacked into his common sense. *Exhaustion, that's all it is.*

Dylan emerged from the lake, clothes sticking to his skin. "I'm sorry, Mariah, everyone." He said the words through chattering teeth, probably as embarrassed as he was relieved.

"I'm the one who's sorry." Mariah hugged him. "If it wasn't for my stupid hat."

Blake stepped away from the couple, numb feet sinking into sand now instead of water, and approached Autumn and Lucy. He must look like a drowned Hulk. Drained of energy, he leaned over his knees. When he lifted his head, Autumn was still staring. Finally, she blinked, blue-green eyes glowing against the growing dark of the storm. "I've never seen someone swim like that."

Blake pulled his shirt away from his torso, but it dropped back and clamped to his skin. "Like what?"

"Like you were pounding through a cement wall rather than water." The tone of her voice untangled the meaning of her stare. She'd been looking at him—still was—as if he were a . . . hero.

Warmth slicked through him, defying the cold and wet and fatigue. "Well, I did what I had to do to keep you from going in." He winked. Probably looked like an idiot.

"Thank you!" Dylan called from where he stood with his arms around Mariah.

"No problem." Truth was, he'd do it all over again for that smile from Autumn. And then, as they turned toward the inn, he reached for Autumn, pulled her to his side, and left his arm around her shoulder.

She gave him a questioning glance.

He pointed his thumb behind them. "They think we're a couple, remember?"

She only laughed. And didn't pull away.

Autumn was as cold as if she'd been the one to barrel into the water. But deep down, emotions sizzled and melted her heart into goo.

She was falling for Blake Hunziker. Hard.

They stood around the island counter in the middle of the inn's kitchen, Lucy wrapped in a Christmas quilt Autumn had pulled from the settee in the fireplace room, and Autumn with a towel hanging around her shoulders. They may not have gone all the way into the lake like Blake, but both had still ended up with wet clothes and damp hair from the sleet.

After they had all warmed up for a bit in the kitchen and ensured everyone was okay, Blake had headed home. And Dylan and Mariah left, too—Dylan with a sort of mortified set to his shoulders and Mariah's eyes brimming with thanks . . . and perhaps apology, too.

"It's crazy how fast it happened." Autumn cupped her mug of hot chocolate. "Sometimes, with the right amount of wind, the lake can get so grabby. I've seen it knock people down and pull them away from shore several times. And to think, all Dylan was trying to do was rescue Mariah's hat."

Betsy ladled hot chocolate into a second bowl-shaped mug. "Thank God for Blake."

Yes.

"He's strong." Lucy said, accepting the cup from Betsy. "You should see his muscles, Betsy. His shirt was all wet, and—"

"I get the picture, Luce." Betsy eyed Autumn.

Who then looked away to conveniently fiddle with Oliver's shoes as he perched on the counter. "Lemme down, Num."

"All right, but we have to leave soon to get you home." As she lifted him from the counter, the stench wafting from his, ahem, backside, assaulted her nose. "Oh, buddy, we have a situation. Bets, did you bring his diaper bag in?"

"Yep, it's on the bench by the back door. I'll get it."

She still held Oliver in the air, his legs dangling.

"Put me down, Num. Down!"

"How many OSHA rules would it break if I changed him in here?"

Betsy chucked the bag her direction. "Hey, as long as you're the one doing the changing, I'm not complaining."

She set Oliver on the floor. He must've known what was coming, because he made quick work of tugging off his shoes. She set the towel from over her shoulders on the floor and tugged Oliver over. He started struggling as she slipped off his pants.

"Come on, buddy. It's not that bad."

He kicked at the air and, while she was busy reaching for a diaper, rolled away and stood before she could stop him.

"Oliver—"

"Noooo!" He ran from the room, giggles bouncing along with his jiggling diaper.

Betsy stuck her hand on her waist. "We've got a streaker."

"Oh brother." Autumn hurried after him, followed him through the dining room and into the lobby, where a trail of puddles still waited to be cleaned up after they tracked in, and . . .

She skidded to a stop.

Someone waited at the desk. A very distinguished-looking someone, with one eyebrow cocked at the toddler now rubbing his hands in the puddle by the front door. The man wore a fitted silver-gray blazer over dark jeans, burgundy newsboy hat covering his head.

Where was Harry?

"Uh, I'm so sorry. Our deskman must be . . . around here somewhere." She slipped behind the front desk, one eye still on Oliver. "It's been a hectic day here."

"This *is* the Kingsley Inn?" The man spoke with the slight lilt of an accent.

She fumbled for a smile. "That's what the sign says."

"I did not see any sign."

Oh, right. The wind had knocked it loose a few days ago, and she'd ordered a new one that hadn't yet arrived. Should arrive by Friday, in time to be installed before Dominic Laurent's Saturday arrival.

Oliver plopped on the floor and pulled his shirt up his stomach. Lovely.

"Anyhow, welcome to our inn."

"You work here." Statement. Not a question. Though, considering the towel over her shoulders and her bare feet, she didn't blame him for wondering.

"I do. My name is Autumn Kingsley. Do you have a reservation?"

"Indeed, although I am arriving early. I hope this is not a problem."

If the man only knew how many rooms awaited occupants.

"No, definitely not a problem. Your name?"

"Dominic Laurent."

Gone. Her breath. Her words, stuck.

And Oliver . . . now naked if not for his diaper, tugging on her pant leg.

10

This was either the best idea she'd ever had . . . or it was so stupid she deserved a snowball in the face.

Autumn's fingers flexed inside her fuchsia gloves, boots crunching over the snow-packed sidewalk—a result of the steady snowfall that had started yesterday afternoon and continued into today. Winter had finally graced Whisper Shore with a wonderland appearance.

Perhaps that would impress Dominic Laurent, if nothing else. Beside her, the man adjusted his plaid cashmere scarf. He'd been in town a little over twenty-four hours. Maybe, just maybe, long enough to have shed what had to be a horrible first impression at the state in which he'd found the Kingsley Inn yesterday.

"I'm still not sure I understand," he said now, pace matching hers as they created a trail of footprints from where Harry had parked on Main Avenue. She'd coerced him into driving them into town in his newer, roomier SUV rather than subjecting Dominic—Dom, he'd asked to be called—to her aging Jetta.

"It's a town-wide event. Used to be tradition every year on the first big snow of the season," Harry explained from behind. "Someone must have resurrected it."

They weren't sure who. Everything Autumn knew was contained in the text she'd received a few hours ago from Tim Jakes.

Snowball fight is on. 6:30 in the square. Spread the word.

And that's when she'd had the idea to invite their international guest, to give him a taste of the Whisper Shore his investment might benefit. Only now, as he fiddled with the top button of his jet-black coat—not a speck of lint nor a wrinkle in sight—she wondered if it'd been such a good idea after all.

Despite her worries, she couldn't help catching the buzz of excitement floating through the town square, like the puffs of white air accompanying her breathing. Harry stepped up beside her, excitedly clapping his hands together as they approached the center of the square.

"The entire town comes out to . . . throw snow at each other?" Dom slipped his fingers into leather gloves that looked as if they'd never been worn.

"Not the entire town." Autumn pulled her wool beret over her ears. "Only the brave ones."

The sun had bedded about thirty minutes ago, leaving the light of the moon, streetlamps, and strings of Christmas lights draped over trees and storefronts to illuminate the town square. The Andrews Sisters sang "Jingle Bells" over the speakers piping into the downtown.

"It's pure Whisper Shore craziness," she added. "I know it sounds weird, but it's just one of our little quirks."

A whistle trilled from the gazebo steps as they arrived at the huddle of townspeople. She'd recognize that shriek anywhere—it was how Mrs. Satterly used to call kids in from recess. The retired schoolteacher stood on the steps, megaphone in hand. "Folks, let's gather for the rules before we get started."

Autumn spotted Blake then, chatting with Tim Jakes over by an evergreen. As if sensing her gaze, he looked over, waved. She waved back.

"Something tells me this is going to be highly amusing." Dom's head was tipped to one side, and if she wasn't mistaken, that was a hint of boyish anticipation on his face. The man might actually have a fun streak. So far all she'd seen was prim and proper. Which was about as foreign in Whisper Shore as his accent.

Maybe it hadn't been such a bad idea, after all.

Mrs. Satterly's voice sounded through the megaphone again. "Now that I have everyone's attention, I'm going to go over the rules. Pay attention." She adjusted the faux fur muffler that matched her coat. "Here's how this is going to work. When I blow the horn, the snowball fight begins. No aiming at anyone's face. No throwing anything other than snow. And for goodness' sake, no tripping anyone. When I blow the horn again, it's all over."

As Mrs. Satterly spoke, Blake joined their group. "Hey, Red."

She read the curiosity he directed at Dominic. "Blake, this is one of our hotel guests, Dominic Laurent. Dom, Blake Hunziker. He's a . . . uh . . ."

"Friend?" Blake inserted, veiled amusement in his half smile. "And partner in festival-coordinating crime."

But Dom wasn't even paying attention, focus still attached to Mrs. Satterly and her megaphone. "That's it?" he asked when she finished. "Those are all the rules?"

"Well . . . yeah." Autumn shrugged.

"Nothing else? No winner? No objective?"

"Dude, *fun* is the objective." Blake rubbed his hands together. Even in the dark, his dimpled smile radiated . . . cuteness.

Oh, Lord, the inappropriateness. He's. A. Hunziker.

It seemed to matter less and less the more time she spent with him.

"On your marks, get set, go." The horn blared over Mrs. Satterly's last word, and the square exploded into action. Dom, with his perfectly gelled hair and shined shoes, gave her a helpless look as a snowball whizzed past his ear.

Autumn swung her hand into the snow and scooped up a pile. "It's a free-for-all, Dom. Go for it." She lobbed her snowball at Tim Jakes's back.

"Hey!" He whirled.

A carefree aura slid over Autumn—over everyone—and laughter bubbled up inside. She looked around, spotted Harry packing his own ball.

A snowball smacked into her shoulder. A few feet away, Dom grinned with pride, then reached for another handful, this time aiming for Harry.

"Now you've got the hang of it," she called.

She shouldn't have worried about bringing him along this evening. Perhaps the intended disorderliness of to-night would make up for the unintended disorderliness of yesterday afternoon. Might even charm the man.

Wet snow soaked through her mittens, and her jeans would never make it through the chaos without getting drenched. She didn't care. The cold barely stung her cheeks anymore.

She packed her hands around a ball and looked up just in time to meet Blake's eyes watching her. A fountain of snow flashed past her face, but Blake's focus stayed on her, an impish grin stretching his cheeks.

Oh no. She whirled and ran, dodging flying snow and frenzied friends.

"Really? You're running, Red? I thought you were braver than that."

Autumn spun on her heel and chucked her snowball. It hit him in the cheek and broke into chunks. She clapped her hand over her mouth.

"You just broke one of the only rules." Exaggerated shock danced in his tone.

She backed up. Bumped into someone. *Oomph.* Almost lost her footing. "I didn't mean to hit you in the face."

"I could report you to Mrs. Satterly. Or . . ." His hand tunneled through the snow. He came up with a handful of snow, rounded it into a snowball. A big snowball.

"I said I was sorry."

He raised his pitching arm.

And then she was running again, squealing, hair flying behind her head. She shook with laughter as she ran, weaving in and out, Blake's voice goading her from behind.

"You're not going to get away."

"I know I told you I'm bad at sports, Blake, but the one thing I can do is run. I—"

She went down. Her hands thudded into the snow, the slick chill reaching up her coat sleeves. She rolled onto her back, giggles racking her body. "Oh my goodness. Oh my . . ."

Blake stood over her, smiling as if he'd just nabbed his prize. He dropped to his knees, snowball still in his gloved hand. "I've got you right where I want you, Red."

She lifted her palms in a surrender pose, out of breath. "I-I give. You win."

"I win? But I haven't even hit you with a snowball yet."

"I've got snow in my hair, down my back, and in my shoes." Laughter still jumbled inside, shaking her torso.

"That's your own fault for running." For one more second he held the snowball over her face, cheeky expression warming clean through her. *Oh, I'm in trouble.*

Seriously in trouble.

Something in his eyes shifted and he dropped the snowball. Her laughter stilled, the squeals and shouts and footsteps crunching through snow all around her fading. Only Autumn. Blake.

And something she shouldn't be feeling . . . at once heavy and weightless.

Blake clasped both her hands and pulled her up into a sitting position, snow-wet strands of hair trailing down her cheeks.

One hand still enclosed in his, she tipped her head to meet his eyes once more. "Blake, you're the one who got the snowball fight started again, aren't you." Was her voice as breathless as she felt?

Snowflakes were catching in his eyelashes. "I did."

"Why?"

"You said the other day you missed it." His smile was so sincere, the magic of the night, the snow still floating from the sky. She—

"Autumn!"

Autumn jerked at the shrill call. Through a kalei-
doscope of color, her gaze landed on Mom, watching
from the curb. As her brain "Maydayed," she heard her
name again, disapproval storming in her mother's tone.

Get up. Explain. You were only—

And then her name again, this time in a gasp from the
person beside Mom. Matching blond hair and a bulky
red coat and . . .

She stood up. "Ava?"

A second later, a snowball smacked into her face.

☙

Blake stood, brushing the snow from his knees as
he watched Autumn trail away between her mom and
her sister.

"Man, you didn't make any friends with that move."
Tim Jakes approached from the side, picked up Blake's
stocking cap from where it had fallen during his chase
with Autumn.

He must have seen . . . enough. "I know. Dunno who
looked fiercer. Victoria or Ava. That *was* Ava, right? My
eyes weren't playing tricks on me?"

The squeals and shouts of the snowball fight continued around them. Ava Kingsley had looked at him as if he
were the ghost of Ryan, come back solely to torment her.
Her stare cut through him until he'd had to look away.

"That was her all right."

He wanted to follow them. Tell Autumn's family it
wasn't what it'd looked like.

Except it was exactly what it'd looked like. If they
hadn't been interrupted, he'd have kissed Autumn.

Provided she hadn't pushed away or slapped him or anything, of course. But from the haze of delight on her face, the way she hadn't moved a muscle as they'd sat in the snow, yeah, didn't seem like she'd planned on fighting it. In those few seconds, their last names, their families' rivalry, none of it mattered.

The heat of the moment still torched his insides.

"I should've at least made sure she was okay. That snowball hit her in the face hard. Did you see who threw it?"

"I saw a little kid run away with a horrified look on his face. Probably an accident."

Autumn was just moving out of sight when Tim elbowed him. "Uh, Blake, you might want to find somewhere else to be right now."

A note of dread hung in his voice, and Blake turned to his friend. "But why—" He broke off at the sight of William Baylor thundering toward them. *Not good.* "Whip out your badge, Tim. Could come in handy."

Baylor reached them. "I was told you started this."

"Um, well, I—"

"Who do you think you are?" The man looked ready to throw a punch.

Blake stiffened. "Look, Mr. Baylor, I ran this by my dad."

"He's not in charge of the parks. I—"

"But he is the mayor, which is about as high of an authority figure as we get around here."

The tick in Baylor's jaw became more pronounced. "I'm sick of your attitude, Hunziker."

Blake pressed his lips, grasping for a calm he didn't feel. This man could coax a pacifist into a fight. "If you want us to stop, I'll go borrow Mrs. Satterly's megaphone and send everyone home. If that'll make you happy. But look around, people are having a great time. Why spoil that?"

"You think you're welcome here, Blake? You're not." Baylor stepped closer, mere inches separating them. Blake could feel his breath, the tension seething from him. "We're not going to forget what you took from us. I won't forget. *My son* won't forget."

The words landed on target, pummeling the last of his confidence. Baylor was probably right. Blake could organize a snowball fight, throw a festival together, maybe even help the town out a little. But that didn't mean he actually belonged in Whisper Shore.

After all, look at the way Autumn's family had looked at him just now—searing accusation.

"Dad!"

Blake's gaze shot to the source of the yell, the voice he still heard calling in his dream. "*I don't see Ryan's chute.*"

"Shawn."

He pushed past Baylor, covered the short distance to his old friend. How many times in these past two weeks had he thought about stopping by Shawn's apartment? He'd even called the Baylors' house, breathing a sigh of relief when Mrs. Baylor had answered instead of William, and asked for Shawn's address.

But as soon as he'd told Mrs. Baylor who he was, she'd hung up. He hadn't had the nerve to ask Hilary for the information.

"Shawn," he said again, now standing in front of his friend. Under the spotlight of a streetlamp, Shawn's eyes darkened.

"Let's go, Dad," he called over Blake's shoulder.

"Shawn, it's been a long time. I've been meaning to—"

Suddenly, like a flare lit and let loose, Shawn pushed both palms against Blake's shoulders. "Get away from me, Blaze."

Blake caught himself before tripping backward, surprise stinging. "Dude, what's the matter with you?"

"I said get away."

But Blake only straightened. He'd had enough of this. "Look, I get it: you blame me for what happened. Newsflash: I blame myself. It destroys me all over again every time I relive it. Isn't that enough?"

Shawn was in his face then. "I don't blame you for what happened to Ryan. I blame you for running away and leaving me to deal with the aftershock."

"Shawn, let's go." William's voice was firm from behind Blake.

But Shawn ignored his father. "You know they all think I was high, too."

Hot memories flickered, one match after another burning through him. Ryan and Shawn sitting in the car for a few minutes before gearing up. Ryan and Shawn laughing in the back of the plane before Ryan's jump. "Yeah, well, for all I know you were. Ryan got the drugs from somewhere."

Before the words were out of his mouth, Shawn's fist connected with Blake's face, the impact nearly as jarring as the hissing voice of the past shaking loose the pain he'd almost started to forget these past few days. He stumbled only for a moment before rushing Shawn.

The fight lasted less than a minute. Maybe only seconds. Because almost as soon as he lunged toward his once-friend, William and Tim jumped in to break it up. Tim's arms pulled him backward, away from Shawn.

Blake's breath heaved, his face throbbing where Shawn had punched him.

And slowly, in moments that dragged like mud under tires, everything came back into view. The snowball fight. The light of Christmas decorations stringing the park. Tim, with one arm still hooked over his. Mrs. Satterly watching from the gazebo.

Shawn, glaring, swiping the back of his palm across a split lip. Then stalking away with his father.

❦

"Mom, I swear, I'm fine. It was an accident." Autumn dropped into a chair at the kitchen table and pointed at her right cheekbone. "See? No bumps, no scratches. No face-altering indentations. I won't need plastic surgery."

Though there *had* been something solid in the snow-ball—like a chunk of ice. The impact had been enough to knock her off her feet.

Mom clucked her tongue and jerked open the freezer. She still wore her ankle-length black coat and the slim black gloves Autumn and Ava used to call her serial-killer gloves. She pulled out a bag of frozen peas. "Here."

Autumn's gaze slid to Ava, slumped in the chair across from hers, veiled disgust rimming her eyes. Autumn had tried to draw her out on the short walk home, but Ava had answered only in monosyllables.

"I can't believe you're here! Why didn't you let us know you were coming?"

"Mom knew."

"How long are you staying?"

"Don't know."

"You should see the inn. We've done a lot of work lately, and it's decorated just like when we were kids."

No answer.

One hand dutifully holding the peas up to her cheek, Autumn used the other to unwind her scarf. She was starting to heat up in the warmth of her mother's kitchen.

And the smolder of Ava's and Mom's matching glares.

It was Blake. It was what they'd both seen. Or thought they'd seen, anyway. Autumn and Blake, only inches apart. The stricken look on her mother's face at that moment had suggested they were standing at the front of a Vegas wedding chapel taking vows—not in the middle of town having a . . . moment.

"What were you thinking, Autumn?" Mom snapped now.

"Mom—"

Mom held up her palm, leather glove creaking. "I don't want to talk about it. You know how I feel about that boy. I'd prefer to forget I just saw you holding his hand."

"You just said 'holding his hand' like it's synonymous with dancing in our skivvies. He was just . . ."

About to kiss her. She could deny it to her mother but not to herself. Couldn't deny, too, the desire she'd experienced in that moment. Like hot water puddling in her stomach.

"Like I said, I don't want to talk about it." Mom tore off her coat.

The dull throbbing where she'd been hit traveled around to the back of her head. Autumn rubbed the side of her head with her free hand. "All right, then."

She looked to Ava. *Try again.* "I'm pumped that you're here, Ava. Just in time for the Christmas party on Saturday and—"

"Seriously? Seriously, Autumn, you want to catch up after *that*?"

Oh boy. "Ava."

"Blake Hunziker, Autumn. Blake. Hunziker."

"I know who he is." And hadn't she run his name through her mind over and over in the past week, reminding herself why she shouldn't be feeling the feelings she thought she might be feeling?

But if she'd realized anything since Blake wandered into her life, it was that they'd been wrong to blame Blake for the tragedy of the past. She'd seen the weight he carried, the flashes of shame he thought he hid. He didn't need the added burden of everyone else's anger, too.

"Yeah, well, you may know who he is but apparently you're forgetting what he did. He ignored you when you tried to tell him how messed up Ryan was. Months later I'm hiding in my car, watching Ryan's hearse travel down Main and I can't even go the funeral because his horrible family blames me." Ava's voice caught at the end, her tight ponytail whipping as she turned her face away.

"Ava, I don't think they really—"

Her sister jerked to her feet. "And you were out there, rolling around on the ground—"

"I was not rolling around." Autumn let the bag of frozen vegetables thud to the table.

"Girls," Mom's voice cut in, admonishing tone suggesting they were teenagers instead of grown women. "Lucy went to sleep early tonight. Do you really want to wake her up with your yelling?"

With one last glare, Ava spun and disappeared from the room.

Autumn closed her eyes, headache pounding anew. This wasn't how their reunion was supposed be. She hadn't seen her sister in a year. There should be hugs and laughter and declarations of how much they'd missed each other.

Mom tugged at the fingers of her gloves, pulled them off, and dropped them on the table. Her shoes clicked over the beige-and-gray tiled floor as she moved across the room. She reached for the electric kettle and turned. "You might have thought of how it'd look."

"I didn't know she was coming home."

"You knew I was here. Did you know I had to find out from Grady Lewis you're working with that boy on the festival?" Mom's pencil-lined eyes were rimmed with frustration.

"I've been meaning to tell you."

Mom didn't answer. Only filled the kettle with water and set it on its base. Soon the hum of water bubbling covered the silence.

Autumn traced her finger through the puddle created by the now-thawed vegetable bag. "He's not a horrible person, Mom. He lost his brother. Ava might have moved away . . ." She might have hardened, become distanced. Poured herself into her new life until there was nothing left for her family. "But she's still alive. Blake doesn't have that."

She waited for Mom to say something, anything. But before she could, a knock sounded at the door. Autumn started to turn, but Mom marched past her. Behind her, Autumn heard the squeak of the door's hinges, a throat clearing.

"Uh, hi, Mrs. Kingsley."

Autumn spun around, knees bumping into the chair behind her. *Blake?*

"Yes?" Her mom's voice held all the warmth of an iceberg.

"Just stopping by to make sure Autumn's okay."

She started for the door, ready to play interference. "I'm fine. Thanks for checking. I—"

Mom turned back to Blake. "She's fine."

"Ooo-kay."

Wait, was his face bruised? His eye . . . "Blake, what happened?"

Mom moved from the doorway, retrieved her teacup, and whisked from the room.

"I guess I shouldn't come in."

Autumn filled the space Mom had seconds ago. "Your eye . . ." She lowered her voice, just in case Mom was listening from the next room. "Did you get in a fight?"

The crisp pull of the cold urged her another step forward, and she lifted her hand, fingers barely skimming the surface of his puffy skin.

"Red, how'd you like to skip town with me?"

11

How in the world had she let Blake talk her into this?

Autumn slung her purse over her shoulder. "We should've called first."

Blake leaned against his open car door. Behind him stretched a field of black Illinois dirt dotted by patches of snow. On the other side of the gravel lane rose a two-story farmhouse, white siding long since stained to a pale gray. Over to the west, a machine shed and a cherry-red barn with white trim settled in front of a grove of trees.

Wind whistled through the quiet.

"Well, like I said, I tried WhitePaging it and came up dry. Mrs. Satterly wasn't even sure the same folks they sold the farm to live here now."

And so he'd decided to make the four-and-a-half-hour drive on a whim. Because he was Blake Hunziker, and he did things like that. And she just hadn't been able to say no to him last night when he asked her to come along. Not with his puppy-dog eyes and bruised cheek and that hint of desperation on his face.

Blake still hadn't told her what had happened. But with both Mom and Ava mad at her, the idea of getting away for a while had sounded like a good idea. She'd left a note for them.

"They may not even be home," she said now, voice muffled by the scarf she'd burrowed into.

"Then it'll be easy to get photos. Come on." Blake's grin held enthusiasm, and only the red circling his cheeks and nose gave any hint of the cold. He didn't even wear a coat.

Crazy man. Dragging me across a state to take photos of a farm. In the frozen tundra that is Illinois.

Not that Michigan was any warmer.

And not that she hadn't secretly loved the idea of spending a whole day with him. In just a couple weeks, Blake Hunziker had turned her everyday life inside out. Even now, when they should've been making preparations for the festival only a week away, they were knocking on the door of someone who, for all she knew, might poke a rifle at them.

And she was enjoying every moment. "I think I watched too many episodes of *Bonanza* as a kid, Blake. I feel like any minute someone's going to screech at us for trespassing."

His eyes twinkled as he climbed the cement steps. "This is no Ponderosa. I think we're safe."

"I'm pretty sure in one episode or another, someone got in trouble for trespassing on *Little House on the Prairie,* too."

Blake grabbed ahold of her hand. "I love your imagination, Red."

Maybe she should've stiffened. Pulled her hand back. But the warmth of his palm through the cotton of her mitten held her in place.

He knocked. "Just think of how happy we'll make Mrs. Satterly when we come back with pictures. You should've seen her talking about her husband. It was like the years faded away and she was right there with him. Right here, I guess I should say." He knocked again.

"Quite the romantic, aren't you, Blake Hunziker."

And for goodness' sake, did he have any idea how adorable those dimples were?

Stop it. The mental chiding was barely a whisper. Easy to ignore as she glanced at their hands.

"Either that or I'm still a first-grader at heart, trying my best to get on my teacher's good side."

The door opened slowly, and a figure appeared. A silver-haired man, probably in his early sixties wearing Levi's and a flannel shirt. "Morning. What can I do for you?" He rubbed one palm over his chin, curiosity bobbing in the movement.

"Hi, my name's Blake, and this is Autumn. We're friends of a woman who used to live on this farm. I know this is completely out of the blue, but our friend said she'd love to see the farm again someday. I wondered if you'd mind if we took a few photos to bring back to her."

Interest lit the man's face, but hesitation held him back. "I don't think that'd be a problem, but mind telling me your friend's name?"

Blake nodded. "Pam Satterly. She's in her mid-eighties now. Back when she lived here, she was married to—"

"Paul Satterly," the man jumped in, grin now complete. "Susie and I loved those two. Come on in. Suz, we've got visitors." He called the words over his shoulder, waving them inside.

Blake squeezed her hand and they entered. A cinnamon scent floated in the air, along with the aroma of coffee. They followed the farmer into a kitchen that likely hadn't seen a remodel since the '70s.

But instead of feeling outdated, the linoleum floor and lace cloth-covered table, aged cabinetry, and deep white sink, all radiated a homey feel—one matched perfectly by the wide smile of the woman holding a coffeepot by the counter.

"Suz, this is Blake . . . uh, didn't catch your last name, son."

"Hunziker," Blake supplied.

"Blake and Autumn Hunziker."

A chuckle tickled through Autumn. "Oh, we're not married. I mean we're not together." She could feel her blush even as she tried to stave it off.

"Look pretty together to me." The man sent a pointed glance to their still-linked hands.

Oh. Right.

Blake released her hand then, but not before a wink that only deepened the heat pooling in her cheeks. She fingered her scarf, suddenly warm enough to ditch the thing. *Not together. Not a couple.*

Even if the idea seemed less ludicrous with each passing day.

Don't be silly, Autumn. Mom would pop a blood vessel at just the thought.

"I'm Vernon, by the way. And like I said, this is Susie. We *are* together. Going on forty-two years now."

Susie rolled her eyes. "Forty-three, and he knows it. Old coot."

Vernon crossed the room and kissed his wife's cheek, then took the coffeepot from her. "I may be an old coot, but you've put up with me plenty long. Now, can I get you folks some coffee?"

"None for me, thanks, but Red here is probably jonesing for a second cup by now."

Susie smiled. "Red? I like that. Because of the hair?"

Autumn unzipped her coat. "That's what he says."

"I'm telling you, when the sun hits it just right, it's red." Blake shrugged and helped her out of her coat.

"Or you're color-blind."

Vernon and Susie exchanged glances before Vernon filled a mug and set it on the table. "Have yourselves a seat. Tell us about the Satterlys."

Susie gasped. "You knew Pam and Paul?"

"Mrs. Satterly—Pam—was my first-grade teacher. I never knew Paul all that well. He passed away several years ago." Blake pulled out a chair for her as he spoke.

Had he always been this gentlemanly? Autumn thought back as she sat. *Come to think of it, yeah.* Even now, instead of sitting next to her, he reached out to help Susie with the plate she carried to the table and then waited to sit until she'd lowered.

The man had manners. And she hadn't even noticed.

"These are Susie's famous caramel rolls. She's known throughout the county, and probably throughout the state, for her rolls."

"Hush, Vern. But do help yourselves. They're still warm."

Autumn's stomach growled as Susie spoke. Breakfast—

a granola bar at 4:30 a.m.—felt like a day ago instead of only hours.

"I remember how Pam and Paul showed us around this place when we were first considering buying." Susie sipped her coffee. "We were just newlyweds then, and I remember thinking, I hope I'm still that happy when I'm in my late forties." She chuckled. "Which, at the time, seemed so old. How is Pam?"

Blake lowered the bite he'd been about to take, a shadow passing over his face. "Actually, she's not doing well. She told me the other day she . . . doesn't have long."

Autumn's gaze shot to his. He hadn't told her that part. Only that he wanted to do something nice for Mrs. Satterly. But she heard the sadness in his tone now, saw it in his face and in the slow hunch of his shoulders. This is why he'd been so eager to come.

Yet another layer she hadn't seen.

"I'm so sorry to hear that." Susie's soft words huddled in the quiet.

Blake blinked. Once. Twice. And Autumn's heart tilted. She inched her hand under the table, feeling for his. She found the ridge of his knuckles and laced her fingers over his. He turned his hand underneath to latch onto hers.

"She's in good spirits and still herself. That's for sure." He lifted his fork once more and took a bite, swallowing before speaking again. "And she talked so much about this farm and her husband. Said she wished she could see it again." He squeezed Autumn's hand. "That's why we're here. We were hoping you wouldn't mind if we took a few photos to show her."

"Of course we don't mind, son." Vernon chugged

down his coffee. "I'll show you around myself. We can photograph every inch of the place, if you like."

Susie grasped her husband's arm. "Oh, Vern, the Bible. We have to give it to them."

"Right, I'll be right back." He practically jumped from the table and disappeared from the room.

Autumn finally took a bite of her own roll, sticky sweetness almost melting in her mouth, a perfect taste for these moments in a cozy kitchen with such a warm couple. And Blake, still holding her hand.

Vernon reentered the room and placed the book in front of Autumn. "You have to take this to her. We found it in the attic and saw Pam's name inside. But we didn't have a way to get ahold of her."

The Bible was well used. The pages crinkled as Autumn bent it open. She glimpsed handwriting on the inside front cover and smoothed the pages back to read the verse scrawled inside.

"'Praise the Lord, O my soul, and forget not all his benefits—who forgives all your sins and heals all your diseases, who redeems your life from the pit and crowns you with love and compassion, who satisfies your desires with good things so that your youth is renewed like the eagle's.'"

"Psalm 103:2–5," Susie said. "I've read that passage so many times since we first found this Bible. It got us through Vernon's cancer scare a couple years back and a farm accident decades ago when our son almost lost an arm."

Vernon traced a wrinkle on his cheek. "And these days I'm loving that last part about our youth being renewed." He placed his arm across the back of Susie's chair.

Blake leaned over her, scanning the page. The smell of him, something spicy and . . . manly, beat out even the smell of Susie's rolls or the coffee she had yet to drink.

Autumn scanned the verse again.

"Who satisfies your desires with good things."

A couple weeks ago, if she'd asked God to satisfy her desire, the good things she'd have hoped for were so simple. The job in Paris. A way to save the inn before leaving. A chance to hug her sister and restore her relationship with her mom.

But now . . .

Blake met her eyes.

Now she couldn't help wondering if saying hello to one good thing might mean a hard good-bye to another really, *really* good thing.

※

"Possibly the only thing I like less than ladders, Blake, is cats."

Blake paused on the top rung of the ladder leading into the barn's hayloft. Floating dust particles were highlighted by sunlight streaming through the crack of a partially open door at the far side of the loft. He blinked to adjust to the dim lighting, then glanced back down to where Autumn still stood below, veiled in shadows on the barn's cracked foundation.

"C'mon, Red. Vern really wants us to 'see the kitties.'" The man had insisted.

"Go up and see the kitties while I do a few chores." Blake had tried to offer his help. After all, the farmer had spent hours whisking them around the property. It'd been a blast of a day.

And Autumn had been the best part. She'd finally stopped checking her iPhone every few minutes for messages from the inn or rattling off festival to-dos to complete when they returned home. She'd been carefree and, frankly, more alluring than ever. Completely at ease.

Until the mention of cats.

He tried to keep the tease out of his grin. "If you come up here, you'll make Vern happy. You'll make me happy. And what's more, I'll promise to stop at that used bookstore on the way home."

If that didn't cinch it, nothing would. He climbed the rest of the way into the barn's second level, the musty smell of hay enveloping him.

And sure enough, seconds later, Autumn emerged into the loft, hefting herself over the opening and standing up beside him. "Cats totally creep me out."

"Kittens are different." Piles of hay scattered across the loft mostly covered the wood floorboards beneath their feet, tiny squeaks and meows filling the quiet. "Besides, think of the bookstore."

He sidestepped a hay bale and found three kittens running around the center of the room. He plopped down and a kitten crawled into his lap. "See? Cute." A second kitten climbed over his leg and clawed up his shirt.

Autumn still stood near the opening, arms crossed. Finally, she dropped her arms and joined him. "The last cat I was around tried to scratch my eyes out. I made the mistake of offering to pet sit for Harry. Pretty sure he got the cat from the fiery pits of you-know-where. If I didn't hate them before . . ."

She knelt in the hay, and a third kitten grabbed for her shoelace.

"Okay, fine, maybe they're a little cute." She lowered to a cross-legged position, and the kitten immediately found its way to her lap. Blake watched her lips spread into a grin, and with the way the sunrays highlighted her profile . . .

Dude, a photographer could have a field day with her.

He gently removed the kitten still trying to make its way up his shirt, then met Autumn's eyes. *Sooo pretty.*

She blinked, cleared her throat, discomfort at once endearing and amusing, just like everything about her.

"Let's name them," she blurted.

"They're barn cats. Not pets."

She practically cooed as she lifted the kitten from her lap, holding it in front of her face. "Even barn cats deserve names."

"Wow, you melted fast. From 'I hate cats' to deeming them name worthy."

"I have my persuadable moments." She was still peering at the cat as she spoke, and he could almost hear the wheels turning in her mind, searching for the perfect name.

But all he could think, could wonder, really, was if that was true—about being persuadable—then maybe all he had to do was wait for the right moment . . .

To tell her what? That sometime in the past two weeks, she'd stopped being a last name to him? That he'd started thinking of her less as a co-event-coordinator and more as a friend?

Just a friend?

"This one is Lucy."

He coughed, causing the kitten in his lap to scurry toward Autumn instead. "After Betsy's sister? Wait, did you leave her alone today with your mom and sister?"

"You make it sound like a terrifying prospect."

Well . . .

"And no, she's been spending mornings at the inn helping Betsy. Besides, I was actually thinking of the Pevensies in the Narnia books. Lucy." She pointed to a black kitten. "And that one is Peter and the one with the white paws is Edmund."

"I thought there was a fourth kid?"

"Susan. But she didn't make it back to Narnia in *The Last Battle*. So I don't feel bad leaving her out."

"Obviously I will never catch up to you on reading."

She lowered her kitten. "Did you know people have actually debated the fate of Susan through the years? Oh, and here's a strange bit of trivia—there was a comic book a few years ago that had Susan Pevensie sharing an apartment with Alice from *Alice in Wonderland*, Dorothy from *Wizard of Oz,* and Wendy from *Peter Pan.*"

"You've got a library in that head of yours, Red." Dust caught in his throat, and he sneezed.

Her "bless you" blended with her laughter, and he sneezed a second time as she asked, "Hey, what do you think that rope is for?"

He followed her pointed finger to the long, thick coil with a series of knots at the frayed bottom. "Have you never hung out on a farm? It's for swinging, of course."

"Swinging?"

"Yeah. I'll show you." He climbed up on a high pile of hay bales. "Toss me the rope, will ya?"

She stood and swung the rope his direction. He caught it and gripped it tight, feet planted on the grouping of knots. "Here I go." He took a running jump off the bales and swung across the loft. "Woo-hoo!" He let go and landed in a heap of loose hay.

Autumn laughed as he stood and dusted himself off. He grabbed ahold of the rope and approached her.

"You Tarzan, me Jane," she said.

He held the rope out. "Your turn."

"Uh, no thanks. Don't want to get my clothes dirty."

He cocked an eyebrow. "Woman, you're wearing jeans and a stained shirt."

"Hey, that pulled pork Susie served at lunch was messy stuff."

"Take the rope, Jane."

She jerked it from him and climbed onto the same pile he'd jumped from. "Fine. But if I crash into the wall or land on a kitten and kill it, I'll blame you."

He gathered all three kittens into his arms. "The animals are safe. Go for it."

She squealed as she flew through the air and dropped, pieces of straw splashing up around her. She popped up. "That was fun."

"See, I told ya." A kitten batted at his ear. He leaned forward to let them scramble away. When he came back up, Autumn stood in front of him.

"You know what's amazing to me?"

She smelled like hay and some kind of fruity shampoo, and something close to wonder dangled in her voice. "What?"

"The same person who has traveled all over the world, bungee-jumped and parasailed and flew planes . . ." She faltered, but only for a moment. "That same person seems to get just as much of a thrill from playing with kittens and swinging on a rope in a barn loft. Or boarding on a sand dune."

He pulled a piece of hay from her hair. "Well, sometimes the adventure isn't in where you are but who you're with." He heard the huskiness in his own tone. Felt the words he wanted to say play through him. *Just tell her.*

You've been the best part of coming home.

When I'm with you, my black eye and reputation don't even bother me.

My favorite time of every day is hanging out at the inn.

But the sentiments couldn't find their voice under the weight of a dozen *why-not*s: It'd only been two weeks. Their families didn't get along. She deserved someone who had made something of himself, not wasted the past six years of his life.

And Ryan and Ava. He couldn't forget how horribly that ended.

Still. Standing there in the hayloft, he could almost ignore all the warning signs.

"Do you really believe that?" Doubt lingered in Autumn's question as she faced him.

He forced himself to focus on her question. Believe what? What he'd said about adventure? "Well, yeah. I'm pretty good proof, aren't I? I have literally been all over the world. And at times, it was great. But there's something to be said for being able to see the potential adventure in everyday life, in the people around you."

Did he sound dumb? Was he making any sense at all?

And was there any chance she read between the lines to the truth he was just now latching onto? *She* was an adventure. Getting to know her excited him more than any continent-hopping trip or crazy stunt.

A mountain hike or bungee jump might momentarily satiate some thrill-seeking bent in him. But this woman who hated cats and loved books, who could probably argue better than that lawyer ex-fiancé of hers and who loved her old inn more than she even realized . . . she fed a longing he couldn't have even named earlier, but that he now recognized for what it was.

A longing for connection. Understanding. The kind of soul-deep friendship he'd watched form between Randi Woodruff and Matthew Knox, the reporter she'd fallen for. And despite the mountain range of reasons why Autumn Kingsley was the last woman he should connect with in that same way, he couldn't deny the desire that made him want to conquer the mountains until he arrived on the other side.

Which is where?

Possibly somewhere miles past "just friends."

"Autumn." His voice was raspy but, amazingly, void of the uncertainty he'd been towing around for days. *Maybe there are a dozen* why-nots. *But what if there's a* why *that's bigger than all of them?*

What if Autumn was the reason God had brought him home?

"Autumn." He stepped closer as he repeated her name. Waited for her to step back. And when she didn't, when her breath hitched and her eyes met his, he leaned his head down.

And then back as another sneeze tickled up the back of his throat.

Autumn jumped at his "Achoo," bumping into a hay bale behind her and toppling until Blake reached out to catch her. "Don't sneeze on me," she squealed, giggles erupting and the potency of the moment fading.

And for a second, disappointment knocked through him.

But only for a second. Because as he righted Autumn and joined in her laughter, suddenly, for the first time in a long time, he knew exactly what he wanted. She was standing right in front of him, ribbons of sunlight winding through her hair and a smile a person couldn't get tired of.

And there wasn't any rush. He wasn't going anywhere.

He sneezed again.

"Blake," Autumn said through fits of giggles. "I think you've got a cold."

He shook his head, hair dusting over his forehead. "Nope. Allergic to hay. Sorta forgot until now."

And that's when she flopped onto a hay bale, her laughter his new favorite sound.

⟡

She had to tell him.

Autumn inched off her gloves while still controlling the steering wheel, puffs of air from the heater in Blake's new-old Jeep warming through her as they traveled toward the beckoning lights of Whisper Shore. She pushed her wind-tousled hair over her shoulder and turned the vehicle onto the road that led into town. The long day, the late hour, didn't seem to matter under the smile of moonlight.

"You know, I totally could've driven." Blake leaned against the passenger seat's headrest, eyes closed.

"Those allergy pills said they could cause drowsiness. We're safer this way."

"Admit it, you just wanted a chance to drive the Wrangler."

Somehow the rustic light-brown Jeep completely fit him. Much more than Ryan's Firebird ever had. Though it still surprised her he'd sold the car. "It does make me feel like MacGyver."

He opened his eyes. "Just wait 'til summer when we can drive it with the top down."

She gulped at his *we*. And there it was again. That annoying inner voice urging her to tell him. But how was she supposed to say it? *Actually, Blake, I won't be here this summer. . . .*

For the hundredth time during the drive, she opened her mouth to let it out. But just like every other time, the revelation stalled in her throat.

After a silent moment, she felt Blake's glance on her, and when she turned, it was to see a grin that oozed satisfaction. "This was a great day." His eyebrows lifted as if waiting for her agreement.

"A really great day." Vern and Susie's heartwarming welcome. All the photos they'd taken for Mrs. Satterly. The books she'd scored at that little bookstore on the way home.

And the haymow. That one intoxicating moment before he'd sneezed.

He was thinking about kissing me.

Maybe more than thinking about it. She'd read it in his eyes and heard the quickening of her own heart. It's what had started the anxious thoughts nettling inside her in the first place. *Just tell him you're moving.*

"Blake, I—" she began, but he said her name at the exact same time.

They laughed and he motioned for her to continue, but she insisted, "No, you go ahead." *Later. I'll tell him later.*

Stars flirted in winks and gleams from a midnight blue sky. "I was just thinking—wondering, I guess. . . . You asked me whether I really believed what I said about adventure and being just as happy here." He slanted another glance her way. "Why'd you ask that?"

The temptation to brush off the question was so strong, she almost gave in. Sure, she could joke and laugh with Blake as if they'd laughed and joked as friends for years instead of only a couple weeks. But share something this vulnerable?

And yet, something had changed today. Something so poignant it was almost tangible. Or maybe it had started at the snowball fight. Or when he rescued Dylan at the lake. But it continued today with clasped hands and that moment in the barn and . . . and now, as a tentative desire to let him in spread through her.

"My parents were going to divorce. Before my dad died, I mean. And he was going to leave Whisper Shore."

Leave me. Somehow she knew she didn't have to say the words for him to hear them. "Oh, Red."

She turned onto Mom's street. "Mom doesn't know I know. I overheard them arguing about it one day. After that, I kept waiting for them to sit Ava and me down, tell us the bad news. But a couple weeks went by. And then Dad . . . the aneurysm."

She blinked in rapid succession, grip tightening over the steering wheel. Telling Blake was one thing. But, please, no tears. Not after a day like today. Not when she wanted to hold on to that feeling of abandon for as long as possible.

"I'm sorry." Blake reached for her free right hand. "I didn't realize . . . I wish I knew what to say."

She blinked again. Swallowed. "It's okay. Really. It's just, I think about it, a lot. Dad wasn't happy here. Even as a kid, I picked up on his wistfulness. As if he felt he was missing out on something." She let go of his hand so she could turn the wheel. "I guess that's why I asked you what I did." She pulled up in front of Mom's house, only a couple lights shining from its windows.

"So you've just pretended all these years you didn't know they planned to split up?"

"Didn't see what good it'd do to talk about it. I mean if Mom had wanted to . . ." Her voice drifted. "I suppose that's part of why Mom and I struggle sometimes. I think if I'm honest, there's a piece of me that's always been annoyed that she wasn't truthful with me. And what's more, from what I overheard, she wasn't going to fight him on the divorce. I wish she would've. I wanted to hear her ask Dad to stay. She seemed more concerned about what was going to happen to the inn than our family."

The truth spilled from her now, more than she meant to share. More than she'd said even to Ellie.

And Blake—kind, surprising Blake—just reclaimed her hand and squeezed it. Listened. He was so good at that. In just a couple weeks' time, he'd found a way to lead her into vulnerable places she'd avoided for years. And somehow, the mental journey wasn't as emotionally taxing with him at her side.

After a moment's quiet, Blake cleared his throat. "So you're going to trust me to drive my Jeep home all by myself?"

She gasped. "Oh, I wasn't even thinking. I'll drive you—"

"Red, I'm completely and totally coherent. And I haven't sneezed in fifteen minutes. Pretty sure I can make the drive." At that, he let himself out of the car. He'd rounded to her side and opened her door before she finished gathering her purse and bag full of books. After she slipped out, he closed her door and reached for her bag.

A motion-sensor light clicked on as their footsteps creaked over the steps leading up to the porch. Autumn huddled into the collar of her coat. "Well, I'd better get inside." She nudged her head toward the door. "Mom and Ava . . ."

"Wouldn't be happy to see me," he finished for her. "Hey, Red . . . ?"

"Yeah?" Her voice was breathy and uncertain.

"Thanks for telling me. About your mom and dad, I mean."

She should be the one thanking him. For inviting her along on his quest. For an entire day free of worry about the inn. For somehow knowing there was a story behind her questions in the barn—and giving her the space to tell it. "Thanks for listening."

"And just to reiterate, I meant what I said—that adventure is more about who you're with than where you are. I wish your dad could've grasped that."

He took one step toward her, closing what little space remained between them, bag of books still dangling from his arm. And as he hooked one thumb in the pocket of her coat, she could feel her heartbeat picking up, beating in sync with the tapping of a branch hitting the roof.

And the voice in her head amped to a command. *Tell him.*

"Um, you know earlier today," Blake spoke again, his breath mingling with her own. "In the barn—"

"Blake, I'm moving."

At her blurted words, his head snapped up. "What?"

No, no, that wasn't the right way.

"Back to your place?" The yellow of the porch light spotlighted his wrinkled brow.

"Actually . . . to Paris."

She could practically hear the bricks of confusion thudding one after another in him. Oh, why had she told him like this?

"Paris." Blake sputtered the word, voice caught in the wind.

Cold wrangled through her, chiding her lack of tact. And her timing, which, oh, had never been so off. Not just her timing in telling Blake about her move. But in . . . everything, this whole friendship.

"Paris?" He said it again, more oomph in his voice this time, and maybe even a twinge of aggravation. "As in Paris, France?" His unshaven jaw twitched.

"Do you know of any other Paris?" She attempted a smile, grasping for their usual banter, but if her face looked anything like her thoughts, the grin came out twisted, her comment gargled. "Okay, I know there's a Paris, Michigan. And then there's Epcot . . ."

No return tease lit his eyes. Only a widening gap between them as he let her bag of books drop to the porch floor with a thump and stepped back, rubbing his hands together—maybe for warmth. Maybe to fill the quiet her lack of words produced.

But what more was there to say?

In a month, she'd be gone. And he needed to know.

Or maybe she needed him to know. Before he kissed her. Before he inched past the last of her reserve.

More like pole-vaulted.

The wind chugged again, the rhythm of the tree branch picking up speed as it hit against the house. "I've been wanting to go for years. Planned to study there in high school even, but then Dad . . ."

He met her eyes once more, slivers of compassion joining the stormy mix of who-knew-what in his dark gaze. "You're just picking up and moving? What about the inn?"

"That's why I'm trying so hard to get everything into place. You know, fix it up, Dominic Laurent—the guy you met yesterday—he's my secret plan. I even had this crazy idea to ask my sister to take over management." She shifted her weight. "I don't want to leave a mess behind me."

"Clearly."

How could one word feel so sharp? "Blake—"

He shook his head. "No, you're being smart, Autumn. Like always. Responsible, checking things off the list. If you're going to walk away from your life here, at least you're doing it the right way."

Then why did his tone suggest the opposite? "You make that sound like a bad thing."

He sighed, raking his hand through his hair, backing down the porch steps.

She marched after him. "Please don't make me feel bad for this. I'm just trying to follow my dream before . . . it's too late."

He looked at her for a long moment, his expression unreadable now that he'd moved from the light of the porch. "Well, congratulations on the job." A forced half smile, the feel of his hand lightly squeezing her arm, neither stopped his words from falling flat.

12

The snow-globe effect glittered the town square. Blake pulled up the collar of his navy blue coat, trapping whatever heat he could. Once the snow they'd hoped for had started falling, it hadn't stopped. It dusted from the sky now and, in addition to the twinkle lights, wreaths and tinseled ornaments dangled from the gazebo and streetlamps.

It was exactly as Blake had pictured it when he and Autumn had started planning for the festival. So why couldn't he shake the melancholy that twisted around him like a scratchy scarf?

"We'll have to be careful not to blow a circuit, but it's doable," Frankie said, gloved hands closed around his Thermos.

He'd arranged for Frankie and Benj, two guys from the city crew, to meet him at the square today to talk about the Christmas tree lighting.

"It's going to be a good display, the perfect kickoff for the festival." He took a sip of the cocoa he'd picked up at the bakery.

"First time we've ever done something like that." Benj's hair poked out from underneath his fur-lined cap. "Reminds me of the tree lighting down in Silver Dollar City."

Maybe wouldn't be quite that spectacular, but still, excitement for the festival had begun to spread through town. Despite the failure of their committee meeting a couple weeks back, folks seemed to be getting on board.

They still had a good week to spruce up the rest of the downtown before festivalgoers descended on the town. And this morning, Dad had approved spending the festival budget—including booth sponsorship dollars—however Blake and Autumn chose.

"When you were appointed the festival coordinator, son, you were given control of the budget. So if you don't want to hire Lillith Dunwoody, don't do it."

They'd had the discussion over breakfast at the kitchen table. "Even if the committee members quit?"

Mom had refilled his glass of orange juice. "If they quit over something like that, they weren't ever committed in the first place, if you want my opinion."

He'd chuckled then, looking between his parents. Mom, spritely and energetic as ever. Dad, grinning. And yet, it wasn't enough to hide the exhaustion circling his eyes. The town economy must be taking a toll on Dad. Serving as mayor while running his own business would be enough to wear anyone out. That and the thought of another election coming down the pike.

But the logic of it didn't erase the worry that thumped through Blake at Dad's appearance. Maybe he should've insisted on working at the hotel, taking on some of Dad's load, instead of doing the festival.

"Do what you think is right as far as the festival budget," Dad had said after swallowing a bite of toast.

Whatever he thought was right.

But that was the problem, wasn't it. How was he supposed to trust himself to know what was right, considering his past? Considering how many times he'd chosen wrong? Considering the years he'd wasted living in the shadow of those mistakes?

And it wasn't the decision on how to spend the festival budget whirling up his worries anyway, was it? Autumn's face flashed in his mind. *She's leaving.*

"So are we good to go here, Blaze?"

He twitched to attention. "Oh, yeah, Frankie. Thanks for all the help."

"Just remember, on the night of the tree lighting, the important thing is that you plug into the right outlet. We're running everything through surge protectors, but even so, if you plug into the extension with the rest of the lights—that's this one here—you could cause a blackout."

"Or worse, a fire," Benj cut in.

"Got it."

He pitched his now-empty Styrofoam cup into the trash bin beside the gazebo and thanked Frankie and Benj again. Another item checked off his and Autumn's list. Wonder how far she was getting on her to-dos. He could text her. Even better, call.

But after last night . . .

"I'm moving, Blake."

His steps dragged. It bothered him that it bothered him. It bothered him that it had kept him awake half the night. He should've fallen into a worn-out sleep after the day of traveling.

Instead he'd tossed and turned into the early hours of the morning, wishing he'd never let himself notice her. Wishing he'd stayed focused on the task at hand, the reasons he'd come home.

Wishing she'd stay.

Wishing he was enough to make her want to stay.

Just as he stopped at his father's hotel, a man stepped from the revolving doors, righted the cap on his head, and turned toward Blake. Wait . . . wasn't that the Laurent dude Autumn had introduced him to at the snowball fight?

The man stopped. "Ah, the younger Hunziker, I believe. We met the other night."

Yes, right before his humiliating fight with Shawn, the evidence of which still ringed his right eye. Though the bruise had already lightened to a brownish yellow.

"Nice to see you again," he said, jutting out his hand. But why was Laurent at the hotel instead of the inn?

The man must've caught the question in Blake's eyes. "Nice hotel. Surprising for this small of a town, really."

"Well, only about ten thousand of us live here, but on a good summer weekend, we swell to close to twenty-five thou."

"So I hear." Laurent tossed his scarf over his shoulder. "I must be going."

Blake swallowed the slew of inquiries tussling his thoughts as he watched the man walk away. A minute later, he approached the hotel's check-in desk. "Hey, Clark," he greeted the concierge who had manned the desk since Blake could remember. "The dude who just left, Dominic Laurent, is he checked in here?"

Clark straightened the rack of brochures at the corner

of the desk. "If he was, I couldn't tell you. Guest privacy and all that. But since he isn't, I can tell you he just came from a meeting with your dad."

"A meeting. With my dad."

"That's what I said."

Blake tapped the desk with his palm. "Thanks, Clark."

Dominic Laurent had a meeting with his father. Uh-oh, had he started comparing investment opportunities? Decided Autumn's lakeside inn didn't measure up to the upscale hotel in the middle of town?

Autumn would be crushed. She'd talked about how important the potential investment was to the future of her inn. And though she didn't say it in so many words, he had a feeling it wasn't just important, but critical. That loan extension might have been enough to get her through a couple months, but the bank couldn't hold out forever.

He angled through the lobby and headed toward Dad's office. He found his father already on his way down the hallway, a grin accompanying his hurried steps. "Hi, son. Banner morning, this. Just got word that two members of the state tourism board will be attending the Christmas festival. Take that, Victoria Kingsley. We'll get our grant yet. But what can I do for you?"

He fell in step with Dad. "The man you just met with . . . Laurent."

"Good guy. Younger than I expected. Knows the biz."

"What was he here for, Dad?"

"Only something I've been working on for months. More than a year, actually. I've been strategically reaching out to LLI ever since I noticed the downtick in tourist numbers summer before last. Finally tempted them to town."

Blake skidded to a halt. "What?"

"There'll be a little give and take if we join their family of hotels, but the bulk of the give would be on their side. In the form of a financial commitment. And it'll blow our marketing out of the water."

"*You* got Laurent to town?" Autumn had talked like the man's presence was some kind of divine intervention. She didn't know why Dominic Laurent had come to their little tourist town, but she was just sure it was an answer to prayer. *Her* prayer.

Instead, if he understood his father correctly, it was an answer to corporate strategy. From the hotel that had eaten away at her inn's business for years.

Dad finally paused. "Yeah, I got him here. But get this, his family has this crazy superstition. They never actually stay at hotels they own or invest in. So he's booked out at the Kingsley Inn. Is that rich or what?"

Dad started walking again.

Rich . . . or something.

How was he supposed to tell Red?

If only Autumn had coordinated her outfit as well as she'd organized the party downstairs.

"You should've let me run to your Mom's house and pick up your own shoes instead of bringing a pair of mine." Ellie stood in the center of the guest room with her hands on her hips.

Autumn placed one tentative foot in front of the other. How did a person walk in spikes like these? It's what she got for leaving in such a frenzy this morning. She'd grabbed her garment bag with her dress for tonight—and mismatching shoes.

She hadn't realized the mistake until just thirty minutes ago, when she'd finally hurried upstairs to change as guests started arriving. No time to run to Mom's place. Thus, the harried phone call to Elle, who hadn't yet left her house. *"Thank goodness, we've got the same size feet. Can you bring a pair for me to borrow when you come?"* Too bad she hadn't emphasized flats instead of heels.

Maybe it would've made more sense to call Mom or Ava, but neither had been particularly talkative when she'd arrived home from the Illinois road trip. She'd tried—again—to talk to her sister. But Ava had closed down the second Autumn admitted where she'd spent her day—or more accurately, who with.

She hadn't seen either Mom or Ava all day today. Had thought maybe one or both of them would offer to come over to the inn, help with final party preparations. Now she wondered if they'd even show up tonight. But how could they not? In all the changes that had rocked their family since Dad died, their annual Christmas party was the one holding tradition. They wouldn't skip it, would they?

"It would've been out of your way to stop at Mom's house," she argued with Ellie now. "Besides, your red shoes look way better with the dress anyway, right?" She tilted to the side. "Even if I can't walk in them."

The sleeves of her black dress reached to her elbows and the top half fit her figure perfectly. The skirt gathered at her waist, then swished out in layers to her knees. The red heels were the perfect accent. Made her feel like Audrey Hepburn ready to take to the lamp-lit streets of Paris.

But it'd be a miracle if she made it through the evening without toppling down the staircase and breaking her nose. Not exactly the kind of impression she wanted to make on the party attendees downstairs—community members, the inn staff and their families, the guests currently filling ten of the inn's rooms. Most of all, Dominic Laurent.

"Are you sure you should even be here, Ellie? Your doctor did order bed rest, right?"

"Mild bed rest. I've already had this argument with Tim. In fact, he called my clinic this morning specifically to get the okay for me to come tonight. I'm surprised he didn't ask for a doctor's permission slip. Made me promise never to stand more than five minutes at a time. Speaking of . . ." She lowered onto the guest bed.

Autumn reached the window, ankles finally beginning to hold up. The perfect winter evening—glimmering stars peeking through feathery clouds, a quarter moon smiling—seemed like Mother Nature's kiss of approval.

She should be dancing inside with the thrill of this evening—a chance to wear a pretty dress, play host to friends, show off her inn looking better than it had in years. Thanks to Blake.

And that would be the reason for the emotional undertow keeping her from floating joyfully on the surface of the night's fun.

"Ell . . ." She turned from the window. "Do you think I'm going to like France?"

Ellie pulled out her ruby earrings. "Like it? Honey, you've been talking my ear off about it ever since Sabine e-mailed you the job description. I'm still a little ticked at her for pulling you away from me. And yet, what kind of best friend would I be if I didn't want you to chase your dream? You're not rethinking the move, are you?"

"Oh no, it's just . . ." With each day she checked off on the calendar, subtle concern joined the swirls of excitement about her upcoming move. There were things she'd miss. People. The pillowy comfort of familiarity. The way temperamental Lake Michigan greeted her every morning. "Just reality setting in."

"You'll probably have a little homesickness when you get there. You might have moments of wondering what you got yourself into. But then you'll go up the Eiffel Tower. You'll take a bus out to Versailles. You'll catch a train some weekend to Spain. And the doubt will fade away.

"'Course, all the rest of us back at home will miss you like crazy." Ellie reached for Autumn's hand and dropped in her earrings. "Here, these will pull your whole outfit together."

"But they're yours."

"Believe me, I won't miss them." She slipped off her matching bracelet. "This too. There, perfect. You are going to be the belle of the ball."

Autumn smoothed her angled bangs over her forehead. "You do realize I'm technically working tonight, right?"

Ellie stepped back, surveying Autumn's ensemble. "Just out of curiosity, which of the guys do you most want to impress? The foreign one with the cute accent and the investment dollars or the handsome hometown prodigal?"

Autumn stepped out of one shoe and rubbed her foot. "Ellie Jakes, Dominic Laurent is a guest. I never fraternize with guests. Especially not ones I hope to form a business relationship with." Although, it was odd that after several days, Dominic still hadn't said a word about the inn. He'd simply greeted her before heading out each day. Complimented Betsy's meals and the view from his suite.

But nothing of a professional nature. Oh well, maybe he preferred to experience their amenities extensively before talking business.

"I just thought perhaps you'd noticed that he's got that suave and mysterious thing going for him." Ellie sat on the bed. "Blake, of course, is about as mysterious as an apple, but still—"

"Ellie." She didn't even know if Blake still planned to come tonight. Not after the way he'd looked at her when she told him about France.

"There's something different about Blake these days, though." Ellie continued, apparently oblivious to Autumn's pinched reaction. "He's focused and determined— still a little quirky, yes, but with a good heart. And when he's not working on the festival or beating my husband at basketball—or whisking you away to Illinois, for that matter—he's here at the inn. Almost as if he's getting a little . . . attached?"

Autumn squeezed back into her shoe. "He does like this place. He keeps giving me ideas for improvements. Yesterday on our drive he was telling me about this reservation software the hotel uses."

"I wasn't talking about the inn, and you know it."

So maybe she did. So maybe she knew exactly what Ellie hinted at.

But what Ellie obviously overlooked was the teensy little existence of the ocean that would soon separate Autumn from Blake.

They'd connected, sure. Found a surprising friend-ship while working, yes. But as soon as she'd dropped that bombshell last night about her upcoming move, everything had changed.

And that . . . was that. No need to dwell on it.

"Come on, Tzeitel, let's go join the party."

Ellie stood. "Reference?"

"*Fiddler on the Roof.* Let's go before I start singing 'Matchmaker, Matchmaker.'"

When they emerged from the room, Autumn balanced herself with a hand on Ellie's shoulder. Even from the sec-ond floor, the smell of the chocolate fondue bar wafted, sweet and enticing. The brassy jazz of Benny Goodman's "Santa Claus Came in the Spring" provided the backdrop for chatter below.

Autumn leaned close to Ellie. "If I fall down these steps and break my neck, promise me you'll name your baby after me."

Ellie's laughter stopped her at the top of the staircase. "If I can make it down the steps with a stomach the size of a watermelon, you can walk in those pumps. Sway your hips and you'll be fine."

Autumn stepped down one stair, ankles folding, and grabbed on to the railing. "The hips are not helping. The hips are not helping."

"On second thought, take off the shoes until you make it down the steps."

"Good call." Autumn stepped out of the shoes and sighed in relief. When they reached the bottom of the staircase, she dropped Ellie's shoes to the ground, eyes searching the crowd for any sign of her mother and sister.

"And here I thought maybe you were going barefoot."

Her focus lurched to the right.

Blake. The bruise still shadowed his eye, but the way his shoulders filled his black shirt, together with light gray pants and a striped tie . . . Well, she could admit it. The man looked good.

And he'd come. Despite the way they'd left things . . . he'd come.

She blinked, grasped for nonchalance. "You try walking down stairs in heels like these and see if you don't give up, too." In place of Benny Goodman's jazz, Ella Fitzgerald and Ray Charles now bantered to the tune of "Baby, It's Cold Outside." Not all that fitting, considering the summerlike warmth in Autumn's cheeks.

Blake's gaze traveled from her shoes to her face. "Did you know seventy-five percent of spinal injuries are due to high heels?"

"I'm a little disturbed you know that," Ellie said. "I'm going to go find my hubby. And a chair. My five minutes of standing are almost up."

"He's over at the fondue bar," Blake called after her, then turned back to Autumn. "Totally made that stat up, by the way."

He would. "Sorry I didn't make it to the meeting with Frankie and Benj this morning. But after being gone all day yesterday, there was so much to do here." She lowered her voice. "Although the one thing I wanted to do, catch Laurent for a conversation about the inn, didn't happen. He was gone all day."

Blake's already dark eyes dimmed. Was he thinking of last night, too?

"Listen, Blake, about last night . . ."

He held up his hand. "Let's not rehash it. I'm glad

you told me." He hesitated. "And . . . as your friend, I'm happy for you."

Friend. The word shouldn't taste so dry.

"Besides, tonight's your night, Red. Let's just focus on now."

But see, when she started focusing on now, that's when she let herself get attached. That's when *friend* didn't feel good enough. "Well, um, I guess I should mingle some." She took a step back, wobbled, and his arm shot out to catch her.

"Whoa, careful. What's bothering you? Nerves?" He looked down with a rakish grin. "Or the shoes?"

He still held on to one arm. "Both." Her answer came out a squeak and his eyes returned to her face. And why was her stomach going all knotty on her? *Friend*.

"Don't worry, Red. Your party is going to be a smashing success. As for the shoes . . . Here." He held out his elbow. "Just hold on. I won't let you fall."

⟡

He'd kept his promise.

Through twenty minutes of fluttering through her crowd of guests—a few moments chatting with Petey from the Snack Shack and his wife, small talk with the ladies from the Chamber of Commerce, catching up with people she hadn't run into for weeks—Blake stayed at her side. Sometimes balancing her by the elbow, sometimes simply moving in sync with her, as if they were partners in a waltz.

"Pshaw, we're not charging you for our services."

They stood with Larry Hinkle from the local radio station now, talking about the AV he'd agreed to provide during the run of the festival. Blake stood close enough she could smell the musky fragrance of his aftershave.

"Now, Mr. Hinkle, we have a budget. We're definitely going to make sure you're compensated."

"Nothing doing, Blaze. Displaying our station banner at the AV table is compensation enough. That and the work you've done on this thing. It's about time someone stepped up and shook this town out of its slump."

By the time the man walked away, he'd offered to run PSAs every day leading up to the festival

Autumn tipped her head up. "Blake Hunziker, you are incredibly good at charming whoever you talk to. Any longer chatting with Larry and he'd have asked you to be the new station manager."

"What's this? A compliment from a Kingsley? Almost don't know what to do with myself." He turned to face her.

"Seriously, you could make a career out of schmoozing people."

"So I should go into politics?" The lights of the dining-room chandelier danced in his eyes. "It'd be a short-lived career if I didn't have my right-hand Red with me."

"A compliment from a Hunziker? Almost don't know what to do with myself." She hugged one arm over her torso, feet rooted to the floor. Without her arm hooked through Blake's, she didn't feel nearly as stable.

"As long as we're at it, you look stunning tonight. Should've said that earlier." Blake cleared his throat. Oh, and a tint of pink found its way to his cheeks. If that wasn't the best thing she'd seen all night . . .

He cleared his throat again and pushed out a funny-sounding chuckle. "If you think I'm a good schmoozer here, you should've seen me as Mr. Randi Woodruff. We had to do these interviews, talk shows and stuff. I practically had people eating out of my hand. I make a good fake husband if I do say so myself."

She grinned up at him. "You're so humble, too."

"Indeed. But anyway, this all just goes to show, we make good partners."

"Who would've thought?" She tried to inject a teasing tone into her words, but instead they came out tinny and timid. "Uh, listen, I need to duck into the kitchen and see if Betsy's about ready to serve dinner."

"Gotcha. I'll be around."

As she moved toward the kitchen, she caught sight of Dominic Laurent over by the fondue table. She hadn't had a chance to talk to him yet, but he wore a look of satisfaction. That was something, right?

She pushed her way into the kitchen. "Hey, how's it going in here?"

A cloud of warmth enveloped her, tantalizing aromas lifting from the oven.

"I'll be ready in five." Betsy wore a black sequined dress under her white apron, matching headband holding her short hair back. "Taste test?" She held out a frosting-coated spatula.

"Don't mind if I do." The taste of chocolate added an extra layer to the sweetness of the night. One of Betsy's two waiters brushed past as Autumn perched on a stool. "If I could live in a house made from this frosting, Bets, I would. 'Course, then I'd earn a reputation as a woman who licks her walls, which would be weird, but also cool in a Willy Wonka kind of way."

Betsy giggled, arranging plates of layered cake garnished

with strawberries and drizzles of white-chocolate sauce on a platter. "You're in a mood."

"The party's perfect. Everything's perfect."

Almost perfect. Still no Mom. No Ava.

"I'm glad. Oh, Lucy's going to help serve, if that's all right with you. Lem went home sick."

"Awesome. About Lucy, not Lem."

"And I decided to serve beets instead of zucchini."

"Check it." She licked off the last of the chocolate. "And gross, by the way."

"Just seeing if anything would phase you. I know how much you love beets."

"You could've said you were replacing the tomato-basil chicken with fish eggs and I'd have been happy. Because like I said, everything's going—"

The back door swung open.

"If that's Lem, I told him not to come back if he's still sneez . . ." Betsy's voice trailed as the figure stepped into the kitchen.

Ava. Wearing a floor-length skirt and ruffled shirt and a tentative expression.

Autumn hopped off her stool, at once happy yet hesitant at the sight of Ava in an outfit that was as dressy as her sporty sister got. She'd always had the model looks of the family but, much to Mom's constant chagrin, tended to hide her lithe figure under athletic clothes and her whitish-blond hair under baseball caps.

"Ava, you came. You could've come in the front door, though."

Ava wore her hair in her usual ponytail, but strands escaped on both sides, framing her face. "We weren't sure . . ."

We?

And then Mom appeared behind Ava, wariness etched across her face. But . . .

"Wow, Mom, you're here."

Mom brushed past Ava, burgundy dress swishing around her legs. "Of course, I'm here. Wouldn't look right not to be."

Mom's tone didn't signal any delight at what the rest of the night held, but her presence, for the time being, was enough. Ava's too. There was hope for their little trio of a family yet.

"Well, what can we help with?" Mom asked.

Betsy waved her hand. "Oh no, we've got plenty of help."

"Ava, you haven't been out to the inn since you've been home." Autumn looped her arm through her sister's. "I'm so excited to show you all the things we've done to spiff it up. Come on out to the dining room."

"Your tour's going to have to wait, Autumn," Betsy countered. "I'm ready to serve. Don't want the fish eggs to get cold."

Ava's nose wrinkled. "Fish eggs?"

"Inside joke. Let's go. You too, Mom."

Mom exited the kitchen, but Ava stopped Autumn with a hand on her arm before they followed. "Can we . . . talk sometime? I know I said some things that—"

"We both did, Ave. But tonight, let's just have fun. All right, sis?"

It's what Blake had said. Just focus on tonight.

She loved tonight.

Hesitance hovered in Ava's smile, but she nodded.

When they entered the dining room, Autumn spotted

Harry over by the bay windows and brought two fingers to her lips, motioning for him to whistle. He shook his head. The man hated it when she made him whistle. She flashed him a saccharine smile and mouthed, *"Do it."*

Harry's piercing whistle brought the room to attention. Autumn moved to the front of the room. "Everybody, thank you so much for coming out tonight. Looking around the room, I'm reminded how much I love the people of Whisper Shore, and how blessed I am to have such wonderful friends."

And family. Ava hung back near the doorway. Had she spotted Blake? *But she's here. Even if she's uncomfortable, she's here.*

And Mom was over with Grady Lewis near the entryway into the lobby. Did she notice the polished floors and new window treatments? Would it make her angry to know Blake had been the one to help hang them?

"Those of us who are from Whisper Shore know this past year hasn't been without hardship. Actually, the past five, six, seven years have taken their toll on our town." Everybody had been affected when Ryan died. And then the economy crashed. And Whisper Shore seemed to lose itself, its personality and charm, right alongside its tourists. "But at Christmastime, we're reminded that behind the industry and economy and business, beyond the pretty lake and sometimes nice weather, there's always something to celebrate."

As she paused, a creak sounded overhead. Who would be upstairs? She'd seen all the current inn guests mingling in the dining room.

"There's Christ's birth. There's friends." She couldn't stop a glance Blake's way. "There's family." Her gaze flitted from Mom to Ava. "Our awesome cook, Betsy, and her staff have prepared a mega feast tonight. She's going to let us know what's on the menu, and then we can all find our seats."

Autumn stepped aside so Betsy could recite the meal items, and guests moved to find places at the gaily decorated tables that filled the room. Except . . . why were there wet spots on the red tablecloths of the center tables? Not the ceiling again.

Autumn started to lift her gaze, when Betsy asked, "Autumn, will you pray for the meal?"

"Of course." Maybe no one else would notice the dripping. She waited until the sound of chairs knocking against the table stopped and folded her hands as another creak sounded from above "Father God, thank you so much for bringing us all here tonight, for the chance to enjoy good food and fellowship."

A longer, louder creak. And then a cracking sound. Worry chugged through her. "Thank you for the meal Betsy has prepared and for each person around the table." Another crack. And—she peeked one eye open, then the other—dust? "Please help us have a wonderful . . ."

But she couldn't go on. Because now everybody's eyes were open, gazes fastened on the ceiling. Another cracking sound, only this time she could see it—one big crack and a hundred little ones branching out. A *thump, creak,* and . . .

Oh, Lord, help us.

A *crunch* sounded as the ceiling broke open, chunks of plaster and insulation hitting the tables in the center of the room, dust and debris fogging the air. People jumped from their chairs, gasps and shrieks drowned out by a final boom and thud as something heavy crashed into the room.

Coughs and a trickle of ceiling rubble hitting the tables and . . .

Autumn forced herself to look.

A bathtub.

A bathtub resting in the middle of the wreckage.

A giant hole in the ceiling.

Either of which she'd gladly climb into.

13

Tiny white flurries sputtered from the sky, carried on a brisk cold Blake hadn't felt in years. It had been so long since he'd experienced a Michigan winter. But there was a zesty feel to the chill, something fresh and glinting, like the string of stars decorating the sky.

"I should really stick around." Ellie stood beside the passenger door of a Nissan. "She's so upset."

Upset was an understatement. The flush of pink had seeped from Autumn's cheeks as her dining-room ceiling caved. The gasps of her guests turned into shocked chuckles and then full-out laughter. Amazingly, no one had been hurt. They'd wiped the dust from their clothes and backed away from the wreckage. . . .

But Autumn had just stood there. Frozen.

And he'd had the craziest desire to pull her close in an act of comfort—like she had for him the other night in her sister's bedroom. But they'd been alone then. So instead he'd watched as she blinked, leaned over to say something to Harry, and then disappeared from the mess.

Blake stuffed his hands into the pockets of his black coat and held his arms tight to his body. "You heard Harry, Ell. She wanted everyone to go home."

Tim held the door open for his wife. "I'll come back tomorrow to help clean up, hon. But you're supposed to be on bed rest."

The glow of the moon lit the mostly empty parking lot of the Kingsley Inn. Only a few cars still claimed spots. He didn't know how he'd ended up being the one to see off all Autumn's party guests. But for whatever reason, he'd stepped into the role when Autumn retreated to the second floor. Probably to assess the damage.

Or maybe have an emotional breakdown in private.

"But I feel bad leaving her here alone."

"She's not alone. I think her mom and sister are still here. I'll make sure she's okay. I promise."

Ellie peered at him through ringlets frazzled by the wind, nodded, and ducked into the car.

Finally, as Tim and Ellie rolled down the lane, Blake climbed the inn's porch steps. Warmth reached for him as he entered. The odor of dust and plaster leaked into the lobby.

Along with the sound of a determined grunt.

He glanced through the opening into the dining room . . . and it took everything in him not to break into chuckles. Autumn, still in her black dress and red heels, pushed against the cracked bathtub where it rested in the middle of the floor, one of the dining room tables broken underneath. Drips of water spurted from overhead. Several chairs were overturned and at least two other tables had been damaged.

"Come on, you stupid thing." She breathed the words through another futile push.

Tendrils of hair had slipped free of her headband and fell around her face. And her cheeks were red from exertion. With a frustrated groan she stepped away from the tub and kicked off one of her shoes, sending it skipping over the floor.

"Whatcha doing, Red?" He stepped into the room.

She turned, her other foot lifted midkick. Instead of chucking off the shoe, she stepped down, now at a tilting angle. "What's it look like?" She shoved the hair out of her face. "Did everyone leave?"

"Mostly. Except for the people who are actually staying here." Thankfully none of whom occupied the room overhead, according to Harry. Where was the guy anyway? And the rest of Autumn's staff? Shouldn't her mom and sister be helping her?

A burst of laughter sounded from the kitchen now. The sound of dishes clinking and the faint strains of music playing from a radio filtered through the door.

"They're still laughing about it," Autumn said, arms crossed. "Everyone thinks it's so amusing. But it's not. It's embarrassing."

Blake took a step closer to her, nudging a table leg out of the way. "Look at it this way. At least no one was in the tub when it fell. *That* would have been embarrassing."

She should've giggled, but the poor woman was wound tighter than ever. She kicked off her other shoe, sending it his direction, then turned back to the tub. He could see the muscles in her legs and arms strain as she pushed against the claw-foot beast. Another piece of hair fell loose and trailed down her back.

His heart lurched at her disappointment "Red, come on. Don't worry about the tub and the ceiling now. Let's go raid the kitchen and get something to eat. We'll take care of all this tomorrow."

"Really? You're worried about your stomach at a time like this?" She pushed again, the tub barely inching.

"There are sharp pieces everywhere, and you're barefoot."

She paused. Score one for his powers of persuasion. Except when she turned to look at him, renewed determination lit her ridiculously blue eyes. "My tennis shoes. They're upstairs in the room I changed in. Could you go get them? Room Seven."

And leave her alone to dislocate enough discs to make a chiropractor's day? He reached out to take her hand and tugged. "Come on."

"No, I'm going to clean this up."

"You'll ruin your dress."

"I don't care." She attempted to pull away, but he held on.

"Well, I do. It's gorgeous on you."

Another yank and she freed her hand. Immediately her arms folded, and she stood as if in cement. He studied her for a moment, then reached into his pocket. "Fine."

"What are you doing?" Her eyes narrowed.

He lifted his phone. "Taking a picture of this. Because one day, Autumn Kingsley, you are going to laugh about the fact that a bathtub fell through the ceiling and landed on your dining room table."

"I will not."

He snapped a photo of the mess. "Pretty sure you will."

"You think you know me so well."

He tipped his phone up to get a shot of the oval-shaped hole in the ceiling. "No, I think I know what's funny. And this is funny."

"Is not."

He pointed the phone at her and tapped to take a photo. "Is too."

She just stood there, rooted to the floor for another couple seconds, until finally her arms flopped to her side and she dropped to sit on the edge of the bathtub. He watched the lines of her forehead smooth away, one corner of her mouth tug upward. She lifted her eyes. "Did you see the way Chester Johnson's eyes bugged?" She gave a squeak of a laugh.

He pocketed his phone as a grin pinched his cheeks. The town's postmaster *had* turned frog-eyed. "I'm surprised he didn't lose his toupee."

"I'm not sure anyone would've noticed if he had. Not with this thing making an entrance. Talk about crashing a party." She bent over, a raspy burst of giggles finally surfacing.

"My mom always used to tell me to wash up before dinner." He sat beside her on the edge of the tub. "This gives it a whole new meaning."

Her laughter mingled with his, rising until she no longer held back.

"Just think if Ellie had gone into premature labor," she pushed out between breaths. "The bathtub would've been right there."

"Oh, Red, get that picture out of my head."

"Hey, you rhymed." She hiccupped.

He steadied himself with both hands on the rim of the tub. "It's a special talent of mine."

She tilted her head back, laughter stilling into a sigh. "My sides hurt." Another hiccup. "You do know I'm going to demand you delete whatever pictures you took of me, right?"

"Not going to happen. I'm going to save them for the perfect occasion."

"You better not." One more giggle, and then she lifted her hands and swiped them under her eyes. A tear escaped down one cheek.

She had either laughed so hard she'd teared up or . . .

Another tear trailed down her face.

"Aw, Red." He reached an arm around her shoulder. "It's going to be okay."

She stiffened only a moment before relaxing into his grip. "I really wanted to impress him." Another hiccup. "First he shows up early and finds a half-naked kid streaking through the place."

Oh. Dominic Laurent. A reminder of what he'd learned earlier today batted his conscience. He'd waffled all day as to whether to tell Autumn the investor she thought she had in her back pocket was really in town for *his* family's hotel.

Would she feel at all better about what had happened tonight if she knew Laurent had never had any interest in the inn?

Not likely. At all.

"And now he sees what truly poor shape this place is in. I thought tonight would be the spark we needed, but . . ." She sniffled, and he wished he had a tissue to offer her. "Maybe I just . . . don't have spark."

With his free hand he brushed a strand of hair from

her face. "Red, you've got spark. Trust me." It radiated from her whether she knew it or not.

She shivered then, and he felt the goose bumps rise on her bare arm under his fingers. The tears had stopped, but not her shaking. How could she be cold when he felt warm enough to heat the room?

And when she was close enough to . . .

His gaze dropped to her lips, and he could feel Autumn tense. But she didn't move. His fingers strayed across her cheek. "Red."

Her voice came out a whisper. "I'm still moving, Blake. And there's going to be an entire ocean—"

"Yeah, well there isn't one now." Despite the mess, despite the wreck of their situation, this moment . . . it felt like a second chance following yesterday's moment in the haymow. *Was that just yesterday?*

"True." The word feathered from her lips just as he tilted toward her.

The kitchen door burst open. "Autumn, Betsy asked me to tell you she's saving some dinner for . . ."

Blake jumped to his feet, and the movement sent Autumn wobbling.

Ava stopped halfway across the room. "Oh."

Blake reached for Autumn's hand before she could fall backward into the tub and pulled her to her feet. She bumped against his side before steadying and practically jumping away.

"We were just—" he began.

"Right. Dinner. That sounds good," Autumn blurted at the same time. She threaded her fingers through a messy wave of hair and brushed past him, disappearing through the door Ava had just entered.

He couldn't read Ava's expression. Didn't have long to try, because she turned to follow her sister.

Leaving him to stand in the middle of the wrecked dining room beside a bathtub, wondering if he had any chance of making things better.

❧

Something tapped in an uneven rhythm, like Morse code against a windowpane.

Autumn blinked one eye open, the glare of sunlight creating a haze around her even as cold burrowed under the blanket covering her.

Where in the world . . . ?

She opened her other eye. Her office at the inn. The couch. She peeled her cheek from its cool leather and lifted her head. Why hadn't she slept in one of the empty guest rooms instead of the office?

The tapping at the window continued as she slid to an upright position, a thrumming in her temple matching the branch nearly beat for beat. That was some wind outside.

"Oh, Lord, please tell me it was a dream." The wish came out a whisper—and a futile one at that. Because she wouldn't have slept in her office if last night's calamity had been the stuff of nightmares instead of pure, pitiful reality. Nor would she be wearing such a mismatched outfit—yesterday's tennis shoes and last night's dress, topped with a sweatshirt that wasn't hers.

Right. Blake's.

She'd stood barefoot at the island counter in the inn's kitchen last night, eating Betsy's fancy dinner while Ava helped Betsy put away unused dishes. Ava had explained

Mom went home with a headache. She'd thought Blake had left, too, until a knock sounded at the back door. They'd all jumped.

Harry answered. Autumn had craned her neck just in time to see Blake hand something to Harry. "She looked cold."

Harry nodded.

"G'night."

The door closed.

She took a bite, and when she looked up, everyone stared at her. "What?"

Harry handed her the sweatshirt and they went back to putting dishes away, a trail of yellow lights through the window signaling Blake's departure.

Now fully awake, Autumn let out a groan and forced herself to stand. "Come on, Kingsley. You can hide away, helpless and distraught, or face the mess head on."

"Talking to yourself?"

She started at the intruding voice, nearly tripping on her untied shoelaces. "Sheesh, Harry, ever heard of a knock?"

He gave her a once-over and snorted. "Ever heard of fashion sense? Or proper pajamas?"

"Just wait. Someday all the models will be wearing sneakers and hoodies with their dresses. Why aren't you at church?"

Harry folded his arms, eyes lit with a curious anticipation. "There's something you need to see."

Autumn walked to the oval mirror hanging on one wall. Framed in ornate brass, the glass reflected a sad state of affairs appearance-wise. No wonder Harry had snickered. Her hair looked like a bird's nest gone wrong, and her wrinkled dress would make an iron cry. The sleeves of Blake's sweatshirt dangled past her fingertips.

How was it the thing could still smell so much like him when she'd been wearing it the past seven or eight hours? Not that it wasn't a good smell. And its soft cotton warmed her upper half clear through.

"Ahem." Harry cleared his throat, breaking her stare.

"Right. There's something I need to see. What now? Did a bed land in the lobby? Better yet, a toilet. Maybe we can turn the whole first floor into one giant bathroom." There, she'd made a joke. Maybe this day wouldn't be all bad.

Harry rolled his eyes. "I never realized how sarcastic you are in the morning."

"I'm overwhelmed. How are we going to fix this? Here, I was actually happy that we're close to fully booked the week of Christmas. Now I'm worried we're going to have to cancel reservations."

Yet in the light of day, with the bright sun streaming in through the window and Blake's sweatshirt cocooning her in warmth, a shred of hope snuck in. If they acted fast, surely they could patch up the hole in the ceiling. Replace the damaged dining room tables. Get the bathtub back upstairs.

Except, with what money? She'd spent most of the bank's loan already.

And who would she call in for help on a Sunday?

And what about their current guests? Where would they take meals?

Her hope dissolved into a puddle of questions. "What are we going to do, Harry?"

"Harrison." He stomped his foot. "And you're going

to follow me." He about-faced and disappeared from the doorway.

Autumn shrugged. She'd have to emerge sometime. Besides, the tempting aroma of coffee trailed through the ground floor. She could be thankful for that anyway.

Harry marched down the hallway and into the lobby. Autumn refused to glance through the opening into the dining room as she followed him to the front door. "Can I grab a cup of straight black first?"

He ignored her, pulling the door open and letting in a sheet of sunlight mixed with cold, piney air. A fresh layer of white quilted the ground. She hadn't even noticed the snowfall last night—and she barely noticed it now. Because in the middle of the yard stood a circle of people she didn't recognize.

"Who are they?"

"I don't know, but they look like they're here to work."

Exactly. They wore work boots and tool belts and stood in a circle chatting. One of the men turned, spotted Autumn, and pointed. The circle broke and then . . .

A woman walked toward her, almost-black hair pulled into a messy bun and jeans tucked into a pair of rugged-looking boots. Her grin was wide and familiar.

Harry's gasp matched her own.

She stopped in front of them. "You must be Autumn. Hi, I'm Miranda Woodruff."

Randi Woodruff, star of *From the Ground Up*, standing on her lawn. Autumn exchanged a shocked glance with Harry, then accepted the celebrity's handshake. "Yes, I'm Autumn."

"Sorry to just pounce on you like this. We would've

called first, except Blaze didn't give me your number and he's busy rounding up the equipment we need."

Autumn blinked, everything suddenly snapping into focus. "Blake called you."

Randi chuckled. "He did. Last night, and he was talking so fast I could barely understand him. Crazy man. Hey, you called him Blake. Is he trying to shake the nickname or something?"

"I guess so." Okay, she had to stop acting nervous. *Being* nervous. Celebrities were just people. And this was just another woman.

A strikingly beautiful woman who pretended to be married to Blake for a month.

It shouldn't bother her so much. It's not like she and Blake were . . .

Suddenly last night's moment in the dining room zoomed into focus, both of them perched on the rim of the bathtub, so close she could feel the warmth of him despite the shivers tickling down her skin.

Last night's near-kiss had been weighty with tension and desire, fragile. And when Ava had burst in and he'd pulled away, her nerves turned to broken glass.

"Autumn?"

"Sorry, um, I'm just . . . massively confused."

Randi only smiled, and beside her, Harry cleared his throat.

"Oh, this is Harrison."

"Love your show. Always DVR it. I'm a fan."

Randi shook his hand. "Thanks. As for us, we're all pretty big fans of your Blaze. He called us last night around eight, and by ten I'd pulled a crew together."

"How'd you get here so fast?" Harry asked the same question running through Autumn's mind.

"We hopped a private jet crazy early this morning. We've only got the day, but from Blake's description of the damage, we should be able to fix you up by tonight. Mind if we go inside and take a look?"

Autumn nodded, shock still holding her tongue hostage.

Harry nudged her as the crew started filing past. "Snap out of it, Kingsley," he hissed.

"B-but . . . money. I don't . . ." *Have any*. The admission was too embarrassing to say out loud.

Randi only waved off her concern. "No worries. It's taken care of."

"But—"

Randi had already turned to follow her crew.

Autumn forced her voice to work. "We've got to let the guests know what's happening. Maybe serve breakfast in their rooms. Or serve in the sitting room."

Harry nodded. "Randi. Woodruff."

She turned to him, grin taking over her face. "I know."

"Will she think I'm ridiculous if I ask for an autograph?"

"Better yet, a photo."

Harry's hands clamped onto her arm. "And she's fixing the inn. Your inn."

He pulled her into a hug, and she nodded against his shoulder. Blake had saved the day. He'd honest-to-goodness saved the day.

"Autumn?"

She broke away from Harry at the sound of Randi's voice. *Look calm. Look professional.* "Yes, uh, Rand . . . I mean, Mrs . . . Miss . . ."

"Randi is my show name," she said, amusement playing over her face. "You can call me Miranda. I just wanted to check if it's okay for us to go into the room the bathtub fell from. I know you've probably got guests in some rooms."

Harry pushed past Autumn. "I'll show you the way to the damaged room," he said, eagerness punctuating his words. "We do have a few guests staying with us, but I'm sure they'll understand. . . ."

His voice trailed as he climbed the porch steps two at a time.

"Oh, hey, here comes Blaze." Randi waved, and Autumn turned to see Blake's Jeep pulling into the lot, followed by a truck. "Tell him we'll be out to unload the equipment in a minute, will you?" Randi disappeared into the inn.

Autumn crossed the yard, sunlight kissing her cheeks and haloing around Blake as he jumped out of his vehicle. He didn't even notice her at first, signaling for the truck to bypass the parking lot and pull up in front of the inn.

But then he caught her eye. Smiled.

The truck driver followed Blake's gesture and pulled in front of Autumn, temporarily blocking her view of him. But as soon as it zipped past, she couldn't help it.

She launched herself at Blake, her embrace voicing the thank-you she couldn't push out. And if she'd thought his sweatshirt smelled good . . .

His chuckle rumbled against her. "Who knew you'd be so grateful for a sweatshirt?" He said the words over her shoulder but didn't let go.

And she'd have been lying if she said she wanted him to.

❧

"It's a Christmas miracle."

Blake watched Autumn turn a slow circle in her inn's dining room. Except for the shine of new paint on the ceiling, no one could have known that less than twelve hours ago, dust and debris and splintered wood had filled the space.

Instead, nicks and dents had been sanded from the now freshly polished floor and the broken table and porcelain bathtub removed. Miranda's crew had repaired, insulated, and resealed the ceiling. And the bathroom upstairs had new flooring and a new tub. All the plumbing and electricity was in place.

And Red . . . She hadn't stopped smiling all day.

"A Christmas miracle," he agreed from the archway leading into the dining room. "Or proof that my former pretend wife never once pretended about her skills."

Miranda had been amazing, directing the repairs while hard at work herself. She was around somewhere, making one final inspection of their day's work. In the corner, a crewman folded up a metal ladder.

Autumn motioned Blake into the room. "Look, they didn't just fix the hole in the ceiling. They repaired every little crack and installed new crown molding."

Actually, he'd done the crown molding. Had followed Miranda's instructions and fit the wood in place all around the room where wall met ceiling, the whole time thinking about those few moments last night with Autumn. And then this morning, when she'd nearly hugged the breath out of him.

He'd felt like a superhero just then. Like, for once, he'd done exactly the right thing at exactly the right time. He'd feasted on the satisfaction of it all day.

Autumn turned to him now. Sometime this morning, she'd run home and changed out of last night's dress, replacing it with jeans and a long-sleeved T-shirt. But she still wore his hoodie, unzipped and loose over her shirt. It was too big for her, practically ate up her figure, but he wasn't about to ask for it back.

Ever since she told him about her upcoming move, he'd been trying to convince himself the sparks he'd thought he felt between them were just his imagination. They were friends, nothing more. The thought that he might be falling for her was the result of spending the bulk of his time with her—that was all.

Besides, who falls for someone in two weeks?

Autumn pulled her hair loose from her ponytail and shook it free.

Fine. Apparently he did. But he'd force himself to brush free of it, like the way Autumn combed the knots out of her hair with her fingers.

"I wish I knew how to thank you, Blake. Or should I say Blaze?" A tease lit Autumn's voice.

Going to be a lot easier said than done.

He shook his head and stuffed his hands into the pockets of his dust-covered jeans. The work of the day had turned his white T-shirt beige, and he hadn't washed the caulk from his hands after working upstairs.

"All my effort trying to get people in this town to forget the Blaze thing and Randi ruins it in one day. But, um, I think it was worth it."

"What was worth what?"

Miranda came up beside them, wiping a trail of dust from her cheek.

"Bringing you here was worth the resurrection of my nickname."

Miranda gave him a playful punch. "Hey, I did my very best to call you Blake. But I can't help that I slipped up all day. I guess you'll always be Blaze to me. Besides, consider it payback for all the terms of endearment you threw at me when we were 'together.'" She accented *together* with air quotes.

"Terms of endearment?" Autumn asked the question while fiddling with the zipper of her sweatshirt. His sweatshirt.

"Punkin, sweetheart, dumpling. He tossed 'em out like candy at a parade."

"To which she usually threatened to fake divorce me." Blake gave Miranda a side hug and mussed her hair. "Wifey, I don't think we were ever meant to be."

Miranda laughed and pulled away. "Pretty sure Matthew would agree." She checked her watch. "Speaking of which, I'm eager to get back and see him. Looks like we're about loaded up. You're driving us to the airport?"

He nodded. "Yep." The crew had taken a private jet into Detroit—since the local airport didn't have a jet runway—and then caught a puddle-jumper to Whisper Shore, thanks to Ike Delaney.

Autumn followed them to the porch, thanking the crew one by one, insisting they could all stay at the inn for free anytime they happened to get up to Michigan. He watched as she hugged Miranda Woodruff, the sheen of celebrity awe still not quite dissolved.

He shot Autumn a "see ya later" smile before following the crew to the porch and out to the parking lot. Minutes later, they motored down the road.

He glanced over to the passenger seat as he drove. Miranda's gaze was fastened the opposite direction, to the dunes rising and falling in the east in ripples of white against a cerulean sky.

"Different view than your mountains back home, yeah?"

"Very different. You know, I'd never even been to Michigan before?"

Miranda's home was in the heart of the Smokies. When he'd been there, the colors of early fall had painted the landscape in a firestorm of hues. He'd only spent a month there, but he'd come to appreciate the place.

Michigan was scenic in its own way, though—coastal blues and greens dancing against the rocky shore. Sunrises worth the efforts of early risers in their unpredictable patterns of color—some mornings a pale palette of pastels and others bold oranges and yellows. *No mountains, but it's home.*

Miranda shifted in her seat to face him. "So when are you going to tell her?"

"Tell who what?"

"Oh, come on, Blaze. We lived in the same house for weeks. I do know you a little."

It was true. The marriage might have been phony, but the friendship had gelled into something genuine over the weeks.

"You like her."

"Randi—"

"She likes you."

His mouth opened. Closed. Opened. "There are extenuating circumstances. Complications."

Her laughter bubbled. "Complications? Let's take

a little trip down memory lane, why don't we. Do you recall that when I fell for a snooping reporter from Minnesota, I was trapped in a fake marriage at the time? Had the whole country believing I was married to, oh, who was it again? You." She punched his arm. "If those aren't complications, I don't know what is."

Fine. So she had a point. But things had a way of working out for some people. People like Miranda Woodruff who, underneath the sham of an identity she'd built for herself, had a sincere heart. People who were worthy of their dreams.

And Autumn . . . she was worthy of her dreams, too. And her dream was France.

Not him.

He might be her hero today, but that would wear off, and he'd mess things up, and one day she'd pull away.

"Sooo . . ." Randi pried.

"I think you've been around your reporter boyfriend too long." In other words, she'd turned nosy.

"I'll take that as a compliment."

"Anyway, she's moving to France soon."

Miranda scoffed again. "For a guy who spent years traveling the world, that should not be an issue. Follow her there."

But he couldn't. No, he'd come home because it was time to settle down. Be responsible. Following a girl he'd only connected with a couple weeks ago halfway around the world . . . That was anything but responsible.

Old, reckless Blaze might've gone for it.

New, dependable Blake?

He flipped down his sun visor. "Anyway, how is Knox?"

"Handsome. Sweet. Getting ready to propose."

"He is? That's fast."

"Yeah, but when you know you know, right? Anyway, he thinks he's being super secretive about it, but I have my sources. Namely, my manager."

"Oh, he's still crashing in the dude's basement?"

She nodded. "Yeah, but not for long if I can help it. Soon as he pops the question, I've got a proposal of my own."

Not hard to read the mischief in her eyes. "You want to elope." Her TV-star status had never quite overcome the woman's need for privacy.

"Yeah, to avoid the media craze."

He turned onto the road leading to the airport. "Funny thing, that. You want to avoid the media. I sort of . . . need it."

"Why?"

"This festival-coordinator gig I told you about? They only gave it to me hoping I'd put Whisper Shore in the headlines. You know, as the guy who, well . . . ."

"Played my stand-in spouse? I can't believe that was only a month and a half ago. It seems a lot longer."

A *lot* longer. "Problem is, the only media I'm getting calls from are crummy tabloids. If we really want to draw people in to the festival, we need attention in tourist mags and travel columns, not—"

He broke off at the sound of Miranda's gasp. Glanced over, then followed her gaze out her window to where the cars filled the airport parking lots. Not only cars . . .

Cameras. Dozens of them.

"Blaze, I think your wish just came true."

14

"Autumn, get in here!"

Harry called the words as he waved at Autumn from the fireside den. But hesitance held her in place at her perch behind the check-in desk. If she abandoned her post, she might miss Dominic Laurent's morning descent from his suite.

She'd promised herself she'd stake out the lobby all day if she had to for the chance to finally corner the businessman. Her plan was simple: boldly ask for a meeting. And then discover whether the off-chance to which she'd tethered her hopes for the inn's future had any possibility of coming to pass.

"Hurry before you miss it!"

Quiet chatter rolled in gentle waves from the almost packed and newly remodeled dining room on the opposite side of the lobby. At least they finally had a full house. In the past couple days, news of Randi Woodruff's one-day stop in Whisper Shore combined with the coming festival had finally pulled in the reservation rush she'd been hoping for.

She had Blake Hunziker to thank for both.

Autumn leaned over, elbows perched atop the desk, head tilted to look around Uri rolling a luggage cart past. "What is it?"

Harry stepped to the doorway as his wave turned frantic. "The commercial break's almost over. They said he'd be on after."

He who? And why was Harry watching the flat-screen in the den? They usually kept the thing turned off in the morning. "Already told you, I'm not leaving this desk until Dominic comes down." She closed her fingers around her almost empty cup of coffee.

"He won't leave before eating. You won't miss him. C'mon." He returned to the den.

Curiosity finally propelled her off her high leather chair. Harrison was right—Dominic would likely stop for breakfast before disappearing for the day.

The jingle of a commercial rang her into the den, and the warmth of an already lit fire embraced her, along with the scent of evergreen from the potpourri they'd placed around the artificial tree. Harry stood in the center of the room, arms crossed over his usual sweater vest—this one in Christmas burgundy and hunter green—and eyes trained on the television.

Autumn reached his side, coffee mug in hand, just as the familiar voice filled the room. Her gaze jumped to the screen. "No way, is that—?"

"Your man Blake? Yup."

It looked like a satellite interview, for Blake stood in front of the gazebo in the town square. The cold of the morning was apparent in the red of his cheeks and puffs of white air when he spoke. "He's not *my*—"

"Shh."

" . . . so we're excited about showcasing our town and giving visitors an event they won't forget." Sunlight glinted in golden flecks in Blake's eyes as he spoke.

She sipped her coffee. It wasn't the first time Blake had been on TV since Randi's impromptu stop in town. He'd been so busy with local and state media she'd hardly seen him. But it was the first time he'd been on a *national* morning news show. And oh, he looked as natural as if he'd been giving interviews his whole life—dark hair pushed away from his forehead and easy smile directed at the camera.

Well, it's not as if this is exactly new to him. After all, he'd done the TV rounds back when he was pretending to be Randi's husband.

"And it's our understanding Whisper Shore recently had a visit from a celebrity you're well acquainted with." The reporter conducting the interview, probably from New York City, appeared in a split-screen shot next to Blake.

Was it just Autumn or did she catch the barest hint of a wince in Blake's expression? The tiniest crack in his camera-perfect pose . . . and then he simply nodded. "Yes, Randi Woodruff did visit. Actually, she stopped at the Kingsley Inn, one of our finest lodging establishments here in town."

Harry broke into a cheer. "Go, Hunziker."

The interview lasted another thirty seconds, with Blake steering the conversation back to the festival. The city council should award him a medal. He'd accomplished what they'd asked of him—used the media's residual interest in him to turn the spotlight on their town. And just in time for the festival.

Though she had to wonder how Blake felt about the community leaders putting more stock in his media draw than his talents. They needed to open their eyes. The man could do a lot of good for Whisper Shore. He had such an easy way with people. He'd proven himself handy around the inn—that's for sure. And he'd taken their nearly extinct festival to a whole new level.

He had a wealth of ideas, but more impressive than that alone was his ability to get things done. She couldn't help wondering what the Kingsley Inn would be like if someone like Blake at been at its helm the past few years—someone more skilled at seeing what the place could be rather than someone anxious to leave it behind.

Harry turned to her. "You're quiet."

"Just wondering what Mayor Hunziker would say about Blake plugging our place instead of theirs." The fireplace crackled behind her, and she pushed up the sleeves of her black sweater.

"I'm sure their rooms were booked long before ours." He lifted the remote to turn off the television.

"And even if not," a new voice sounded from behind, "the man's so smitten it probably didn't even occur to him that his own family may not like him promoting the competition."

Autumn turned. Her sister leaned against the doorframe with arms folded, but the casual pose contradicted the testiness in her tone. After Saturday's party, things had somewhat settled with Mom and Ava—as if someone had dropped a gauzy sheet over the wrinkles in their past. See-through enough to know the problems were still there, but a soft enough cover to "pretty up" the mess.

But it appeared the smooth sailing of the past couple

days might be coming to a choppy end. Ava's eyes were still on the now-black screen.

Probably best to ignore the "smitten" comment. Ava was wrong, of course. Blake's kindness in securing Randi's help and comforting Autumn after the bathtub incident didn't erase the impracticality of anything more than a friendship.

Just like Harry turning off the TV doesn't erase that image of Blake smiling at the screen? The kind of smile that could convince single girls from across the country to travel to Michigan for a chance at the man.

Autumn gulped the thought down, opting for a "Hey, Ava" that came out feeble and unconvincing. "What brings you here so early?"

"Coffee. Mom's out."

Uh-oh.

Harry made the apology for her. "You may be out of luck. Our inventory is due in today. 'Til then, we've been rationing."

Autumn held out her mug. "Only had half a cup myself. There's a swallow left if you want it."

Ava's sigh matched the exasperation in her eyes. She straightened, uncrossing her arms and holding out a stack of envelopes. "Here. I met the mailman on the way in." She handed the bundle over. "And I'll take that drink."

Autumn relinquished her cup and started flipping through the mail on her way back to the lobby. Bill, bill, advertisement, travel mag, bill . . . bank envelope. She didn't need to tear into the thing to know what it held. A reminder of the short-term loan payment due next month—or of the mortgages payments that were past due.

Oh, why had she given Ava the last of her coffee? She could've used a dose of steely resolve in caffeinated form right about then.

She deposited the mail on the desk, looking up to see Ava gazing into the dining room. "If you're thinking about stealing a leftover cup of coffee from an empty table, don't."

"How'd you know what I was thinking?"

"Because I was considering the same thing a few minutes ago. Bad form, though. Maybe instead we talk Harry into making a bakery run."

Harry joined Autumn behind the desk. "I'm not your errand boy."

"Caramel macchiatto for me," Ava said.

"Hazelnut blend, black." Autumn tucked the bank envelope to the bottom of the mail pile. "Pretty please?"

Harry looked between the sisters before letting out an exaggerated moan and reaching for the coat he'd stashed behind the desk. "Fine. But you both owe me. You can pay up by figuring out which bulb is causing that entire string of lights on the porch to flicker."

Autumn wrinkled her nose. "Scratch the plan. I'll go to the bakery."

But Harry had already reached the door. "Too late. Besides, you need to wait for Laurent. See ya."

A burst of cold rushed in when he opened the door, and Autumn instinctively huddled into the bright pink scarf around her neck. "I hate it when Harry makes a good point."

Ava trailed over to the desk. "Laurent. That's the guy from lodging biz, right?"

Autumn nodded.

"I saw him drive away in a rental car when I pulled in."

Autumn slapped her palms atop the desk. "Seriously?" She'd missed him again? It was feeling less and less likely that the man had any intention of conducting business while in town. Maybe he really was just on vacation. "This *day* . . . I want a redo, and it's barely eight a.m."

She trudged past Ava, yanked her coat from the coat tree and slipped outside, wishing the view were enough to calm the wavy tension rolling in her stomach. Minutes later, after checking outlets and extension cords, she settled on the porch bench, strand of lights in her lap, and fingered through the bulbs one by one.

She heard the front door creak open, footsteps over the porch boards. Quiet dangled in the air, like the icicles hanging from the porch roof. And then Ava sat, picked up the opposite end of the flickering strand, and started jiggling bulbs. The wind chimes in the corner made up for the lack of conversation. Until . . .

"It's really that bad?"

"The inn, you mean? Yeah." The sound of lake water wrestling with the wind chugged in. "Truth is, I almost feel guilty about Blake getting Randi Woodruff here, all the work they did, when we could be closing up come New Year's."

She could feel Ava bristle beside her. Both Ava and Mom had stopped by the inn on Sunday as soon as they heard a celebrity was there. But if Autumn wasn't mistaken, both had done a masterful job avoiding Blake that day . . . and every day.

"Look, I know you and Mom don't like Blake. But he's been more help to me than . . ." *You or Mom.* She cut off before the biting words escaped.

But Ava seemed to hear them anyway. "That's not fair."

Maybe not, but it was the truth.

Another rustle of the wind chimes. "Autumn, you could've told Mom you didn't want to run the inn. You could've walked away any time."

Autumn twisted another bulb. Resisted the urge to chuck the whole string to the ground in frustration. "It's not that easy. I felt obligated."

"Why? No one else in the family did. Not even Dad." Ava's words along with a snagging chill scraped over her.

"What's that supposed to mean?"

"Come on. You know as well as I do Mom and Dad were on the brink of splitting up before he died."

She *knew*? And all this time, Autumn had thought she was doing such a noble thing by pretending . . .

"He was ready to leave this place behind. And Mom . . . she signed it away as soon as she had the chance. I don't know why you're holding on so tightly—especially when you've got that opportunity in France."

How about their employees, for one? The historical significance and family legacy, for another. And maybe just the idealistic desire to leave something sweet and successful behind her—rather than broken-down evidence of her own shortcomings.

But the arguments clogged in her throat. Instead, she watched as Ava tested one bulb, then another. Three. Four. Five. It added up to the total amount of times she'd seen Ava since her sister moved. Five Christmases. No shared birthdays or Thanksgivings. After Ava first moved, Autumn had repeatedly offered to fly out and visit. Ava found an excuse every time.

Ava looked up now to catch her staring. "What?"

"Why me?"

Ava's brow wrinkled as she pushed back her hood. "Huh?"

"I get why you moved away, I do. I get that you were hurt. But why did you push *me* away? You didn't even come for my college graduation." Now that the dam burst, she couldn't stop the flood. "It really hurt." Years of bottled emotion released in three little words.

She'd imagined this conversation with Ava so many times. Always pictured her older sister apologetic and emotional, their certain embrace like a sentimental scene from a Hallmark movie.

Instead, Ava only directed her gaze to the lake as she dropped her end of the lights into her lap. Shutting down once again. Once again leaving Autumn to wonder what she'd done wrong.

To wonder why Ava, just like Dad, had decided she wasn't worth sticking around for. Frustration pumped through her, and her palm stung where she'd grasped the wired lights, pointy bulbs poking into her flesh.

Then, finally . . . "It wasn't about you."

"Felt like it. Were you mad I couldn't talk Blake into helping Ryan?"

"Wasn't about Blake either. But you know what, let's talk about him. He's a bad idea."

"Ava—"

"I saw the way you were smiling when you saw him on TV. Don't give up the dream you've had your whole life for a guy who'll only break your heart." The clanging of the chimes accented her words.

"He's not Ryan."

The words suspended in the air for what felt like a full minute before Ava jerked to her feet, her end of the stringed lights dropping to the ground. Autumn waited for her argument. Even in the midst of the shards of sharp emotion, a sliver of hope suddenly glinted.

After all, they were sisters. And sometimes sisters fought. Better that than continued distance. Maybe on the other end of this conversation the pieces of their relationship might finally fit back together.

Or maybe that was wishful thinking. Because seconds later, Ava stalked out of sight, only those stupid chimes filling the silence.

Where is Autumn?

From his perch behind the waist-high wall around Whisper Shore's outdoor rink, Blake watched the colorful flock of skaters circle, blades scraping over ice. Overhead, the rickety lights fastened to two poles flickered on, the sun having started its slow descent.

She'd said she'd be there. An hour ago.

"So your little town does this festival every year?"

Blake's focus snapped back to the reporter beside him—the one with the nasally voice and toothy grin and digital recorder pointed at his mouth. One day before the festival, and he'd spent most of it giving interviews while the volunteer committee did the actual work. Didn't feel right.

But at least the city council had finally gotten what they wanted—media attention. It had ratcheted up to dream levels in the four days since Randi Woodruff's appearance in town. He only hoped it wasn't too late to impact the festival. This afternoon's appointment with the entertainment columnist from Chicago was the final step in the PR effort to pull in last-minute travelers.

And he'd wanted Autumn to be a part of it. After all, she'd done just as much work as he had.

But she hadn't shown.

And he was torn between worry and irritation. *Probably busy at the inn or working on last-minute festival stuff.*

Hands clasped over the edge of the wall, he attempted to concentrate on the reporter's questions. She'd asked to do the interview "somewhere Whisper Shorey." Her words. "Yes, the festival is an annual thing. Although this year we're doing quite a few new events."

He launched into the same spiel he'd given the travel blogger from Detroit yesterday, the morning show anchor this morning—all about the tree lighting, the winter sports, the food stands, the musical entertainment.

When he realized Sissy—yep, really her name—had stopped taking notes, he trailed to a close. "It's going to be great." He hoped, at least. Assuming he and Autumn hadn't forgotten anything. Assuming Mother Nature cooperated and they got another batch of snow tonight. Assuming everything went as planned.

And then he'd get that Chamber job. Prove himself dependable. Finally be taken seriously.

"Now, readers of this article will mainly recognize your name due to your 'connection' with Randi Woodruff."

Oh well, so much for being taken seriously. "That is probably true."

"Tell me how a man goes from television fame to small-town event organizer."

He gets home and realizes he doesn't know what else to do.

The thought plunked like a kettlebell. One he hefted away as soon as it landed. Because it was all sorts of untrue. The job with the city was a perfect fit for him. It was everything he'd prayed for leading up to his return—a normal, sensible, respectable job here in his hometown.

Sounds boring.

He blinked. Was boring so bad?

"Blake?" Sissy's bleach-blond ponytail swayed as she prodded him. In her white parka and hot-pink earmuffs, she reminded him of a rink bunny at a hockey game.

"Truth is, I fell into that role. And while both Randi and I have acknowledged the situation certainly wasn't honest—I'm thankful for the opportunity I had to make such a great friend." He recited the same shtick he'd given during each interview that wandered into Randi territory. He paused, gaze drifting to the rink, the swirl of colors moving in disjointed circles. "But at the end of the day, this is where I belong. Whisper Shore is home. And this festival is a big part of our community."

Sissy chuckled and lowered onto the bench behind the rink. "You've got the art of the subtle redirect nailed."

"I'll add it to my résumé."

"Perry, are we set for photos?" She directed the question at her photographer on the bench beside her.

He nodded. "Mostly. Could use a few more skating shots."

Blake almost sighed in relief. So they were almost

done. "In that case, I'll lace up my skates." He wobbled to the bench on his blade covers and sat.

"Wait, one more question." Sissy waited until Perry moved into place by the wall, prepping for his shots. "I did a little pre-interview Googling on you. Got curious when I came across an online obit . . . for your brother."

The biting cold found flesh. Sissy's surprise comment iced through him, freezing any response or smooth topic switch of his own.

"I realized why your name sounded so familiar to me back in October when I first saw it in headlines. I went to U of M. Two years older than your brother. I was at the game when he led the team to the Big Ten championship. He was only a sophomore then, right?"

Blake chucked off his blade covers, letting them clatter on the cement. He nodded.

"I remember reading a few years later about him . . . passing away." She inched closer on the bench. "The obit said it was an accident. Car accident?"

He shifted, and his blades scraped against the cement. Ever since the media circus began, he'd been waiting for—no, dreading—questions like this. Amazing that they hadn't come earlier. After all, when Ryan first died, it had been all over the sports news. One of the country's most promising athletes . . . gone.

"Not a car accident." He heard the tightness in his voice, felt his nerves pull taut.

Sissy's mittened palm found his knee. "Whatever it was, it must have been difficult for you."

It was all he could do not to jump away. "Difficult. Yes." And then he did move away—just enough that her hand slipped to the bench—as if physical distance could also protect him from the pain her questions threatened.

"No wonder you left the country . . . and then took up with Randi Woodruff. You were looking for distraction, weren't you? Poor man."

And that's when he heard it—the lilt in her voice pushing through her reporter's probing. She wasn't digging for information about Ryan's accident.

"You could've found distraction a little closer to home, you know."

She was . . . flirting.

And what had started as snaking hurt slithered into anger. He jerked upward, ankles holding steady over the blades of his skates. "Listen—"

"Blake Hunziker, this is how you celebrate our month anniversary? Skating without me?"

Blake glanced over his shoulder. Autumn, fists on her waist and pout on her face. She gave the quickest wink. He read the *Play along!* in her expression as she came up to his side and gave him the kind of smile that, on another day, would've started a fire in his senses.

And on another day, he'd have slipped into the charade with gusto.

But thought of Ryan dissolved any playfulness he might've otherwise felt. His "of course not" came out feeble and dry, not at all worthy of the ruse he knew she was putting on just to save him from Sissy's flirting.

Despite his poor performance, though, it worked on Sissy. In less time than it took Autumn to drop her skates to the ground and wind her arm through his, the reporter muttered a "thanks for the interview" and hustled off to join Perry the photographer.

As soon as they were out of sight, Autumn dropped to the bench and pulled off her boots. "I am gooooood."

"You're also late."

"Yeah, sorry about that." She jutted her right foot into her skate. "It's been . . . a day. But I'm here now. And I just provided an exit route from what looked like an overly friendly interview." Left foot. "Unless . . . Wait, you weren't into her, were you? You looked uncomfortable, but—"

"I was." Except *uncomfortable* didn't begin to describe the tornado of emotions in the last ten minutes. Enough to induce a pounding headache and an energy drain that not even Autumn Kingsley's presence could revive.

Autumn stood. "As long as we're here, we might as well skate, right? Let's go."

As if on autopilot, he followed her into the rink, blades scratching over the nicks and grooves of well-worn ice. The laughter and Christmas music, the buzz of the overhead lights, it had all felt merry and carefree when he arrived an hour ago.

Now it goaded him, pulsing like the pain in his temple.

Autumn looked over her shoulder. "C'mon, Blake, keep up."

A kid slicked past him, bumping his side and throwing a "sorry" behind him. Blake could practically hear his own scowl. And Autumn's confusion as she watched and waited for him to catch up.

But instead of moving his feet to slide toward her, he fisted his hands inside his gloves and scraped his way to the rink's exit, ignoring Autumn's voice calling after him.

Why were sounds coming from the inn's kitchen at ten p.m.?

Autumn paused halfway down the open staircase, her palm sliding to a halt. Betsy had gone home an hour ago, but Autumn had stayed behind—hoping paperwork might help her forget about that mortgage statement from the bank, the fact that she'd once again failed to talk with Dominic Laurent . . . and Blake's disappearing act at the rink. It had been a déjà vu moment—too similar to Ava walking away from her earlier in the day.

But when she realized she'd been staring at the same spreadsheet for fifteen minutes, she'd finally given up and padded upstairs to turn out the lights and be on her way.

But then the sound of movement in the kitchen . . .

She heard the tap of a cupboard door closing—as if the intruder was trying not to be heard. She took another furtive step, turning her head to peer over the railing toward the kitchen. The line of sconces along the wall offered little light.

Maybe it's only Harry.

Except he'd said something about catching a movie tonight. Reaching the bottom of the staircase, she rounded the corner, hesitance slowing her movement. What if someone had broken in?

Autumn dropped her hand from her throat, padded to the recreation closet in the hall. She inched the door open, wincing when it creaked. They'd moved all the summer equipment to the outdoor shed earlier this fall, but maybe, if she got lucky, she'd score a left-behind baseball bat.

Autumn felt around the closet, fingers connecting with a handle. She pulled it free, stepped back into the light. A badminton racket. About as threatening as a baby bird.

Make that birdie. Ha. She clamped her fist to her mouth. *Hel-lo, burglar. No time for lame jokes.*

She lifted the racket and with one hand pushed herself through the swinging door. "Who's there—"

A grunt and a shower of white. Cloudy flour fell in a haze all around her. Only when the foggy white cleared did she see him.

Blake. Empty hands posed midair. Empty bag of flour at his feet. Narrowed eyes.

Autumn brushed the flour from her shirt. "W-what are you doing here? Raiding our pantry?"

Blake crossed his arms, his navy blue shirt stretching across his shoulders.

"I was not raiding your pantry. I brought my own flour, thank you very much." Which he'd very obviously dropped when she'd very obviously surprised him.

"How Betty Crocker of you. But why?"

He stepped aside, arm gesturing to the counter behind him. She stepped over the powdery puddle at their feet to survey his spread. Skillet. Eggs. Butter. Sugar.

"Crepes, Red. I was going to make you crepes."

"Crepes."

Blake sighed, ruffling the flour out of his hair. "The other day you said it's one of the things you couldn't wait for . . . for France."

Her eyes flitted to the creased paper on the counter— a recipe, one he must've printed from the Internet. She spun around to face Blake, badminton racket still dangling from her hand.

"I felt bad about abandoning you at the rink."

"If this is how you do apologies, you should ditch me more often." And after the day she'd had, his gesture felt all the weightier. She almost hugged him—even let herself picture it for an undisciplined moment: arms around his neck, chin against those ridiculously broad shoulders and forehead brushing against his scruffy cheek. Warmth trickled up her neck and into her face.

Suddenly the phrase "be still my heart" made all kinds of sense. "I, um, I . . . thank you," she finally forced out, then lifted her racket. "Guess I don't need this."

"Impressive choice of weapon, though."

"I thought you were a burglar."

"And you were going to attack me with that? Gutsy, but maybe consider a tennis racket next time."

She thwacked him—lightly, laughing—then abandoned the racket to the flour-covered floor.

"So how clean is the floor? We've missed our five-second-rule window."

Even after her ruining his surprise, he still wanted to make the crepes? She should back out, use her need for sleep as an excuse. Because every hour spent with the man was one more challenge to her ability to think logically—*I'm leaving, he's staying, it wouldn't work.*

But the words wouldn't budge from her throat. Not with his slightly crooked smile flashing her way and a streak of flour across his cheek. Instead, her feet carried her toward the pantry. "No worries. We've got all-purpose flour, bleached, non-bleached, whole wheat."

"Not whole wheat," Blake called after her. "I'm all for healthy eating, but *not* defiling crepes."

Autumn returned with an unopened bag. "How'd you know I'd still be here?"

"Your car's in the lot.

Blake cracked two eggs into the bowl. While Autumn watched, he added flour, milk, water, a pinch of sugar and salt, then whisked the mixture. "You'd make Betsy proud."

"I like to cook. I can make lasagna that'll have you feeling like you're in Rome sitting across the table from . . . um, some famous Italian. I can't think of any. Mussolini?"

Autumn leaned over the counter. "He was a ruthless Fascist. And he was executed."

He dropped a dab of butter into the skillet. "Please don't tell me your book collection includes a biography on him."

"Mussolini's favorite drink was a strawberry sherbet frappe. Doesn't sound very dictatorial, right? And near the end of World War II, someone was supposedly lynched by an anti-Mussolini mob just because he ordered the man's favorite drink."

Blake pointed a spatula at her. "Okay, you seriously need to get out more."

"What? I like reading biographies. I like learning about other people's lives, what makes them tick. I picture myself in their shoes." She leaned her chin on her fist. "I'd like to live a life worthy of a biography."

Blake stirred the batter. "You don't think you already do?"

She chuckled. "Um, no. Not a biography. Not even a . . ." She stopped.

"What?" He used a measuring cup to pour the thin, whitish-yellow batter into the skillet.

She slid onto a stool. "Well, my dad took thousands of pictures in all his travels. He had shoeboxes full. And

I remember when I was kid, sitting by him while he sorted through all the photos, organized them into piles and years, filed them into photo albums." The albums still lined one of the hallway shelves in Mom's house. "Some evenings he'd pore over those pictures for hours, entertain Ava and me with all his stories."

Blake looked up from the skillet, his eyes like dark chocolate, sweet and serious at once. "And you don't think you've lived a life worthy of a photo album."

He'd seen right through her. Did he have that ability with everyone . . . or just her? In the skillet, the batter crackled, tiny bubbles popping to the surface. "Let's just say I've never gone to scrapbooking night at the church."

She tried to infuse her voice with lightness, but it didn't blot out the intensity of Blake's study. She moved from the counter, looking for a broom to clean up the floor. And before he could carry the conversation further, "Want to tell me what happened at the rink today? Why you left?"

"Nope."

"Blake." She swatted the broom at the white powder covering the floor.

He ignored her, slid a spatula underneath a paper-thin crepe, and flipped it. It landed with a slap, and he gave a self-satisfied smile. "Hey, if my city job doesn't pan out and Betsy ever quits, you should hire me."

She stilled her broom and leaned against it. "You're not going to answer me, are you."

"The reporter bugged me. That's all." He reached for a banana.

Had to have been more than that. But as she watched him peel the banana, slice it into perfect rounds, she got the sense all the pushing in the world wouldn't make a difference. And maybe this, tonight, was as much about Blake distracting himself as apologizing to her.

The thought pulled at her heart. Blake carried more hurt inside him than he wanted anyone to see. If he wanted to ignore it, she'd pretend she couldn't hear the pulsing of his pain. Autumn finished sweeping while he flipped another crepe.

Then they worked together to slather Nutella over the thin pastries and dot them with sliced bananas before rolling them up. Blake plopped hers on a plate. "You first. Take a bite and tell me it's a masterpiece."

She bit into it—sugary bursts of perfection. Swallowed. "Whoa. Uh, yeah, masterpiece."

Blake nodded. "Good."

"No, like, for real—masterpiece." She pointed to the plate. "This is what you should be famous for, Hunziker. Not a silly fake marriage or town festival. I'm going to call that reporter and tell her about your crepe-making skills. Headline worthy."

She offered up the playful compliments through another sweet bite. But why wasn't Blake smiling? She was on her third bite when he spoke.

"She asked about Ryan." Blake's eyes were fixed on the counter top, but clearly it wasn't speckled granite he saw. "She asked about Ryan, and just like that . . . I was there."

Autumn swallowed, the crepe's sweetness melting away under the heat of Blake's honesty. Understanding swept in, and she set the pastry on her plate, debated less than a second before placing her palm on his arm. She felt the tick of his muscle at her touch.

"I thought it was what Ryan needed. Even though I did everything right—made him get a doctor's okay before we went up. You know, his knee injury and all." He raked his fingers through his hair, leaving a streak of white from flour. "What an idiot—worried about his knee when really . . ." He turned to her, downward gaze fastening on her. "He was such a mess. And I took him up in a plane and told him to jump. *I told him to jump.*"

"Blake—"

He spun away from her. "The second he stepped out the airplane door, I knew. Don't know how, but I did. And then Shawn . . ." He leaned over the counter, hands latching onto the edge and head down. A shudder rippled down his back.

And her heart split. She was at his side in a moment, one arm reaching behind him and her cheek finding his shoulder. She brought her other hand to his chest in a steadying side hug.

He took a shaky breath. "Oh, God, I wish I could take it back. He needed help, not a stupid, reckless—" He broke off suddenly, shifting into her embrace, arms crushing her to him. Autumn tasted the salt of her own tears as they stood there, Blake's breathing heavy enough to tell her he was trying so very hard to hold on to the last of his defenses.

Just let go, Blake.

She ran her palm up and down his back, wished for words to take away the pain. How could she have ever blamed Blake for all that'd happened? What kind of fool pointed fingers at a man like this, tenderhearted and hurting and—

He lifted his head, breath warm on her face, but arms loosening around her.

And something in her dreaded the release. "Blake—"

"Please don't say it wasn't my fault."

It came out a desperate whisper, halting her response and pulling her in until she did the only thing she could think of. Stood on her tiptoes, tilted her head . . . kissed him. Once . . . and then again, one hand finding his face, her thumb sliding over his cheek.

And then his hold tightened once more, and he kissed her back with a fervor that both scared and thrilled her. *Such a mistake. I'm leaving.* But she couldn't pull away. Her hands locked together behind his neck, and she melded to him.

Maybe I don't have to go.

The thought thumped through her at the same time as a cell phone blared into the silence. It was enough to thrust them apart, their shared surprise so tangible she could almost hear it along with the ringing of Blake's phone.

He pulled it from his pocket and checked the display. He jerked it to his ear. "Hey, Mom. Aren't you usually asleep by now?"

Autumn watched as the color drained from his face, his obvious alarm spreading to become her own.

"I'll be right there."

15

Why did her bedroom smell of bleach? A pang traveled through Autumn's neck and down her shoulders, but she couldn't make her eyes open.

You're not in your bedroom. You're at Mom's. . . .

But no, she wasn't there either, was she. Something jabbed her arm, and she realized it was her own knee. Why was she all pretzeled up?

Autumn forced her eyes open. The bright lights of the hospital waiting room fuzzed into view. Vinyl-backed chairs and waxy plants peppered the room. And she'd somehow slept through the low drone of the television hanging in the corner.

"Oh good, you're awake."

Autumn untangled her limbs, straightening in her chair, the voice behind her not registering. She rubbed the back of her neck, then turned as the woman sat down next to her.

Francie Hunziker. Though her hair was pulled into a neat braid and her clothing unnaturally unwrinkled, the tiredness in her eyes spoke of the long night she'd spent in the hospital.

"Um, is it morning?"

Mrs. Hunziker pointed to the clock above the waiting room's one window. "If you count four thirty a.m. as morning, then yes, it is. I still consider it the middle of the night, but I'm strictly a night owl. Blake is our resident early bird."

Autumn hadn't talked to the woman in years, though she sometimes caught glimpses of her on Sundays. They attended churches located just across the street from one another. Every once in a while Autumn had pulled out of Christ Community's lot just as the Hunziker SUV waited in First Church's drive.

How many times over the years had she silently chastised the Hunziker family? Wondering how the same family who'd publicly humiliated her sister sat in church Sunday after Sunday.

Her conscience needled her now for her harsh judgments. "How is Mr. Hunziker?"

"He's as stubborn as ever. Woke up an hour ago and insists he's ready to go home. We're so grateful—it was a very minor heart attack."

Autumn felt her breath release. "Oh, I'm glad. I didn't know if . . ." Her voice trailed as she thought back to last night. How long had she stayed awake waiting for Blake to reappear in the waiting room? The last time she remembered looking at the clock, it had been after one a.m.

"You mean no one gave you any kind of update?" Francie shook her head. "Blake came out here once, around two, and I assumed . . ."

She must have already been asleep. Though, come to

think of it, she'd dreamt of someone holding her hand, breathing her name . . . kissing her forehead? Maybe it hadn't been a dream.

"Well, good then. I was sticking around last night just to make sure everything would be okay. I guess I should be going."

Autumn reached for the purse she'd been using as a pillow, but Francie's palm on her arm stopped her. "Let me go get Blake. I'm sure he'll want to see you out."

And suddenly the events preceding last night's rush to the hospital came racing back in. Blake baring his heart. And that sizzling kiss. *Kisses.* Oh goodness, just the thought sent shoots of heat straight to her toes. Did Mrs. Hunziker notice the blush that surely had to be breaking over her cheeks?

And then he'd gotten the phone call. His face had gone white.

"I have to go," he'd said, thrusting his phone in his pocket and yanking the skillet off the stove.

"What's wrong?" She abandoned her broom.

"My dad. Heart attack."

He lunged for his jacket, thrown over the back of a chair, and started for the back door. She'd followed, not bothering to ask if he wanted company for the drive.

They'd left the place a wreck of spilled flour and burnt crepes. She should get back to the inn and clean it up before Betsy arrived and sprained a muscle at the sight of her kitchen.

Autumn stood. "I really should get—"

"Frankly, I'm almost more worried about Blake than I am Linus."

Autumn paused, purse pulled only halfway over her

shoulder. Francie stared at the TV. Her eyes glazed, and biting her bottom lip, she suddenly looked less the put-together wife and all the concerned mother.

Autumn lowered back into her chair, and at the movement Francie shifted her focus from the TV to the window. "He looked exactly the same last night as he did the day we picked him up after Ryan's accident. Pure shock and . . . shame. As if it were his fault. . . ."

Autumn's emotions curled, past and present swirling into one. Maybe it was the lack of sleep or the tears now pooling in Francie Hunziker's eyes, but suddenly all Autumn wanted was to find Blake. To make sure he was all right. To gather up all the hurt he'd ever felt and force it away.

Francie shifted in her seat, knees turned toward Autumn. "Why couldn't we see then how much he hurt? Ryan was already gone. All our attention should've turned to the son we had left. Instead . . ." A sob gurgled up her throat. "We let him feel like he was to blame. Everyone, this whole town and his own family and . . ."

Ava. Her mother. Autumn.

The truth of it slammed through her. Oh, sure, unlike Mom and Ava, she'd gone to the funeral. But she'd given Blake the scorching looks. Even without words, she'd contributed to the weight he carried—the hurt he'd exposed last night.

"I'm certain he knows you don't blame him. And he knows you love him, Mrs. Hunziker. He came back, didn't he?"

Francie pulled a Kleenex from her purse and dabbed her eyes. "But he's not the same person. He's caged up his free spirit. He's still taking on responsibilities that aren't his own. And he has no idea how desperately he's loved. No silly town festival or job or whatever misguided sense of the picket-fence life he thinks he needs could possibly add any more to that love."

"So maybe you should tell him that. You've shown him your love by throwing him a party and giving him a plane and when Linus talked the city into considering him for a job. But maybe he needs to hear the words."

Francie stilled then, smudged mascara raccooning her eyes until another swipe of her tissue cleared away the color. "From the mouths of babes."

"Huh?"

"Wise words, dear."

Oh. "Well, I'm twenty-eight, so I'm not sure I'd call myself a babe."

"My son sure would."

Autumn's jaw dropped at Francie's droll statement, especially on the heels of such emotion. But the woman's lips spread into a slow smile, despite the left-behind trails of her tears.

"I, uh . . ." The exit sign over the waiting room doors flickered and buzzed. Words gummed in her throat. "I really should get going. I left the inn a mess. Would you tell Blake I'm praying for you guys?"

Francie nodded as she stood. Autumn rose, and when Francie opened her arms, they hugged.

"Mom? Autumn?"

Blake.

She saw him over his mother's shoulder and pulled back. Disheveled hair, wrinkled clothes.

Francie glanced over her shoulder, then back to Autumn. "You know, dear, it may not be a bad idea to take a dose of your own advice." And then she turned, footsteps tapping as she moved down the corridor to Blake. Their brief words carried.

Linus was awake. He was asking for her.

And then Blake moved to Autumn as his mother went back. "Sorry you were here all night. I should've taken you home or something."

"I drove, remember?"

He looked to the floor, and she followed suit, her blurred reflection staring back at her from the waxed surface. There was last night between them. There was the oddity of her being here with his family. There was his mother's statement.

"Take a dose of your own advice."

As in, use words? But to say what? Any words she might offer would be tangled in a knot of confusion and uncertain feelings.

Except not as uncertain as you think.

Because Autumn could deny it all she wanted, but it didn't change the truth embedded in the whispers in her heart. Last night had been about more than comforting a hurting man. It'd been about her own desire, too.

Blake raked a hand through his hair. "I can't believe the festival starts tonight. There's so much to—"

She stopped him with her hand on his arm. "Don't worry about it. I'll take care of it all."

Because, Lord help her, she cared that much.

He should've seen the signs. Why hadn't he seen the signs?

The monitor beside Dad's hospital bed pulsed, its

numbers and lines Blake wasn't entirely sure how to interpret—and yet his anxious glance returned to them time and again in between staring at Dad.

Dad with the tubes in his nose and the IV in his arm.

Dad with the sallow skin and disheveled silver hair.

Dad who had been inching toward this heart attack for months, according to the doctor.

And Blake hadn't seen it.

His legs ached, and he stood, stretching, forcing himself to look away from the monitor.

Earlier, Dr. Trainor had said, "He's going to be fine as long as he slows down and modifies his diet. In fact, he should be able to go home tomorrow afternoon. Or, well . . ." He glanced at his watch. "Make that today."

Mom had listened calmly, taking notes and probably already formulating a new dietary regimen for Dad. It wasn't until the doctor left and he'd downed an entire cup of coffee—the first time he'd ever made it more than a few sips into the beverage—that he'd remembered Autumn.

He'd found her curled in a waiting-room chair and spent twenty minutes sitting at her side. He leaned over once to brush the hair from her forehead and press a kiss in its place.

She'd barely stirred.

"Francie?"

Dad's voice, raspy and weak, now sounded from the bed.

Blake dropped back into his chair. "Mom went out for a couple minutes, Dad, but I'm here." It was only the second time his father had awoken. "But I can go get her."

"That's okay." Dad shifted, turning his head toward Blake. "So I'm still here."

"And will be until this afternoon if Dr. Trainor has his way."

"He forgets I serve on the hospital board. If he . . ." He paused, waiting for his breath to even. "If he wants funds for that second X-ray machine, he'll release me when I say I'm ready."

For the first time since Mom's phone call, Blake smiled. "My father, playing dirty politics."

"And I'm not even ashamed of it. Hand me that glass of water, will you?"

Blake reached for the water and waited as Dad took a drink, then replaced it on the stand next to his bed.

"So I'm going to be okay?"

The monitor continued its rhythmic tune. "You are. Mom may never let you eat bacon again, but you're going to be okay."

The tease filtered from Dad's face. "I need you to do something for me, Blake. I was supposed to meet with Dominic Laurent this afternoon."

A groan rolled up from Blake's stomach. He still hadn't found a way to tell Autumn about Laurent.

No, instead he just lost it on her last night . . . then kissed her like a man starved. He didn't even know what to feel about that. Awkward? Embarrassed?

Thrilled?

Dad shifted against his pillows. "I don't want to put him off—not when we're this close to closing the deal. I need you to take the meeting."

His father was in a hospital bed. Of course Blake would do anything he asked. But why this? Why the one thing that was sure to disappoint Autumn?

"I haven't had much to do with the hotel. I'm not sure I'm the best person to—"

"He said . . ." Dad struggled to rise to a sitting position. Blake helped rearrange the pillows behind him. "He said one of the things he likes most about our hotel is we have the amenities of an urban hotel in the comfort of a small-town location *with* the feel of a family establishment. It's important."

Blake rubbed his hand over the stubble covering his cheeks, fatigue pulling at his mind and body. He wasn't the right person to represent the family in a meeting with Laurent. These days he felt more familiar with the running of the Kingsley Inn than his own family's business.

And if Autumn knew . . .

"Will you meet with him, son? One p.m. at the hotel. My accountant will be there as well."

He exhaled, the sigh coming from deep inside. This was why he'd come home. To be the responsible, dependable man Ryan would've been. To make up for lost time. "Of course, Dad. I'll be there."

"Good." Dad leaned back against his pillows. "Now tell me about the Kingsley girl."

Dad might as well have jumped from his bed and done a headstand. "What?" It's not like Blake had made an attempt to hide the amount of time he'd spent working with Autumn from his parents. But he hadn't figured it'd be a popular topic of conversation either.

"Come on, my health may need a little fine-tuning, but I'm not an idiot, son. You spend fifty percent of your time at her inn and the other fifty percent dragging her around town helping with the festival."

"Not dragging. We made a deal. I help her, she helps me. That's all."

"You mentioned her inn on that news show."

He'd seen that? "Yeah, about that. Sorry—"

Dad's laughter was hearty, despite his slight rasp. "And then there was your little road trip to Illinois."

Yeah, he seriously needed to get on that finding-his-own-place thing. Although it probably wouldn't make much difference. Whisper Shore operated like one big society page in an old-school newspaper. "Dad, I know what you're insinuating—"

"Oh, I'm not insinuating anything. I'm just plain asking. You two a couple?" A hint of sunrise filtered through the window blinds, washing over Dad's face in stripes.

"We're not." *Right? Then what was that kiss?*

"Well, if that changes, just know I . . ." Dad broke off for a moment, expression thoughtful. "I still regret how I reacted to Ryan and Ava's relationship. And I won't be making that mistake again. I never should've blamed her. But I think maybe it was easier pretending she pulled him away from the family, dragged him to all those parties . . . than acknowledging the truth. That the son I loved was making his own poor choices."

Blake rubbed his eyes, sleep tempting every muscle in his body even as the import of this conversation weighed on him. "I think I did the same thing, actually. I think it's why I didn't listen . . ."

His words jammed. He'd never told Dad or Mom . . . never told anyone, really, about that conversation with Autumn. But suddenly he needed to let it out. Confess.

He looked at Dad's pale cheeks and grayed eyes. Since

coming home, father and son had enjoyed a newfound bond. What he was about to say might ruin it all. Still . . .

"Back before Ryan's accident, Autumn came to talk to me. Her sister asked her to. Ava knew about Ryan's painkiller addiction, and she suspected it had escalated into heroin." Blake had later learned that was common for prescription medicine addicts who ran into trouble securing meds. "Ava didn't think I'd listen to her, so she sent Autumn."

He could still picture Autumn, her obvious discomfort. She'd been trying to be a good sister.

If only he'd followed her example. "I completely ignored her, Dad. I told her it was ridiculous."

Autumn had stood there, agitation expanding until she finally gave up.

And maybe it was the memory of that failure—*his* failure—more than anything that convinced him things couldn't work between them. Because he'd always remember how she'd given him a chance to help . . . and he'd brushed her off.

He looked at Dad now, waiting for the sigh of disappointment that was sure to come. But instead, Dad reached for his water glass. "Son, I think you need to know, *Ava* came to us. To your mom and me. We had the exact same opportunity as you. We had the exact same incredulous doubt as you."

Blake swallowed a gasp. "She did?"

"We didn't believe her, but we called him that same night. Asked if what his girlfriend told us was true. He denied it all, and I'm pretty sure that's the night he broke things off with her."

Shock bullied through him . . . and the tiniest taste

of relief. Didn't negate his own failure to help, but it certainly changed the flavor of his guilt.

"Thing is, Blake, your mother and I decided several years ago to stop focusing on what we'd lost and instead focus on the now. Dredging our shortcomings and regrets gets us nowhere. It's why I decided to run for office—do something new, you know?" Dad shifted in his bed once more. "And that's why I asked about Autumn. I want you to know you can have a 'something new' too."

His father's words cushioned the intensity of these past minutes. Dad cared, so much more than Blake had ever taken the time to grasp. "I do. That festival, the job the council mentioned. I'm finally focusing on my career."

Dad should like that, right? Why, then, the slight frown? "Yes, but . . . are you sure you're not just launching yourself at the first thing in front of you? Isn't that how you ended up in the Randi Woodruff mess?"

"What do you mean? It's a good prospect, settling down and working a good job. Finally contribute something to this town."

Dad lowered against his pillows. "I'm just asking if it's what you really want. Maybe I'm asking if you even know what you really want. I'll tell you this—whatever it is, it can't begin and end with trying to make up for a past you'll never change."

The statement cut through him, probably sharper and more biting than Dad had intended. He had no idea that he'd just told his son his entire reason for coming home was pointless.

That the one goal he'd set for himself was unattainable.

"Just think about it, will you? What do you want, son?"

And it was so clear then, the truth: *I don't know.*
He was still a drifter.

⟡

"Where have you been?"

The strain in Harry's tone skirted the edge of annoyance. Autumn's snow-covered boots tracked puddles into the inn's lobby, which probably wouldn't help the man's attitude. But she didn't have time for moods or complaints, joking or otherwise.

"The festival starts tonight. I haven't exactly been lazing around." Did her words come out as panicked as she felt? Blake had been telling everyone she was the so-called brains behind the festival operation. But the truth of it was, he was the leader. Blake might think this town doubted him, but he had a charisma people couldn't help but follow.

Autumn? All the volunteers had looked to her out at the town square and she'd only stuttered and fumbled, then escaped under the guise of picking up supplies.

I'm trying, Blake, but failing.

Then on top of it all, Harry had called her, insisting she hurry to the inn. Wouldn't tell her why over the phone.

"You look frenzied," he offered now from behind the front desk.

"Thanks, Harry. You're always so encouraging." Fire barrels. Somehow she needed to come up with five more fire barrels. And extension cords. "Everything's going wrong with the festival setup. We've bought out the hardware store's entire supply of extension cords. Please tell me we have some extras here. And . . ."

She paused at the sound of voices on the stairway. Guests. Guests who shouldn't see the inn's manager losing it in the lobby while she melted underneath the weight of her winter coat and the town's expectations.

Not to mention her own desperate desire to make a man sitting with his father in a hospital waiting room happy.

She gulped down the freak-out wiggling its way toward freedom and turned on a manager-like smile. "Afternoon, Mrs. Mills, Mr. Mills. Watch out for the wet floor."

Mr. Mills held his mother's elbow as they made the slow descent. The older woman and her devoted son were two of her favorite winter regulars, pure sweetness and smiles, the both of them. "Been playing in the snow, Miss Kingsley?" Jerry Mills paused as his mother stepped onto the same stair as him.

What Autumn wouldn't give for the money to put in an elevator. "You know me. Making snow angels, building snow forts."

Mrs. Mills laughed as the mother-son duo reached the bottom of the stairs. "Oh, Jer, I haven't made a snow angel in a decade at least."

The smell of Betsy's apple cider drifted in, along with the sound of Harry clacking away at his keyboard. Over the Mills's shoulders, she could see the fire crackling in the den's fireplace.

And suddenly all she wanted to do was sink into the inn's embrace—the warmth, the familiarity. Forget the burden of the festival and saving jobs and prepping for France. Just hole up in the three-story haven that, despite all its cracks and wrinkles, had an uncanny ability to soothe her nerves.

Had Dad ever felt this way? In all his desire to slip into his old life of travel and freedom, did he never hear the beckoning whisper of this place?

"Mother, remember your hip." Jerry's voice broke through her murmured thoughts. "I don't think making a snow angel is the best idea." The man led Mrs. Mills around the water-splotched entryway and toward the front door.

"I'm seventy-four, Jerry James Mills, not one hundred and four. I don't have a foot in the grave yet."

"But your hip—"

"Then *you* make one and I'll watch."

"You forget, Mother, I'm fifty-four, not . . . four."

Their voices trailed as Jerry helped his mother over the threshold and onto the porch. Reminded her of Blake walking Mrs. Satterly up the town square gazebo the night of the snowball fight.

"I'd like to see the looks on the faces of our other guests if we find Mrs. Mills and her son making snow angels on the front lawn," Harry mused from the front counter, chin perched on his fist.

"I'm just happy we have other guests at the moment. Now why the frantic phone call? Doesn't look like the place is burning down." And extension cords. Where could she find extension cords?

"Meeting room."

"Huh?" The small room at the back of the inn with the *Meeting Room* placard on the door hadn't held a meeting since . . . well, okay, never that she could remember. Instead, it was where they stored old furniture and items guests left behind. Dad used to call the place the "vacation graveyard."

"Go on back. You'll see."

"Seriously, I don't have time for mysteries. Especially not pranks."

"Kingsley, trust me. Shut up and go to the meeting room."

With an exasperated huff, she spun toward the hallway. Since when did employees boss around the boss? She should've demanded he tell her what was up before hurrying out. For all she knew, the festival setup had come to a grinding halt, and with the thing set to kick off in less than six hours. . . .

She stopped at the meeting room's cracked-open door, sunlight leaking through the sliver of an opening. Huh? Usually boxes were piled so high in the room, they blocked the window.

She pushed the door open.

And gasped.

Someone had cleared the room of its clutter, the gray-topped table and six leather chairs around it miraculously visible. A marker board spanned one small wall—had that always been there?—and a coffeepot gurgled from the corner.

"Total transformation, huh?"

Ava appeared from behind a white projection screen set up on the wall opposite the marker board. She walked through the tunnel of light from the wireless projector atop the table and approached Autumn.

"You did this?"

"Not just me. Lucy helped me empty the room, dust, and vacuum, and Betsy brought in the coffeepot." She held out a laminated and spiral-bound packet. "And you can thank Harry for this, believe it or not."

"'Kingsley Inn Report: History, Financials, Proposal.'"
She read the title, then met Ava's eyes. "A proposal for LLI?"

"Dominic Laurent will be here in about ten minutes.
Sorry you didn't have more notice, but turns out the
guy has an appointment this afternoon. And the festival
is going to keep you busy from tonight on. Better now
than never, right?"

Autumn dropped into the first chair in sight. Emotions
danced inside her—spinning too merrily to identify by
name, but each one engaging her heart. She was finally
getting her meeting with Dominic Laurent. Not because
of anything she'd done . . . but because of the people
around her who loved and supported her.

"I don't know what to say." She looked up at Ava,
holding her sister's gaze. "I mean, other than thank you."

Ava lowered into the seat beside her. "After yesterday . . . Well, I know this doesn't make up for anything,
but . . ." She shrugged, her voice trailing.

Autumn's own voice came out a whisper. "You do
know I just want to be sisters again. Like we used to be."

Ava leaned toward her, their shoulders bumping. "I
think we might be off to a good start. Brutally honest
conversation yesterday. Me doing a nice thing for you
today. Tomorrow you can braid my hair or something."

That was the old Ava peeking out, always reaching
for humor over emotion. But Autumn didn't miss the
softness in her sister's eyes.

"By the way, you also need to thank Mom."

A whole new layer of surprise draped over her.
"Seriously?"

Ava nodded. "I talked to her when she got home this
morning. I honestly don't think she realized how dire

things are here. You should've seen her jump into action. She'd be here still except she's meeting with some state tourism board members—guess Linus Hunziker invited them. She wasn't too happy about that. But helping you . . . It lit her up, Autumn."

It's like someone had flipped a switch in her family, and the joy of it flooded her heart with light. "Mom helped with all this?"

"We hatched the plan together and she got everyone else involved." Ava stood. "I know you've got this hankering to leave Whisper Shore, sis. But boy do you have a lot of people who love you here. Even snarky Harry."

Yes, so many people.

Hot tears pooled at the back of her eyes, and she blinked them away. *Not going to cry. Not now. Not when Dominic Laurent will be here any minute and this is my chance. . . .*

Her chance to thank Mom and Ava and everyone else. And she wouldn't let them down.

"Ten minutes, you said?"

Ava nodded again. "Might want to lose your coat, chug a coffee, practice your speech."

She'd been practicing in her head for weeks.

"I'll go wait for Dominic."

But before her sister left the room, Autumn looked up. "Hey, where'd you put all the stuff that was in here?"

Ava grinned. "Hauled it out to the cottage. Harry said once you leave, it'll probably serve as storage anyway."

Her cottage. Storage. Made sense, she guessed.

Didn't sit well, though.

She shook her head, shrugged out of her coat. Never mind. Time to make her pitch, make her friends and family proud. And save the Kingsley Inn.

16

Just finish this tour and then . . . sleep.

Exhaustion trekked through Blake, weighting his limbs and fuzzying his brain. He'd only slept a couple hours last night, folded like a piece of origami in the chair beside Dad's bed. The lack of rest taunted him now.

"How often do you host events in these meeting rooms?" Dominic Laurent peered into the largest of the Hunziker Hotel's conference rooms, his voice echoing against the beige walls rimming the spacious room.

Blake's focus fell to the iPad in his hand, on which Dad told him he'd find everything he needed to know about the hotel operations. So different than the little notebook Autumn carried around in her back pocket.

Even as his finger scrolled and tapped through the documentation, stubborn thoughts of Autumn refused to subside. How hurt she'd be if she knew he was conducting this tour. How angry.

True, he got a kick out of winding her up, watching

those sapphire eyes flash and a feisty response bubble from her.

But this was different. This was the stuff of betrayal. Harsh word, yes, but it was exactly what he was doing. After weeks of helping Autumn prepare her inn for the man who now strolled through the conference room—just a day after kissing her—he was stealing her financial opportunity right out from under her nose.

Never mind it had apparently never been hers to begin with.

"We draw two to three larger events and meetings per month. Smaller gatherings also reserve the space now and then—local groups, civic service clubs, that kind of thing. This room can be divided up into separate spaces, as well."

The Kingsley Inn had nowhere near this kind of meeting space. But what it lacked in corporate draw, it more than made up for in charm. The inviting den with the oversized fireplace, the comfortable dining room with its lingering welcome, a stunning view of Lake Michigan from every window on its north and west sides.

Stop comparing.

And stop with the guilt already. What was wrong with helping his father? Was it so horrible to look out for his own family's business, too? While Dad slept this morning, Blake had glanced through the budgets saved on the iPad, checked out reservations for the coming months. Things weren't nearly as dire as at the inn, but the hotel wasn't raking in the income either. Made him wonder how in the world Dad had afforded that plane still sitting in its hangar.

Dom strolled back to his side, a nod signaling his

satisfaction. "Very good. I appreciate the tour, especially considering your family emergency. I trust you will keep me apprised of your father's condition."

"Apprised. Right. Yes."

He finished the tour with Dominic less than ten minutes later, reciting the last of the information his father had provided and handing over a packet of financial information. They stopped in the hotel lobby, where guests milled at the full-service coffee bar lining one wall.

Dominic's phone rang then, and he excused himself to answer. Only when the man stepped away did Blake's focus shift to the scene outside the hotel windows, where festival preparations were in full swing.

That was where he needed to be. Helping Autumn. Making sure the festival went off without a hitch.

"Blake, my boy, what are you doing inside with all that's happening over in the square?" Kip Gable ambled over from the coffee bar, white apron peeking from underneath his winter jacket.

"Better question is what are *you* doing here?"

Kip held up an empty tray. "Guess you all were running short on pastries at your coffee setup and your chef was caught off guard. Hail the hometown baker. I was helping with the festival crew when I got the call."

"How's it going out there? Is Autumn overseeing things?"

"You should've seen her. Took charge like she was Wonder Woman."

Through the lobby's elongated windows, the colors of activity moved against a backdrop of white—clusters of volunteers setting up booths and arranging decorations, the square transforming in front of his eyes.

And somewhere in that organized mess of people, Autumn directed it all.

She's doing it for you.

The whisper glided in from who knew where, sending shoots of warmth from his core to his fingertips, despite the brimming argument that no, she was doing it for the town. To fulfill her responsibility as the co-coordinator.

She's doing it for you.

And here he was, giving a tour to the only man she was convinced could save her business.

"You should see her telling everyone what to do." Kip was still talking, hands swinging as accents to his words. "Hilarious. And then, of course, soon as we found out the electrical circuits couldn't handle any more, she got this idea for fire barrels."

Blake glanced over. "Fire barrels? In the middle of the park?"

Kip held up his palm. "Don't worry, she checked on ordinances, fire code, all that. Long as the barrels are grated at the top, we're okay."

But all that grass, the trees, wooden booths, the gazebo . . .

He shook the silly concern away. This was Autumn they were talking about. Smokey the Bear had nothing on her safety-wise. While he covered for his dad, she covered for him. And gratitude didn't begin to cover the range of emotions swelling in him.

Dominic returned then and Kip waved a good-bye.

"Thank you again for everything, Blake." Dom held out his hand and Blake accepted the shake. "I will look through these papers, but I'm confident your father will be pleased at the offer LLI is prepared to make. Please let him know he can expect to hear from me with a final proposal by Christmas Eve."

Blake's hand fell to his side. "Really. Christmas Eve." His words came out flat, more statement than question.

"No rest for the wicked, isn't that how the saying goes? Anyhow, we'll be in touch."

The man was halfway across the lobby before Blake blinked. "Wait, Mr. Laurent . . . Dom." He skirted around a startled guest, offering a quick apology as he lunged past.

Dominic turned, revolving door humming behind him, along with the clamor of wheeled suitcases rolling over the metal divider between door and floor.

Blake halted in front of the man, breath tight with hurry and doubt. *Dad wouldn't like this.* No, he'd hate it.

But the impulse was too strong to ignore—anchored in emotion and the scene outside the lobby window and the realization that Autumn had become as important to him as family. Uncanny, yes, but undeniable.

The woman who opened her home to a friend in need, who couldn't bring herself to follow her own dreams until everyone around her was secure, who spent her free time volunteering and talked about traveling with the wistfulness of a little kid standing outside a locked amusement park . . . She'd seen him. All of him—not just the Blake who'd early on earned a rep as the wild one, who globe-trotted and graced tabloid covers and flew the plane his brother had jumped from.

She'd crept past the barriers in his heart and taken up residence.

It couldn't be permanent residence. He'd have to let her go. He knew that. But right now, he couldn't detach himself from the idea that he owed her this. She'd offered him friendship. She'd given him a peek into her heart. She'd *kissed* him last night when he'd fallen apart in her kitchen.

He couldn't just sit by while her hopes dissolved.

"Yes, Mr. Hunziker?" Dominic's folded arms hinted at slight impatience.

"I wondered if you've given any thought to investing in the Kingsley Inn. You are staying there, after all, and . . ." He should've thought this through before blurting it out. But he couldn't let the man walk away without at least asking.

"You too?" Dominic's impatience slid into surprise.

"Me too?"

"The inn staff fairly ambushed me this morning. Pulled me into a meeting in a space they consider a conference room."

So Autumn had finally gotten to him. Was that pride pooling through him? "It's a great little place, don't you think?" Still needed some repairs, sure, but nothing a few more weeks and a good investment couldn't solve. In fact, he could list off exactly where he'd start with the larger of repairs right on down to the details.

Dom unfolded his arms. "Tell me something. Why ask me this? You are rival businesses, no?"

"Historically, yes. But a town like Whisper Shore can easily accommodate two upper-end lodgings. And Autumn is . . ." *Adorable. Stubborn. Perfect.* "A friend."

"I find business peers do not often make good friends."

"I find good friends more important than business."

"I see."

Blake doubted it, if the man's expression was any indication. Still. He hadn't turned to leave yet. Consideration— or maybe simply curiosity—held him in place.

"Look, I wouldn't ask this, except that I know how hopeful Autumn is to settle the inn's affairs before leaving. She wants to insure the Kingsley Inn stays open and is prosperous in her absence."

Dom's eyes rounded. "She's leaving?"

"She didn't mention that?"

"So she's looking for a financial investment to secure her own departure."

"What, no, that's not . . . She's had a great opportunity land at her feet." He could admit it, even if it bothered him.

"Owning a business is a great opportunity. Choosing to leave it behind is telling." Dominic's stance firmed. "Besides, I've seen the numbers. If I wasn't certain before, I am now. It would be a horrible investment."

Shock charged its way through Blake. He hadn't expected such outright refusal from the man, nor the lackadaisical disdain written in his features.

"And if you ask me, you'd be better off looking out for your own interests and that of your family's business rather than wasting it on an inn that will close by the end of next year's first quarter."

Blake felt the tick in his jaw intensify. He pushed out his question, voice raspy. "Did you . . . tell that to Autumn?"

Dom's stance loosened and he waved one hand. "Of course not. She will receive a polite letter of decline after I check out."

"Coward."

Slick with frustration, the word escaped before Blake could stop it. Heat coursed through him, and if he wasn't working so hard to keep his hands at his side, he'd be yanking loose the ridiculous tie around his neck.

"I'm sorry you feel that way." The calm in Dominic Laurent's voice was unnerving. Cold. His eyes narrowed. "I'm sure your father will be sorry as well."

The slap of the man's shoes sounded as he made his retreat.

Would it jinx things to call tonight perfect?

Autumn's gaze traveled across the town square. Christmas classics played over the speakers, and strings of lights hung around the gazebo and from every lamppost standing guard around the square. The rainbow lights ribboning the massive evergreen, though, wouldn't be lit until the tree-lighting ceremony later in the evening, when darkness veiled the park.

Fire barrels dotted the square and served as gathering spots where townspeople warmed their hands. The streetlights, too, glowed against the almost-dark sky.

And so many people. Families, groups of teens and adults, kids threading through the park. It was . . . perfect.

"Gotta love a town where we mix fire barrels and pine trees in the same event." Ava linked her arm through Autumn's. Lucy walked on the other side.

"People are having a good time, aren't they?"

"I'd say so. What'd you do? Spike the apple cider?" At Autumn's gasp, Ava giggled. "Just kidding. They're having a good time because this is an awesome festival. You did you a good job, you and . . ." She hesitated. "Blake."

Autumn dropped Ava's arm and turned to face her.

"Oh my goodness. Did you just say something halfway nice about Blake Hunziker?"

Ava cocked her head. "Halfway? I was downright complimentary. Which is how I *know* you spiked the cider."

"I just wish Blake could be here to see all this."

Lucy jumped in. "He is here. With his dog."

"I didn't realize. . . ." Autumn's fingers went to her hair, nonchalantly threading out wind-mussed tangles.

Ava cast her a wry grin. "I'd say something snarky, but you'd only deny it, so . . . never mind."

Fun seeing Ava so carefree. The shift felt seismic. "Ave, if I didn't know better, I'd say you were enjoying yourself here at home. Ever thinking about moving back?"

"You kidding? Coach Mac—he's the head football coach at the college—let me stand on the sidelines for every game this fall. I'm practically an unofficial member of the coaching staff. Got a good thing going there."

Autumn laughed at that. "I had no idea your football obsession would eventually turn into a dream job."

"Some people have dreams their whole lives. Others discover their dreams along the way." Ava shrugged. "C'mon, Lucy, let's go get some more of that cider."

Ava retreated with Lucy in tow. But before following, Autumn turned a full circle, gulping in the sight of Whisper Shore in celebration and Ava's words still knocking around in her mind.

"Some people have dreams their whole lives. Others discover their dreams along the way."

So what happened when lifelong dreams collided with—her gaze landed on Blake over by Petey's booth— new ones? She hugged her arms to herself and swallowed, suddenly tasting cold loneliness instead of her exhilaration from just seconds earlier.

Blake reached across the table and accepted a Styrofoam cup from Petey. Kevin stood obediently at his side, looking less a stray these days and more as if he'd belonged all along. *Maybe a little like the man himself?*

"He turned out mighty handsome, didn't he?"

Autumn dipped her gaze. Mrs. Satterly looked up at her from where she leaned on a cane. "Oh, Mrs. Satterly—"

"Don't even try to deny it, young lady. Eyesight's as good as ever since my optometrist upped my prescription. That boy could pose on the cover of a magazine."

He has. "Or star in a production of *Seven Brides for Seven Brothers*." The bottom of his plaid flannel shirt peeked out from underneath his coat, and he wore boots with his jeans. He obviously hadn't shaved since his night spent at his dad's bedside. Only needed a fur hat to complete the handsome lumberjack look.

She watched as Blake accepted a handful of marshmallows from Petey, then leaned down to let Kevin eat them out of his hand.

"Sweet of him bringing back all those photos of the farm." Mrs. Satterly nodded, then turned back to Autumn. "Even blew one up and framed it."

Autumn could believe it. That was exactly the sort of man Blake was—conscientious, caring, always going the cliché extra mile in a completely non-cliché way.

"Can I get you some hot chocolate, Mrs. Satterly?"

"I've already had three cups, my girl. No, you go talk to your man."

"He's not my . . ." *Oh, never mind.* First Ava, then

Mrs. Satterly. She might as well go talk to Blake. If she didn't, surely someone else would come along to prod her into it. Besides . . . she wanted to.

Just to see how his dad's doing. That's all.

Right. She couldn't even talk herself into believing her own lie.

With a steadying inhale, she moved forward until she'd reached him. She leaned over to pet Kevin first. Then, "Hey, Blake." She straightened, waiting for him to turn.

As he did, there was no missing the spark of pleasure flickering in his eyes. "Hey, Red." His gaze swept from her face down to her boot-covered feet and back up.

Kevin poked her leg with his nose, apparently hungry for more attention. She knelt and let him lick her cheek. "I didn't think you would be able to make it."

"Miss this? Dad's doing fine. And I couldn't have stayed away if I wanted to." He took a sip of his hot chocolate. "And I didn't, in case you're wondering. Want to stay away, I mean."

He'd slipped into rambling, and she had to work to hold back her own nervous giggle. *Don't be ridiculous. This is Blake. You've worked side by side with the man for almost a month now.*

But things were different under the moonlight. And a kiss they hadn't talked about—but which had lingered in the back of her mind all day. When Kevin backed away and she rose, she caught a whiff of Blake's subtle cologne floating on the breeze. "So what's up with your dad?"

"Came home this afternoon. He's worn down, but Mom will make sure he rests. Probably force-feeding him fish right about now."

Autumn wrinkled her nose. "Poor man."

"Poor Mom. I have a feeling she's in for a battle." He took another drink of the cocoa, then set the cup down. "Dance with me?" He nodded to the wooden dance floor set up in the corner opposite the grand tree.

"But the program's going to start soon. I should find—"

"Doesn't start for more than an hour. There's time." Blake reached for her gloved hand. "Petey, can I leave Kev with you for a sec?"

At Petey's nod, Blake tugged Autumn forward.

Over the speakers, Bing Crosby crooned "White Christmas" while couples moved in slow turns on the dance floor. Snowy boots shuffled and winter coats swished. Not exactly ballroom elegance, but the charming atmosphere mixed with the anticipation of the tree lighting filled the space with a merry aura.

"Did you know Bing Crosby originally sang this song in *Holiday Inn* before *White Christmas*?" Autumn asked as Blake pulled her onto the floor. She moved into his hold, one hand encased in his, the other on his shoulder.

"Nope. I'll store that away, though, in my trove of fun facts courtesy of Autumn Kingsley." They moved along perfectly in sync, melding into the dance with ease. "You dance well, Red."

"Even in snow boots?" Her black pants were tucked into the white fur-trimmed boots, which matched the glowing white coat that traced her figure to her waist, then fanned to her knees. Though she'd doubted he would make the festival opening, she'd dressed carefully—just in case.

"Even in snow boots."

They moved through the rest of the dance in silence

until the last strains of Bing's voice faded away. They were halfway through a second song when Blake spoke again. "Red?"

She looked up and for the briefest moment lost herself completely in Blake's dark-eyed gaze. "Yes?" Her breathy word seemed to teeter in the crisp air.

His hand slid down her arm until their fingers laced. "Come on, I want to show you something."

"But, the tree lighting—"

"They won't start without us. We're the coordinators, remember?"

He nudged her forward, stopping at Petey's booth to get Kevin, then pointing to his Wrangler. "But where are we going?"

"Patience, pumpkin."

She'd barely buckled her seat belt before Blake hit the accelerator, leaving the lights and sounds of the festival behind them. "This could be considered kidnapping, you know."

He flashed her a crooked smile. "I don't recall any real resistance, sweetheart. You could've called for help. You could've kicked me in the shin."

"Could've. Probably should've." And yet, there was no denying the delight puddling in her.

Didn't take them long to reach his apparent destination—the baseball diamond on the edge of town? "There a winter ballgame I don't know about?"

"The water tower, Red." He pointed to the gray structure profiled by silver moonlight. "Surely you came here in high school."

Uh, yeah. Not really her thing. She shook her head.

"I thought every Whisper Shore kid at one point or

another climbed the tower on a dare. Or . . . for something else."

Oh, now he got polite. "Just say it, Blake. It's the prime make-out spot in the county."

His exaggerated gasp fueled her laughter. "It's true. Some towns have theaters or scenic overlooks. We've got the water tower. But I promise, no funny business. I just want you to see the view from up there."

He didn't think she'd actually climb that thing, did he? "Yeah, not happening."

"You owe me. I made you crepes last night." He slid from the car but then ducked his head back in. "But if you're scared—"

She stomped from the car. "I'm not scared."

His head appeared over the car's roof. "Prove it."

"Fine."

"Really?"

"I said I'd do it, didn't I?"

She craned her neck to look at the thing once more. Her eyes trailed the narrow metal ladder that scaled the side of the tower to a small landing rimming the round structure at the top.

Blake's long strides led the way to the tower, hesitance dragging her own steps.

Oh, why couldn't she just tell the truth? That she'd rather roll around in a patch of poison ivy than climb that thing. Shave her head. Get her tongue pierced.

"It's not as bad as it looks," Blake said into her ear. Irritating how well he could read her. "There's nothing to it. Just don't look down and you'll be fine."

"It's going to be freezing up there. And with the snow, it could be a slippery climb. Is that really safe?" But Blake just kept walking. Autumn tipped her head back as they reached the tower's base and he stepped back and waved her forward. *Stupid, stupid, stupid.* "Aren't you going to go first?"

"I thought I'd go behind you. You know, just in case you need a little extra encouragement on the way up."

He couldn't go a minute without flashing that smug grin of his, could he. Her common sense told her to flee to the warmth of the car and climb in the back seat with Kevin.

But then she remembered Blake convincing her to sand-board. To spontaneously road trip with him to Illinois. To swing from a rope and land in a pile of hay. Every experience was one she knew she'd file away among her favorites. The man hadn't steered her wrong yet.

So with a deep breath she placed her foot on the first rung, hoisted herself up, and began climbing. One rung down. Two. Three. This wasn't so bad. Four. Five. Six. Halfway up she made the mistake of looking down. *Oh boy.*

"Just keep going," Blake called. "You're doing great."

"Tell me why I'm doing this again?"

"Because you trust your good friend Blake."

"Why is my good friend Blake talking in third person?"

"Why is my good friend Autumn not climbing?"

She tore her gaze away from the ground and kept climbing. A cold wind teased her cheeks, and the metal rungs chilled her fingers. But the exertion of the climb, the nervous fear burning through her, countered the cold.

And the knowledge of Blake climbing below her provided just enough security to keep her moving. Finally she reached the top of the ladder and pulled herself over the final step and onto the metal landing. The ladder jerked with her movement. Seconds later, Blake's form hauled over beside her.

"See? Easy-peasy."

Autumn huddled against the tower while Blake plopped down, letting his legs dangle over the edge of the landing, hands on the lowest bar of the railing encasing them. Finally Autumn moved from her crouched position to sit, legs crossed, and braved a look.

Though dusk shadowed the sky, the lights of the festival glowed from the center of town. Several blocks of dotted color and movement. And then off to the west, moonlight glittered against the lake. Stars peeked like distant pearls poking through the sky's blue-gray canvas.

The view was startling, perfect.

Blake dropped his arms from the railing, a satisfied smile stretching his cheeks.

This was perfect.

Almost enough to blot out the cold heaving past the fabric of her coat and clothes. Almost. She scooted forward, let one leg dangle, then the other, and huddled next to Blake. Eyes still on the landscape, he pulled her hand through his arm.

At least the cold was good for something.

They needed to get back.

But the festival had never seemed less important than in these past fifteen minutes. With Autumn tucked at his side, Blake could have stayed up there forever. Not the same as flying a plane, perhaps, but awfully close. The sky. The freedom. The peace.

The only thing blocking him from full contentedness—the remembrance of why he'd brought Autumn here. To tell her about Dominic. To spill the truth in a kinder way than a letter of rejection ever would. To break it gently.

But the soft sigh Autumn released into the breeze held him back. She was so . . . happy.

I don't think I can do it to her, God.

"Hey, Red—"

"Do you think—" She spoke simultaneously, breaking off just as he did, her hand still locked around his arm.

"You go first." Anything to put off the disappointment he dreaded.

"I was just going to ask, do you think Ryan and Ava ever came up here?"

"Oh, I know it." The landing jiggled under his laughter. "Once, Shawn, Tim, and I actually followed them here during spring break. As soon as they made it up, we started catcalling and whistling."

"Awfully mature of you."

"Dude, I was like nineteen at the time, and my brother was neck-deep in a forbidden romance. Of course I was going to heckle him."

"Forbidden, huh."

"Hey, don't tell me your mother liked the idea any more than my parents. It was a Montague-Capulet situation if there ever was one."

"You mentioned Shawn. He's the one who gave you the black eye, yeah?"

"You heard."

"It's Whisper Shore. Gossip is like oxygen around here."

"True." And yet, five years away had leached any disdain for the place right out of him. Maybe because for every harsh memory there were a hundred good ones. His first flying lesson with Ike. Summers marked by camping trips and games of pickup basketball. He and Ryan, never, ever bored.

And sitting with Autumn Kingsley atop the water tower. She was probably chilled to the bone, and yet she hadn't complained.

Either tell her or get back to the festival.

Can't do it. Not here. Not now, when everything felt so right. He'd tell her tomorrow. Or maybe Sunday, when the festival was over.

Maybe it wouldn't even matter to her as much as he thought. Maybe in her excitement for France, she'd shrug it off. Maybe.

He didn't like the idea, though.

The breeze played with her hair, stray strands tickling his cheeks. "Red, we should probably get back. The tree lighting and all that."

She nodded against his shoulder, another sigh feathering from her. And on impulse, he kissed her forehead. Grinning at her look of surprise, he pushed past his reluctance and scooted toward the ladder. "Follow me?"

She nodded.

No conversation on the way down. Just the clinking of their shoes against the metal rungs, the barest whispers of distant festival noise. Within minutes his feet sank into a blanket of snow, followed by Autumn's landing seconds later.

She turned from the ladder to look up at him. "Thanks."

"For forcing you to brave your fear of heights?"

"For reminding me how pretty Whisper Shore is."

Whisper Shore and something, someone, else.

And despite the choir of voices clamoring in the back of his head, belting out reminders that she'd be gone soon, that this friendship-turned-something couldn't possibly have a happy ending, he couldn't help what he did next.

He pulled her to him, lowered his head, and kissed her. Softly at first, but then with a surprise desperation that pulsed through him. And then she was kissing him back, her arms pinned to his chest as his tightened around her.

So maybe last night in the inn's kitchen hadn't been a fluke.

Her hands slid behind his neck, and in those seconds, completely lost in the feel of her, he could almost forget . . .

She's leaving.

You're staying.

With one palm holding her to him, the other combed through her hair as he kissed her again. Her lips, then her cheeks, her nose. "Stay . . ."

He whispered the word before realizing what he'd said. Or that he'd said it aloud. But as soon as it slipped from his lips, it just hovered there, the moment frozen.

Autumn blinked, breaking away but still so close he could feel her breath. "What?"

"Stay here. Don't go to France."

She lowered from her tiptoes, surprise—maybe closer to shock—drifting over her face. The cold tried to squeeze between them, but the warmth of her, the lingering feel of those sizzling kisses still heated through him.

And the burning request that he hadn't meant to make.

But that everything in him begged an answer for. Not just an answer. A *yes*.

"Stay, Red. Please."

17

Was it possible for one night to be both the best *and* most confusing Autumn had ever had?

Hand on the inn's front door handle, she glanced over her shoulder to see Blake's Wrangler motoring down the lane. Desperate to draw out their few minutes closed into the small space of his vehicle, she'd asked him to drive her out to the inn so she could pick up her car before returning to the festival. She'd left it at the inn earlier, having caught a ride to town with Ava.

It had been a flimsy excuse. As if five extra minutes, or ten, could help her make sense of her battling desires.

Autumn pulled the door open and stepped into the warmth of the inn. She closed the door behind her, then leaned with her back against it, biting her lip, remembering . . .

"Stay, Red. Please."

"Are you serious?"

As if sensing the import of this moment, the breeze had stilled, allowing her question to idle between them.

"I wouldn't ask if I wasn't."

She hadn't been able to look away, focus captured by the earnest glimmer in his eyes. She had the sudden urge to trail her fingers across his shadowed cheeks and jaw. And the realization of her longing caused her own flush to deepen. At least, in the dim of dusk, he couldn't see it.

But had he seen the trail of her emotion, its path dividing so many directions she didn't know which to follow? A piece of her longed to swoon in the romance of the moonlit night. Another piece moaned at the timing of it all. And then there was the piece that only wanted to kiss him again.

"I shouldn't have asked."

His words had been as soft as the snowfall salting the air around them. A snowflake landed and caught in his eyelashes.

"Don't say that."

"Wasn't fair to ask you."

Maybe not. But hadn't she lain awake each night for the past week wondering what it'd be like if she weren't going to France alone? If a very specific someone were to show up in Paris to take in all the sights and experiences and adventures with her?

But each night, she'd battled to silence her imagination. Because Blake had made it clear he had returned to Whisper Shore to stay.

His hold on her had eventually loosened, and what had been only a sliver between them widened into a gap. "I should take it back." He turned. "Forget I—"

And then instinct had taken over. She stumbled around him, hurrying to face him once more. "No, don't take it back."

"Don't?"

"Don't. Let me . . . let me think, all right?"

"Red—"

"Just don't take it back."

He swallowed, nodded, and held her gaze for another second until his lips spread into a slow smile. "So I kiss that good, do I?"

And then she'd thrown her glove at him. He'd caught it with one hand, and minutes later they were headed to the inn, the atmosphere between them crackling with tension.

"You all right, Miss Kingsley?"

Jamie's voice pulled her back to the present, hand still on the door handle behind her and the inn's heat layering over the warmth of her winter coat. Her college-student deskman had been working extra shifts now that he was on Christmas break.

"I'm fine. Just stopped by to pick up my car. Thought I'd check on you too."

Jamie's brow furrowed. "Check on me?"

Oh, the kid had no idea. A playful laugh escaped from her. "Jamie, it's time I let you in on the secret. I check on you most nights."

His eyes widened.

"It's important to me that you get a little sleep each shift. Don't want you falling asleep on your way to class."

She watched his jaw go slack and his cheeks turn pink. The guy had to be a heartbreaker at college. "I am sooo sorry. You can dock my pay."

"No way."

"But you know I sleep when—"

He broke off, and they both turned at the sound of

footsteps coming down the stairs, along with the thump of luggage banging against each step. Huh, she'd thought most, if not all, of their guests were still at the festival.

When the guest came into sight, she froze. Dominic Laurent . . . looking for all intents and purposes as if he planned to check out.

But she hadn't had a chance to follow up with him after the presentation. *Whoa*. Had that been just today? Yes, she'd woken up in the hospital this morning, given a surprise presentation to Dominic around lunchtime, spent hours at the square . . . then the water tower . . . and Blake.

Blake and his request.

"*Stay*."

"Dom, are you . . . going somewhere?"

He stopped at the front desk. "Yes, I have a red-eye flight to catch. I'd like to check out." He turned his focus to Jamie, as if dismissing her.

But . . . it didn't make sense. She'd asked him today if he planned to go to the festival. He'd given an off-handed "yes." Of course, then he'd run off for some other meeting . . .

What other meeting would he have had in Whisper Shore?

And for heaven's sake, why was he checking out now?

"I thought you were going to the festival. The tree lighting should be starting in about fifteen minutes. I have to hurry back myself. I could give you a ride, and—"

He slapped his room key on the counter and turned to her. "Thank you for the offer, but as I said, I have a flight to catch."

Maybe he planned to follow up with her by phone. Or e-mail. Yes, maybe that was it.

"Well, I truly appreciate the time you gave me today."

"Oh, speaking of that." He reached around to the leather computer bag hanging over one shoulder and pulled out the spiral-bound packet she'd given him today, the one Harry had put together. "I might as well give this to you now."

He wasn't taking it? "Oh, but it's yours to—"

His sigh broke in. "Miss Kingsley, I planned to have my secretary contact you, but, well, since you're here it may be best just to tell you. Laurent Lodging is not interested in your inn."

All the warmth, all the giddy hope brimming in her from earlier in the evening, now fizzled. "*Not interested in your inn.*"

"I know we need a few repairs, and the financial statements don't look wonderful but—"

He plopped the packet on the counter. "You don't seem to understand. I didn't come to Michigan to see your inn." He spoke slowly, as if giving her time to swallow and digest each word. "I came to look into the Hunziker Hotel. We've been considering a Great Lakes location for some time now and that property seemed promising."

"Oh."

Oh.

The Hunziker Hotel. He'd never had any designs on the Kingsley Inn.

"Although, if it makes you feel any better, it's looking unlikely that I do any future business with *that* hotel. Not after the way Blake Hunziker treated me today."

Her breath seized. Blake? Today? No, he'd been at the hospital all day today, hadn't he?

"One minute he was giving me a tour. The next, he was hurling insults."

Autumn barely heard the last part, her mental wheels stuck and skidding on the first. "He gave you a tour?"

"He did, yes."

And the truth of it came barreling in. "So he knew . . . he knew you never intended to invest in my inn."

Dominic nodded slowly. "That would seem to be the case."

He knew . . . hadn't said a word. Even when she'd told him all about today's presentation while they drove back from the tower.

The scent of the potpourri on the front desk, or maybe the overbearing spice of Dominic Laurent's cologne, assaulted her senses. And the heat she'd felt earlier turned to an icy chill.

"Miss Kingsley?" Jamie's voice.

But she couldn't answer him. Because any attempt would spill the agony pooling inside her.

Laurent turned away from her. "I'd like to check out, please."

And she took the opportunity to make her escape.

"Where've you been?"

Tim Jakes met Blake seconds after he parked his car and slid from the front seat.

In the hour since he'd left the festival, dusk had turned to full-on dark, streetlamps and Christmas lights now carrying the load of lighting the festival grounds. And the fire barrels, too, drawing clumps of people who mingled and laughed.

"Seriously. Where ya been?" Tim matched Blake's pace as they crossed the square.

"Oh, man, things are happening. Big things." Things he hadn't planned on.

Like kissing a beautiful woman silly and then asking her to forget France and stay in Whisper Shore, with him.

Crazy.

Just like he'd promised himself he wouldn't be anymore.

But it had felt so right.

And she hadn't said no.

After dropping Autumn at the inn, he'd stopped at his parents', let Kevin into the house, and checked on Dad before returning to the square. Snowfall had thickened on his drive back to the festival, turning the grounds into a picture of winter perfection. When they got the tree lighting going, it would be all the more picturesque. He could already taste the success.

Except he still hadn't had a chance to chat with the state tourism board members Dad had invited. Soon as the tree lighting was over, he'd find them.

"What things are happening?" Tim asked the question as they reached the gazebo.

"Awesome things." Awesome if Autumn decided to stay, that is. And, well, maybe even okay if she didn't. Because those kisses . . . Oh boy . . .

"The tree lighting was supposed to start fifteen minutes ago. People are getting antsy."

"Dude, chill. We just have to wait for Autumn to get back from the inn. She should be here any minute."

"Then as long as we're waiting, wanna tell me why you're grinning like an idiot?"

"Been a good night. That's all."

"Really got the cryptic thing going on, don't you."

No, he just didn't kiss and tell. Not when the woman in question had completely captured his heart. And apparently his common sense. To think, he'd actually taken her to the water tower with the intent of telling her about Laurent.

Oh, but this was so much better.

"Hey, wasn't your dad supposed to emcee the ceremony? Who's going to do it now?"

"Guess I will."

"Know what you're going to say?"

"Uh, thanks for coming?" And then he saw her, Autumn, marching all cute and determined his direction.

Only she wasn't smiling. None of the blush in her cheeks or soft delight in her eyes. She looked . . . angry.

Tim whistled beside him. "Looks like you're in trouble, Blake. What did you do?"

He had no idea.

Okay, not true. He knew what he'd done. Bundled up all his feelings into the one wild request he'd laid at her feet. "*Stay . . .*"

But she hadn't seemed upset by it. Not then anyway.

"Look, I'll go tell the AV guys we're about ready to get started." Tim jogged from the scene, disappearing just as Autumn reached him.

"Hey—"

She cut him off with a chilling glare. "How could you?"

Perhaps it was a slow reaction. Perhaps the reality of

what he'd asked her simply hadn't set in until now. But was it any reason to get mad? "I thought . . . I know it was sudden, Red. You told me not to take it back, though."

She shook her head, hair spilling over her shoulders. "Not that. Dominic Laurent."

Oh.

"He was checking out when you dropped me off at the inn."

Blake felt like decking the guy.

He felt like decking himself.

He should've told her. He should've told her the day he found out. "Let me explain—"

"Explain what? That you conveniently decided not to tell me you knew the man had no interest in my inn? No interest whatsoever. His words, not mine."

People were starting to turn. Autumn's voice raised with each hurled sentence.

"All those times you let me go on talking about it—my hopes, all the work we were doing solely to impress him."

"Red, can't we talk about this later?"

"And stop calling me Red. Did you think if I knew I'd try to steal him away? Should I be flattered that you actually thought of the inn as competition?"

And now his own anger reared its ugly head. "You don't seriously believe all that, do you? After all the ways I've helped you out. The repairs. The bank loan."

That froze her in place.

"Yeah, I made the call to Hilary and then her brother who got the loan officer on board. After all that . . ." Not to mention, his conversation with Dominic today, when he'd put his father's own goals in danger by asking Laurent to consider the inn.

And she was standing here, accusation radiating from her. Just like . . .

Just like the day of Ryan's funeral. When her burning expression had drilled into his after the service, when she'd spun on her heels and retreated before he could talk to her.

He didn't deserve it. Well, maybe then, but not now.

"We're not doing this now, Re . . . Kingsley. We have a tree to light."

"I don't care about that."

"Well, I do." He marched past her, eyes on the extension cord and the outlet. They'd skip the fancy speech. The lights and music would have to be enough, because no way could he push out a slew of pretty words when his insides burned. He nodded to the AV guy.

"Blake, I need to know why you didn't tell me."

He ignored her, swiped the plug from the ground, and knelt near the power strip. He raised his hand to signal the deejay. The first line of Christmas music rang out. And he jabbed the plug into the first outlet he saw. Mere feet away, the tree lit up their surroundings, with bright white and patterns of color. And the *ooh*s and *ahh*s of the crowd joined the strains of music.

And the crackle of sparks.

Oh no. No . . .

He jumped away from the power strip on instinct, sparks leaping from the thing.

And the crowd's cheers turned to gasps. He heard Autumn's squeal behind him.

In nightmarish slow motion, the sparks leapt from his feet with another large pop and landed on one of the evergreen's branches. At the same time, bulbs popped one by one as too much electricity pulsed through the wires.

He heard someone yelling to call 9-1-1. Felt the movement all around him as people sprang into action, parents gathering their kids, a general sense of panic spreading.

And in front of him, the centerpiece of the Christmas festival, the historic evergreen, caught on fire.

*

The smell of smoke and ash hovered over the town square like a foggy morning mist. Blake rubbed the back of his neck.

The lingering smolder burned his eyes—or maybe that was the lack of sleep. Cold had long since given way to numbness.

The sounds of the fire crew packing up echoed in the background, but they moved as if in a hush. They'd fought the blaze valiantly, but fire had gobbled the tree as if starved. Now, two hours later, all that remained was a pile of burnt wood and a stump, embers still flickering in tiny dots of orange.

A palm clapped onto Blake's shoulder. "Two of our guys will stick around 'til morning to keep an eye on things, Hunziker. You should go home now." Soot marred the face of the fire chief in streaks of black. He squeezed Blake's shoulder. "It could've been a lot worse, son."

As the man walked away, Blake took in the rest of the park. After the initial rush of the fire's outbreak, the festival attendees had been surprisingly ordered. Booths were moved, people ushered away, the gazebo doused in water to prevent the fire's spread.

Blake bent over to pick up a toppled chair and set it upright.

"He's right, you know."

Blake turned. *Mrs. Kingsley?* Autumn's mother stood a few feet away, white hair glinting in the dark and long coat whipping around her knees. "Excuse me?"

"It could've been a lot worse. No one was hurt. All we lost was a tree."

Victoria Kingsley wasn't seriously trying to cheer him, was she?

He shook his head. "A tree and all the revenue we could've made tomorrow."

She crossed the distance to stand in front of him. At closer range, he saw the barrette loose in one side of her hair, the dirt streaked across the front of her coat. Had she stayed all this time helping clean up?

"Tomorrow's still going to happen. I was just talking to some of your committee. They're—we're—going to work through the night."

"But . . . but who's going to come? People will hear about the fire and assume—"

"Don't you use Twitter? Facebook? We'll get the word out, Blake. Besides, the fire probably has people more interested than anything. Someone told me a video of the sparks hitting the tree is already on YouTube."

Great. Another public memento of another public failing. His lot in life, it seemed.

And why on earth was Victoria even talking to him?

"I heard about Linus. I hope . . . he's all right."

He wouldn't have been more surprised if one of the firemen had turned a hose on him. Had the fire affected Victoria's memory? Did she not remember the way Dad lambasted the Kingsley family and their inn countless times over the years? Used his role on the city council to deny their requests for things like parking lot expansions or zoning changes? Probably worst of all, kept Ava from Ryan's funeral?

But she just stared at him now, waiting for a response. "Dad's . . . all right."

"Then I wonder if you could tell him something for me. The reason I voted to table Whisper Shore's funding request to the tourism board wasn't out of spite. If the city just would've waited, they would've received a memo asking them to reapply at the start of the state's budget year—when our allocation dollars would be refreshed. What's left in this fiscal year's pot isn't worth competing for. Plus, we're moving to a new granting system next year—fewer awards, larger amounts."

Blake tried to make sense of her words. If he understood correctly, she was saying she'd been trying to help the city all along. "So, Dad prompting the board members down here . . ."

She shrugged. "Premature."

And maybe, probably, much worse considering what they'd seen tonight. If he hadn't felt horrible before . . .

But Victoria's expression held sympathy rather than judgment. Maybe even . . . compassion. Somewhere, beneath the humiliation he wore like a straitjacket, curiosity beckoned. But he was too exhausted to follow up on it. Instead, he only nodded. "Thanks. I'll tell Dad."

Victoria started to move away, seemed to think better of it, and halted. "Tonight was a blip. Just . . . do better tomorrow. That's all you can ask of yourself." With that, she retreated.

And Blake's gaze returned to the pile of rubble that was once the centerpiece of their festival, guilt and disappointment cavorting through him. He raked his hand through his hair, ash on his fingers when he pulled them away. That's when he noticed Autumn—white coat and boots now splotched with dirt and ash as she sat on the steps of the gazebo.

Have to talk to her sometime.

Had it only been a few hours ago he'd sat with her atop the water tower? Kissed her? Asked her to give up her dream for . . . him? What a joke. A man who couldn't even pull off a little community event.

Still, you have to talk to her.

His feet propelled him forward. When he reached her, Autumn looked away, eyes glassy—from smoke or tears? Probably both.

He sat down beside her. Instead of the magnetic pull between them from earlier in the evening, a seemingly uncrossable gulf expanded in the inches separating them on the step.

"I'm sorry, Autumn. I know it doesn't change anything, but I am sorry. About Laurent." And everything.

She opened her mouth. Closed it. Opened it once more and sighed. "I know you are. What I don't know is . . ." She finally looked at him. "What I was thinking. What we were thinking."

"Red—"

Her eyes pressed shut.

"What I said earlier—"

"I have to go, Blake."

And he knew she didn't mean now. She meant weeks from now. *Go* as in *to France*. "I know."

Really, he'd known it all along.

Didn't lessen the sting of it, though. Or his need to say the words he should've said earlier, in place of his stupid request for her to stay. "I've traveled all over the world, Autumn. Had some incredible experiences. But I . . . I still felt empty after it all. It's why I came home."

The sound of one of the town's fire engines groaning to life rumbled through the park.

"The truth is, I would've felt empty anywhere. I realize now that through a million moments of adventure and excitement, I was only trying to make up for the one moment I wanted to forget." He heard her intake of breath. Couldn't look at her. Forced out the kicker. "The difference between you and me is, I was running away from something. You're running toward something. To a future and a dream you deserve."

He watched a lone tear track down her cheek. But she didn't argue. And as much as everything in him begged to reach for her, he grasped for self-control. This was right, this good-bye. Any kind of physical contact at all would only make it worse.

So he stood, chill upon chill heaping through him. "Bye, Autumn."

She looked up, sniffled once more. "Bye, Blake."

And before he lost his willpower, he turned, feet crunching through snow and debris, breathing tight—each inhale hurting his chest. Then, because he needed the distraction to block out his conflicting emotions, he pulled his phone from his pocket. He checked the time. He checked his texts. He checked his voice mails.

And felt the last of his resolve crumple at the last one. Kevin's owners wanted their dog back.

18

"Does everything make sense, Autumn?"

The papers in front of Autumn were a jumble of numbers and legalese. Grady Lewis had reviewed every line with her in between sips of coffee. Autumn's own mug was empty. For once, the smell of the brew didn't tempt her—nor did the scent of Betsy's cooking wafting from the kitchen.

Probably one of the last meals she'd cook there. The full staff would gather in the dining room at noon. One more meeting. During which she'd spill the news they surely already knew.

"Autumn?"

She started at Mom's voice beside her, the hand on her knee. "Yes, it makes sense."

She should've done this in the privacy of Grady's office. But something in her needed to do it at the inn. Needed the cold, hard dose of reality.

Without the investment from LLI, she had no way to make her bank payments. So as of January 15—two days from now—her loans would go into default. The bank would begin the foreclosure process. Grady had explained that she could fight it, could request extreme measures. He believed the small-town bank might still work with her. But she'd tried. Failed. It was time to move on.

And by month's end, the Kingsley Inn would close its doors.

Out in the lobby and over in the den, Harry, Uri, and Charlotte worked together to dismantle the Christmas decorations. She'd left them up longer than normal—in a feeble attempt to squeeze every last ounce of cheer she could from the holiday season before facing the inevitable.

The glint of sunlight bouncing off layered snow flooded the dining room. Autumn blinked against the assaulting brightness and did her best to take in the rest of Grady's explanation of what would come next. But emotion made it difficult to pay attention. She was so tired.

Thank goodness Mom had offered to help with the transition—especially with Autumn moving a continent away next week.

Fifteen minutes later, Grady was packing up his brief-case, offering them one more consoling nod, then leaving through the lobby. A hush fell over the table, only the muffled sound of Harry disassembling the Christmas tree from one direction, pots clanging from the other.

Mom rose. "Come on. Let's take a little walk."

"And go where?"

"Just come."

And because arguing felt like too much work, Autumn

stood and followed Mom from the room. She trailed her through the lobby—past the check-in desk, where they'd stopped taking reservations—up the staircase, her hand gliding over the banister Charlotte insisted on polishing even though it wouldn't matter any longer. Instead of stopping on the second floor, Mom continued to the third.

She opened the door to the suite where Dominic Laurent had resided during his stay. All the furniture sat in its usual place, a listless pallor clinging in the air.

But Mom seemed to take no notice as she padded across the carpet Blake had helped lay in the days before Dominic's arrival—adding an extra sting to the day. Autumn hadn't seen him for nearly three weeks.

Three stretched-out, achy weeks accented first by Christmas and then New Year's. She'd done her best to smile her way through the holidays—chuck off the heaviness of losing both Blake and the inn. She'd celebrated at home with Mom and Ava on Christmas, attended a party at Betsy and Philip's on New Year's Eve, hung out with Lucy, and attempted to be as excited as everyone else during the countdown to midnight.

After all, this coming year should be *her* year. Would be. She just had to get through a slew of good-byes. Starting with a farewell to a brick-and-mortar friend.

Mom stopped in front of the panoramic windows with a spectacular view of the lake. She pushed aside the sheer curtains, letting in a hazy light. "Always my favorite spot in the inn. Your dad and I actually spent our honeymoon in this room."

Autumn reached Mom's side. "Really? Didn't know that."

Fingers still wrapped around the curtain, Mom spoke with her gaze on the view. "He really loved this place at first. But after a few years . . . all he felt was resentment. And he started talking about selling."

After only a few years? That meant Dad had already been unhappy at the inn when Autumn was a kid. And she hadn't realized . . . "Why didn't he?"

Mom lowered to the window seat. "Because every time he brought it up, I argued. I'd talk about his grandparents and how hard they worked to build it. I think I thought holding on to the inn meant . . . holding on to him."

Mom's confession landed smack in the middle of Autumn's own resentment, causing cracks in what she finally recognized as her own complete misread. All these years since she'd overheard that conversation between Mom and Dad, she'd wished Mom would've made some kind of stand, wondered why she seemed to care more about the inn than her broken marriage.

But it was so clear now. Mom had been fighting all along, in her own way trying to hold on to her husband.

Autumn sat. "Mom, I—"

But Mom shook her head. "The thing is, I've been doing the same thing with you." She let go of the curtain and turned. "Signing the inn over to you was my way of holding on. It wasn't fair to you. And I'm truly sorry."

A honeyed feeling drizzled through Autumn, sweet, filling gaps in her understanding and oozing over the emotional dents of these past few years. How many times had she wondered if God still saw her, tucked away here in Whisper Shore, and yet . . . had she ever really seen Mom?

"I know you and Dad were talking about splitting up

before he died." She said the words softly, looking for surprise on Mom's face.

But Mom only nodded. "I wondered."

"And Ava left so suddenly." Although this last time, there'd been something different about the good-bye after Christmas. It had been a long time since she'd seen her sister loosen up, slip back into life in Whisper Shore while home. It seemed Ava was on her own journey these days. "Anyway, I'm sorry I'm leaving now, too, and—"

Mom stilled her with one palm raised. "No, don't apologize for stepping into your new adventure. It may have taken me a long time to let go—not sure I actually have just yet—but I'm proud of you. As for your father . . . it wasn't the first time he talked about leaving, Autumn. He always changed his mind. I like to think he would've changed again if he hadn't . . ." Mom's voice cracked, and Autumn inched to her side of the window seat, placed her arm around Mom's shoulder.

The stillness of the room, the gentle snowfall outside the glass doors, matched the peace trickling through Autumn. One conversation and she felt closer to Mom than she had in a decade. And something told her even her upcoming move wouldn't change this.

"Mom . . . thanks." *And thank you, God. I needed this so much.*

Those few minutes with Mom felt like a direct answer to prayer. And the kind of reminder she couldn't ignore. God hadn't forgotten her. He knew exactly what she needed.

And when she needed it. She'd thought losing the inn meant leaving a mess behind her, glaring and public evidence of her failure to live up to the Kingsleys who'd come before her. Yes, it'd take a while for that sting to ease. But a new place in her relationship with Mom was a better soothing salve than she could've imagined.

A couple quiet moments later Mom took a deep breath and straightened her shoulders. "I can smell Betsy's meal. Your staff is probably gathering."

"Stay for the meal and meeting?"

Mom grinned, closed the curtains and stood. "I'd love to."

After so many seasons away, Blake had forgotten the way winter had of teasing its way over the landscape . . . and then suddenly pouncing and holding tight in an icy vise grip.

The same cold that turned Lake Michigan to a bed of white stung his cheeks as his boots crunched over the latest round of snow. He burrowed his chin into the high neck of his warmest coat, its collar brushing against his stocking cap. At his side, Kevin bounded along—one of Christmas's better presents. When he'd talked to the dog's owners, they'd expressed only frustration about the hassle of a pet. Somehow by the end of the phone call, he had himself a permanent canine pal.

Sunlight sparkled against the snow, off the surfaces of gravestones peeking through the cover of powder. His nose and cheeks were nearly numb. Probably would've been smarter to drive out to the cemetery, but he'd needed the time the walk provided. He'd put this off ever since coming home. It wasn't an errand to fit in or a to-do to check off a list. But somehow he felt he owed it to

Ryan—especially since he hadn't stayed in town long enough after the funeral to even see the gravestone.

His footsteps and Kevin's paw prints marked a trail along the east edge of the cemetery, past the veterans' memorial near the center, down to the curved black granite stone resting underneath a bare-branched maple tree.

His steps slowed as he neared the stone. Snow covered the beveled surface of the gravestone and fell in a curtain over its face.

Blake came to a stop. With one gloved hand he cleared the top of the stone, then brushed his palm over the front until the words came into view.

Ryan Hunziker
December 27, 1985 – June 24, 2008
Beloved Son, Brother, and Friend

He'd expected the lurch of emotion—it's why he'd put this off so long. But not this searing, gut-wrenching pain. "Ryan." He whispered his brother's name at first, and then repeated it. Louder this time. Almost a croak as his throat caught. "Ryan, why didn't you tell someone?"

The gravestone only stared back at him.

"We would've helped you. *I* would've helped . . ." The rush of anger wasn't anything new. But allowing it to soak in this time instead of pushing it away, that was new.

"I'm mad at you. Do you hear me? So . . . mad . . ."

If Ryan had only told someone.

If Blake had listened to Autumn.

If God hadn't taken him away.

Why did you take him away?

Suddenly he was on the ground, knees digging into

the snow as liquid pooled in his eyes. *He was my best friend. My brother.* And then his face was in his hands, the leather of his gloves catching his tears as sobs shook his body.

He didn't know how long he'd knelt there, hurt squeezing his lungs and wringing his heart, twisting until he was one giant open wound. Raw and emptied.

Finally, he swiped the back of his glove over both eyes, tears forming icy flecks on his eyelashes. He squeezed his eyelids closed, waiting for the last shudder to peel through him. Beside him, Kevin nudged his nose into Blake's arm.

He took a long breath, reached one hand to touch the stone. "I miss you."

I miss him, God.

A breeze sifted through the trees dotting the cemetery, carrying the whisper. "*I know. I see you, and I know you.*"

Blake tipped his head back, letting the cold sweep over his cheeks. It was true, wasn't it? He could run to any corner of the earth or escape to his lakeside home. It didn't matter. God still saw him. Knew him. Intimately, even more than Ryan ever had. More than Autumn. More than his parents.

You see me and you know me. You know the hurt I've been running from.

He wiped his eyes once more and stood, brushing the snow from his knees.

And you love me.

He swallowed.

"And I saw Ryan. And I knew him. And I loved him."

The assurance feathered through him. He'd spent years blaming himself for not recognizing the signs. Not seeing what was really happening with his brother. But Ryan had never been invisible to God. Oh, how he hoped Ryan had known that in the end. That somehow, even in a drug-induced haze, he'd felt God's embrace in those last moments.

"Son."

Blake jumped, snow squeaking against the soles of his boots as he turned. Dad strode toward him, his Ford sedan parked on the gravel road.

"Dad, should you be out here?" It had been weeks since the heart attack, but Mom still barely let him out of her sight.

"Somehow both you and your mother missed that part about it being a 'minor' heart attack." Dad gave Kevin a pat. "Oy with the hovering."

Blake felt a smile surface as Dad reached him. He had no doubt his face betrayed his emotion of only minutes ago. In fact, for all he knew, Dad had watched the whole thing from his car. If he wasn't so . . . hollowed, he might feel embarrassed.

As it was, any need to hide the fact that he'd lost it moments ago just wasn't there.

"You came out to wish your brother happy birthday, too?"

"Actually, I hadn't gotten to that part yet."

Dad shuffled to his side, and they faced the gravestone together, his father's palm on his shoulder.

"Dad, how did you . . . heal? You and mom?"

"Not quickly. That's for sure." Dad paused. "At first I threw myself into my work. Then the election. But at the end of the day, the only thing that really worked was just . . . forcing myself to trust God. Choosing to believe that He can bring good out of pain—that those aren't just trite words people offer in horrible circumstances, but actual truth. And that there's always hope—" Dad's voice caught as he finished—"that I'll see my eldest son again."

His grip on Blake's shoulder tightened.

"In my most broken state, God saw me. I believe He even grieved with me. And then He started putting me back together, slowly, piece by piece. His heartbeat pulsing inside me when my own was broken."

"Maybe if I'd stayed home, the same thing could've happened for me. I wouldn't have wasted so many years."

Dad clapped his shoulder once more and then let his arm fall to his side. "They weren't wasted years if they brought you back home. Especially if they brought you to your knees."

He met his father's eyes then, and next thing he knew, Dad pulled him into a hug. The kind of father-son embrace Blake hadn't even realized he'd been missing. And when he stepped back, he saw the emotion on his father's face, etched into every line and written in his eyes.

"Well, shall we sing?"

Blake cocked his head. "Sing?"

"To your brother. 'Happy Birthday.'"

"You're serious."

"As a heart attack."

"Not funny, Dad." But the laughter ringing through the cemetery said otherwise.

❧

"Mom, you promised!"

An announcement over the Grand Rapids airport's intercom system drowned out Autumn's gasp, but surely the look on her face spelled out her shock. Her gaze flitted from face to face. Tim and Ellie with little Oliver, Betsy and Lucy, Harry, Jamie . . .

"I promised not to throw you a going-away party. Didn't promise we wouldn't all show up at the airport to see you off."

"You all drove all this way without me knowing?"

"It was only a forty-five minute drive, silly." Betsy waved her hand in the air. "We carpooled in the inn's van, by the way. I was a little worried you'd pass us along the highway. But thankfully your mom sent us on our way early enough."

"And then drove me here without so much as a word." Autumn stepped aside as a group of students passed, what looked to be the only other large group in the place. The airport in Grand Rapids served just seven airlines and on its busiest day was a nap compared to Chicago—which is where she was headed next. Then on to Atlanta. And, finally, France.

This was good. It was right. A dream finally coming true.

And all her friends had come to see her off.

Well, almost all.

She shouldn't have expected to see Blake's face among the group of friends. They hadn't even talked to each other since that night at the festival. Not that she hadn't pulled out her phone umpteen times since, fingers poised to tap out a text or even call him.

Especially these last few days, as she'd placed her belongings in storage, packed her suitcases, said her goodbyes one by one. But every time she ended up dropping her phone back into her purse.

Maybe it is better this way.

"Let me go get checked in and drop off my baggage, and then we'll do another round of good-byes, okay?"

She lugged the larger of her two rolling suitcases to the desk. Mom pulled the smaller one behind her. Autumn laid her driver's license and passport on the desk, waited as the ticketing agent printed her boarding pass.

Minutes later, she returned to her well-wishers and the hugs began. She'd already said good-bye to each of them earlier in the week, but this last chance meant the world. She hadn't known she was this hungry for one more taste of home before leaving.

"Nervous?" Mom whispered in her ear as they embraced.

"Like crazy."

Another hug.

Ellie burst into tears.

Oliver followed suit.

Harry tried and failed to hide a snicker.

The security line awaited.

"Well, bye again. And thanks so much coming, you guys. You don't know how much it means."

She gave Mom one last smile and turned.

He could still show up.

Autumn closed her eyes, shook her head, nudging the thought free as she forced herself to make her way to the cordoned maze leading through security.

"Autumn, wait!"

Ellie's voice pinged off the waxed floor, and Autumn halted, spinning to see Ellie hurrying her direction. "I can't believe I almost forgot. I would've hated myself."

"Ellie, calm down. If you go into labor right now,

you'll scare the security guard." As she'd doled out hugs minutes ago, she'd seen the guy at the entrance to the security line watch Ellie in her nearly-ready-to-pop state.

"Hey, if he's that freaked out by a pregnant lady, he might need a lesson in the realities of birth."

"Hmm, pretty sure none of us needs that lesson. Not in an airport anyway. Why the last-minute chase?" Back where she'd left them, the rest of the group watched.

Ellie pulled a crumpled—and stained—envelope from her pocket. Was that jelly on the seal?

"Sorry, Oliver got ahold of it at the breakfast table this morning. Anyway, Blake"—Autumn's heart hitched at his name—"gave it to Tim, who gave it to me. I was supposed to give it to you and almost forgot."

A letter passed through mutual friends. "Kinda junior-highish, isn't it?"

Ellie shrugged and handed over the envelope. "I was thinking more along the lines of sweet, but make of it what you will. One more hug?"

She leaned in for the embrace, then patted her friend's stomach. "Don't forget to name her after me."

"Of course."

Autumn stared at the envelope until the security guard's voice poked in. "Miss?"

She stuffed it in her pocket.

Where it stayed as she moved through security, found her gate, waited to board her plane. It wasn't 'til she'd stuffed her carry-on in the overhead compartment, settled into her window seat, and buckled the strap across her waist that she pulled it out again. Finally ready to read whatever he had to say.

She slipped her finger under the envelope flap, tore

it open, and reached inside, expecting a sheet of paper, maybe more.

Instead she pulled out a photograph. The image was grainy, but it wasn't hard to tell what it was. That stinking porcelain bathtub sitting on her crushed dining room table.

And scribbled on the back:

Told you you'd laugh about it eventually. Have the adventure of a lifetime, Red.

Blake

Only she didn't laugh. More like snorted—a half-chuckle, half-cry. And there'd have been tears, too, she knew it, if not for the college-aged girl who plopped into the seat next to her just then.

"Hey." The girl bent to stuff her duffel bag under the seat in front of them.

"Hey."

The girl lifted her head and held out her hand. "I'm Lindsay. Guess we're seat buddies."

Autumn bent her arm at an awkward angle in the tight confines of the seat to shake the girl's hand. "Autumn. Where are you headed?"

She took a band from her wrist, then pulled her long blond hair away from her face and formed a ponytail. "All the way to Paris, baby. I'm studying abroad for the semester."

"That's where I'm going, too." A fresh round of nerves, but a little excitement, as well, whooshed in to take the place of her emotions over the photo.

"This will actually be my third time there. Parents took

me a couple times. But this is my first time on my own. Who's that?" Lindsay pointed to Blake's name scrawled on the back of the photo. "Boyfriend?"

"Nah, just . . . a friend."

Only, if she was completely, brutally honest, there was no "just" about it, was there? In less than a month, the man had flat-out stolen her heart, whether she wanted to admit it or not. She could only hope the adventure, the excitement of her new life would eventually dull the ache she finally realized for what it was.

She missed him. Already.

Autumn slipped the photo back into the envelope. "So is Paris as amazing as everyone says it is?"

Her seatmate's eyes lit up. "Better."

19

Surely a crepe was the perfect cure for the lingering melancholy even the park's unobstructed view of the Eiffel Tower couldn't shake. After nearly three months in France, her taste buds still hadn't tired of the treat.

"Bonjour, Freddy."

The older man with the Cary Grant chin and oversized metal spatula in his hand tossed her a smile as she approached. "Ah, my American friend. Your usual, no?"

Autumn bit her lip, sun kissed by the warmth of an early April sun and stomach gurgling impatiently for her daily lunch. The sweet smell of the crepe stand flowed over her until she could almost taste the thing before Freddy had even prepared it. "I don't know. Maybe I'll opt for out-of-the-box today."

Freddy's forehead wrinkled in confusion. Apparently American clichés didn't translate.

"I mean, maybe I'll finally try something different."

"You surprise me!"

She could try berries and cream. Or apple and cheese. Her stomach growled again. If she ate this way at home, she'd have gained twenty pounds in her first week in Paris. Thankfully, here she walked everywhere. "Oh, never mind. The usual."

Freddy wagged his finger in the air before going to work. "Every day I think perhaps she will try something new. Every day it is the same." How many times had Petey at the Snack Shack said almost the exact same thing when she ordered her usual ice cream cone?

"Sorry, Freddy. What can I say? I'm a sucker for Nutella."

A minute later, he handed over the treat folded in white paper and accepted her four Euros. "Until tomorrow, my friend."

She bid him another "bonjour" and started toward the hotel, having lingered extra long at the Parc de Champ de Mars during her noon hour today. She bit into the crepe as she walked, willing the burst of sugar to soothe the prick of emotions. When she turned the corner and found herself facing the sun, she slipped the sunglasses from her head and tipped them over eyes puffy from lack of sleep.

This couldn't be homesickness, could it? Not after so long in Paris. After all, once the jet lag had worn off that first week, minor jitters had faded into pure excitement. She'd settled in. Learned her way around. Even discovered a little church that offered a service in English on Saturday evenings. Along the way, she'd found herself more and more craving alone time with the God she'd for so long assumed didn't really see her.

Maybe she'd simply needed the major life upheaval to realize she was the one who'd had her blinders on.

However it happened, she was grateful for the slow unfolding of a new closeness with God, like the white flowers opening a little more each day on the trees in the park.

Why, then, the needling undercurrent? Why the tossing and turning at night?

Autumn waved at the florist arranging a display in the window next to the hotel, then pulled on the oversized gold handle to let herself in. The lobby sang with movement—bellboys rolling suitcases over the marble floor, a half-dozen concierges working with guests at the oblong desk lining one wall.

Autumn wove through the busy room, slipped behind the desk and through a door marked *Employés de l'hôtel*.

"So she shows up."

"Good afternoon to you, too, Sabine."

"Are you not sick of those yet?" Sabine gave a pointed glance to Autumn's mostly demolished crepe.

"Never." Autumn took her final bite and tossed the paper in the garbage bin.

Amazing how quickly she and Sabine had picked up where their high-school friendship had left off. Of course, it helped that Sabine spoke English better than some Americans. Autumn hadn't realized how elementary her French vocabulary really was until her first day in Paris.

"You didn't go up today, I see."

Autumn stopped in front of Sabine's desk and put her hands on her hips. "How do you know?"

"How do I know? Your hair." Sabine pointed a red-painted fingernail to her own. "If you'd walked or ridden up the Iron Lady, you'd have wind-blown hair."

Autumn groaned and plopped into her chair. Fine.

So she still hadn't gone up the Eiffel Tower. She'd stared at it plenty, had gone to see it her second morning in France, actually, and every day since. She'd memorized the look of it from every angle from every bench in the garden-bordered Champ de Mars.

But every time, she stopped short of buying a ticket and riding an elevator to the top.

"By the way, you were supposed to have a sixty-day review last week," Sabine said now, pulling the pencil from behind her ears and squinting at the calendar beside her desk through red-framed glasses. "April second was your two-month mark."

Two months on the job. Almost three in the country. The time had flown.

The time had dragged.

Oh, Lord, what is wrong with me? This is France. France. The adventure she'd dreamt about, prayed for, for years. She should be exploring Paris to her heart's content, booking weekend trips to other European countries, planning a summer vacation on the Mediterranean coast.

Instead, she walked through the same park every morning. Bought the same crepe at the same crepe stand. Worked in a hotel office not all that different from back home.

Her gaze darted to her desk. It looked as if she'd worked there two years rather than two months. Files and notebooks, a computer screen she rarely used because she was so busy working with guests. Framed pictures of Mom and Dad, Ava. Little Oliver and his new baby sister. A photo of Betsy and Philip in front of their house. Cards from Lucy and Fletcher and others from her old reading group at Hope House.

And that photo from Blake, note side facing out. *"Have the adventure of a lifetime, Red."*

"Autumn, did you hear me?"

She glanced up.

"I said, as far as I'm concerned, you've been an amazing asset to the hotel." Sabine perched on the corner of her metal desk now. "Consider this the review. I just need you to sign the evaluation I'm required to fill out. Also, I'm supposed to give you an opportunity to voice any concerns about the position and whether or not it suits you."

The position? It suited her perfectly. An office in a beautiful hotel, working with travel agencies to book rooms and coordinate tours for guests from all over the world. No more playing amateur handywoman like back at the Kingsley Inn. No leaky roof to fix or cracked siding she couldn't afford to replace.

No, if she had any concerns, they weren't about the job, but about the feelings pricking her from the inside. The loss of the inn still weighed on her, even though she'd told herself it was just one more sign she was meant to leave Whisper Shore.

But it was more than that. It was leaving Mom so soon after they'd finally found some common ground.

It was a twinge of disappointment that her grand adventure didn't seem to be living up to her imagination. It was annoyance that it was probably her own fault for letting silly emotions dictate her enjoyment of her new life.

It was missing Blake.

Oh, she could deny it all she liked, but in her most honest moments—tucked under the quilt in Sabine's second bedroom, sitting in the pew of that little chapel on Saturday nights, staring at the Eiffel Tower alone in a crowd of tourists—she had to admit it. Even all these months later, any thought of Blake, the man who sheltered a compassionate heart and craving for purpose underneath an adventurous exterior, still dissolved her into a pool of yearning.

And it always left her with the same question: Had she followed the wrong dream?

But why would you give me this dream to travel, God, only to replace it when it's finally come true?

"I think that crepe put you in a sugar coma, Autumn." Sabine's voice crept in. "Your eyes are glazed."

"Sorry."

"Thinking about home again?"

That and something else. Someone else. "I'm that obvious?"

"You talk about that inn you own all the time."

Owned. Soon the bank wouldn't own the inn anymore, either. Grady Lewis had e-mailed that a developer had shown strong interest in the property. "Sorry. Again. Guess I miss it more than I thought I would."

"Excuse me." One of the English-speaking concierges poked her head in. "There's someone here to see Ms. Kingsley."

Autumn acknowledged Sabine's curious glance with a shrug. She stood. "Maybe the Tottenheimers? They had questions about a riverboat tour and—"

A figure pushed past the concierge. "Yes, I'm at the right hotel!"

Shock propelled Autumn forward at the sight of her sister, duffel bag over one shoulder, clothes wrinkled, and blond hair pulled into her usual ponytail. "Ava, what are you . . . Why . . ." She abandoned the questions as Ava pulled her into a hug.

◈

Blake wouldn't have blamed Shawn Baylor if he slammed the door in his face.

But instead his old friend offered only a wary "Oh, it's you."

Better than a punch, at least. The bruises might have faded, but the memory of their public fight hadn't.

He hadn't exactly been looking forward to this encounter. But in the four-plus months he'd been home, there hadn't been a day he didn't think at least once of Shawn. And after today's meeting with the city council, with all about his life that felt up in the air and uncertain, maybe this was one thing he could resolve. Or at least attempt to.

Shawn's bulky frame guarded his doorway, but the fact that he still stood there offered a glimmer of hope.

The smell of cigarette smoke mingled with a flowery air freshener in the apartment complex hallway. "So . . . can I come in?"

Shawn shrugged, something close to curiosity hovering in his eyes. "I guess." He moved aside to let Blake enter.

The inside of Shawn's apartment smelled better than the hallway, but its sparse décor and bare walls begged for attention. The only hints of hominess were the couple framed photos sitting on what looked like a hand-me-down end table. One held a photo of Shawn and his family. The other . . .

Wait a sec . . .

Blake brushed past Shawn to pick up the photo.

Four faces ogled the camera—Shawn, Tim, Ryan, Blake. Goggles in place, in their skydiving gear. This had to have been taken on one of their college breaks. He glanced up at Shawn.

His friend wore a "So what?" expression. Arms crossed, lips pressed.

Blake replaced the photo. "Nice place."

"It's a junk heap."

Oo-kay. "Well, I don't see rats scurrying across the floor or anything, so that should comfort you, at least."

And like he'd hoped it would, the words caused the tiniest chink in Shawn's demeanor. His friend was notoriously spooked by rodents. He, Ryan, and Tim used to mock Shawn mercilessly about it.

"Haven't seen one yet," Shawn acquiesced.

See, they could do this. Have a normal conversation. And when the moment was right, Blake would say what he'd come to say. He'd practiced the words in his head on the drive from the city offices to Shawn's place.

"So, what're you here for?"

"Not into the small-talk thing, huh."

Shawn's arms dropped. "I would've thought you and I were past small talk."

"You're right." Blake ran his hand through his hair. "Man, I just came to say I'm sorry, all right? I'm sorry about all of it. The fight. Not . . . keeping in touch all those years. Being so stuck in my own anger and hurt that I didn't even consider how you were doing back home."

"Blaze—"

"And what I said back in December—suggesting you

. . . and the drugs . . ." He still couldn't believe he'd even hinted at that. "It was low and uncalled for. Anyway, that's what I wanted to say. I'm . . . sorry."

Shawn worked his jaw, indecision clear on his face. Finally, he let out a sigh. "I'm not good at this stuff. Probably why my marriage is a mess."

"Well, who is? I fumbled through that apology like . . . name a really bad NFL player."

"Man, you spent too many years out of the country."

Shawn's laughter was like aloe over a sunburn. "I haven't seen the past six Super Bowls." Hadn't watched this year's because he'd been too busy sulking about Autumn leaving, wondering what to do next.

He'd assumed he was out of the running for the city job after the festival fire fiasco and had instead settled in helping Dad out at the hotel—started learning the financial side of the biz, covered the odd shift at the front desk, discovered he got a kind of kick out of welcoming guests to their little corner of the world.

Whisper Shore didn't have the dazzling architecture of European cities or the ancient artifacts of the Middle East. No jungles or mountains or even famous landmarks. But it had personality. Charm.

It was home. It felt right to stay.

If only he was as certain about the job the city had offered him a few hours earlier. Yes, the meeting with the council had taken him completely by surprise. Turned out they thought he was a good fit for the Chamber role, after all. Forget the fire, they'd said. Unfortunate mishap. He had the youth and the vision to help reverse the slide of their town's main source of revenue.

He'd walked away from the meeting with only one question: Did he have the desire?

"Uh, want to sit down?" Shawn interrupted his thoughts.

Blake plopped onto the plaid couch edged up to one wall. "Isn't this the couch we used to sit on in your parents' basement while we played Nintendo?"

"Yeah. And actually, I've got the Nintendo too." He hesitated for only a moment. "Want to play?"

"Oh yeah." Because he could think about the job later. He was here for Shawn.

"Mario Kart?" Shawn handed him a controller.

"Bring it on."

Half an hour later, Blake's fingers remembered every button on the game controller, and they'd found their way to comfortable conversation as Shawn obliterated him at a decades-old version of the racing game. And Blake's sinking into the caving couch, throwing out joking insults, and downing A&W felt less forgotten than familiar.

"I don't know what happened." Blake dropped his control on the floor after another loss. "I used to rock that game."

"Well, I'm not sure keeping up my video-game skills is all that much to brag about." Shawn went to the fridge for another soda.

"Listen, Tim and I are shooting some hoops tonight. You in?"

Shawn returned, nodded, an actual smile stretching his cheeks now. "Taking the boys to McDonalds, but after will work."

At the reminder of Shawn's sons, Blake debated for

a moment before offering the question. "About Hilary. Any chance you two . . ."

"Might get back together?" Shawn saved him from finishing the question. Stood. Paced the room. "Hope so. I gotta get my act together."

"I talked to her today. And if it helps any . . ." They'd stood outside the city offices after the council meeting, marveling at the onset of an early spring and then somehow slipping into a conversation about Shawn. And how much Hilary missed him. And how, if Blake could find a new sense of healing, maybe Shawn could too. "She's not going anywhere, Shawn. I think . . . she'll wait."

His friend didn't say anything. Just stood in the center of the room, rubbing one hand over the opposite arm, gaze distant. And then, "I think maybe we're going to be okay."

Blake almost asked which "we"—Shawn and Hilary or Shawn and Blake. But maybe, probably, he meant all of them. And finally, one piece in Blake's messy puzzle of uncertainty fell into place.

"I missed you, man." Even more than his earlier apology, these were the words he'd been working up to.

"You too."

He stood and slung one arm around his friend—the embrace a little awkward . . . but a lot needed.

"I should've never blamed you."

Blake wanted to argue. After all, hadn't he spent plenty of years blaming himself? But it seemed they were all moving past blame these days, perhaps his own family most of all. How many times had he tried to apologize to Dad for ruining the Laurent investment? And every time, Dad assured him all was in the past, forgiven.

"Means a lot, Shawn." They exchanged nods. "Seven o'clock, high school court."

"I'll be there. Do we need a fourth?"

"Already on it. I've got this new friend named Fletcher. You'll like him." Blake turned for the door, but Shawn's next words stopped him.

"What about Autumn?"

He about-faced. "What about her?"

"The old Blaze wouldn't have let a girl he was into take off across the ocean without going after her."

"Not sure I'm still 'the old Blaze.' And besides, how do you know—"

"About the two of you? Dude, this is Whisper Shore. Talk spreads at light-year speed. Most of the town knew you dug her before you did."

Wasn't any point in arguing. But what the town didn't know was that their friendship went beyond a little crush. He'd gotten to know Autumn enough to realize she needed the chance to pursue her dream.

It might make for a cute rom-com script to chase after a girl and convince her to stay. But maybe the grander gesture was letting go, finding a slice of joy at the prospect of her finally having her big adventure.

Even while, back at home, he worked through the ache of her absence.

Anyway, he hadn't gone after her, and she was gone, and he needed to figure out exactly where to go from here. Ike Delaney's words came back to him: "*You don't have to see every open door on the way to your end goal—just the one staring you in the face.*"

Was the city job the open door staring him in the face right now?

"It's too bad about her inn," Shawn said now.

"I know." Losing it to the bank had to have been a major sting.

"I heard a developer or two has been looking into it. Word on the street is whoever buys the property won't want the business. Probably tear down the inn and turn it into a strip mall or something."

"Where'd you hear . . ." He broke off at Shawn's rolling eyes, and they said together, "It's Whisper Shore."

The thought of it—Autumn's inn stripped and torn down—pummeled him. All his work helping her fix it up for naught. That inn wasn't just a business. It was a legacy. One he'd come to feel part of during his weeks spent there. And it was interesting how many times in the past few months he'd found himself attempting to incorporate some of the inn's friendly touches at his father's hotel.

If only Autumn's financial advisor had been able to find someone interested in preserving the Kingsley Inn's heritage. A buyer who could see past what it lacked to what it could be. With a little TLC and the right renovations . . .

He froze in Shawn's doorway.

"I don't think I need a few days after all."

Shawn's brow wrinkled. "Huh?"

"To consider the city job. I know what my answer is."

"I have no clue what you're talking about."

Blake rubbed his hands together, anticipation blending with his whirling thoughts. "I think there might be a different open door staring me in the face." And with that, he turned and started down the hallway.

"Still no clue what you're talking about," Shawn called after him.

He only lifted his hand in a backward wave . . . and picked up his pace.

⟡

The view from the Eiffel Tower's second landing was enough to steal Autumn's breath. Unending city lights and the Seine wiggling through them. Stars already peeking through the dusty pinks and oranges of dusk. She could feel her senses gulping it all in.

"Totally worth the seven hundred and nineteen steps, right?" Ava snapped a photo with her iPhone. "Somehow it's even prettier now than it was when I came here sophomore year of college. So. Beautiful."

Beautiful, yes. "Do you have any idea how jealous of you I was when you went on that trip?"

"Probably about as jealous as I've been of you these last few months. You *live* here now, sis. You're like Sabrina Fairchild."

"Which one? Hepburn or . . . ? I don't even remember what actress played her in the Harrison Ford version."

"Then Hepburn it is."

But in the movie, Sabrina eventually went home. "I still can't believe you're actually here. It feels surreal."

Ava had explained earlier about her Tuesday-Thursday teaching schedule this semester. She'd caught an overnight flight Thursday after class, planned to fly back Monday afternoon.

But Autumn had decided not to let herself think further ahead than the next seventy-two hours. She meant to enjoy every moment of her sister's surprise visit. It had started with a repeat visit to Freddy's crepe stand, an early dinner at a sidewalk café, and now—finally—the Eiffel Tower.

"What made you decide to come all of a sudden?" she asked now, a cool evening breeze ruffling through her hair. "Thought we'd talked about you maybe visiting for a week or two over summer break?"

"You kept talking about crepes in your e-mails, and I couldn't stand it any longer." Ava shifted, one elbow leaning on the railing as she faced Autumn, expression softening. "And in between all the crepe talk, you sounded lonely."

And here she thought she'd masked it in her chatty e-mails. "So you hopped on a plane."

"I hopped on a plane." Ava turned back to the railing, threading her arm through Autumn's. "Figured it was time I start taking my big sister role a little more seriously. Not that you needed it. I mean you've got Betsy and Ellie and—"

"I needed it."

She didn't have to look over at her sister to feel her smile. The blink and twinkle of lights and stars mixed in the distance.

"Man, I can't get over the view," Ava said after moments of quiet. "It's magical up here, yeah?"

"Yes." *But also . . .*

Ava slid her a glance. "Don't tell me you're let down."

"I'm not, really, it's just . . ." She didn't even know what.

Maybe it was the metal bars boxing them in. The press of bodies around her. The smell of cigar smoke from a group of college students a few feet away. Giggles from the girls as the inexperienced guys in the group tried to figure out how to light their cigars.

"I'm just moody. Tired. Haven't been sleeping well."

"You're tired? I'm the jet-lagged one who's been up since yesterday." When Autumn didn't answer, Ava elbowed her for a second time. "What is it, little sister?"

She scanned the view, tilted her head, focus latching on a couple in the corner, fingers laced, leaning into each other as they took in the darkening horizon.

Ava followed her sight. "Oh, now I see."

Autumn jerked. "What? No, I'm just . . ." She let the sentence drop.

Ava zipped up the jacket she wore over her U of M T-shirt. "Did I tell you when I came here on that college trip, I never made it up to the third landing?"

"No, why not? Get scared?" That'd be funny. Ava, the one who'd never been scared of anything.

"Ha, and no. Ryan and I had started dating the year before that, which you know—"

"Much to the chagrin of Mom and Dad."

"And his parents, too. Anyway, I'd wanted him to come on the trip. It was spring, not like he'd miss any football games. But the team was in conditioning whenever they weren't playing, so he said no. I pouted for a while, but finally decided, fine. I'll show him what he's missing. I sent him postcards every day, sometimes multiple times a day. Posted all these photos online of the fun I was having. Even though inside I was, like, miserable."

"My lovesick sister." It amazed her, really, that Ava was talking so openly about Ryan now. Maybe it was the Paris effect.

"The worst was when I came up here. It was so gorgeous, but I kept thinking, 'I shouldn't be here without Ryan. Doesn't feel right without him.' Made it up as far as the second landing but couldn't make myself go up to the highest point. I decided I'd wait and come back someday . . . with Ryan."

Her voice softened at the last part, cracking when she said Ryan's name. Autumn leaned toward her sister, reaching her arm around her waist. She took in the glassy sheen in Ava's eyes. And yet, something peaceful had settled over Ava's face.

"Oh, sis."

Ava shook her head. "It's okay, really. Healing's been slow, you know. But it's . . . good. And I didn't tell you this so we could get all morose." She met Autumn's eyes. "Just wanted you to remember I know what it's like to love a Hunziker boy. And to hurt over it."

Autumn inhaled sharply. "Ava, no. I—" Ava's soft laughter cut her off. From almost tears to giggles? Her sister *was* jet-lagged. "What's so funny?"

"You are. Listen, we don't have to talk about Blake if you don't want."

"I don't want."

Ava nodded. "Okay then." Pause. "So when are you going to go back home and tell him how you feel?"

"Ava!" She yipped the word, arms folding. The laughter of the college students turned rowdy. "Look, I can't go home. I might be a little homesick now and then." Or a lot. "But this is my dream. It's what I wanted. I'd be crazy to give it up."

"Sometimes what we think we want and what we really want are two different things."

"Thanks, Socrates."

"If you're appointing me a philosopher's name, I'd prefer Aristotle. And you're welcome." Ava allowed another drawn-out pause before speaking again. "So . . . there's another reason I came. Wanted to give you something."

Ava reached into her pocket and pulled out . . . a bracelet? "I found this the other day. Went looking for it, actually, after your latest e-mail. Mom sent it to me one year for my birthday. At the time I thought, 'There she goes again. Trying to cutesy up her tomboy daughter.' But then I took a closer look at it, saw the inscription." She held out the bracelet for Autumn to look at.

Autumn fingered the narrow silver plate, read the inscription out loud. "'Hope does not disappoint. Romans 5:5.'" She looked up. "Mom sent this?"

"Yeah, and I think she was trying to send me a message. Wasn't really ready to hear it then, but I did look up the verses. I read them again recently, this time in *The Message* paraphrase. Talks about being alert for whatever God is going to do next." She handed the bracelet to Autumn and pulled out her phone. "Here, read it on my phone."

Bible study with her sister at the Eiffel Tower. Hadn't seen this coming.

"In alert expectancy such as this, we're never left feeling shortchanged. Quite the contrary—we can't round up enough containers to hold everything God generously pours into our lives through the Holy Spirit."

"Don't you love that?" Ava pocketed her phone. "Autumn, I think if you're honest with yourself, you're having a hard time here because you're wondering about what you're missing out on at home. And you're scared of going home because of what you'd miss out on here."

Frustration scraped over her. "Aren't those valid concerns?"

"Not if they've got you trapped in a constant state of what-if. You said once in December that you want adventure, freedom. Maybe the real freedom is in letting go of the *what-if*s. Choosing hopeful expectation over worry that life is going to shortchange you."

Hopeful expectation. It sounded great, but . . . "What if I'm not sure which thing to hope for? What I want anymore?"

"Maybe you start by thinking back to the last time you can remember when everything felt right. Like you were exactly where God wanted you to be. When you wouldn't have changed a single thing about that moment."

Before Ava even finished saying the words, Autumn was there. Sitting atop the Whisper Shore water tower, legs dangling from the railing, Blake's hand over hers. Moonlight glinting over Lake Michigan and the town bordered by shadowed fields.

Not everything had been perfect in that moment. After all, Blake's father had just had a heart attack. They'd spent the night before in the hospital.

But even then, there'd been a rightness. She'd felt so much a part of Blake's life, waiting in the hospital, just . . . being there. For him. She'd felt more purpose slouched in that waiting-room chair than she'd even begun to feel here.

It'd been the same feeling she had making final festival preparations, helping Blake pull the town together for one more event of the year. And Christmas night with Mom and Ava . . .

And at the inn. Laughing and sharing pranks with

Harry. Ducking into the kitchen for Betsy's food and advice. Catching Jamie asleep on the night shift. Talking with Uri about his late wife. Even climbing around the roof patching those stupid holes.

Slowly, like the fading of sunset's colors, it all came into focus. No, it hadn't been homesickness she'd been feeling. It was the ache of two desires vying for top billing. But suddenly—finally—she *knew*.

She loved that old, broken-down inn.

She loved her quirky little town.

She loved . . .

Blake's face filled her mind. His annoyingly perfect smile and constant tease and dark eyes that danced with playfulness. Ava was right. She didn't just miss the man. She kinda . . . loved him.

Oh, Lord, I think I really do.

And she'd given it all up for some misguided definition of what her life should look like lest she miss out. A shake rattled through her.

"Autumn, are you crying?"

Hot tears tracked down her cheeks, too many for her rapid blinks to hold back. "Yeah, but . . . it's only 'cause I figured it out."

"Figured out . . . ?"

"Let's go."

"Uh, up to the third floor? Sure. Though, we may have to wait awhile for the elevator."

"No, I mean, let's *go*."

"Where?"

But she was already moving, gaze searching for the elevator, the answer to Ava's question pushing her on.

Home.

20

The sky's embrace had never felt so warm. The pull of the clouds, never so intoxicating.

Blake inched his plane into an angle with his right rudder pedal, gaze swooping from white wisps outside the windshield to the instrument panel he knew like a favorite childhood book.

"I told you it'd come back easy enough, Blaze." Ike's voice was muffled through his headset.

Blake let his grin answer for him and pulled back on the steering yoke to lift the plane's nose. It may have taken years and a few too many false starts to find his way back into the cockpit. But now that he was there, with the turquoise swirl of Lake Michigan beneath him and the open expanse all around, he could practically taste it—the freedom.

Not that it had been an easy feat, even today. First he'd had to get through an hour's walk-around with Ike, proving he still knew his way around the aircraft, naming every piece of equipment and reciting rules that had somehow stuck in the back of his brain since his original training for his commercial-pilot certificate.

But the hardest part had been takeoff. He'd taxied for a good twenty minutes before finally lining up on the runway and letting instinct take over.

Now he wondered what he'd been waiting for. Exhilaration ribboned through him as he handled the plane, pushing through the sky in angles and waves. *Wonder what Ike would say if I attempted a loop.*

He glanced over at the older pilot. Ike had abandoned his clipboard with the checklist of items to "test" Blake on. Ike met his eyes. "Don't even think about it, kid."

That transparent, huh? "Think about what?" He donned an innocent smirk.

"You've got the same look you had twelve years ago. Only your fifth or sixth time up, and you got the hankering to try some aerobatics. Right then and there, I knew I had trouble on my hands."

Blake's chuckles rang out. Months or even weeks ago, Ike's words might've stung. But sometime between sobbing at Ryan's grave and now, he'd let go of the regret, the label *trouble*.

Or maybe he'd allowed the grip of his shame to start loosening even sooner. It'd started that first day home, when Mom and Dad had welcomed him with open arms. And continued when Autumn Kingsley walked into his life and took up residence in his heart whether he liked it or not.

Funny thing was, it wasn't 'til she walked *out* of his life that it hit him: Their friendship—relationship?—whatever it was, it'd bloomed long before he'd done anything to earn it. Same with his parents' forgiveness. And, well, God's acceptance, right?

That was the kind of truth that filled a man with confident expectation.

That got him out to the airport, into the cockpit, up in the skies.

That fueled newfound dreams.

Speaking of . . .

His gaze darted to the clock on the instrument panel. He was supposed to get an ad to the newspaper by noon to make this week's issue. And he'd been hoping to finish painting today.

In the two weeks since he'd landed the loan and signed the papers to become the new owner of the Kingsley Inn, they'd made progress on renovations. But they still had a long way to go if they wanted to be ready for tourist season kickoff in May.

"Come on, Ike, one loop and then I'll take her down."

"Nothing doing, Blaze. You want me to sign that endorsement to keep your certificate current, you keep this flight standard."

"Boring, you mean."

"Stuff it, kid. You know you're not bored."

Not even close. Every muscle and nerve breathed with life today. And it wasn't just this flight, but anticipation at what the coming months held. It still amazed him the bank had agreed to a loan. That they'd accepted his offer over that of the developer who'd also bid on the land. Dad's cosigning probably had something to do with it.

And the town of Whisper Shore had changed since winter. Somehow the festival had brought the little community back to life, sparked a new appreciation for its history and tradition, revived the charm. Maybe that's why the people at the bank had opted for preserving the inn rather than letting a developer tear it down.

And they'd trusted Blake to do it.

He just hoped he could live up to the promises he'd made. To do all he could to turn the business around and build it back up to the draw it'd once been. He had bold plans and a hopeful outlook.

The one chink in his confidence? Wondering what Autumn would think of the inn's new owner. A tremor of turbulence rocked the plane, but only for a moment. Blake's knuckles tightened on the yoke and he held steady, eyes on the altimeter.

He assumed Autumn knew about the sale. Certainly Victoria had told her. Maybe it wouldn't even matter to her. It's not like she'd be around to assess his progress.

But he couldn't help hoping there was at least a piece of her that was happy, maybe even grateful, that some-one—even him—had saved it. That the new owner loved the place and meant to preserve its legacy.

"Shifty wind," Ike grumbled. "Crept up out of no-where."

"That's Lake Michigan for you." He lifted one hand from the yoke and clamped Ike's shoulder. "All right, a half-loop. What's it called? An English something-or-other?"

"English bunt, and I don't think so."

"Dude, it's child's play."

"It's not on the checklist."

"Neither was bringing you donuts this morning, but I did that, didn't I?"

"Now you're just playing dirty." Ike's sigh rolled like

the propeller's spin. "Fine, do the stunt. But up your altitude first."

"Aye, aye, Captain."

Ike only rolled his eyes, and Blake once again pulled on the yoke to push the plane higher in the sky.

"Not too fast or you'll stall."

"Got it. I'm not a total newbie."

"Look who's all cocky all of a sudden."

"Not cocky." Blake reached good height and gave the yoke a gentle push until the wings leveled. "Just . . ." He shrugged. "At home."

Ike's nod spelled understanding. "All right, then. Do the stunt."

The thrill tickled through Blake as he increased the plane's speed, the hues of the sky blurring. He pushed the yoke forward, gently at first, then with more pressure until the plane swooped, drawing a half circle in the sky. For mere seconds, they dangled upside down, Ike's whoop ringing through the cockpit, until Blake righted the plane and slowed.

The beat of his heart put rhythm to the laughter lost in the hum of the engine.

"You nailed it."

"Told ya."

"Okay, take her down."

Minutes later, the plane descended at the Whisper Shore Municipal Airport, the bump of the wheels against pavement barely jerking the inside of the cockpit. Once they came to rest outside the hangar, Blake cut the engine and turned to Ike.

"So . . . I'm good to go?"

"I'll type up and sign the endorsement today. Once

that's done, your certificate's considered current again. Good to go, indeed."

"Sweet." He unbuckled his seat belt and removed his headset.

"One more thing, kid."

"What's that?"

"Assuming you're going to be sticking around—"

"Oh, I'm definitely sticking around."

"Then we need to assign you a long-term hangar."

Long-term. He liked the sound of that.

The two weeks of her two-week notice at the Paris hotel had felt more like twenty. And the flights—oh, she could've sworn they'd circled the globe at least a dozen times. Then the drive from Detroit in a compact rental car she couldn't drive fast enough.

But now that Autumn was finally home, nerves had turned her into a knotty, immobile mess. Jittery emotions propelled her past the turnoff into town—and Blake— and she headed toward the inn. Or at least where it used to be.

What had she planned to do, anyway? Show up on Blake's doorstep? And say . . . say what? Why hadn't she thought further ahead than the travel portion of her impulsive return?

She stepped out of the car, the lake's foamy smell instantly pulling her in, the call of a sea gull and the water's lapping the perfect soundtrack to the assurance she'd hoped for. This is when she loved Whisper Shore best, just waking up after winter, a lingering calm rolling into anticipation as tourist season waited on the horizon.

The thought of tourists tugged her gaze from the lake, over quartz-gleaming sand and past the vibrant spring-green span of grass to where the inn still stood. Even from a distance, the grin of the old place was more vivid than ever—repainted shutters glinting in the sunlight and whitewashed porch stretching like a toothy smile. The new owner was making the changes she hadn't been able to manage.

Maybe now's the part, God, where you show me what to do next. You got me home. I think I might know why you got me home.

And it wasn't the inn. Still . . .

She knew every inch of the place, all its weathered nooks and crannies. She'd long ago memorized the sound of the lake's nighttime lullaby from the dilapidated porch. She knew which creaks belonged to which stairs and could feel the design of the wooden banister without even running her hand along it.

She may not have appreciated it while she'd been there, but the time away, the distance, well, it cleared her perspective.

On the inn.

On a lot of things.

Autumn closed her car door and several tentative steps later climbed the porch stairs. The smell of paint lingered in the air as she reached for the front door, the jingle of the bells such a familiar greeting she almost didn't notice.

And a familiar voice, too.

"No, we're north of Grand Rapids." Pause. "Yes, south of Mackinac Island. Uh, no, east of Lake Michigan."

Autumn covered her mouth to stop an outburst of laughter.

Harry glanced up, irritation smoothing into an actual smile as he covered the phone's mouthpiece and whispered. "This is why GPS systems were created."

"Hello to you, too, Harry." Shouldn't he look a little more surprised?

"Harrison." He shook his head and returned his attention to the caller. "Yes, if you're coming from the west, take exit 51." Pause. "Yes, on your left."

Seconds later he hung up and rounded the desk, arms outstretched. "I knew you'd come back."

"No you didn't." She stepped into the hug. "I didn't even know until I did."

"Come on, I'll take you back to meet the new owner."

"Oh, no, that's not why I stopped by." That would be way too awkward. Possibly emotional. Not that she didn't wonder about the new owner. . . . But it was going to be awkward enough at first, living in town and not working at the inn—let alone owning it. "Harry, I don't—"

But Harry ignored her protests, slinging his arm around her shoulder, guiding her down the hallway and toward the back door. "You've got no reason to be nervous, Kingsley." He opened the door and nudged her out. "Trust me."

The door closed.

"Right. Trust the guy who just pushed me out the back door. Who once left me stranded on the roof, ladderless." A spring breeze messed with her hair. No matter, the flights and drive had flattened and tangled it already. She'd fix it up at home before finding Blake.

And it's not like the new owner would care about her appearance. "Except where are you, Mr. New Owner? Or Mrs., Ms. Whatever."

"Talking to yourself, Red?"

Autumn spun at a voice. *The* voice. Blake. And oh, she could just melt into the dew-tipped grass—her and her airplane hair.

He was as good-looking as ever, even in paint-speckled jeans and T-shirt. Of course, he'd once again opted for the not-so-clean-shaven look. And of course, his grin was as much teasing smirk as anything.

Nerves dashed through her—a completely different kind than the ones heckling her as she'd thought about meeting the new owner. Oh no, these ones were all . . . warm.

He stopped in front of her. "Anyway, you're right on time for the interview."

"Interview?"

"I realize I'm not really dressed for it, but I'm trying to finish painting all the shutters today. Front and west sides are done. Got one more on the east side and then all the back ones. So . . . what do you think of my place?"

Clunky realization set in. *Blake* was the new inn owner? This was . . . somewhere between ridiculous and unbelievable. "What? Y-you bought m-my inn? I mean, your inn now, but . . . you? How? When? *Why*?"

"You should've been a reporter. I think you covered almost all the five Ws there."

Enough with the joking. She folded her arms. "Explain yourself."

"Bossy. Which, come to think of it, is probably a good trait for a manager to have." He took a step closer. "Which is what I meant by interview. You totally want the job, right?"

She inched back. "It may be the jet lag, but I am so confused."

And oh, with that annoying, dimpled smile again. And he smelled like, well, Blake . . . and paint. And . . . she couldn't think. Stupid, knotty emotions.

"I'll keep the jet lag in mind during the interview. But come on, say you'll consider it."

"How, uh, how many other people have you interviewed?"

"You're the only one."

"Have you advertised for the position?" Did her voice seriously just squeak?

He pulled a crinkled paper out of his pocket. "I was supposed to drop an ad at the paper by noon. But I had this meeting first thing today—with your mom and my dad, if you can believe it. There's this grant thing, and, well, then I took *The Blaze* out for a quick flight."

He'd *flown*? And he was working with Mom?

He chuckled now at her confusion. "You look like I felt coming home after six years."

"Yet it was only a bit over three months."

"Anyway, my point is, I didn't get the ad to the newspaper. Kind of happy about that at the moment." And for the first time, he actually appeared nervous, the tease in his eyes dissolving.

"Blake."

Wind played with his dark hair. "All right. Yes, I bought the inn. Put my plane up as collateral, got a loan, even put together a business plan. It happened fast, but if all goes well, we might make a go of this place yet."

Impossible to miss his *we*. "But your family's hotel?"

"Nothing wrong with a little healthy competition, right?" He chuckled. "And anyway, Dad was fine with it. Funny thing is, he's actually thinking of selling the hotel and retiring."

"So . . . you plunked down the money, just like that, because you *like* the place?"

He took another step forward, and this time, she didn't step back. "And because you love it."

"Blake—"

"Look, I bought it because I honestly believe this old inn still has stories to tell—however sentimental that sounds—and I realized I want to be a part of telling them." He angled toward the inn, arms sweeping as if showing it off to someone who didn't already have its outline memorized. "I like how rooted it is. I like the challenge of fixing it up and luring tourists. I like the hundreds of ideas in the back of my head for expanding it."

Whoa. This hadn't been some impulsive decision. He really had a plan, and there wasn't even a whisper of doubt in her mind he'd make a success of it.

"I bought it for all those reasons. But, too, I didn't want you to come home for a visit, on holidays or whatever, and see it torn down. Even had the crazy thought that maybe someday you'd come home for good. I wanted it to be waiting for you."

She let that sink in, tingles running through her. And goose bumps on her arms, despite the sunlight, despite the flush heating her neck.

"I bought it for me, yeah. But I also . . . I bought it for you, Red."

She unfolded her arms. "*I bought it for you, Red.*" She could replay those words a hundred times in her head and they wouldn't get old.

He held out the typed ad he hadn't delivered to the newspaper office. "Here, you can keep this."

"Um, why?"

"You told me months ago you didn't feel like you'd lived a life worthy of a scrapbook—which I completely disagree with, by the way. But regardless . . . I can pretty much guarantee from here on out you'll want a photo album. I think you can make digital ones now, though, so you can still get out of going to ladies' craft night, if you want. The ad should go on the first page—a memento of your impromptu interview today."

"Is that so?" She couldn't stop looking at him, grinning like an idiot.

"I mean, that is, if you're here to stay. It's not a holiday, so that's not why you're here. And—"

"I'm moving home, Blake."

His smile could have kindled a campfire. "*I bought it for you, Red.*" And that's when she couldn't hold back anymore. She lifted her arms to throw them around his neck. "Thank you. *Thank you.*"

His arms closed around her, and he just held her there, a cocoon she had little desire to ever leave. Oh yeah, she'd be sticking around.

"So tell me," he said into her hair. "What are your greatest strengths as a potential employee of the Kingsley Inn?"

She tightened her hold around him. "Well, I ran the place for three years."

"Good point. And?"

"I already have a name tag . . . if I can find it. And business cards."

"Also good. Because after we get done hosting Dylan and Mariah's wedding reception—"

"No way."

"Well, I did save the guy from drowning." His voice brushed over the tips of her ear. "You wouldn't believe my powers of persuasion."

Except that she would. Easily.

"So you're going to need those business cards when a hundred other couples in need of a wedding venue come banging on our door." He pulled back then, only far enough to meet her eyes, his hands still on her waist. "Why'd you come back, Red?"

He really had to ask?

"Because I couldn't make myself go up to the third landing of the Eiffel Tower."

Sunlight and confusion swirled together in his eyes. "I don't get it." But he didn't wait for an explanation. Only leaned in, and everything around her stilled and faded.

But before he could kiss her, a whisper escaped. "So I've got the job?"

"Honey, you always had the job." He kissed the tip of her nose.

"Best. Interview. Ever."

"You can say that again." Her cheek.

"Best interview ever."

"Now stop talking so I can give you a proper welcome-home kiss."

And while the old inn watched and the lake and the breeze sang together, that's exactly what he did.

Acknowledgments

One of my close friends (she knows who she is!) once made fun of my hugging. She actually called me a weak hugger. To which I said . . . challenge accepted. I've worked hard on my hugging skills these past couple years. Problem is, now I have all these people I want to hug who I don't see all that often. . . .

So to everybody who helped make this story possible, please accept this written embrace and know that next time I do see you you're totally in for the real (and recently improved) version.

Many, many thanks to:

My family: Mom and Dad, you continue to be the greatest supporters and encouragers in my life, along with simply being the best parents ever. Thank you, too, to my siblings, grandparents, and extended family. Love you all.

My agent, Amanda Luedeke, and my editor, Raela Schoenherr . . . aka a writer's dream team. Getting to work with both of you is beyond fun. I'm grateful for all you do, for the ways you've helped my dream come true . . . and most of all, for your friendship.

Editor Karen Schurrer, I really can't tell you how thankful I am for your expertise and keen eye. Thank you for giving this story such time and care.

My craft partner, Lindsay, and our other two GLAM girls, Gabrielle and Alena. (Um, I'm the M for anyone stuck on the acronym.) Man, did God ever know what he was doing when he connected the four of us. I think we should have a writing retreat every month! P.S. Notice how I'm resisting the urge to say anything about wood ticks. . . .

The My Book Therapy team: Susan May Warren, Rachel Hauck, Lisa Jordan, Beth Vogt, Edie Melson, Michelle Lim, Alena Tauriainen, Reba Hoffman, David Warren. I love the laughter and tears we share every time we see each other.

Artist Jenny Parker, who created the cover for this book. Oh, how I squealed when I first saw it. It's so adorable . . . and I'm so grateful.

Everyone at Bethany House, including the marketing and sales teams who get books into the hands of readers. I still sometimes can't believe I get to be a part of your publishing family.

Cara Putman, I don't know if you realize how much

that fifteen-minute mentor appointment we had at ACFW meant to me . . . or how much your encouragement impacted me. It felt like a calming inhale of fresh air during a season when I couldn't seem to catch my breath. Thank you for the chat and the prayer.

There are so many more people I want to say "thank you" to—other writing friends, both online and local; my co-workers; girlfriends who I don't get to see often enough; the amazing launch team for my first book; endorsers and reviewers whose words do an author's emotions good.

And readers . . . thank you so much for taking the time to hang out with my characters. In a way it's sort of like you're hanging out with me—without the downsides of seeing my messy home or frizzy hair. Thank you!

But most of all, I have to say thank you to God . . . for the ways you worked in my heart during the writing of *Here to Stay* and for reminding me the best dream I could ever have is you.

Melissa Tagg is a former reporter and total Iowa girl. In addition to her homeless ministry day job, she is also the marketing/events coordinator for My Book Therapy, a craft-and-coaching community for writers. When she's not writing, she can be found hanging out with the coolest family ever, watching old movies, and daydreaming about her next book. She's passionate about humor, grace, and happy endings. Melissa blogs regularly and loves connecting with readers at www.melissatagg.com.

More from Melissa Tagg

Visit melissatagg.com for a full list of her books.

On a visit home to Maple Valley, Iowa, political speechwriter Logan Walker meets intriguing reporter Amelia Bentley. She wants his help on a story, and he wants to get to know her better. Their attraction is mutual, but what will happen when he tells her the real reason he's returned?

Like Never Before

Kate writes romance movie scripts for a living, but after her last failed relationship, she's stopped believing "true love" is real. Could a new friendship with former NFL player Colton Greene restore her faith?

From the Start

If you enjoyed *Here to Stay*, you may also like . . .

Genealogist Nora Bradford has decided that focusing on her work is far safer than romance. But when a former Navy Seal hires her to find his birth mother, their connection is undeniable. The trouble is they seem to have met the right person at the worst possible time.

True to You by Becky Wade
BRADFORD SISTERS ROMANCE
beckywade.com

Nurse practitioner Mia Robinson is done with dating. Instead, she's focused on caring for her teenage sister, Lucy—who, it turns out, is pregnant and plans to marry her boyfriend. Mia is determined to stop the wedding, but she's in for a surprise when she meets the best man.

The Two of Us by Victoria Bylin
victoriabylin.com

◈ BETHANYHOUSE